D0065555

Donated by the
Carl & Verna Schmidt
Foundation
2010

ALSO BY JULIA GLASS

I See You Everywhere
The Whole World Over
Three Junes

The Widower's Tale

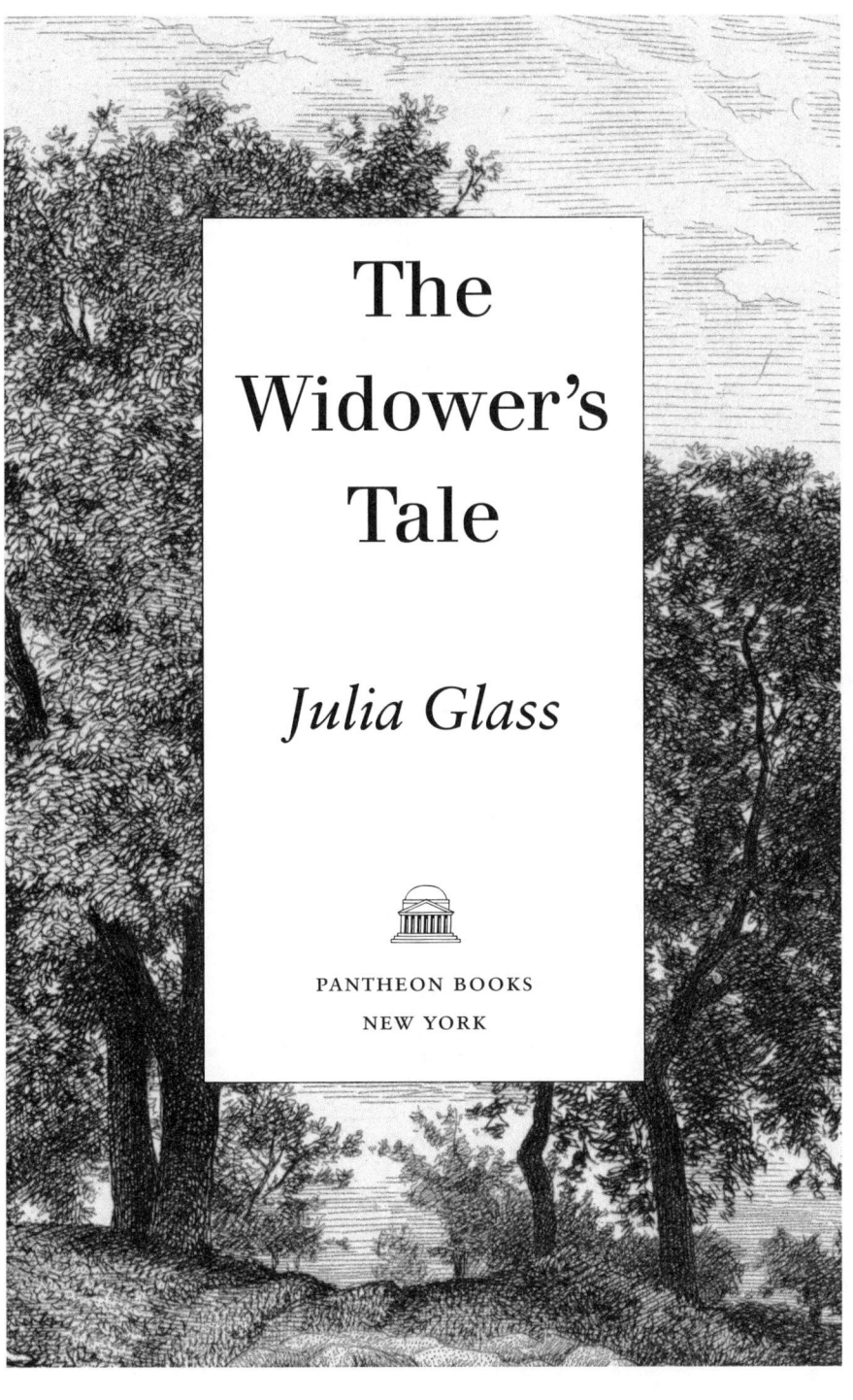

The Widower's Tale

Julia Glass

PANTHEON BOOKS

NEW YORK

Copyright © 2010 by Julia Glass

All rights reserved. Published in the United States by Pantheon Books,
a division of Random House, Inc., New York,
and in Canada by Random House of Canada Limited, Toronto.

Pantheon Books and colophon are registered trademarks of
Random House, Inc.

Library of Congress Cataloging-in-Publication Data
Glass, Julia, [date]
The widower's tale / Julia Glass.
p. cm.
ISBN 978-0-307-37792-0
1. Widows—Fiction. 2. Grandsons—Fiction. 3. Preschools—Fiction.
4. Family secrets—Fiction. 5. Ecoterrorism—Fiction. 6. New England—
Fiction. I. Title.
PS3607.L37W56 2010 813'.6—dc22 2010002854

www.pantheonbooks.com

Printed in the United States of America
First Edition
2 4 6 8 9 7 5 3 1

For my parents
and
my three Jewish mothers

In the way that a gambler who has lost can easily imagine himself again in possession of his money, thinking how false, how undeserved was the process that took it from him, so he sometimes found himself unwilling to believe what had happened, or certain that his marriage would somehow be found again. So much of it was still in existence.

JAMES SALTER, Light Years

The Widower's Tale

1

⁓

W hy, thank you. I'm getting in shape to die."

Those were the first words I spoke aloud on the final Thursday in August of last summer: Thursday, I recall for certain, because it was the day on which I read in our weekly town paper about the first of what I would so blithely come to call the Crusades; the end of the month, I can also say for certain, because Elves & Fairies was scheduled, that very evening, to fling open its brand-new, gloriously purple doors—formerly the entrance to my beloved barn—and usher in another flight of tiny perfect children, along with their preened and privileged parents.

I was on the return stretch of my route du jour, the sun just gaining a vista over the trees, when a youngster who lives half a mile down my street gave me a thumbs-up and drawled, "Use it or lose it, man!" I might have ignored his insolence had he been pruning a hedge or fetching the newspaper, but he appeared merely to be lounging—and smoking a cigarette—on his parents' hyperfastidiously weed-free lawn. He wore tattered trousers a foot too long and the smile of a bartender who wishes to convey that you've had one too many libations.

I stopped, jogging in place, and elaborated on my initial remark. "Because you see, *lad*," I informed him, huffing rhythmically though still in control, "I have it on commendable authority that dying is hard work, requiring diligence, stamina, and fortitude. Which I intend to maintain in ample supply until the moment of truth arrives."

And this was no lie: three months before, at my daughter's Memorial Day cookout, I'd overheard one of her colleagues confide to another, in solemn Hippocratic tones, "Maternity nurses love to talk about how hard it is to be born, how it's anything but passive. They explain to all these New Age moms that babies come out exhausted from the work they do, how they literally *muscle* their way toward the light. Well, if you ask me, dying's the same. It's hard work, too. The final stretch is a marathon. I've seen patients *try* to die but fail. Just one more thing they didn't bother to tell us in med school." (Creepy, this talk of muscling one's way toward the *dark*. Though I did enjoy the concept of all those babies toiling away, lives on the line, like ancient Roman tunnel workers, determined to complete their passage.)

As for the youngster with trousers slouched around his bony ankles, my homily had its intended effect. When I finished, he hadn't a syllable at his service; not even the knee-jerk "Whatever" that members of his generation mutter when conversationally cornered. As I went on my way, energized by vindication, I had a dim notion that the youngster's name was Damien. Or Darius. I put him at fifteen, the nadir point of youth. Had he been a boy of his age some twenty years ago, I would have known his name without a second thought, not just because I would have known his parents but because in all likelihood he would have mowed my lawn or painted my barn (gratefully!) for an hourly wage appropriate to a teenage boy's modestly spendthrift habits. Nowadays, teenage boys with wealthy parents do not mow lawns or paint houses. If they stoop to any sort of paid activity, they help seasoned citizens learn to navigate the baffling world of computers and entertainment modules, charging an hourly wage more appropriate to the appallingly profligate habits of a drug dealer in the Bronx.

Damius or Darien might indeed have been the one to coach my own seasoned self through the use of my new laptop computer (a retirement gift that spring from my daughters), and to fleece me accordingly, had I not been the fortunate grandfather of a very intelligent, very kind, adequately well-mannered boy of twenty who was, at the time, an honors student at Harvard. A "good boy," as parents no longer dare to say, cowed by advice from some celebrity pediatrician who's probably fathered two or three litters with a sequence of abandoned wives. But that's what Robert was, to me (and still is, or is again, despite everything that's happened): a Good Boy, on the verge of becoming a solid, productive citizen. "My grandson is a very good boy," I used to say, with pride and confidence, especially within earshot of his mother.

Robert had inherited his mother's passion for science, and I had begun to assume, with mixed feelings, that he planned to follow in her professional footsteps. A successful oncologist in Boston, Trudy has become marginally famous as a media source whenever some new Scandinavian study pops up to hint at anything approaching a cure. One day, watching her as she explained a controversial drug to that life-size Ken doll on the six o'clock news, it occurred to me that my younger daughter entered my living room more often as a guest of NBC than as my flesh-and-blood offspring. I saw Robert far more frequently.

Robert stayed in close touch with me as contractors, carpenters, plumbers, and electricians jacked up and tore apart my barn so that it could become the new home of Elves & Fairies, Matlock's favorite progressive nursery school. (Simply to look out my back windows that summer felt like spying on the public humiliation of a loyal friend, an ordeal I had engineered.) When these callow strangers—few of whom spoke English by choice—were not perpetrating their mutilations, buttressings, and vigorous eviscerations upon that stately structure, they treated my entire property like an amusement park. During breaks, they would kick a soccer ball back and forth by the pond, and while there were plenty of other shady spots in which to lounge, they ate their lunch on the steps of my back porch, their laughter and indecipherable chitchat echoing throughout my house. I could not even identify the language they shared. It might have been Tagalog or Farsi.

Fortuitously, despite my protests, Robert had insisted on setting up an e-mail account when he tutored me on the use of my laptop. After decades at a job where the King Kong shadow of technology loomed ever larger and darker over the simple work I loved, I had fantasies of a quasi-Luddite retirement: I would revel in the pages of one obscurely significant novel after another, abandoning the world of gigabytes and hard drives. Cursed be the cursors; farewell to iEverything and all its pertly nicknamed apps.

In a word, ha.

That summer, as it turned out, I found my sleek, alarmingly versatile computer a blessing—chiefly because it meant that I heard regularly from Robert, who was working at a coastal conservation outfit up in Maine. He kept me sane by sympathizing with my fury about everything from the cigarette butts and gum wrappers I found in the forsythia bushes to the dozens of alien soda-pop cans I had to haul, along with my own recycling, to the transfer station. Most insulting was the altered view from my desk: my copper beech so rudely upstaged by a large blue closet concealing a toilet.

That Thursday, finally, the blue john was carted away. The workmen were gone. My good deed was coming to fruition, and I was determined to put myself in a positive frame of mind. Yes, I was irritated by the youth in the baggy trousers and all that he personified—but he was just one sign among many that the world was changing its colors without my permission. Yes, I was apprehensive about the looming loss, possibly permanent, of certain privileges I had long taken for granted: peace, privacy, and (my daughter Clover had recently informed me) swimming naked in the pond before dark. But I had been led to expect these vexations. And I was excited to learn, from Robert's latest e-mail, that he was now back in Cambridge, preparing to start his junior year.

So when I came downstairs after showering, reading two chapters of *Eyeless in Gaza,* and shooting an e-missive to my grandson inviting him to lunch, I was almost completely happy to find my elder daughter in my kitchen. Almost.

There she sat, at the same table where she'd started each day for the first seventeen years of her life, eating a bowl of yogurt sprinkled with what looked like birdseed, drinking tea the color of algae, and paging through my copy of the *Grange.* For the past year, she'd been renting part of a house across town, yet she continued to make herself at home without announcing her presence. I knew that I ought to feel an instinctual fatherly joy—here she was, safe and hopeful at the very least, possibly even content—yet most of the time I had to suppress a certain resentment that she had made such a wreck of her life and then, on top of that, made me feel responsible for her all over again.

Like her younger sister, Clover hadn't lived under my roof since a summer or two during college—unless one were to count the recent period (though one would like to have forgotten it) during which she had languished here after the histrionic collapse of her marriage. For six months, until I helped her move across town and convinced my friend Norval to give her a job at his bookstore, she had gone back and forth between my house and her sister's.

"Hey, Daddy." Clover beamed at me. "How was your run?"

"Made it to the Old Artillery," I said. (Wisely, she paid me no condescending compliments.)

She stood. "Can I make you a sandwich?"

"Thank you," I said.

"Turkey? Peanut butter? Egg salad?"

"Thank you."

Clover laughed her deceptively carefree laugh. At an early age, my daughters learned that I do not like unnecessary choices, yet they tease me with them all the same. My favorite restaurants—if any such remain— are the ones where you're served a meal, no questions asked (except, perhaps, what color wine you'd prefer). You can carry on a civilized conversation without being forced to hear a litany of the twenty dressings you may have on your salad or to pretend you care what distant lake engendered your rainbow trout.

As Clover assembled my lunch, she told me in meticulous detail about the last-minute touches she and her new colleagues were putting on the barn to prepare for the open house that night. I sometimes wondered if she could appreciate the depth of the sacrifice I was making—all of it for her.

While she twittered on about the final visit from the fire marshal, how she'd held her breath as he peered upward yet again at all those hundred-year-old rafters, my attention wandered to the newspaper, open to the police log. In any given week, the most notable incident in Matlock might be *Loud voices reported 2 a.m. on Caspian Way* or *Pearl earring found under bench at train depot.* But then there were such delectably absurd items as *Woman apprehended removing lady's-slippers from woods off Mallard Lane* or *Caller on Reed St. complained wild turkeys blocked access to garage.* A recent standout was *"Bonehead driver" reported at food co-op transfer site.*

That week, our fearless enforcers had coped valiantly with a Shetland pony wandering free behind the public library, a 911 hang-up, the report of a *weird man on a bike* riding along a perfectly public road, a complaint about *extensive paper detritus* blowing across a hayfield, and a car left idling for twenty minutes at Wally's Grocery Stop. But then I came to the listings for the previous Saturday, a day of the week that, in the police log, tends to be dominated by reckless driving at the cocktail hour. This time, however, the first entry for Saturday read, *Motor vehicle vandalized and filled with vegetable refuse reported at 24 Quarry Rd. at 6:05 a.m.*

I burst out laughing. Clover stopped talking and turned from the counter to face me. "You find vaccination records a source of amusement?"

I tapped the paper. "This is priceless. Did you read this?"

She struggled not to look annoyed. Carrying a plate on which she'd placed a sandwich made with burlap bread, she looked over my shoulder. I read the item aloud. " 'Vegetable refuse'? Now there's something new."

"You didn't hear about that?" said Clover.

"How would I? I'm no longer on the soirée circuit. I've been branded the town curmudgeon."

"You have not. In fact, you are the town savior, in the opinion of seventy-three parents arriving to see their children's fabulous new school this evening."

"Until someone's precious little Christopher Robin breaks a toe on the flagstone walk or falls off that fancy jungle gym."

Clover uttered a noise of exasperation, but she spared me the usual dose of her newfound philosophy about the magnetic effects of negative thinking.

"But this." I pointed to the paper again. "This wins a prize."

She sat down across from me and told me that some fellow named Jonathan Newcomb had awakened to find his brand-new Hummer filled with corn husks. "Like, jam-packed with the stuff. And there was this big sign pasted over the entire windshield, and it said, ETHANOL, ANYONE? And they put it on with the kind of glue you can't get off—in New York, they use it to glue on notices when you don't move your car for the street cleaner."

"Who is 'they'?"

"The police, Daddy."

"No, I mean the 'they' who filled that car with corn."

"Just the husks. Nobody knows."

I laughed loudly. I might even have clapped my hands. "That's the most creative prank I've heard of in ages."

Clover did not partake in my amusement. "Well, Jonathan is on the warpath. He made sure they fingerprinted everything in sight. Like even the hubcaps. He missed a plane, too. His company had an important meeting."

"Wait. Quarry Road? Isn't Newcomb the fellow who put down three acres of turf where all that milkweed used to grow like blazes? The field where I used to take you and Trudy to see the butterflies? You *know* that scoundrel?"

"He's a *dad*," said Clover.

I was baffled by this non sequitur until I realized she was referring to E & F. No doubt Newcomb paid the full, five-figure tuition. Probably times two, for a brace of hey-presto fertility twins.

"Can you imagine," she said, sounding deeply concerned, "getting all that corn silk out of the upholstery?"

"No. I cannot imagine that." I used my napkin to conceal my smile.

The minute I finished my sandwich, Clover reached across the table and touched my hand. "There's something important I have to ask. How would you feel if the two older classes built a tree house in the beech tree? They wouldn't harm the tree, I promise."

"Four-year-olds with hammers and saws? That makes sense."

"They'd be the helpers, the apprentices. They do have wood shop, you know. In all the years of E and F, no one's ever lost a finger or an eye. And we have this amazing new teacher—the first male teacher, in fact! He has just the most wonderful concept for the project." She proceeded to describe how the older children—the Birches and the Cattails—would be "studying" architecture.

"Whatever happened to construction-paper collages and masks made from paper plates?" I raised my hands in surrender. "No, don't tell me. This is the twenty-first century! Rubber cement went out with the typewriter! Wake up, you old coot!"

Clover smiled, indulgently. "Actually, they do lots of collages. But now the kids have glitter glue. It comes in every color of the rainbow."

"Will wonders never cease," I said. Though I was glad to see her cheerful again, I'd begun to feel as if we now suffered from what I could only call a humor gap. Unfairly, perhaps, I blamed it on her psychotherapist, whom she liked to quote as if the woman were Jefferson or Gandhi.

Clover sat back and folded her arms. "Daddy, it's time you took the tour. Really. You will be so amazed. I think you'll really like it. You will."

"Will I." But I gave her my least sardonic smile.

"I promise."

"Then let's go." I stood with a purpose—my hamstrings issuing a sharp rebuke for the last half mile of my run.

As I followed Clover out the door, I could see how attractive she remained, even from behind: she had her mother's airy grace, the straight spine, that enticingly hapless thicket of hair. She'd let it go from ginger to a golden, variegated gray, a choice Poppy did not live long enough to make. Clover was on the cusp of forty-five, a birthday eight years beyond Poppy's final age.

Because I'd seen so much of Clover since her return to Matlock, weeks would go by during which I did not consciously notice this daughter's resemblance to her mother; and then, whenever it rose to the surface again, I felt the familiar, vertiginous tumble of emotions: relief at the presence in the absence (that something of my wife remained) and sorrow at the absence in the presence (that my daughters would always remind me their mother was gone). And the ugly sense that I held a bottomless debt of repentance: for even while I'd maintained my solitude, had never come close to marrying again in the thirty-two years since my wife's death, still that solitude had been ample with pleasure.

When Poppy was alive, the barn loft was her dance studio. She taught little girls and women of all ages, even a few renegade "sensitive" men. Back in the no-hassle sixties, it was a cinch to turn your barn into a backyard business, to add a bathroom here, a tiny kitchen there. In fashionably rural Matlock, it became a fad. Several architects set up shop just out their kitchen door; art studios proliferated; for a few years, we had a local dairy store, the Mootique. (Trudy and Clover loved to visit those smelly cows and sample the eccentrically seasoned cheeses.) The Episcopal minister's wife taught natural-childbirth classes in the barn behind the rectory—a place that had been used to store outdated prayer books and props for holiday pageants. She swept out the dust and painted a giant blue dove on the siding that faced the town green. On brilliant cloudless days, it took on a trompe l'oeil effect, as if you could see through the barn right out to the sky. Poppy called it "our very own Magritte."

I wonder if the zoning board of yesteryear devoted its meetings to getting high. Because all of a sudden, not long after Poppy's death, everything changed. By the late seventies, well, good luck to you if you wanted to put so much as a spare bedroom over your garage! By the dawn of the new millennium, spaces zoned for commercial use had become as rare in Matlock as families with middle-class incomes. Which meant that Evelyn Fougère—E & F's legendary progenitor and directress—found herself in a grand pickle when, at the end of a ten-year lease, she and her school were politely banished from the parish house of the Congregational church. The deacons had voted to take in a non-profit organization that found homes for refugees from African countries where chopping your neighbors into little pieces had become a way of life. Many heated letters appeared in the *Grange*, but the CC deacons held fast to their conviction that the town must extend its evanescent goodwill much farther afield.

According to one rumor, Evelyn's persistence in attending the Episcopal church across the green from the CC had tipped the scales against her, but what was the point of parsing the verdict? She was desperate, and she did her homework. My barn, grandfathered as an "educational facility" thanks to Poppy's classes, was the answer to her most secular prayers.

I had kept Poppy's studio exactly as she left it: the long mirror spotless, the barre polished, the festive Mexican rugs rolled tightly and stacked in a corner. After her death, it took a good ten years for people to stop asking me if they could rent or even borrow the barn (about the same duration it took for them to give up on me as the perfect partner for yet another nice, bookish woman who'd missed or been jettisoned from the marriage trolley). I knew perfectly well what people thought: that it was a shrine to my guilt. I didn't care what they thought. I would have the studio cleaned every few months and visit just often enough to check for invading wildlife. Otherwise I never expected to see it altered. But Clover's crisis changed all that.

Evelyn Fougère had the nerve to pick up the phone, call me, and ask outright. (Whatever happened to the discretion of making such requests by mail?) "Percy, you've heard the news, I'm sure," she said, "so I'll get to the point. I need your barn. The children need your barn! I do not have to tell you how essential this school has become to the town. I know that sounds conceited in the extreme, but it's simply a fact. You owe us nothing; you don't even have a *grand*child who needs a space—and believe me, I'm not above such incentives!—so all I can do is throw myself on your mercy . . . and maybe remind you of my longtime friendship with Clover? Remember the summer you rented us a pair of ponies?" Her laughter was nervous and imploring.

I had been waiting for a pause in which to concisely, not too impolitely, demur—it did not help her case that she so readily addressed me by my first name when I had always been Mr. Darling to her—but then her suggestion of an "incentive," followed by her reminder that she and Clover had been girlhood chums, set my rusty mental cogs in motion. *Bargain with the devil!* warned a shrill inner voice, yet it so happened that I had just hung up from another painful conversation with Clover, who'd told me that what she now felt certain she wanted to do (yes really really certain this time!) was "something with little children." I had listened sympathetically, but forgive me if I also rolled my eyes, suspecting that what she "really really" felt certain about was that she should never have abandoned her husband and her *own* children. What she felt was nostalgia and remorse. But I'd kept these thoughts to myself.

So after letting Evelyn's laughter dwindle to silence, I said, "Make me a proposal. And maybe I'll make you one in return." From her involuntary gasp, I knew that, in exchange for a five- or ten-year lease on my huge, picturesque, appropriately zoned barn, she would gladly hand over not just her firstborn child (a comely aspiring actress at Juilliard) but her island house in Maine. Instead, I secured a decent job for my confused, rootless daughter. And I agreed to keep the rent low as long as Clover hung on to that job. If anyone could keep Clover on track, it was the shrewd, creative, nurturing Evelyn. Maybe that's what Clover needed: a boss who knew what made small children tick, how to make them happy, how to help them grow. Because that's how I secretly saw my daughter—as a small child in the body of a forty-four-year-old woman.

But a bargain with the devil it certainly was. All summer long, I refused to go anywhere near the barn, let alone set foot inside. I knew my resistance was petty, but I could not yet relinquish my need to preserve the one place where my wife's spirit still reigned supreme. On many a day, I turned up Beethoven to drown out the whine of electric tools, the hollow tumbling of two-by-fours, the merriment of hardworking men telling lewd jokes in a foreign language.

One day, while I was reading Trollope in Poppy's old dressing room (from which I had no view of the architectural assault), I was startled by a quivering brilliance on the ceiling, the kind caused by reflections off jewelry or rippling water. I went to the window and looked down just in time to see the sections of that great, long mirror pass by, strapped faceup to the top of a van, hurling sunlight back at the sky. I was seized with a possessive panic, as if I had happened upon a burglary in progress. I made it halfway downstairs, at a clumsy gallop, before I realized that I had no use for those mirrors. Someone had taken the care to remove them intact; perhaps they would go somewhere they were needed. Perhaps they would once again reflect the limbs of young, supple dancers. It had not occurred to me before that my hoarding them in that deserted barn had been selfish.

After I knew that the contractor had finished the taking away and begun the bringing in, I asked Clover about the rugs; I would find a good home for them, too. Poppy had collected the rugs over two trips we took to Mexico, one to cavort on the beach, one to see archaeological ruins. On the second trip, she was pregnant with Clover. The rugs were primitive, brightly striped and flowered squares woven with a soft, furry wool—perfect, said Poppy, for "barefoot work" in the winter.

"Oh, Daddy, they were destroyed by moths," Clover told me. "They fell apart completely when I untied them. We had to throw them away. I hope you don't mind." She searched my face—worried, I could see, that I might be angry.

"I suppose they would be," I said, speaking gently. "I ought to have wrapped them up, years ago." What a waste.

Why should I give a hoot about those old rugs? Why wasn't my entire, loving focus on Clover, my oldest child, the one who needed my help—far more than I or anyone could give!—and who, right then, was genuinely excited to be the new assistant to the esteemed director of Elves & Fairies?

That Thursday in August, as I followed Clover down the long slope from the house to the barn, I had to admit that she looked as proud of this fresh endeavor as I'd seen her look about anything since the first few years of her children's lives.

New grass already grew where stacks of lumber and the trampings of workmen had stripped my lawn bare. I noticed for the first time that the jumbled stones in the walkway had been evened out, that an apron of dark green rubber formed a subtle patio at the entrance to the barn. My driveway no longer petered off into dandelions and timothy but lassoed back on itself, forming a loop where parents could drive through to drop off and retrieve their progeny.

Was I ready to face the mutation of my wife's favorite refuge into a warren of crayon-colored nooks and crannies, where the closest thing to Merce Cunningham or Balanchine would be a game of musical chairs? And what if this were something I should have done long ago, by way of atonement?

Yet I would not allow my good mood to be shattered by feelings of futile guilt. I retraced my attention to the image of that wretched Hummer—the automotive equivalent of a big-city cockroach—stuffed to the gills with corn husks. Someone in Matlock had a fine and devious sense of humor. Perhaps there was a God.

When I muttered to myself, "Ethanol, anyone?" Clover turned around and gave me a funny look.

I said, "Lead on, my dear."

Because the barn was set into the hillside descending toward the pond, one entered the loft from ground level on the side that faced the house. The old double door still served as the main entrance (though reinforced and painted that lurid purple). Above it, a faux-rustic sign bore the school's wincingly adorable name. (Efforts by the school's lone set of gay parents to change the name, because of its homophobic associations, had been squelched. Evelyn had published a letter in the *Grange* about protecting "authentic" fairies from the evils of political correctness.)

"So, get ready!" Clover opened the doors dramatically, like that vapid young woman on *Let's Make a Deal*, a show that Poppy and I used to laugh at together, only half watching, as we danced around the kitchen making dinner.

Clover's promise held: my admiration escaped me in a simple, wordless exclamation. It was, indeed, amazing. Evelyn's husband, Maurice, was the architect given free rein—and when I saw what he had done to my barn, I understood why a small hush fell over any gathering into which he walked (and I understood, too, why they could afford a waterfront house in Vinal Haven and a ski hut in Vermont). The man was a master of light.

Predictably, yet logically, a long hallway bisected the space, beneath the spine of the roof. The classrooms to either side were partitioned with walls containing doors and windows of widely varied dramatic shapes: not just the shapes you might expect (star, crescent moon, hexagon, diamond) but elegantly simplified silhouettes of a turtle, a bear, an owl, a howling wolf! There were new skylights, too, which admitted vertical rivers of light.

"Good Lord," I exclaimed, irresistibly moved.

"You see? Isn't it just heavenly? And it's all super-safety glass," said Clover, knocking on one of the windows. "Practically impossible to break."

Along the outside walls, shelves painted in a dozen shades of green and purple held plastic bins of wooden animals, silk scarves, pom-poms, crayons, miniature scissors . . . all the tutti-frutti paraphernalia of a childhood pictured in magazines. On the paneling between the skylights hung posters of wildflowers and exotic birds; on the floors lay soft multicolored mats; in smart blond shelves stood books with extravagantly artful jackets. From the angled ceiling of each room hung a fan. Swiftly yet almost silently, they stirred and cooled the air.

"Good Lord," I said again. "And to what slum did we send you and your sister for nursery school?"

"There was no Elves and Fairies then," said Clover. "There was just Mrs. O'Connor's playgroup in the basement of the Artillery." She turned to look at me. "Which was just fine, Daddy. We loved it."

She led me down the long hall toward the back; halfway there, to one side, I glimpsed an alcove holding three elfin toilets. The tiles formed a glittering mosaic of the sky: midnight blue and gold, van Gogh's cosmos boiling with comets.

I remembered then that Maurice's firm specialized in art museums. He'd designed a wing at the Fogg during my final years at Harvard.

"Come see the view," my daughter urged.

Filling the back wall of the loft, from my waist to well above my head, was a vast triangular window. Below us lay the pond as I had never seen it, for this wall had always been solid, opaque. I felt almost dizzy as I surveyed it—not because I have a fear of heights but because it seemed inconceivable that I could view this place I knew so well, better than almost any other place in my entire life, in a way I had never viewed it before.

"How can this be?" I muttered.

Clover laughed, misinterpreting something I hadn't meant to say aloud. "How it can *be*," she said, "how it came out like this, was through the incredible generosity of all the people who wanted us to get it exactly right. Not to mention you, Daddy. Without you, God knows where we would be. *If* we'd be!"

I did not look her in the face, not wanting to share her raw emotion. Instead, I continued to survey the landscape stretched below me. I saw that the maples on the far side of the pond were already hinting at fall, a blush of orange in their crowns I would never have seen from the ground. I saw the roofs of the Three Greeks, a trio of Greek Revival houses that shared the opposing shore. I saw the pale hot summer sky as the wide plane of water so faithfully portrayed it. And for the first time, I saw the exact shape of the pond, not just as it is pictured on maps of the town but as it exists in nature: a paisley, an attenuated raindrop, a tear.

A phone rang. Clover went back down the hall. I heard her voice: "Elves and Fairies! Clover Darling here! May I help you?"

"Good heavens, Poppy," I whispered. "What a world."

"What a world indeed."

My heart seized as I turned around. Smiling at me from inside one of the classrooms was a pixieish young man, wiry and slight as a gymnast, his hair a compact yellow shrub.

"Ira Schwartz," he said. "I didn't mean to make you jump."

We shook hands. Churlishly, I withheld my name. Pointlessly, too.

"You'd be the heroic, legendary Mr. Darling," he said, cocking his head slightly. "I'm the new guy here, but I know all about *you.*"

Rampant freckles, a coy smile: the perfect Puck. Then it came to me. I laughed. "Ah yes. You'd be the fellow who wants to turn my poor old tree into a high-rise hotel."

"Oh that *tree,* can I tell you . . . rarely have I met a tree like that. It's so"—he shook his golden head—"so royal."

"Yes, it is."

"But I assure you, Mr. Darling, that what I propose to do—and only if you're willing—won't compromise your tree in the slightest. Not one bit."

Down the hall, I could hear Clover involved in a conversation about toilet training (apparently now called toilet *learning*).

I leaned toward the pixie and said, "Do you know why I've allowed my life and my property to be thrown helter-skelter by this endeavor?"

Finally, I'd silenced the fellow. He regarded me unwaveringly, however, eyebrows raised, respectfully attendant. "Well," he finally said, "I'd be curious to know, but only if it were my business."

"It's not, but I'll summarize. Family. Not money, not altruism, not—*not*—a nostalgia for the company of children."

He nodded, but his hands stayed in the pockets of his rather tight blue jeans. "Mr. Darling, I can take no for an answer."

"Young fellow, I'm not giving you an answer. I'm giving you a context." I spoke cheerfully, not disdainfully.

"I didn't mean to confront you," he said. "I'm sorry if it seemed that way. I guess I interrupted your tour. . . ."

I looked at my watch, if only to give us both a graceful out. "My people will be in touch with yours."

It took him a moment, but then he burst into courteous laughter. "And my people will be ready to negotiate. I shouldn't tell you this, but they're softies."

He went back into his classroom, and I retraced my steps down the long, lovely hallway. Clover, still on the phone as I passed her office, made a desperate face, but we waved to each other. I blew her a kiss.

Outside, the afternoon heat struck me like a mallet, and I decided it was time for my final naked daylight swim. From mid-May to late October, I swam virtually every day, rain or shine or fog, and I hadn't owned a pair of swimming trunks in God knew how long. A week before, Clover had told me in no uncertain terms that I was to give up this habit; never mind that I made my way between the pond and the outdoor shower in a towel.

I do not believe in ghosts. Yet undeniably, over the years since Poppy's death, there were times when I swam in the pond and felt haunted: not by Poppy herself (that might have felt merciful, in a way) but by the doubts that I would never, ever share with anyone about the way in which she died. Swimming, for me, has always been a kind of meditation, not a form of exercise. The wild silence of "my" pond was a part of that meditation. Crickets, frogs, songbirds, peepers—each in its season—set the rhythm of my breathing and my brain. (I had learned to shut out the occasional distant mower.)

Half an hour later, as I drifted placidly on my back, watching the clouds above me do the same, a whole new sound invaded my world: from open windows, the bantering of the teachers as they readied the loft—the school—for the inaugural gathering that night. Voices carry surprisingly far across water. Except for Ira, the would-be tamer of my tree, the voices belonged to women, all maternal in the extreme, blessed with sunny outlooks and sunny laughter to match. "Did you fill the sand table, Joyce?" "Oh, aren't these new smocks adorable!" "I love watching the first-time dads scroonch down in the tiny chairs, don't you?" And then the pixie spoke: "Do you suppose that if Dick Cheney and all those joint chiefs were forced to hold their meetings in preschool chairs, maybe we wouldn't be in this ghastly war?" Uproarious laughter followed. One of the women said, "Ira, that is a beautiful thought."

I beheld a sudden mental projection of my heirloom beech wearing, like a turban, a miniaturized Guggenheim Museum.

I rolled over and swam the length of the pond, back and forth several times. I tried to concentrate on the pleasure of my increasing fitness rather than the treacly human birdsong that was, I feared, to taint a ritual whose importance to me no one else could ever know.

As for my running routine, that was exercise pure and painful. I had decided to make it a daily obligation in April of that year, on the day after my seventieth birthday, a month after my retirement from Widener Library: a time in life when it's easy to see yourself as headed downhill fast. And so, though I would vary my route in other ways, I always turned left at the foot of my driveway, aiming myself up the long hill toward the old meetinghouse and the town green.

Not long after settling into my regimen of touring the nearby streets on a regular basis, I began to notice a number of onerous signs that the character of my town was under siege. Especially disturbing was that I did not know whether these changes had been going on behind my back for years or had arisen recently, even suddenly; whether I could hope that, if the latter was true, the changes might somehow be reversed.

I noticed the first affront in May, the day I decided to turn onto Fox Farm Lane—a road I had not taken in years, since it is a self-referential loop serving only its residents. I'd passed but a handful of houses when I noticed that several wore new coats of paint in highly untraditional colors, that a cobbled drive had been laid where I remembered a long dirt track, that two dozen young maples had been planted at robotically regular intervals along the boundary of a lawn, each one cabled and braced, replacing a good length of the tumbledown antique stone wall flanking the road. I was thinking what a pretty penny those trees must have cost, what a tasteless shame it was to have dismantled that wall, when I rounded the first sharp curve and saw it.

I would have been no more shocked to come upon a trailer park than I was to behold the addition on the Harris Homestead: a vast, malignant cube of clapboard and glass jutting abrasively into the surrounding woodland. It was nothing short of a cardinal sin against the soul of that fine, stoic saltbox.

The Harrises have not lived in their eponymous house for nigh on two centuries, but this was the sort of town—or had been the sort of town—where people who bought such a house, formerly the sole dwelling on your typically rugged New England farm, regarded themselves not as owners but as stewards, keepers of the historic flame. The addition featured an aggressively shiny picture window and bulbous skylights—three!—as well as a new chimney in a rough stone that clashed with the center chimney of faded brick.

Had our relationship been true to its cordial façade, I would have rushed home and called my next-door neighbor—Laurel Connaughton, chairwoman of the Historical Forum—to inquire about this atrocity. The opening of Elves & Fairies in my barn was hardly the crux of our covert feud; there was her Nosey Parker quest to open a wall in my own ancient house (in which she believed there was a "secret passageway," based on her furtive, inebriated knockings at a Christmas party many years past) and, dating even further back, our endless dispute over the maintenance of shoreline on our side of the pond.

Year after year, Mistress Lorelei insisted on "grooming" the tall grasses and thickets on her part of the perimeter, imperiling the communities of bullfrogs and birds that relied on this tangle for habitat. Without my permission, however, she could not spray for mosquitoes. In part just to irritate her, I had installed half a dozen bat houses on the trees that divided our two lawns. (Actually, my grandson Robert installed them.) She was terrified of the creatures and tried to make an official protest. Hal Oxblood, director of the Conservation Commission, informed her that bats consume several times their body weight in mosquitoes on a daily basis, thus fulfilling her ultimate objective. I did not correct him on this point, though Robert had told me it's a modern myth: a useful myth, he pointed out, since bats need all the good PR they can get. (In fact, he told me, their appetite tends toward moths and beetles.)

Alarming discovery number two occurred a week or so after my unsettling tour of Fox Farm Lane. The first premature heat wave had struck, and the sky was clear, yet all of a sudden I felt rain as I ran onto Wharton where it forks away from Quarry. Puzzled, I stopped. I held out my hands. Lo and behold, the people who'd bought the Weisses' house (people who lived a quarter mile from me but on whom I had never laid eyes in their year-plus of residence) had installed an in-lawn sprinkler system. Where did they think they were living, Grosse Point? Yet I had seen no complaints about this—or about the architectural ravaging of the Harris Homestead—in the pages of the *Grange*. Was I the only citizen who regarded these developments as vulgar and outlandish, a sign that the end of Matlock as I knew it was surely at hand? Perhaps the absence of outrage in the letters column was in itself another sign of the end.

I began to hunt for further aesthetic offenses—and therefore saw one nearly every day that summer, from the faux Williamsburg streetlamps planted in front of our nineteenth-century meetinghouse to the sudden, stunning absence of the magnificent alluvial boulder that had rested literally forever at the bottom of Cold Pond Way. (Who in the world had removed it? Where in the world had it *gone*?) Yet what convinced me we had crossed a line was something far less monumental: my sighting in July of two Bernese mountain dogs, a pair of opulently pampered creatures as black and shiny as limousines—and good Lord, nearly as big—fancy-pantsing along my road with their nymphet owner, her derriere barely the size of a grapefruit, her mane a cunningly gilded fleece, her T-shirt flecked with *rhinestones*.

Clover had mentioned the dogs earlier that month, gushing on about what gorgeous animals they were, but my gut response on seeing them in the flesh was not so admiring. I looked at their collars—green bands printed with rows of red lobsters—and at their owner's cantaloupe-colored loafers and in a synaptic flash recalled what old Ben Stewart had whispered to me at the candlelight service two Christmases past, just before his final heart attack. "Percy, mark my words: our lovely village has become, alas, an enclave." I had humored him with agreement, though at the time I thought he was merely bitter about his sons' insistence on selling his house, the surefire real estate bonanza out-stripping all fondness for their childhood home, with its wide lazy porch and its pocket orchard of eight wizened apple trees that bore fruit with-out any coddling.

As soon as I got home that day, the day of the dogs, I went straight to my *OED* (which Robert irreverently calls my "big dic"). I did not even pause to shower; sweat dripped from my bushy eyebrows onto the mag-nifying glass as I scowled down at the page. *Enclave: a portion of terri-tory entirely surrounded by foreign dominions.* Ben was an English teacher at our top-notch elementary school, so he used words like surgi-cal instruments.

I sat down and began to take a mental tour of Matlock's sinuous roads. Our one gas station, manned for decades by Vince Kaliski, a vet-eran of Okinawa whose wife ran the Girl Scout troop, had closed ten years before. Even the nearby house where Vince and Mary brought up their boys had been razed. More recently, Coiffure Cottage, a beauty salon dating to Cretaceous times, had morphed into a modern art gallery. Buck and Calvin, the plumber and the electrician I engaged to keep my house in working order, had sold their own houses and retired to Florida, none of their numerous sons willing to succeed them—or able to afford our rapidly bloating taxes. Since their departure, I had been forced to employ tradesmen from several towns away, fellows I would never encounter with pleasure at the P.O. or the deli counter at Wally's. Some might have referred to Vince, Buck, and Calvin as "ordi-nary fellows" or "salt of the earth." Such terms are merely code for men who've led lives in which boyhood dreams become a luxury, a whim, before boyhood even comes to an end.

Where were these men now? Were they still alive? Even our elementary-school teachers, the Bens, could no longer afford to live among us.

When I e-mailed Robert about the dogs, I typed into the subject line *Scylla and Charybdis.* During my evening swim, I had a grandiose vision of myself as a lone, graying knight in his drafty castle, surrounded on all sides by Philistines of a novel variety: well schooled, well nourished, well informed (with information convenient to their collectively blink-ered conscience), and sure of the ergonomic traction with which their stylishly countrified shoes met the ground.

I was so worked up that night, I could not resist calling Robert's mother as well. Trudy listened—she's a good listener, which I'm sure makes her popular with patients—but she was hardly sympathetic. When I told her how much I missed Vince, Buck, and Calvin, she pointed out that I'd never socialized with them.

"Socializing is not the only sign of kinship," I said. "You women are not so aware of this. We knew what it was to have a meeting of the minds without some knitting circle. And now it seems as if whatever men I do see about town—and let me tell you, it's rare to spot a man under sixty by daylight!—these men hold down hocus-pocus jobs. They're 'derivatives traders' or 'IT consultants.' They have squeaky-clean nails and flannel shirts that came straight out of a mail-order parcel from L.L.Bean—which of course now belongs to some retailer run by the mob in Bayonne, New Jersey."

"Dad, those guys are prosperous, and so are you. You hate to hear it, but you have more in common with them than you ever did with Mr. Kaliski or the guys who cleaned our oil tank."

"No, I disagree with you there, my dear. And if you want to discuss income—isn't that what you mean when you refer to prosperity?—I'm sure I never made half what Buck did! I understand he bought quite the boat after selling his house and cashing in his retirement savings."

"I'm not talking numbers, Dad, and you know it. It has to do with . . . station in life."

"Class, is that what you mean?"

"Yes. Exactly."

"But that's my point. This used to be a town with many classes."

"Barely."

"We lived comfortably together, so you wouldn't have noticed. We did not need 'great rooms' and three-car garages and central air and—"

"Now you're talking values," said Trudy. "Which have changed since the days you're talking about. You think Mr. Kaliski, if he were still around, wouldn't want a hot tub?"

"I wish you could have seen this town when your mother and I found this house—for a song! The roof was about to cave in, and anyone else would have given up on that barn. But not your mother. She said we would make this a 'house for the generations.' Some of our neighbors, people who didn't know us from Adam, volunteered to pitch in. It was like an old-fashioned barn raising."

"Dad, I've heard all this before. It's sweet. You and Mom lived in a different time, believe me. But you know what? Let it go. Because listen, can I tell you something, Dad? You are turning into a crank! You've always been on the verge, but now it's finally happening."

The tour of my barn that was no longer a barn left me restless, despite my swim. So there I stood, just a few hours later, in The Great Outdoorsman. This establishment is the linchpin of business in motley downtown Packard, a town twenty minutes from Matlock that might as well be on the other side of an ocean. At its center, threatening to topple into a sluggish forgotten waterway, huddle three vast, mostly abandoned brick buildings that once housed shoe factories and a mill; only one has been renovated, bravely declaring itself to be the Packard Arts Center. The town's houses, though old, are weary, not stately; its woods are more weedy than sylvan. Packard is like a poor relation to Matlock, invited to share a cup of grog at the gift-giving holidays; which is to say that Matlock residents fill The Great Outdoorsman and Packard's other modest shops when their pockets are feeling a mite shallow. It also boasts a DMV office with a blessedly short line, a consignment shop whose furniture is perfect for your children's first dormitory rooms, and a small, struggling cinema with third-run movies and lumpy velvet chairs from which the occasional spring protrudes to rip an unmendable hole in your trousers.

But TGO, as it's known, is one of my favorite stores, because it's bright, filled with unpretentious useful things (from long johns to snowshoes), and still run by the family that founded it sometime around the Great Depression.

My mission that day was to procure the swimming trunks with which I had promised Clover I would henceforth gird up my loins. I must have looked a little lost as I ran my hand through a rack of repellently slinky, skimpy garments, because a young woman came over and asked if I needed help.

"Let's see," I said. "If you have access to a time machine that could transport me back to an era when men wore bathing suits that actually concealed something, the answer would be yes."

She laughed. "Oh, these are just the Speedos."

"As opposed to the Slomos?"

She laughed again, her amusement genuine. I felt pleased with my sly little quip. "That's very funny," she said. "But follow me."

For the second time that day, an attractive woman was leading me forward toward the future. This one took me all the way across the store, through aisles filled with clothing for climatic conditions at the opposite end of the seasonal spectrum. TGO was not air-conditioned, and I began to perspire at the mere sight of all that fleece and flannel.

"Here are the more traditional trunks," she said when we reached a rack near the fitting rooms. "There's not a lot left, I'm afraid. But all the swimwear's half off now."

"Doesn't anyone get a yen for a new suit in the midst of a heat wave like this? And do you honestly believe that someone's going to purchase anything made of suede?" I pointed to a row of jackets lined with sheepskin.

"The world is a strange and often illogical place," said the young woman. "The answer to both of those questions would be yes."

This was not your typical sales gal.

I turned my attention to the three swimsuits left in my size. At least they were cut to my expectations—and dirt cheap—but there was nothing subdued or solid. Two were faux Hawaiian, the third printed with a madras plaid I associate with people who join country clubs. I pulled out the two Hawaiians.

"Well!" I turned toward a full-length mirror outside the fitting booths.

"Don't you want to try them on?" asked my handmaiden.

"Not necessary. But lend me your opinion."

With a comic flourish, I struck what I imagined to be a surfing pose, legs akimbo, knees bent. Waistband stretched between my thumbs, I held one and then the other suit in front of me. "Devil? Or the deep blue sea? Pull no punches."

She stood back and narrowed her eyes. I noticed that she did not look like one of the freckled Irish wives from the large family that usually staffed the store. She was about Clover's age, deeply tanned, and her hair was strikingly dark. I wondered if she cared that anyone could see it was dyed.

"Hmm," she said. "The pink pineapples would be a daring choice. You would turn heads in that one. . . . The hula girls are actually more conventional."

The pink pineapples (depicted on an aqua background) were indeed quite gaudy but ornamented a suit with a longer cut. Perhaps it would seem irrational to make the demure choice after having swum buck naked for so long, yet such was my preference. "Daring it shall be," I concluded.

"You won't regret it." My handmaiden held out her hand, and I extended mine to shake it. But she was merely reaching for the hangers.

"Silly me," I said when our hands collided awkwardly. "I thought I was to receive your congratulations. I will have you know that this is the first swimsuit I have purchased since I was in college."

"Well then, I'm glad you're headed back to the water," she said.

I was about to explain my situation to her when I stopped myself. I laughed and shook my head.

"What's so amusing?" she said.

"I'm having one of those—what youngsters so blithely call 'a senior moment.' I thank you for your cordial assistance."

"A genuine pleasure," she said, and she seemed to mean it.

At the cash register, I counted out exact change and told her I didn't need a bag. I also remarked that I had not noticed her working there before.

"I started last month," she said, "and I'm just part-time."

"Well, I hope to solicit your sartorial discretion in the future."

"What a charming thing to say."

"Likewise," I told her. "There is a dearth of compliments in the world these days."

She expressed her agreement and handed me my new suit, neatly folded, along with the sales receipt. Then she said, "It's always nice when the last customer leaves me smiling. Thank you for that." I glanced at the large school clock on the wall; it was nearly a quarter past five. Almost any other clerk would have rushed me out by now.

She locked the front door behind me and waved through the glass as I settled myself on the red-hot vinyl upholstery of my car. Whatever refreshment I'd gleaned from my earlier swim was moot. All the way home, I kept the windows wide open and drove as fast as I dared along the country roads. (*Daring, yes that's me!* I thought, laughing at the image of myself all decked out in oversize magenta pineapples.)

As I approached my driveway, I was chagrined to see the bunch of balloons tied to the much larger mailbox now adjacent to mine, the one that blared **elves & fairies** (purple letters, sans serif, lowercase). I groaned. "Now it begins," I muttered. In two hours, the place would be crawling with E & F's eager-beaver parents. I'd rented the movie *Cape Fear* (I was on a Mitchum kick) and planned to watch it, with my dinner, in front of a fan in Poppy's dressing room. Never mind the heat up there; no one would spy on me.

The second thing I saw was the dark-skinned fellow who showed up at Mistress Lorelei's every so often to tend to her flowers and shrubs. In recent years, master shyster Tommy Loud (a grade-school classmate of Trudy's) had expanded his snow-and-tree-removal business by importing a literal truckload of foreign workers to mow lawns, build showy walls, and maintain swimming pools (another distressing new trend). Generally, they were dropped off by the half dozen, along with an armada of high-powered mowers, blowers, and trimmers. You could hear their work a mile away: a plague of locusts on steroids.

But this fellow arrived solo, worked hard, and then seemed to vanish as if into thin air. Once in a while, I'd nodded to him through the trees. He had nodded back.

Now he paced at the foot of Lorelei's driveway, looking at his watch and wiping the sweat from his face with a gray rag. He appeared agitated, and I could hardly blame him. Thanks to Lorelei's passion for keeping nature at bay, the foot of her driveway—paved, of course—was bathed in late August sun.

I parked my car by the house and walked back. "Hello!" I called out. "Need anything there?"

He looked startled to be addressed, and I wished that I had some language other than poofy French at my service.

"Sir," he said, and he bobbed his head.

For a moment, we stared at each other in perplexed silence. Then he said, "I have been waiting for the truck nearly an hour. Could I . . . telephone?" His accent was strong, yet all I could tell was that it wasn't French.

"Of course," I said. "Come on over."

"Thank you." He made a great fuss of wiping his feet at the front door.

"Oh just come on in," I said. "I'm the world's worst housekeeper."

He entered and gazed slowly around. I pointed to the phone. Still he paused, looking at his hands, which were covered with Mistress Lorelei's high-class topsoil. He held a large rumpled paper bag.

"Listen," I said. "Come wash up and get a drink. You look like a fugitive from the Foreign Legion."

Insistently, I beckoned him toward the kitchen, where I poured him a glass of Clover's mint lemonade while he washed his hands at the sink.

"I thank you," he said before he drank the lemonade—which he did in one long draft.

"Now don't get brain freeze, young man."

He stared at me for a moment. He must have thought me mad.

"Oh don't mind me." I handed him the cordless phone Robert had attached to the wall by the fridge.

I left the room while he made his call. A moment later, he came into the living room. "They forgot me." He smiled calmly. "I'll go wait again."

"Please wait on my front porch, in the shade," I said. I saw him out the door, and I pointed to the wicker chairs. "Here. I insist. You don't even have a hat. You can see your ride pull up right through those trees."

Tentatively, he sat. He looked older than most of the boys I'd seen on Tommy's trucks; late twenties, perhaps. He had an unmistakably Mayan profile, dignified yet vaguely equine. I wondered what long, sad journey had landed him here, a lawn serf in Matlock. I didn't want to know how little he was paid by Tommy Loud. I hoped he didn't have children. Not yet.

"What's your name?" I said impulsively, holding out my hand (and thinking, fleetingly, of my gaffe at TGO). "Mine's Percy."

He took my hand firmly, held it more than shook it. "Celestino."

"Well then, Celestino," I said, "make yourself at home. Seventy-three strangers I've never so much as shaken hands with are about to do the same."

I left him on the porch when the phone rang.

"Robert!" I said when I heard my grandson's voice. "I have something hilarious to recount." I went to the kitchen table and found, just where I'd left it, the town paper open to the police log.

～

Every Thursday for more than forty years, the *Grange* had arrived on my doorstep by 6:00 a.m., almost always before the *Boston Globe*. The paper had been through its ups and downs, but during the past few years its subscription rate had risen to record levels, since the latest editor in chief was a retired Pulitzer winner from the *Wall Street Journal*. (Yes, only in Matlock.) Which meant that the news, provincial though it was, would be delivered with efficiency, taste, and very few typos. (And that editorials, though eloquent to be sure, would bellow, COLOSSAL IF DODDERING EGO!) Yet there was still gossip, triviality, and quaintness aplenty. Christenings and confirmations (High Episcopalian) appeared on the same page as the obituaries—right across from yard sales and the scores of high school lacrosse games. Once, even Girl Scout and 4-H badges had been listed. Our resident columnist, holding forth for the past twenty years, called herself the Fence Sitter, though she was anything but. If opinions were underdrawers, she would be Fruit of the Loom.

When Poppy was alive, I saw the paper first, before I left for Cambridge. I would circle for her the funniest or most bucolic item I could find. When I returned in the late afternoon, she would have countered by circling for me another source of amusement. I would find the paper folded open to her selection, beside it my glass of red wine, on the long rough-hewn table in the kitchen. As I took my first sip, I would gaze over the lawn toward the barn and, beyond it, the glassy veneer of the pond. Even in winter, with all the windows shut tight and glazed with frost, I would hear the music, and sometimes Poppy's voice, strident or praising or keeping time in song. Poppy taught her lessons—always sold out, often with waiting lists—until the very day she died.

Left to raise our teenage girls, I kept many of our rituals intact—even those that hadn't involved our daughters. So I continued to circle my favorite item in the paper every week, to leave it displayed on the table. Perhaps I was hoping that when I came home, Trudy or Clover might have taken up her mother's side of our frivolous duet. But no. The paper would be in the garbage by the time I returned—or buried beneath a haphazard stack of textbooks and schoolwork, a plate of Oreos, a balled-up sweater. What a silly hope that was. I had so many silly thoughts and hopes about the girls back then—and no one to help me sort them out. Once, quite recently, when I hinted at regrets about those times, a much older Clover said, "Oh Daddy, you were deranged, and you deserved to be." Well, I thought unkindly, and you would know about derangement, would you not?

When the girls were small, I heard Poppy tell one of her friends, "I don't see how you could ever have a favorite when there are just two: one will always and forever be your first, the miracle baby, the one who paves the way, strikes out for adventure—the intrepid one, the one who teaches you how to do what nature intended all along—and the other, oh the other will always be your baby, your darling, the one you surprised yourself by loving just as desperately much as you loved the first."

Pursuant to such sentimental partition, Clover ought to have been the intrepid one, the maverick, and Trudy the eternal infant, the one to cuddle, to indulge your adoration. It did not turn out that way.

Poppy and I had named our daughters not by consulting our family trees but by following our passions and then our ideals. When Clover was born, Poppy and I still felt like newlyweds; in the hospital room, as I beheld this new creature, this bundled beauty, I kissed my wife and said, "Flower from a flower." We swept aside Rose, Iris, and Lily for a wilder, less pretentious cousin.

Not fourteen months later, our second child arrived the day after Jack Kennedy was murdered. Such a solemn, bittersweet occasion, that birth. "We must give her a strong, virtuous name," said Poppy. Tearful over the violence and calumny of modern times, we named her for the first woman who had lived in our ancient house, in what we fancied an era when goodness had been essential to human survival. Truthful and Hosmer Fisk had settled here, next to Hosmer's older brother, Azor. From records in the library, we learned that Hosmer and his bride struggled to grow potatoes, turnips, and pumpkins in Matlock's stony soil; four of their seven children reached ages at which they, too, could work the farm. Two lived on to have children of their own. Hosmer's descendants had persisted in our house for three more generations.

Over our friends' polite bewilderment, over our mothers' united dismay, we named our second daughter Truthful Darling. To us, it was a gorgeous, steadfast name, one that mingled courage and honesty with tenderness and love. Alas, it became a source of profound embarrassment to her the minute she set foot in school; even professionally, in her byline on dry articles in lofty medical journals, she has never used it.

Shortly before my retirement, Trudy had been appointed chief of breast oncology at the leading cancer hospital in New England. Her picture appeared in a national magazine, in an article about groundbreaking female physicians. There she was, my own daughter, the baby of the family, posed in her office, an expression of businesslike dignity on her face, a stethoscope sprouting like a silver orchid from a pocket of her white jacket. My phone rang itself silly. I heard from friends I hadn't seen in years—friends of Poppy's, that is.

Clover had led a much more varied life than her little sister—but that variety reflected a series of false starts, not bold adventures. After college (where she majored in sociology, a subject whose revelations she never shared with me), she worked as a waitress in a coffee shop, a gymnastics instructor, a ticket vendor in a Broadway box office, a clerk in a pharmacy, and, perhaps most memorably, as a uniformed parking valet at Boston's most expensive seafood restaurant, less than a mile from her sister's medical suite. Through her twenties, Clover lived with an equally eclectic succession of men, most of them with equally unfixed ambitions. And then she married a supremely decent fellow with a steady job as, of all things, an accountant. She met him when he kept her out of jail for having failed to pay self-employment tax for several years running.

Marrying Todd and having children seemed to cure her of her peripatetic predilections; I made the naïve assumption that Clover had found her vocation in family. Leander and Filomena were the normal, healthy "perfect" set of New York City children, to whom my daughter appeared to be devoted. I have a photograph of them on their prosperous Brooklyn block, little Filo sitting in a stroller, clutching a stuffed penguin, while her brother, Lee, rides shotgun on some skateboard contraption at the back. Clover stands behind and above him, her smile grand, even grateful (Todd the photographer, surely).

Filo and Lee were six and nine years old—both, finally, in school for a good deal of the day—when their mother began to lose her way. I must speak in such hazy terms because she did not confide in me; only later, from Todd, did I glean any reliable information—though even he was not terribly specific. I thought he was simply respecting her privacy or, poor man, embarrassed. At any rate, I believed my daughter's life was just swell until the night, three years ago now, when Todd called me to say that Clover had apparently "run away." He stated this with so little panic that I laughed. And then he asked if she'd spoken to me. Was she even, perhaps, on her way to Matlock?

He had come home to find the children alone in the apartment. They reported that their mother had brought them home from school and, while fixing them a snack, had accidentally dropped a pile of plates, which smashed on the floor. She had begun to cry hysterically and then had shut herself in her bedroom. Eventually, she had come out with a suitcase, assured Lee that his father would be home within the hour, told him to stay inside with the door locked. She said she would return in a few days.

Five hours later, Clover turned up at Trudy's house. She stayed for two days, after which we talked her into returning home. What ensued was a horrendous month during which Clover slept a good part of every day and ate very little. Todd, whose composure rivals that of Mount Rushmore, became frustrated and impatient. Nearly every call he made to me began with "Has she told you anything?"—as if I would be my daughter's prime confidant.

Finally, under pressure from her sister, Clover agreed to see her gynecologist; Trudy had a theory that the emotional turmoil was biologically based, hormones gone haywire as Clover entered the "change of life," and that the problem might call for a pharmaceutical fix. The gynecologist, whom Trudy later branded a hyperfeminist charlatan, agreed that Clover was experiencing a traumatic "perry" menopause (whatever in God's name that might be). Instead of drugs, however, she prescribed an all-female therapy group. After four months, Clover announced that she needed to take a "sabbatical" from marriage and motherhood.

I heard only bits and pieces of this mortifying drama, much of it (to my shock) via young Robert, who was still in high school at the time. Often at first, and then only rarely, Todd continued to telephone me. I began to realize, from the jargon he used, that he was already consulting a lawyer.

And then, one February evening, an alarmingly thin Clover showed up on my doorstep: torrents of tears, no suitcase, not even a decent coat.

How hard I struggled to hold this daughter and console her, rather than shake her till her bones rattled, ask her what was missing in that brain of hers, why she seemed chronically unable to take responsibility for the lives of herself and her children. What kept her from becoming— and this was stunningly unkind, but it passed through my mind in the worst moments of the crisis—the sort of übersuccessful, überconfident, überenlightened grown-up that nearly every other child from her generation raised in this town had become? Now, and the irony did not escape either of us, she was about to start looking after the freshest generation of these children, the charmed little darlings of Matlock.

Filo and Lee were now nine and twelve. They came north to visit their mother every other weekend, every other major holiday and school vacation, and for most of the summer. Over and over, their father drove from New York to the same pizza parlor in Hartford to deliver them to their wayward mother or pick them up again. Logically, I ought to have seen more of them than I would have if Clover had stayed put, but she tended to keep them close when she had them, as if to make up for her lack of presence in what I'm sure they regarded as their "real life" in New York.

As I spoke with Robert on the phone that evening—heard about his new classes, the apartment he was renting off-campus with one of his pals—I carried the phone onto the porch outside the kitchen. When I opened the screen door, a long cylinder toppled against my foot and rolled across the boards.

Half listening to Robert itemize his classes, I picked up the object: a cardboard tube, on which was written this note. *Dear Mr. Darling: Enclosed are the tree house drawings. I hope you'll be intrigued. I hope you'll approve! I am open to suggestion. Yours, Young Man Ira.*

Audacious, the pixie.

I returned my attention to Robert, though the scene before me proved yet another distraction. The pond, mimicking the sky, was already tilting toward a robust persimmon. The days might still be scorching hot, but they were becoming noticeably shorter.

Down at the barn, Clover was busy affixing a welcoming banner over the door. As she stood on a step stool, reaching as high as she could, I fought against the judgment that her short flowery dress was unbefitting her age. Clover had always been one of those spritelike girls who simply never stop being girls. And why should they? It's the girlishness that gets them what they need: everything except true independence, or what we used to call maturity. She was a puzzle, this daughter of mine.

Robert was describing an "ethnic studies" course with some trendier-than-thou title like Issues of Immigration in Modern Society—something to fulfill a certain necessary requirement, to help make him a well-rounded student—when I realized that Clover could use my assistance. I told my grandson I had to get off the phone. I called down the hill, "Hang on there, daughter!"

Considering all her shortcomings, all her failures, you might assume that I did not love Clover as much as I loved her sister. Wrong. Call me arrogant, facile, even ostentatious in my disapproval, but one thing about Clover that always touched me deeply back then, that moved me to private tears, was this: she did not blame me for her mother's death or for the mistakes I must have made in trying to become, thereafter, both parents in one.

Countless times I had wondered, as I did on that pink, hazy, tropically warm evening just over a year ago, how Poppy would have handled this daughter differently; if she would have steered Clover to steadier ground—yet not as often as I had wondered what I might have done (or not done) on another, equally sultry summer night to alter whatever simple chain of events had led to Poppy's drowning in the pond.

2

ombre!" Tom Loud leaned across the front seat and opened the passenger door. *"Muchos apologias."*

Celestino climbed into the cab and nodded at Loud. "Thanks."

"Gil must be a little sunstruck today." Loud tapped his large bronze forehead. As he pulled into the road, he glanced at the purple mailbox and laughed, a grunt. "Elves and Fairies come to roost at Old Man Darling's place. How perfect or what." He cocked his eyebrows at Celestino, as if the two men could share in this vision of justice, whatever it was.

Celestino did not know whether he disliked Loud more because he exploited people or because he, Celestino, was obliged to be grateful that the man had noticed his particular talents and raised him above the other guys in status and pay. This "special treatment" made Celestino more of an outsider than he had already been. Gilberto had not forgotten Celestino because of the sun; he had ditched him, knowingly left him to roast by the side of the road. The Brazilians—and even the Quiché *chapines,* the ones who spoke fluent Spanish—had known he was different from the start. Sometimes he was certain they could sense that he'd had a big advantage and he'd blown it. When Loud had sent him out to work by himself in the spring, he'd been relieved.

Still, Loud was an *hijo de puta,* so to owe him a debt was, equally, to wish him eternal damnation. Now the *hijo de puta* was chattering on, like a parrot, as much to himself as to Celestino, about the threat of water restrictions, the problem of keeping his clients' lawns green without sprinklers. At least he'd abandoned the slopbucket Spanish. Celestino examined the man's soft, fiercely tanned face, greasy with sweat, his thinning yellow hair. The devil would have a fine time with this one.

"You're mighty silent, *hombre,*" said Loud as they entered the train station lot. "Jobs go all right?"

"Yes, everything."

"You plant those hydrangeas today?"

"Yes."

"They'll need the soaker hose. This fucking weather's like Vegas."

Celestino said nothing. He had set the soaker hose, as instructed. Of course he had. He had fertilized the tomatoes. He had baited the Havahart trap for the woodchuck at Mrs. Bullard's. (She'd make sure he delivered the animal to the wildlife station; she wouldn't hear of poisons, death of any kind.) Tomorrow he would climb a tall cherry tree split by lightning, remove the burnt limbs, then bolt the trunk back together, in hopes that the tree could grow around its wound.

Celestino did whatever Loud asked him to do. More.

Loud pulled up at the platform. "Okay then, *hombre*. Tomorrow, six. I'll make sure Gil is here on time. Damn sure."

Celestino might have echoed Loud's tone, smirked and said, *We'll see*, but he simply said, "Yes." He made sure to smile. The less he said, the less he would have to hear in return. He could always pretend exhaustion, at least at the end of the day. Though Loud knew otherwise, most people Celestino met as he did his work believed that he spoke little English. He liked it that way. For now.

"You're a curious fellow, my man," said Loud as Celestino closed the door.

Through the open window, he made himself smile. He answered his boss, "Curious, maybe I am. I don't mind."

Loud laughed. "Well, it won't win you many fans or congregants, as my mother likes to say." At last he drove off, waving carelessly out his window.

This much you could give the man: he had a tough hide and an easy temper. He wasn't sensitive, didn't care what anyone thought of him. He was rich, and his wife was a beauty, slim as a fisher. He had a swimming pool, big cars, a big house: he aimed for these things and wouldn't have hidden these desires from anyone.

Celestino forced himself to return the wave.

On the train, other passengers kept their distance. He always stank of the day's sweat, even if he changed his shirt. Not that the train was crowded; he had what Loud called the anticommute. Away from the city early in the morning, evenings headed back in. This, too—his train pass—was a "gift" from his boss, the cost (at a discount) deducted from his pay each week. The people on the trains he took were an unpredictable mix, but he had never once seen another man who looked like he worked all day in the sun and the dirt.

Celestino was the only worker in Loud's operation who did not live in one of the houses their boss owned in Packard. He had seen them, once, early on, when Loud insisted he'd get a better deal than in Lothian, the crowded, ugly town where Celestino lived. The rent in Loud's houses was low, and they were clean enough, but they weren't much different from dormitories: two men to a room, a few bathrooms shared by many. Celestino's place—the attic of a rundown house, with a corner kitchen, a toilet, a shower—was frigid in winter, beastly hot all summer. Often, it leaked. But the woman who lived in the rest of the house let him stay there cheap in exchange for doing repairs and for making it clear to the neighborhood punks that a man slept under her roof. Years before, Mrs. Karp had hired an aunt of Celestino's cousin's wife to babysit her children, all moved away now, her husband dead. This arrangement, though it meant extra work on top of too much already, allowed Celestino to keep to himself.

No friends, no temptations, no involvements with other people's mess-ups, tragedies, injustices, schemes. Celestino had his own: his mother in Antigua; his father only God knew where, probably murdered; his two younger sisters working at the tourist hotel. Like him, working too hard, paid too little—but safe. Celestino tried not to think about their village, what had become of it since the raids.

The more Celestino lived on his own, the more he felt, and was ashamed of it, that each person stands alone and ought to be responsible for himself alone. Or herself. Except that when it came to women, that's not how he'd been raised. Why couldn't he have brothers instead of sisters, young men he could leave to their own designs, trust to care for their mother without his help? He could have stopped sending money to his sisters and never heard a word of complaint, but his dreams would not have let him sleep. He yearned to hear that Marta and Adela had married, found men to shoulder this burden.

Where he came from was beautiful; where he worked now, beautiful too. In summer here, there was something of the jungle in Matlock: its tall, muscular, enfolding trees; the still, humid air held close by the canopy of leaves; the swamps that nurtured flowers and mosquitoes alike. Things grew too well, all the wild greenery eager to choke out the tame. This was how Loud made his biggest money. *Landscaping,* he called it, this beating back the wilderness from large, luxurious homes.

Yet the more he learned, the more this work satisfied Celestino, and sometimes—after hours laboring alone—it made him secretly proud. Or not so secretly; he knew Loud had sensed this about him months ago. That was when Loud began sending him to work on the gardens and lawns where the owners needed someone who knew the ways of delicate flowers and elegant trees, places where imagination and cunning (and always a good deal of money) had gone into making a paradise. Many of these people were away from home when Celestino did his work. They left their garages and toolsheds open so that he could help himself to shovels and shears. Loud's work trucks—the ones that carried teams of men and boys who mowed, pruned, and raked with indifference and speed—carried tools of the trade, but nothing refined or specialized, like the dibbles, cultivators, and strangely shaped hoes at Mrs. Anderson's place. Mrs. Anderson, a twig of a woman, old and dramatically thin, had introduced dozens of tools to Celestino as if they were her children, slowly repeating their names and functions. Celestino did not report this to Loud, for fear he would see it as "fraternizing with the client."

When someone was home, it was almost always a woman. She might bring him cold tea or juice, offer sandwiches, or simply place food and drink on a table beside a pool or under a tree. Loud's policy was that only he, not the people whose property he tended, gave instructions. He never said so, certainly not, but it was assumed among his workers that to break this rule—to forge any direct relationship with Loud's customers—might lead to deportation. There was talk everywhere now of immigration raids—not here, perhaps, where the rich were rich enough to be generous, where their complicated jobs were not threatened, but as near as New Hampshire. The mayor of a small town just north of the Massachusetts border had begun to stop cars of brown-skinned men at random. *Live Legal or Get a Boot in the Ass:* this should be the new slogan on the New Hampshire license plate.

Silence was more than golden; it was survival. To the white women who made the white sandwiches, all the men in Loud's crew, like members of an army, were anonymous, changeable one for the next. A few weeks back, as he'd walked up a driveway, Celestino had heard a woman say into her phone, "I have to go. My lawn soldier's here."

These women would smile at him in a furtive, hopeful way, then pantomime eating or drinking. Sometimes he would go along with this absurdity, nodding or even miming back, as if he were not just foreign but deaf and mute as well; but mostly he would assure them that he did speak their language—a little. Enough. He did not invite conversation. He liked the solitude of his work. His father had preached the importance of doing "civilized work, work commanding respect." Celestino had come to see his work in this way, but his father would not have agreed. In the final year Celestino had watched his father at work, Raul had been *patrón* to more than a dozen men.

Celestino had been three or four years old before he understood that their village was different from other villages—but this had not always been true. Only a few years before Celestino was born, life for his father, for their relatives and neighbors, had changed. By a celestial stroke of fate, as Raul saw it—dumb luck, Loud would have said—a band of archaeologists had made their village the base for an excavation. Raul had been twenty, just married to Celestino's mother, when these men drove into the jungle from Flores. They were white, friendly, talkative. Many spoke Spanish—university Spanish. Raul and some of the other villagers knew a bit of Spanish from working on the logging crews near the Mexican border.

During his childhood, Celestino heard his father tell the story many times. The men drove brand-new jeeps, pulling trailers from which they would later unload tools, books, and tents that, once stretched on their frames, made the villagers' houses, however colorful, look small, even squalid. They arrived two days before Buena Noche, the village hung with clay ornaments to celebrate the Nativity, mingled with masks and flowers made of woven palms.

Such processions of cars had been seen before—they carried the tourists who came to see the fallen temples—yet always they passed through. Rarely did they stop. Amid the nervous curiosity surrounding these strangers who did stop, Raul joked that the Three Kings and their courtiers had arrived a bit early this year. This was before General Lucas, before the government raids reached their part of the country; by then, the sound of approaching vehicles inspired only fear.

As they were to learn, Dr. Lartigue had already spoken to authorities in Flores. A state official stood by his side when he called a meeting in the square, as soon as the last stall in the market had closed for the day. Standing on a poultry crate, he described the archaeological dig that was about to begin, a magnificent project that would grow for years and years. Raul loved to tell how the white man who spoke city Spanish held up a smooth stone face that he claimed was the face of a god. It had been discovered not far from the village, he said, and if there were more treasures to be found, they would go to nearby museums, would draw more tourists from distant countries who wanted to learn about the traditions and the artistic genius of the villagers' ancestors.

Then he told them how they, the villagers, could make a good living working for the archaeologists, how there would be many jobs. They could earn enough money to support their families through the seasons when the archaeologists would go back to their universities and teach their students about their discoveries. They would also pay a few men to protect the project while it lay waiting for their return.

Unlike Celestino, Raul was never shy. Before the end of that first season, he was directing a small crew (mostly cousins and friends), wielding machetes and shovels according to the archaeologists' directions. Some of these men had worked before as loggers; they said this work was safer and kinder: better pay, shorter hours, many breaks.

Dr. Lartigue liked Raul. It wasn't just that other men listened to him, or that he spoke Spanish and could read well enough. "I made him know he could trust me, and he could," Raul would say when he told the story.

Celestino was born in 1981, during the fourth season of the dig. By this time, Dr. Lartigue had made sure that the village had a good teacher for the children, a man from the city. There was electricity for everyone, more reliable plumbing. There were jeeps left behind when the archaeologists returned to the States. Celestino and his sisters learned Spanish, lived comfortably, and they would accompany their mother, who cooked for the Americans, into Flores when she shopped for provisions.

After the day's work was over, Dr. Lartigue often invited Raul and a few others to his tent. He wanted to hear what he called "local tales"; in exchange, he gave lessons in English and archaeology. He showed them large books of photographs—the pyramids and temples of Mexico, Honduras, and their own part of the world, El Petén. They learned how to mark off excavation pits with stakes and string, how to use measuring tools, how to tell fragments of pots and statues and buildings from ordinary stones. Dr. Lartigue explained how projects like this one attracted thieves, how it was important to be careful when strangers showed up. He kept a gun in a locked box under his cot.

Dr. Lartigue's wife was one of a few women who came along with the foreign men, though she would come for only a few weeks. She would help Celestino's mother and aunt do the shopping and cooking. Sometimes his family shared their noon meal with the archaeologists; once he was in school, Celestino could translate from his mother's tongue to Señora Lartigue's Spanish. By the time he was old enough to sit still, Celestino was welcome in Dr. Lartigue's tent along with his father.

"You will learn English, too," Raul told his son, "and you will do this work, too. We are lucky. We work with men who use their minds. Men who use reason as a muscle." He had squeezed his thick arm to demonstrate.

Celestino took for granted the dependable cycle of work, just like the changing of seasons for those who grew coffee or mangoes. Five months of orderly, well-paid work were followed by seven months when the project slept. During the rains, there were occasional visitors, often in the company of Dr. Lartigue or a government official, but mostly the village returned to a slightly modernized version of its former simple self. Raul and a few other men patrolled the site. A locked shed held the most valuable tools, the maps, books, and other papers sealed in plastic tubs. Celestino was too young to understand that the excavation gave their village invisible protection from the war, from the military raids that had stretched by now far into the mountains and jungles.

He joined the excavation crew when he was twelve. But Dr. Lartigue had other ideas for Celestino, ideas beyond the slashing and digging, the sifting of the clay they dried in wide trays, in the sunlit clearings. The year Celestino turned fifteen, Dr. Lartigue told Raul about an exchange program for Spanish-speaking natives ("indigenous peoples") that would permit his son to go to the United States for four months and attend an American school. An immersion program, Dr. Lartigue called it. One of the schools that sponsored the program was near his house; Celestino could live with Dr. and Señora Lartigue and their two children. "My daughter is just a year younger than you are," he said to

Celestino. "She'll show you the lay of the land. She knows her way around, *ma fille.*" He'd laughed. "Perhaps too well."

Raul could not believe their good fortune. He had dreams that Celestino would beat a new path on which his sisters would follow. What a life they could have—all of them—if Celestino went away with Dr. Lartigue.

As Celestino's train made its way toward Boston, it would pass one or two trains on the outbound track. They were filled, you could tell as they hurtled by, with people dressed for office jobs. Some of these people were hurtling toward the gardens he'd spent his day watering, weeding, and cajoling into bloom. Would the man in the huge white house, the farmhouse that no longer sat on a farm, notice that his peach trees had been trimmed today, the rotten fruit discarded? Would Mrs. Connaughton's husband see that the sunflowers had been straightened, secured to wooden stakes? Celestino had never met these men; he could only imagine their existence.

Was he praised? Hardly ever. But that wasn't what he aimed for. What he aimed for was a life of not working for Tom Loud or anyone like him. Yet it became increasingly clear that Loud, or someone like him, would have to be the one to help Celestino break free. He would have to have a sponsor; he would have to become valued, indispensable. Perhaps this was the humiliation God would exact from Celestino; it was only fair. That he would have to become like a loyal, skilled hunting dog to the *hijo de puta.*

He would have to be nicer to Loud; he must make himself do this. *My stubborn one,* his mother called him. Also *my quiet one.* Stubborn and quiet: these were not qualities that married well if you wished to find favor. They were qualities you had to mold: *quiet* into listening and learning, *stubborn* into work.

Celestino was more frugal than Loud's other workers ("your *compadres,*" Loud called them when he spoke of them to Celestino). He did not have a cell phone. He did not gamble on cards or buy lottery tickets. He'd found free clothes, decent clothes, left in bags behind a church on the block where he lived. He often wrapped and saved for later the sandwiches he was given by the women whose gardens he tended; once in a while, Mrs. Karp gave him a dish of leftover chicken or lasagne. If she traveled to visit one of her children, she told him to take food from her refrigerator, to keep it from spoiling. He drank one beer, or none, each night. Every so often, he went to Mass.

He sent half the money he saved to Marta and Adela, who lived with their mother. Because of pain in her back, Mamá could no longer work at the hotel. She could not lift the thick mattresses on the fancy beds or carry stacks of linens, bath towels the size of blankets, down the endless halls (once the halls of a monastery). She could not walk all day on the hard stone floors that the tourists found so charming. She could not bend to clean a bathroom tub—or get up again once she had. From what his sisters had told him, during the phone calls he made every few months, Mamá sat in their apartment and watched soap operas all day long—while claiming that her Spanish was too poor for any job not requiring exertion. Sometimes she made weavings that Marta and Adela took to the hotel shop, where tourists bought them to lay across their dining tables in London or Miami Beach.

When Celestino thought of Dr. Lartigue, he felt rage as often as pity. It was not right to be angry at someone for dying, especially dying too young, but this was how he felt when he was awakened at night by the teenage boys who played ugly music in the street or cruised noisily back and forth on their skateboards. He would lie awake and imagine his way through Dr. Lartigue's house in Cambridge: its winding stairs with the beautifully carved railings, the silver kitchen with its long green table where Señora Lartigue arranged every meal so artfully, fancy or plain (every meal delicious, served with wine or juice she had squeezed from fresh fruit). Dr. Lartigue's study, filled with so many books that they overflowed the shelves and stood in stacks as tall as a school-age boy; stone sculptures, frayed textiles, paintings of pyramids and tattooed gods that leaned against the towers of books. The porch surrounded by Japanese maples. Celestino's room on the third floor the first time he stayed there: a small room, like a bird's nest. Later on, the larger room on the second floor, the room left behind by Etienne, Dr. Lartigue's son. Isabelle's room, next to Etienne's, her white bedspread with the blue-flowered squares. Isabelle's voice. Isabelle's eyes and hands and feet, everything between.

If not for Isabelle. If not for Dr. Lartigue's heart attack. If not for

Señora Lartigue's anger. If not for his own childish fear. If not, if not, if not. How useless these words, these dead-end wishes. His sister Marta, who knew about these wishes, told him they proved he'd been tainted by his time in America. People with too much money bought themselves regret along with big houses and cars, she said once. Regret was a disease, a fever. (But the money that went with the illness—this she liked, didn't she?)

On his way from the station in Lothian, Celestino bought eggs, an onion, a potato, and a pepper. The fat green ones tasted raw, unfinished, but they were the cheap ones. Mrs. Marsh, whose vast vegetable garden Celestino weeded and watered twice a week, had told him to help himself to her tomatoes that morning. They were spectacular tomatoes, some purple, some striped like flames, others yellow as taxis. When he shook his head, she said, "Don't be ridiculous. All I did was plant them. You're the one who keeps them growing." He had carried the bag of tomatoes with him to Mrs. Connaughton's, his afternoon job, but then, stupidly, had left it beside the kitchen sink of the man who'd let him call for a ride. He should have walked to the train station, to hell with Gilberto. He had been lazy.

In his kitchen, he turned on the radio—the volume low. He was careful to keep Mrs. Karp happy, to jump when she needed him and otherwise to intrude on her life as little as possible. She was kind enough, but she could raise the rent at her whim—or decide she didn't need him. And what if she should sell the house? Would he be forced to join his *"compadres"* in Packard?

He listened to the news while he cooked. The war, always the war in Iraq. More suicide bombings. Children blown up on their way to school. I could have family *there,* he thought. He enforced the habit of reminding himself how his life could be so much worse, how Guatemala was said to be peaceful now, no more soldiers burning down villages, raping and killing the women. Even in the city, his mother and sisters were safer now. Mrs. Connaughton had insisted on showing Celestino her photographs from a tour she took the year before. "Your country is divine," she declared. "I have never seen people who have such an exquisite sense of *color.*"

As he chopped the pepper, he pictured the tomatoes he'd left on that kitchen counter. Mrs. Connaughton's neighbor—Percy—had reminded

Celestino of Dr. Lartigue. He was tall, his eyes the same silvery blue. But more than these features, he had that scholar's air about him, the same clothes: khaki shorts and a thinly striped cotton shirt with the sleeves rolled up, the same shirt you could wear with a tie and a suit. As if such men must always be prepared to dress up at a moment's notice for a party or a business meeting. The first time Celestino had gone to live in Cambridge, Dr. Lartigue had bought him some of these clothes.

The rooms Celestino had passed through, on his way to Percy's kitchen, were old in a vain sort of way. The dark rafters hung below the ceilings, and the floorboards slanted this way and that. The rooms were stuffed with old things, decorated with flowery patterns the sun had faded long ago. You could not have fit in one more stack of books or historical picture: so much like Dr. Lartigue's study. There was a portrait in a gold frame over a fireplace, the paint so crackled and darkened by smoke that all you could really see was the man's moonlike face, its attitude grim, and a white patch of shirt inside a black, or blackened, coat. Throughout the rooms, a lime-colored dusting of pollen lay across every surface, from books to sofa cushions.

That part, the dustiness, wasn't like the Lartigues' house. Señora Lartigue kept the rooms as clean as could be. Her conscience, though—could that be clean? Did she think of him, ever? Wonder where he was? Probably not.

Celestino tried so often to bury the fantasy, stale by now, of returning to that house as a man with his own business—not the archaeologist he'd dreamed of being when he was small, nothing so far-fetched, but a designer of gardens, even parks—and seeking Isabelle. But surely Isabelle was living elsewhere, possibly married. She would be twenty-five.

Celestino was twenty-six. He had not been back to Guatemala in seven years, not since before Dr. Lartigue had died, not since Señora Lartigue, two months later, had guessed correctly that he and Isabelle were sleeping together under her roof, had coldheartedly ambushed them in bed. How stupid that had been, how reckless. It did not matter that, as Isabelle had shouted to her mother, they were "old enough!"

In a panic, certain that in her fury Señora Lartigue would have his student visa canceled, make sure that he was sent back to his country, his village, forbidden ever to set foot here again, Celestino had run. He had taken a bus to New York, where an older cousin drove a gypsy cab.

For two weeks he had stayed in the cousin's apartment, hardly going outside, as if Señora Lartigue might descend from the open sky, a scornful black eagle, swoop him up and deliver him to his punishment. One day his cousin told him he had to leave or work. So he'd worked, a few months here, a few months there: busboy, night clerk in a bodega, janitor in a dress factory. Finally, he mowed lawns in the Bronx, for Spanish-speaking families who'd made enough money to buy houses. He worked almost mindlessly for two years before he realized that this, too, had been stupid and reckless.

Some childhood vision of Señora Lartigue as an all-powerful goddess—like the Aztec goddess who ate warriors whole, the one in the stone relief on Dr. Lartigue's desk—had blinded him to reason. She had been free to kick him out of her home, but could she really have taken away his chances at finishing college? Even though Dr. Lartigue was no longer around to help with his tuition, wouldn't the school have taken pity on Celestino, helped him stay, given him work to pay for his classes? All this had not occurred to him until it was too late. And when he thought of Isabelle, how his fear of her mother had outstripped his desire to be with her, he had to wonder whether he'd deserved all his good fortune in the first place. Maybe Dr. Lartigue had been a poor judge to see Celestino as "a boy with potential."

In the Bronx, there was a fancy estate on the river where people went to admire the flowers and picnic on the lawns. A woman whose grass he mowed had told him they taught classes in gardening there. By that time, his cousin had found a girlfriend and had two babies. Celestino had moved into a place of his own: small, sooty, looking through a fire escape onto the roof of a dry cleaner. The smell from the vent was stifling, the fumes of hell. He could not afford the classes at the estate, but sometimes, on weekends, he went there and walked around, studying the labels beside the plantings, watching the gardeners do their work. A few of them were friendly, so he forced himself to speak up, to ask questions. He learned how to test soil, how to deadhead roses and divide tubers, how to train a fragile vine, how to deepen the roots of saplings so that they would grow tall and hold fast against the wind. He learned about slugs, earthworms, nematodes, aphids, about blights and beetles that threatened the strange northern trees with which he'd become familiar.

He was twenty-four when he'd found the courage to return to

Boston. His cousin knew someone who had a job in a fish-processing plant in Gloucester. There were workers who spoke their language, not just Spanish. But as soon as Celestino arrived in the bus station, he'd taken the T to Harvard Square. Everything seemed shinier, more modern than he remembered—the subway train, the tiled platform, the escalator that carried him into the open air. Even the red brick sidewalks that were meant to seem ancient looked as if they'd been scrubbed. How had so much changed? How had the years passed so quickly? Yet the prosperity he saw made him hopeful. He looked for Isabelle as he walked among the college buildings, toward her family's house—where perhaps he would find her on the shaded porch.

Nothing had changed in the elegant neighborhood where the Lartigues lived. Perhaps the cars, which seemed larger. And the young trees planted along the narrow street: they were taller, dense with leaves. Now he knew the names of these trees. Sycamore, linden, magnolia, spruce. From his time at Wave Hill, he could even identify the different magnolias that flourished this far north, the ones whose late flowers were rarely damaged by frost.

The Lartigues' driveway was empty. The garage was closed. The front curtains—and with a jolt he recognized them, the same blue pattern of country scenes in France—hid the grand rooms within. The mailbox beside the door was stuffed with mail, as if no one had checked it for a couple of days.

He'd stood on the street a long time before daring to walk around the side of the house. He looked about in every direction first, to make sure that no one could see him, call the police. His heart beat hard, warning him away.

The gate, the brick path, the rhododendrons with their rubbery, almost tropical leaves: all of it the same. At the back of the house, he walked close to the edge of a window. The same green table ran from one end of the kitchen to the other. The same green cooking pots hung from a copper rack, like musical instruments waiting to be played. But now there was a dog, which jumped up at the window. It wasn't a menacing dog, but it started barking loudly.

Celestino retreated quickly to the front of the house. He hurried back the way he'd come, back toward the Square. He could still hear the dog barking as he rounded the corner onto Brattle Street.

After stopping to catch his breath, he had walked to the Charles River, a place that would always remind him of Isabelle. What was he doing? Was this folly all about her? He had been with other girls in New York. None for very long, but his life hadn't been suited to settling down, nor had he wanted to settle down. Not there. Unlike his cousin or the other *chapines* he'd met, he wanted more than a shabby apartment in Queens or the Bronx. He did not feel right in the city, and he certainly did not want to have children in the city. He could read the news, see what became of so many children born to people like him. For this reason, he could never completely trust the girls he knew. So many of them seemed to be prowling, like panthers scouting the shadows for mates. (Animal nature, hardly wrong.) The ones he liked, who did tempt him— eventually, they saw that he was not to be caught. A few raged and called him names. Sometimes he told them they were right. This he had learned from Isabelle, to know when you deserve someone's anger, even if you cannot choose to be any different.

Standing by the Charles River, watching two sculls pass by, the rowers bending together like parts of a wooden toy, he remembered going to watch a crew race with the Lartigues. That was during his first visit, when he was fifteen yet felt, in this place, so much younger. They'd had a picnic on the green riverbank. They had introduced him to pâté and capers and cheeses from France.

He thought of going back to the house, waiting for Señora Lartigue. Why? To ask her forgiveness? He laughed. What would it mean after all the time gone by? Dr. Lartigue hadn't even left a will, nothing to show that he'd regarded Celestino—or so he'd said—like another child.

Soon after fleeing to New York, Celestino had telephoned his family. His father had refused to speak with him until he came home to account for his rash behavior. He let a month go by before phoning again. His father held firm. And so it remained, each time he called. Then, just one year after Dr. Lartigue's death, his mother told him that the dig had shut down—almost without warning. For one season, other men had carried on Dr. Lartigue's work, a younger professor in charge. But the following year, as Celestino's father and his crew had prepared for the start of the season, only a few archaeologists came. They had come to close the dig and take their stored belongings away. Their grant had ended, and without Dr. Lartigue's leadership, it would be hard to renew. They assured

Raul that another group of archaeologists, from a museum in Antigua, would soon take over the project. There were no grand speeches to the villagers this time.

Six months later, Celestino got a short letter from one of his sisters. They were moving. A band of thugs had come to the village; there was a panic, fear that the raids had started again, even with the new government in power. People fled, or they hid. It turned out the thugs were looters looking to scavenge the site. Loyal to the end, Raul and two other men tried to defend the locked storeroom. They were beaten. The thieves were angry that the shed contained nothing but tools, books, and papers. They claimed they would return to find out where the valuable things were hidden.

Raul told his wife and daughters that what he had to do was go directly to Antigua and find the museum, tell the archaeologists there about the looters, demand to know when they would come to continue the work of Dr. Lartigue. When the women had not heard from Raul for four months, they decided to travel to the city and find him.

Of course, they never found him. They found a museum that displayed relics like the ones Dr. Lartigue had been digging up near the village, but no one at the museum had heard of Raul—or of plans to continue the dig. The women were lucky to find jobs at a tourist hotel. What was the point of traveling back to their village? The trip they'd taken to reach the city had been risky enough.

That day in Cambridge, as Celestino walked along Brattle Street, past the regal many-windowed houses of the richest, most successful people, with no idea where he was headed or what he intended to do, he noticed two separate groups of Latino men working on the lawns. He listened to them speaking with one another. They were Mexicans, Indians from a region just a few hours from where he'd grown up. He knew their way of speaking from back in New York.

This, he thought, I can do: work on the gardens of the rich and make them grow. I will not have to keep a baseball bat on the floor beside my feet. I will not have to scrub inside the rims of toilets. Dirt, digging in the ground, he did not mind. He knew dirt well. So, it occurred to him, had his father when he had labored for those university men and believed the work would last forever, even change the fortunes of his children. Like father, like son: dreamers in the dirt.

This was how, last spring, he had found his way to Loud, joining a group of men who waited on a city corner every day to be picked up and taken out to the country for work.

He knew that the gardening would end with the first snow—he'd been through two years of this work in the city, under less successful men—and he had to wonder if winter would, once again, throw him back with all the others, sent out to shovel and blow away the snow. A season of misery. But Celestino, who had seen his first gray hair that morning in the small mirror over his sink, was determined that by the time the last leaves fell, things would be very different. He wasn't sure how, not yet, but they would be. They simply had to be.

3

~

From: Trudy Barnes, M.D. <tbarnes@mattmed.org>
To: Robert <baobabbob@econet.net>
Subject: your aunt's birthday

hi robert: don't forget clover's bday dinner fri. pls do
me a favor & buy nice earrings from the upscale hippie
shop nr chauncy: dangly/sexy, don't worry cost, will
reimburse. clara can advise? dad will pick U 2 up at your
house 6:00. granddad bringing cousins—surprise so do not
tell!
xxx mom
p.s. clover's new favorite color is orange

"Hey, Clara," said Robert without turning from the screen. "Mom thinks you've got better taste in earrings than I do."

"Of course she does." Clara lay on Robert's bed, reading her geo textbook.

"Because you're a girl, that what you mean?"

"Because I'm, one, a woman; two, a woman with a sublime sense of fashion; three, the woman your mother hopes you will marry."

Robert laughed. That his mother approved of his girlfriend almost *aggressively* was an open secret; the closed secret was that he had no intention of marrying Clara, or anyone, anytime soon. He was not opposed to marriage—not personally or politically—but nowadays it was little more than a declaration of the intent to have kids. To include kids in any plans for the immediate future would have been reckless in the extreme. Never mind that his mother had given birth to him when she was still in med school. Totally insane.

He spotted an e-mail from Granddad as well, subject *Friday Night's Festivities*. And zap, an IM from Turo: *mtg7! dnt fgt!*

Robert knocked loudly on the wall between their bedrooms. "Hey Turo, F to F, you droid!"

At the end of their sophomore year, it had been Turo's idea that they move off-campus together. Robert had loved their monastically snug yet privileged life in Kirkland House, their narrow beds, their institutional desks, but Turo's passionate conviction, as usual, won him over in the end.

"We'll live economically, willfully," said Turo. "We'll partake of the community as we choose, not by daily coercion."

Robert had glanced out his window at Kirkland's courtyard, where half a dozen half-naked girls were determined to bask in the April sun. "If this be coercion," he said, "then dude, free will be damned."

Turo had laughed. "And look at it this way. A place of our own would give us a certain edge. I mean, if all you can think of is sex, my friend."

Robert admired Turo's urge to resist convention, and once he'd pointed out to his dad that they'd save significant money by living off, even his parents were cool with the plan. But while the choice had been a good one for Robert (that part about the "edge" was true; even Clara seemed to crave him more for his independence), he wasn't sure it was great for Turo. Lately, he'd become so mega intense, so involved in what he called "the underground" (as if they lived in the 1960s, as if anything metaphorically subterranean, truly hidden or secret, were possible now) that he had practically forgotten how to just *be* with other people. Just sit around the kitchen and talk. Sports, girls, parties, profs, just stuff. Between high school and Harvard, Robert had spent a long summer working on a nature preserve in Costa Rica. Not like he'd lived a third-world life (he was just another baby fatcat, no fooling himself about that), but he definitely felt as if he'd opted out of so-called civilization: basically powered down. After the initial freak-out of going offline cold turkey, he'd concluded that plain old-fashioned hanging out, ears off the iPod umbilical, phones and laptops away, no narcotizing of any kind (okay, maybe that great *cerveza* the locals drank), was crucial to your baseline sanity. "I did a low-tech detox," he joked once he returned.

He wondered what it meant that people were so busy reminding him where to be and when. Was he unreliable? Flaky? Hostile to commitment? *Negativo*, as Turo liked to say.

Vertebrates started in half an hour. He spun his chair around. "Cla-*rah*," he whispered. "Rah-rah-*raaah*."

Clara looked across the horizon of her tome. She wore a drab, almost colorless dress, yet it was amazingly hot: so flimsy that Robert could see her navel through the fabric across her belly. Between the top of one long black stocking and her rucked-up hem, he could see two inches of thigh.

Robert began to crawl across the bedroom rug on all fours.

Clara rolled her eyes, but she was into it. She closed the book gracefully, marking her place with the highlighter pen, then swept back her fine yellow hair, exposing her delicate collar bones. "Purr," she commanded. She gazed imperiously at Robert, over the edge of the bed. She inched her body down just enough so that she could reach the door with one foot. She closed it.

Robert purred. Clara laughed her Tinkerbell laugh.

"Now, bobcat," she said, pointing a finger at him, "behave yourself."

Robert counted: twenty-three people, and the meeting was supposed to have started fifteen minutes ago. Twenty-three wasn't so bad, though two and possibly three of these people were clearly crazies, the straight-up, non-PC term for the rootless if not homeless townies who showed up anywhere they could hope for a free snack or cheap vino. (They'd be disappointed tonight.) Or even just a chance to spend time under a ceiling. It didn't have to be too cold or hot outside. These early October nights were perfect still, the air like bathwater, soothing and romantic if you were comfortably off, had a home and bed waiting at the end of your day. During his time in Costa Rica, sleeping in tents and hammocks in the great tropical outdoors, Robert had learned this: no matter how beautiful or temperate your surroundings, if you've grown up mostly indoors, you begin to miss that sensation of being enclosed. Four solid walls and a ceiling kind of define the space you consider "normal." Pathetic but true. So some of the crashers at the meeting were, whether they knew it or not, just clocking free indoor time.

Turo stood at the table in front of the chalkboard, chatting with the speaker he'd invited, a woman named Tamara ForTheEarth. She was a freegan, one of these new extremists who tried to live their lives without consuming anything new: everything tangible, including food, was scavenged. According to Turo, Tamara had even rejected her surname as opportunistic (her dad was some well-known judge in Boston).

Turo kept checking the clock on the wall. Robert knew he was disappointed by the turnout; he'd put posters up all over campus, and he claimed that the new Web site was getting a lot of traffic. He had support from the Environmental Action Committee and even (weirdly) the antiwar coalition. Little more than halfway through their freshman year, Arturo Cabrera had been profiled as a Difference Maker on Harvard's TV station. Robert met him just after that, volunteering to post *Reuse Awareness* flyers beyond the fringes of campus. He'd quit his job in the student laundry to join Turo's campus recycling project.

"Hey, everybody," Turo said at last, waving at the small audience. "Thanks for showing up tonight. Two quick points of business before I turn it over to our visitor. First, let me remind you that donations are always welcome." With mock affection, Turo leaned sideways to put his arm around a supersize mayo jar sitting on the table. "Our intradorm recycling project is up and running again, for the third year, and we need funds to keep renting our storage pod and the van. I'd also love to draft more troops. Not to align myself with the powers that be—or should I say *betray*—but it doesn't hurt to see our undertaking as a war against complacence."

He turned back and smiled at the guest. Tamara ForTheEarth was suspiciously gorgeous. That is, and Robert would never have confessed this to anyone, not even Clara (especially not Clara), she was so picture-perfect, with her red hair and her long legs (shapely ankles in mismatched socks), that a certain unappealingly caveman reflex told him she had to be about surface much more than substance. (But oh the substance *of* that surface.)

While Turo introduced her, Robert sized up her breasts. *Those* were no hand-me-downs. He wondered if she'd be in Turo's bed that night, on the other side of the wall. Ah, well, Clara was no consolation prize.

". . . and I haven't set foot in a retail outlet of any kind for at least two weeks. Here's a tip. Carry a counter in your pocket"—she held up a small metal object, like a stopwatch, which she clicked a few times—"and register every time you make a monetary transaction, plastic included. You will be shocked at the level of your dependence on money. My housemates and I have given up credit cards altogether. We do pool some necessary cash for mega containers of aspirin and baking soda and things like that," she said. "Baking soda's what we use for toothpaste.

Food staples—bread and butter and crackers and things like that—we get from restaurants that toss them out for frivolous Health Department code restrictions, some of them completely random. They're designed to beef up the profits of the food suppliers, not protect the health of consumers. If you send an articulate rep to these places, they'll set food aside for you on a daily basis."

She described how she and her housemates had found their furnishings on the sidewalk, how they had a whole library of nothing but tossed-aside books. (Tamara ForTheEarth shared an abandoned house in Everett with nine other people, all of whom had adopted the same surname.) Another tip: college campuses, especially in May, were a gold mine. "Outside the dorms, you've got these Dumpsters filled with treasures. I mean, here at Harvard? I don't want to get insulting, but you guys are major waste-rels, throwing away perfectly functional TVs, microwaves, hairdryers, things like that. Even laptops!"

Someone in the front row muttered loudly, "Freegans use microwaves and hairdryers?"

"Good question, because, actually, no," said Tamara. "In my house we do have a toaster—we use electricity, I admit that—but the frivolous stuff, the TVs and microwaves and things like that, we just liberate from the Dumpster so *somebody* can use them, so they don't go to a landfill. It's called waste reclamation." She wrote on the blackboard DUMP-STER DIVAS and spoke about a group of women who called one another whenever they spotted a Dumpster that could be mined for usable goods. The ones who could drop everything would convene at the Dumpster once it was dark, sort through the contents, and arrange them on a nearby sidewalk, making it easier for passers-by to take these treasures home.

Robert thought of the desperate urban characters who laid such objects on a bedspread on the sidewalk and tried to sell them for the cash that this woman despised so much.

"You have to learn to embrace the random. That's key." Eagerly, she turned to the board and made a list of Web sites and activist groups: freecycle.com, freegan.info, Really Really Free Markets, Trash Talk, swaporamarama.org. . . . Trash Talk, she explained, was a monthly meeting, over a gourmet potluck meal made from grocery-store and restaurant refuse, about how to minimize all interaction with corporate

America. "And as should be obvious, the less you spend money on, the less you have to work. Two years ago, I was a paralegal, totally enslaved. Now I'm almost finished with my first novel."

Robert raised his hand. "Are you going to sell your novel to a publisher?"

Slowly, catlike, she smiled. "Good try. But no. I'll be printing an on-demand limited edition myself. On the backs of term-paper drafts and classroom handouts, thanks to Turo here." She turned her sly smile on Turo.

Turo stepped closer to her and said, "All that paper we're collecting from your rooms? We reuse as much of it as possible. So don't crumple!"

Murmurs of approval.

Robert had to give it to Turo: he was learning to walk the talk. But he was also getting way too obsessed with *preaching* the talk. And who came to these meetings? Aside from the crazies, the Birkenstockers, the neo-lefties, the rich kids who wanted to stick it to their Republican parents . . . until it was time for the LSATs. Nothing wrong with spreading the word, but Robert had yet to see Turo actually reading for his courses. When Robert mentioned this, Turo admitted he'd "fallen a bit behind."

"WTF, man! Already?" said Robert. "You cannot 'use the system' if you opt out of it."

"*Negativo* on the stress," said Turo. A nicer way of telling Robert to mind his own business, stop acting like a mom.

Robert could already predict that night's kitchen conversation (unless Tamara FTE wound up in Turo's bed). Turo would say that his guest speaker proved you could make a difference while opting out. He was prey to that kind of elastic logic. Like "embrace the random." Couldn't you argue that was sort of what Bush had done when he'd pulled his Jesse James act on Iraq?

But Robert applauded, along with everyone else. He had to admit this woman was impressive as well as hot. When someone asked if she had handouts with the Web sites and other information she'd written on the board, she shook her head vehemently. "But Turo's got scrap paper and pencils," she said. "Be sure you pass it all on. Recycle the politics along with the paper." With her hands, she made an aggressively enthusiastic circular motion in front of her very fine breasts. It was stagey, ritualistic. Which bugged Robert all over again. Her gesture reminded him of the way football players thrust their arms in the air after making a touchdown. Except even that was more spontaneous.

Robert watched Tamara ForTheEarth as she picked up her child-size backpack (sporting Dora the Explorer, clearly a "find") and shook Turo's hand, businesslike. She'd talked about riding her bicycle everywhere—avoiding even public transit unless the weather made it too dangerous to bike—so Robert wondered how ostentatiously "free" that was, too. Maybe she had a Barbie bike, just a little too small, with pink tassels on the handlebars. A Ninja Turtles helmet.

"I can tell, just from your wiseass expression, that you're overanalyzing again." Turo had somehow sneaked up on Robert after seeing Ms. FTE out the door. He spread one hand across the top of Robert's head. "*Haya paz,* dude."

Robert laughed. Sometimes he wondered if he should steer toward psychiatry, once he got to med school. If he got to med school. Weirdly, his mother didn't seem to care one bit whether he became a doctor. She hardly ever talked about it and never gave advice. Maybe she was cleverly steering his course by mostly leaving him alone.

"Hey," he said to Turo. "So if she's squatting, how do they power that toaster?"

"They borrow the juice."

"What?"

"They siphon electricity from a hardware store on the same block."

"Wow. I get it. No buying, but piracy is cool."

"It's a huge chain. Ace or something."

Robert snorted. "Excess justifies the crime?"

"But it does, you know? Think of it as a rad form of economic sanctions. And Tamara, she is the real deal." Under Turo's left arm was the mayo/money jar. It contained five or six bills and about a cup of loose change.

"Maybe so," said Robert, "but meanwhile, I'm going home to cook up some capitalistically store-bought spaghetti."

"Count me in. And then let's drive out and sneak a swim in your granddad's pond."

"Hey," said Robert, "some of us plan not to flunk out. Not yet."

"And some of us like to live on the edge." As they crossed Mass. Ave.,

Turo shifted the jar to his other arm. The loose coins rattled against the glass.

The expression *chump change* lit up in Robert's brain. God but we're spoiled, he reminded himself.

They'd been waiting in the front of My Thai for fifteen minutes—Robert, Clara, his parents, and his aunt—when Granddad strolled in. He was grinning blandly, and he was alone. Robert saw his mom flash Granddad a look of frosty panic. But Clover hugged her father tight. "Daddy, we have got to buy you a new watch," she said.

"Watches are for working people," he said. "And in any case, I have two excellent reasons for being tardy." He walked back to the door and held it open.

In walked Filo and Lee, giggling.

Clover nearly flung her kids to the ground, she hugged them so hard. "Oh my *darlings*!" she cried out, turning heads in the dining room. "This is the best birthday present *ever*!" Robert saw Lee, in the crush of his mother's arms, grimace. Lee looked about two feet taller than when Robert had seen him last. It was as if his cousin had aged six years in the space of one. He was twelve now, twelve on the verge of fifteen.

At the table, there was a flurry of contention over who should sit where. Clover insisted that Granddad, not she, take the head, and then there was a kind of Chinese fire drill to get Filo next to her grandfather, Clover between her children. Robert's parents ended up next to each other, Clara at the foot of the table by default. Granddad hardly acknowledged Clara's presence. Had he even greeted her? Sometimes Robert had the bizarre sensation that his grandfather was actually jealous of his girlfriend.

Once seated, Clover clamped an arm tightly around each of her children, as if they might otherwise flee. Even when the waitress passed out menus, she did not loosen her grip.

"I've heard their pad thai is just out of this world!" Clover turned toward her son. "Lee, I'll bet they have those spring rolls you love so much at that place in Chelsea. Oh, if I'd known the two of you were coming, I'd have chosen the French place. But I'm just so glad you're *here*." She had tears of elation in her eyes, which made Robert feel happy for his aunt but also a little embarrassed. How awful it must be to know that when half the world looked at you, they couldn't help wondering how you'd fucked up so hugely that you'd given up custody of your own kids. Robert figured he didn't know the whole story, but he knew enough to wonder why she wasn't trying to go back to New York, at least to be near them.

"Order whatever you wish, all of you," Granddad announced. "It's my treat. Do you suppose the Siamese people serve anything approximating good champagne?"

"Let's order a whole bunch of adventuresome things and share all around," said Clover. "And I need no champagne to feel high on life right now."

"It's your day, my dear," said Granddad, though Robert heard a note of exasperation. Nowhere was Granddad more of a geezer than in a restaurant.

"I love that crispy whole fish. Do they have that here?" said Robert's mother. "It's usually sea bass. . . ." She scanned the menu.

"Is sea bass one of those overfished species we're supposed to boycott?" said Clover, and then she blushed. "Oh never mind, never mind. Like Daddy says, everyone should have whatever they want most. What about you two?" She pulled her children closer.

"Mom, you're like totally squishing me," said Lee.

Robert's father pulled a small notebook from his pocket, along with a pen. "Why don't I write it all down, make life easy for the waitstaff?"

"My organizer-in-chief," teased Robert's mother.

The waitress was an alarmingly skinny woman who looked about sixteen years old. She arrived at the table with a bottle of Korbel and a pitcher of orange juice. A waiter who looked even younger—surely not much older than Lee—followed her with a tray of those thick, shallow glasses from which, according to Robert's mother, the "less privileged" drank champagne.

"Just leave them here and I'll do the honors," said Granddad, clearing space on the table. "Let's get our food orders in, shall we?" He turned in his chair to face the waitress. "Well, a proper good evening, young lady. We are here to celebrate my daughter's birthday." He nodded toward Clover.

"Oh. Is happy birthday," the waitress said, bowing slightly, her smooth face crinkling with nervous laughter.

"Thank you," said Clover. "It *is* happy. Very happy."

The waitress pulled out her pad and said, with servile cheer, "Any question?"

"I do have a question," said Granddad. He pointed at the menu. "How does one pronounce the name of this dish, number forty-three?"

The waitress bent to read the menu. "Is shrimp. With lemongrass and basil. You like spicy?"

"Ah. Well that does sound enticing, but to order it, I'd like to be able to pronounce it correctly."

"Pronounce?" said the waitress.

"Dad, just say you want the lemongrass prawns. Or number forty-three. That's why they have the numbers," said Robert's mother. She looked at the waitress. "He wants the prawns. Not too spicy."

The waitress said the name of the dish in her native language, giving him the answer to the question he'd asked in the first place.

"That sounds positively melodic. You must be Thai."

"Yes."

"Do you have a green card?"

"Dad!" barked Robert's mom.

"Green card—yes." The waitress wore a terrified smile.

"That is fortunate. There are many opportunities hereabouts. You've landed in an excellent region of the country. Are you taking classes?"

Now Clover chimed in with her sister. *"Dad!"*

"My dear daughters, this young woman will want to practice conversation. How else will her English improve?"

Under the table, Clara was squeezing Robert's hand. He could feel her trembling, trying desperately not to laugh. Robert was used to Granddad's extremely warped M.O. Unless you broadened your sense of humor, it could look demented or just plain rude. But Robert knew that his grandfather really and truly meant the things he'd said; he suspected that even the waitress, at some deep intuitive level, understood this, too. But not Robert's mom, who for a number of reasons (some understandable; others a complete, ridiculous mystery) had a low tolerance level for her father's idiosyncracies.

"I am so sorry," she said to the waitress. "Ignore him and do your job. I will have the whole sea bass, number fifty-one."

Robert's dad ordered a spicy beef dish. To compensate, Robert ordered tofu. Clara ordered noodles with mushrooms. By the time the waitress took their order to the kitchen, Robert was ravenous. He whispered in Clara's ear, "Food doesn't get here fast, I might eat you."

She laughed softly. The beads that dangled from her earlobe tickled his lips. He pulled his napkin securely across his lap.

His mother leaned toward them. "You two seem to have a secret."

"The secret is that we skipped lunch," said Robert.

"Oh Trudy, these are simply"—Clover had just opened the agate earrings and was holding them up to the votive candle before her—"these are just luscious, like . . . mm, like giant jeweled candycorns." Playfully, she touched one of the earrings with the tip of her tongue. Robert had picked them out (defying the notion that only Clara could exercise good taste) and didn't mind the comparison, but he saw his mother wince. Maybe she had germs on the brain. Doctors were like that. Doctors who were mothers were the worst. The smell of Dial soap, to Robert, was the core odor of childhood.

"I'm so glad you like them," said his mother. "I did get a little help from Robert and Clara. The gift is from all three of us. But now—now tell me all about the school, how it's going in the barn." She flashed a smile at Granddad, as if to let him know she'd forgiven him for his behavior toward the waitress.

As Clover talked about the first month of school, all the adjustments, the reactions of the older children who'd known the space at the church so well, she looked happier than Robert had maybe ever seen her. Teaching seemed like a cool thing to do, but Robert couldn't understand getting excited about the bureaucratic stuff: ordering supplies, putting together a nursery school newsletter, organizing parties to basically beg for money that would pay for, what, crayons and gluesticks? There was going to be some glitzy auction the following spring, and Clover was already looking into music and a caterer. "I am psyched," she'd told him while they were waiting for Granddad.

Robert leaned across the table. "Hey," he said quietly to Lee, "so how's the bad old city treating you these days?"

Lee shrugged. "Fine." But he was pleased to be noticed by his older cousin. "I'm doing soccer and tae kwon do. My dad's also making me work with him at a soup kitchen. Like every other weekend."

"That's cool. That's good," said Robert.

"It's okay. It's weird to see the same guys you see sitting on the street asking for money. Like, I don't know if I'm supposed to act like we know each other when I'm handing them a plate of food. Not that we do."

"But look," said Robert, "to me it would be the only way to live in a place like New York and hold on to your conscience." Although, it occurred to him, how was New York different in this respect from Matlock, or Newton—or Harvard, for fuck's sake? And was he, Robert, ladling soup for the crazies? Was going to college a legit excuse for giving it a pass? Not according to Turo. Nothing entitles you to take a break from your debts to the real world, he would say, not in times this dire, this have-or-have-not.

Lee had no reaction to Robert's statement. He ate a bite of his spring roll and said, "Dad's taking us to Washington, D.C., for Columbus Day weekend."

"See the monuments, stuff like that?"

"Yeah. Museums and stuff. But we get to stay at a hotel with a really huge pool."

"Cool," said Robert. Turo had blogged a whole diatribe on the evils of swimming pools: the energy, the chemicals, the waste of so much money and water. But Robert had promised his mother not to talk politics at his aunt's birthday dinner. Not like Clover was a Republican, but his mom always feared that politics would send Granddad into some devil's advocate spiel that would embarrass her in a room full of strangers. She was weirdly adolescent that way.

Granddad was asking Filo about third grade. Robert heard her talking about the classroom cockatiel, whose name was Jacaranda Star Wars. He tried to remember if he'd ever been in a classroom with a pet. Why couldn't he remember such a thing? He tried to summon third grade. Mr. Redmond. Who smelled awful but told great jokes and gave out treats if the Red Sox or the Bruins were riding high. Those were the kinds of things Robert retained from elementary school. What happened to the stuff you supposedly "learned"? Did it fill some deep-down reservoir in your brain, like an aquifer of knowledge from which you could draw only without being conscious of it? What the hell was the crux of education? He felt like he'd learned more when he was helping build that lodge in Costa Rica than he had in his first two years at Prestige U.

The food arrived in a rush of steamy warmth, the dishes set down on the table by their waitress plus three helpers. "Oh my gosh!" exclaimed Clover, pressing her hands together, such a corny kid-gesture. Maybe if you worked at a preschool, you picked up four-year-old gestures and expressions. You probably had to train yourself to say things like "Feathers!" and "Shoelace!" instead of the instinctive obscenities. What did that do to your brain? (Though maybe it made you age more slowly, too.)

"But first I am opening *your* gift." Clover smiled at her children.

Inside the colorful box they'd brought was a pair of dark green leather gloves, long and slim. Immediately, Clover put them on, raising her suddenly stylish hands high above the table, careful not to dip them into the various dishes of open food waiting to be eaten. "Oh my gosh," she said again. "How. Exquisitely. Elegant." She waved her hands in the air, like fluttering birds. "I feel like . . . Helena Bonham Carter!"

She kissed her children and slipped the gloves back into their box. Robert noticed that Filo and Lee looked just the tiniest bit perplexed, and he didn't think it was the reference to Helena Bonham Carter. He wondered if they'd had anything to do with picking out her gift. His mother had a theory that their father was still in love with Clover and always would be, even if the guy had confessed to her that maybe he was gay.

Robert hardly knew his cousins, not just because they were so much younger or lived in New York, but because now there was this weird psychological barrier caused by the fact that he couldn't help wondering if they "knew" about Uncle Todd (technically, Ex-Uncle Todd). Robert wished he knew more than what he'd overheard, and probably he could have asked his mother outright, but he didn't want to. In any case, when Robert saw Filo and Lee at holidays and tried to "get to know them" (as his aunt, not his mother, encouraged him to do), they had these stiff conversations about sports and movies and how cool New York was and how lucky they were to grow up there.

What made it worse was that Robert had heard his parents completely dissect his aunt's entire life again and again and again, supposedly because they cared for her and wanted her to be happy, yet usually sounding more like they were movie critics and Aunt Clover's life, sad to say, wouldn't be up for any Oscars or Golden Globes unless she fired the writers, the cinematographer, and definitely the continuity guy.

In fact, Robert had heard way more than necessary about his aunt's split from Ex-Uncle Todd because of what Robert's dad did for a living.

He was a divorce mediator. Two years ago, when the guano really hit the fan, Aunt Clover had stayed at their house a lot, mostly weeping on the couch. Several evenings in a row, Robert's parents sat with her and discussed her "situation." Robert had been up in his room most of the time, doing homework or phoning friends, but who wouldn't have listened in on the family drama? Robert, unlike his parents, really did love his aunt, no judgment attached, and felt completely sorry for her. He hadn't lived on his own yet back then, but you'd have to be an idiot not to see already that life—that Rubik's Cube of huge decisions and risks—could paralyze you totally.

If she'd asked for Robert's advice, he'd have told her to steer clear of his parents, not because they weren't smart, even wise (their lives seemed so well organized and carefully run, it was spooky), but because he knew they disapproved of her choices and didn't appreciate her spirit.

On Christmas Day when he was seven, Robert had been struck with Cupid's arrow for the very first time. Beautiful, colorful, carefree Aunt Clover had given him a red wooden sled and taken him to the big hill in Matlock where she and his mother went sledding as girls. She had wrapped her arms and legs around him and shrieked at the top of her lungs all the way down to the bottom—several times over. When they returned to Granddad's, she'd made him hot cocoa from a Swiss chocolate bar and swirled in whipped cream with cinnamon. For months after she returned to New York, he'd sent her drawings with scrawled captions. She replied to him with postcards of the city, with promises to show him all the sights if he came for a visit.

The next time she'd come to Massachusetts—it was during a croquet game at Granddad's as she helped Robert send his dad's ball far into the bushes—he had asked her if she'd marry him when he grew up. She looked him in the eye, without laughing, and told him they would discuss it later, in private. He didn't know it, but she had just become engaged to Todd. Alone together by the pond, later that day, she'd explained this to Robert as if he were otherwise a viable suitor. "But you will always be special to me, forever and ever," she'd said, and she'd given him a ring with a pair of clasped hands, which she took right off her pinkie. Robert still had that ring, in a box in his sock drawer in Cambridge.

As far as Robert could tell, Clover had never told a soul about his crush, not even his mother. So it had pained him, over the past few years—even in the car on the way out of the city that night—to hear his parents discussing Aunt Clover as if she were a wayward child.

Robert knew firsthand that only children hear far more than they should, especially on long trips in the car. Where siblings might have been occupied fighting about whose legs were bumping whose, or singing stupid car songs, or playing hangman, Robert had often been distracted from his comic books, plastic Transformers, or the latest Harry Potter when his parents began to discuss people he knew. So he'd heard about Clover's falling in love with her yoga instructor and actually confessing this to Todd—which apparently led to Todd's even bigger bombshell, that lately he'd been wondering if he was more attracted to men. Then nothing at all happened with the yoga instructor, but the cat was out of the bag—or the closet. ("For God's sake," Robert's mother had said, "we all have urges and infatuations. If my sister had enough self-control, she'd have kept that one to herself, and maybe things would have smoothed themselves out!") Clover became incredibly depressed, Todd clammed up, and their marriage went from okay to dismal to flatlined.

Robert was practically out of high school by then, so maybe his parents figured it was no big deal if he overheard all this sordid stuff. They'd made it clear that they knew Robert might not be a virgin and that he'd drunk beer at his friends' houses. They liked to describe themselves as "realistic" parents.

But at a much younger age, he had heard them talking in the front seat about family matters that he found not just unpleasant but disturbing and sad. Mainly about Granddad. Robert's mother, back when he was in fifth or sixth grade, actually seemed unhappy that Granddad continued to live alone in his house. Granddad's friend Norval Sorenson had tried to fix him up with a woman Robert's mother thought was "just ideal for him," but he refused to even ask her on a date.

Till then, it hadn't occurred to Robert that his grandfather was someone who could "go on a date." And why should Robert's mother *want* him to? But of course, riding in the backseat on the way home from Matlock (probably his mother thought he was asleep), he had found out why.

"What is he going to do in twenty, thirty years with no one but us to look after him?" Robert's mother had said to his father. "And by 'us,' I mean you and me, Douglas. He's going to fall down those crooked back stairs one day, and lie there, unable to get to the phone, and—"

"I can understand your fear of catastrophe, but I think you're a little hard on your dad," Robert's father had said.

"Look. I love that house as much as he does. It's all that remains of my mom, in a way—not just her things but the way she arranged them. But it's not reasonable for him to stay there forever! If he's not going to find a mate and share the place, and if Clover's not going to move up from New York—and she isn't, Todd has a very sound business there—well, why doesn't he look into one of those great condos they're building near the green? He could walk everywhere, even to the train. He wouldn't have to deal with snooty Laurel Connaughton or the upkeep of the barn. The good things in his life could all remain the same."

"He wouldn't have his swimming routine. That's important to him."

This had silenced his mother for several seconds.

"It's his life," Robert's father had said, very gently.

"I know that, Douglas. But if it weren't for him, Mom might still have hers. I'm sorry."

Dad had sighed, but he'd said nothing at all in reply. Robert lay on the backseat and wished for the conversation to continue. But it didn't. There was so much more to know, but what? It occurred to Robert that whenever he heard Mom talk about Granddad, she almost always had that same tone, one of sadness, frustration, and anger all bundled together. He understood that the visits they made to Matlock were, for her, more obligation than pleasure.

At that age, Robert thought his mother was as close to perfect as a mother could be (mostly, he still did), but he'd felt suddenly, deeply sorry for his grandfather. Hadn't he been a good father? He must have been. After all, as Robert's mother had explained to him when he put together that his lack of a grandmother equated his mother's *loss* of a mother, Granddad had become "both parents rolled into one." So how could she be so critical? Not that Robert dared to ask.

It was then, just as he began the normal adolescent disentangling from his parents (which, unlike so many of their friends, they would take in gracious stride), that Robert resolved to be an actual *friend* to his grandfather.

~

Platters of confetti-like food traveled up and down the table; small piles of bean sprouts and dried chilies gathered slowly at the edges. Granddad had coaxed Filo into talking about her gymnastics. Robert's dad was trying his best to have a baseball conversation with Lee, about what it felt like in Boston and New York now that the Red Sox and the Yankees had swapped slots as the Charmed Team and the Losers-Despite-Themselves. Clover, Trudy, and Clara were talking about Hillary Clinton's bid for the White House. (Robert's mom couldn't stand her and didn't trust her; Clover said she was the victim of rampant misogyny, from women as well as men; Clara was pretending to be neutral when Robert knew she agreed with his mom.)

Robert slipped away to the men's room and then checked his phone. Turo had borrowed his car again, asking permission after the fact. Robert was beginning to regret that he'd given Turo the extra key. He hadn't confronted his friend, but he knew that Turo used it more often than he let on. Robert knew this because his father, after helping him buy the car on craigslist, had given him one of those dad talks. Among other gratuitous bits of advice, he'd said, "Every time you turn that key, make a habit of checking the gas gauge." Somehow this nugget of Mister Rogers had stuck. More than once in recent weeks, Robert had started the car and noticed that the tank was *more* full than he'd left it.

Robert texted Turo, *HIT THE BKS NOT THE RD!* The guy didn't even have a girlfriend this year. He was practically married to his campus recycling program, and he was talking about joining a committee to advise the university on becoming carbon neutral. Now *there* was a mission for zealots.

When Robert returned to the table, Granddad was telling a story. Everyone was listening.

". . . so this time, someone managed to fling patches of manure—pig manure, the most objectionably pungent sort—across the front yard of our newly elected selectwoman, who just installed a brand-new sprinkler system." He laughed with delight. "A sign was posted reading, IRRIGATE FARMS, NOT LAWNS. It makes me want to dance with glee."

Clover looked quite ungleeful. "Daddy, vandalism is vandalism."

"Oh pish-tush, daughter. Someone's taking a stand against the bourgeoisie."

"Of which you are not a member?" Robert's mother wore a playful smile.

"Of course I'm bourgeois, but I'm *bas*-bourgeois," said Granddad.

Clara and Robert's father laughed.

"This was in Matlock, untouchable Matlock?" said Robert. "Turo would so love this."

Clara nodded. "And how. It's right up his alley."

"We had a similar incident in Newton," said Robert's mother. "Last week someone came home from a party to find their hot tub filled to the brim with what looked like steaming blood. It was terrifying."

"Blood?" said Robert. "Whoa."

"It was red-wine vinegar, but still."

Robert started laughing. "We know them?"

"The parents of that girl who asked you to the prom, but you said no."

"Ooh," said Robert, "the Morriseys in the McChâteau. The wine distributor dude."

"And I think there was a sign there, too," said his dad.

"Yes," said his mother. "SMALLER FOOTPRINTS, DIONYSUS."

This time everyone laughed.

Clover stopped first. "We're complacent now, but just you wait."

Granddad took a sip of his wine. "Rumblings of a revolution, is that what you're alluding to, my dear? I'll toast to that."

Robert saw his mother roll her eyes. "These notions of 'going green' are not so simple. If you knew what it takes to run a safe, hygienic hospital—"

Granddad turned toward Robert. "What do *you* think of this suburban sabotage, young man? Serves us right, yes?"

"Yeah, well, I'm not exactly weeping buckets here."

Clara poked him in the leg. "Robert's getting political these days," she said. "He's branched out from biology into the more progressive social sciences."

Now everyone stared at him. "What?" he said. "I'm taking one course on the politics of immigration. Not like I'm off to a training camp in Peshawar."

"But that's a scorching-hot topic," said his mother. "I didn't know you were taking that."

"It was a last-minute switch." Robert wondered for a moment if his mother was offended that there was something she didn't know about his current life. That wasn't like her.

"Anyway," he said, "we have to write a term paper that involves a first-person source. We have to interview an immigrant, someone who grew up in another country but now lives here. They can be legal or not."

Granddad waved a hand toward the kitchen. "You're at ground zero, I venture to say. Shall we—"

"No, we shall not," said Robert's mother. "You've probably caused a major panic in this place as it is." She held up her watch, tapped it, and sighed. "I'm sorry. I fly to Chicago at dawn."

Clover looked at her children. "Dare I hope you're here for the weekend?"

Granddad said, "I negotiated a swap with Todd. I hope that works for you."

"Oh you know me," said Clover gaily. "I believe in the pleasures of the present moment."

"Well good for you, Aunt Clo, good for you," said Robert, standing up. He hoped she would miss the look on her sister's face. To someone who didn't know his mother the way he did, it would be easy to miss the compassion cloaked as dismay. She wasn't a pessimist, his mother, not at all, but she had a clearer eye than most, wherever she went, for the worst-case scenario. Robert had always assumed it came with her professional territory—though maybe it was the reverse: maybe her nature had led her to her vocation.

"Sit down, children," Granddad said loudly. He got up and went to the kitchen. He leaned his head through the door and called out, "Young people in there, we are ready now!" And in a moment, out came Clover's birthday cake, a most un-Siamese confection glistening with chocolate icing and candlelight.

Robert was pretty certain that what tipped him over the Harvard admissions bar was the essay he wrote about his mother. His grades were practically perfect, but that was true for many of his classmates at Newton South, his psychotically overachieving high school. He wasn't from Tulsa and had not the slightest ethnic tint to his blood. (Turo was half Filipino, half Guatemalan. His mother had drummed it into him, from the nanosecond they arrived in the States, that his exotic mongrel status was a key to open many doors. Not to mention borders: the guy had three passports.) Robert had played soccer (like who didn't?) and tennis and had been on the traveling debate team, but he hadn't been the captain or the director or the mastermind of anything extracurricular, or done anything admirably weird, like competitive skeet shooting or breeding llamas. Unless you counted the Lego workshop he ran one summer for kids at the elementary school. Doubtful. Had his grandfather's position as a librarian at Widener (one of about three thousand) made a difference? Also doubtful. Very, according to Granddad, who honestly seemed to believe that Robert was genius material.

His mother did not ask what he wrote on his college applications. She was a hands-off-the-small-stuff mother, not just because she was this medical hotshot and had no time to hover but because—and she told this to Robert himself, when he wondered once why all the other kids had karate and piano and chess club practically every afternoon in junior high—she believed children should be responsible for their triumphs as well as their failures. She also told him, as if it were a well-known law of nature, like gravity or centripetal force, that creative thinking blossomed in what others might see as idleness. (Later, he wondered how this applied to doctors, who weren't even allowed to sleep for about three years of their education, never mind be anything approaching "idle.")

"Do you *want* to take piano or karate?" she had asked him across the kitchen counter that day. He was eleven. "Say the word and I will sign you up for anything that strikes your passion."

Well, no, he had told her. Though maybe guitar. And the next week a shy, bearded guy had shown up one afternoon with two guitars. When Robert decided to quit, three years later, his parents had expressed no disappointment. They continued to let him steer his own course, though now and then they would throw out bits of general advice, most of it pretty duh in nature. Like "Actions speak louder than words." "A bird in the hand is worth two in the bush." Robert's dad liked proverbs and sayings. He was the parent who clocked more hours at home because that's where he worked. He saw his clients in an office that you entered on the basement level. There was a magnet on his filing cabinet that read, GO OUT ON A LIMB. THAT'S WHERE THE FRUIT IS.

Once Robert reached the age when he was horny 24/7, he began to wonder how divorcing couples might interpret this witty little saying, attributed on the magnet to Will Rogers. Out of curiosity, Robert looked him up on Wikipedia, expecting to find out that, like most celebrities, Rogers had failed at marriage several times over. But no: he'd been married just once and had three children. So apparently the fruit wasn't sexual.

When it came to sex, drugs, and cigarettes, Robert's mother had an uncanny sense of timing in her habit of leaving "literature" on these topics lying around the kitchen. The words made less of an impression than the graphic pictures of lungs brutalized by smoking; of young men tattooed with cancerous lesions from AIDS; of other young men curled up in alleys, destitute, miserable, and lost to the world in a heroin fog. Robert would never know if his dutiful abstinence (well, of everything but safe heterosexual sex) was the product of his mother's leafleting program or his own nature.

When he'd arrive home from school, sometimes he'd hear the raised voices of his dad's clients—shrill arguments in that *You did too! I did not! You did TOO!* type of tone, always man versus woman—through the living room floor. He had never heard his parents argue like that. Maybe all those hysterical clients had the same deterrent effect on Robert's dad that the vice squad medical brochures had on Robert. Or maybe his parents just understood each other. Not that they never disagreed.

Another weird thing was that, because they were both so ethical about keeping their clients' lives private (at least when Robert was around), they almost never mentioned work. They talked about politics, friends, and families, and they genuinely liked to hear about Robert's schoolwork. Yet they gave him the same degree of privacy they gave their clients.

So they never saw the essay that went like this:

> Imagine growing up the only child of a parent who strives to save lives every day—but who does it by making them sicker than they've ever thought they could stand. Imagine how she gets up while it's still dark and has her coffee and does her exercises and then makes breakfast for

you and your father. Sometimes you are not even awake when she leaves for work, but the table is set and there's a note saying when she'll be home and what things you might need to know about your own life that day. When you're little, she's a doctor but still in training, so she's hardly ever home to cook your dinner, but she does her best to read you at least one story every day. Sometimes she comes home for lunch, just to hold you in her lap.

But by the time you're in junior high, she has her own office in a major hospital downtown. She juggles hundreds of patients, but now she comes home for dinner nearly every night. After dinner, while you do your homework, she works too: she reads journals, she goes over notes, but she also talks to patients on the phone. If you pass her study, you can hear her voice, quiet and calm. You know that almost all her patients are women. They have breast cancer. Some of them know they're probably going to die of their disease.

When you're seventeen, she asks if you'd like a summer job in her office. She explains that you'll be doing trivial tasks, like refilling the snack baskets and the refrigerator in the chemo clinic. Everything is miniature: mini crackers, mini bagels, mini packages of jelly and cheese. Tiny water bottles. The coffee and tea come in individual pods. It's as if the food respects people's privacy, too. You keep the copy machines filled, carry batches of patient folders from one station to another, empty recycling bins. The biggest challenge is boredom.

But here's what amazes you. Even though she spends most of her time behind the closed door of her office or exam room, you see your mother in action. You knew she'd be good, but you didn't know how outgoing she would be. At home she's more reserved. Everything she does seems carefully planned. In the hospital, she comes through the waiting room and says something special to each patient; she asks about their children or pets. She'll remember a dog's name. She tells them she's spoken with a doctor, refilled a prescription, ironed out kinks with their insurance. After she goes through, they're all smiling, even the ones who look so thin you worry they might actually break into pieces if they tripped and fell. For a minute, it feels like your mom is the president of a tiny, happy country.

Except that there's a lot of sickness there. The few times you enter the "suites" where they do the actual chemotherapy, you can't help looking for your mother. You see her talking intensely to people who have all these drugs going into their bodies through long tubes. It's like a sci-fi movie, like everyone's on a spaceship headed to a planet where you need to be vaccinated with these chemicals.

One day you are taking crackers to the kitchen by the chemo suites when something dramatic happens. An old man is walking along a hall pushing his IV pole. He groans and falls down. There's a huge crash, because of the pole, and he's curled up on the floor tangled in the tubes.

And like a bullet train, your mother shoots down the hall out of nowhere and practically throws herself onto the man. She pushes on his chest and breathes into his mouth. You've never seen CPR; it would look disturbing even if this weren't your mom. She calls out code words, for help, in a calm but incredibly loud voice you've never heard before. The old man is not her patient, but for now he is. Even when his doctor gets there, she continues to do this incredible work on his body: it feels like forever.

Then she sits on the floor and props him up between her legs. When a gurney comes, the old man clings to her like a life preserver. "I'll go with you," she says. She untangles his IV lines and straightens his shirt. She and his doctor help the orderlies get the man on the gurney. She holds his hand and talks to him. You never knew before that being a doctor could be so intimate.

Everything goes back to normal. You put the crackers in the right basket and the coffee pods in the right drawer. You realize that your own mother, who's biologically yours and yours only, could be Mother to the World. You see what's possible for you, and it feels amazing. Huge. It sounds corny to say, but it's true: you know now what inspiration means, what it means to live out your convictions. Now you'll just have to find out what they are.

Of course, in reality it wasn't so simple. That summer, as it happened, was when things started going wonky for poor Aunt Clo. The weekend after the I-love-my-yoga-instructor/I-might-be-gay explosion, she'd arrived unannounced in Newton. Robert's mother's life couldn't accommodate a whole lot of spontaneity, but this was her sister in a crisis. So she canceled a trip to be the pink-ribbon cutter for a breast-cancer 10K in Baltimore.

"Honey, just head out and do your thing. This is going to be messy," she told Robert after breakfast that Saturday morning.

And messy it was. That night, after Robert got back from hanging out at a friend's house, he found his mother and her sister together in the living room, his dad nowhere to be seen. Aunt Clover had been crying.

He waved awkwardly when they looked up, then went to his room. Later, he heard their voices rise in anger. He heard Aunt Clover wail,

"You DO NOT know what it's like! You had that ABORTION because you couldn't deal with a little uncertainty! Maybe even ONE PERFECT CHILD is more than you ever wanted! Don't you DARE give me advice about being a MOTHER!"

Robert heard his mom shout the F word, which was something on the order of getting to see Halley's Comet.

Two days after that, Robert rode to the hospital with her, as usual, in their ancient but well-preserved Mercedes. If he got a ride home with her—which he did only half the time, because often she worked until seven or eight—that was when they talked. In the morning, they shared the car in harmonious silence, both sipping coffee, cushioned in the crimson-leather seats. On the Mass. Pike, he found himself staring at his mother's profile, her face calm, the way it always was in concentration.

He told himself that if she noticed, if she turned and asked why he was staring, he would dare to tell her what he'd overheard. He would ask her about the abortion. He was old enough, now, to love being his parents' one and only offspring, to see what a hassle siblings could be, but when he was much younger, he'd asked again and again for a little brother or sister, the way other kids asked for a puppy.

His parents had both told him that in a world so overpopulated, especially in a country where people's everyday habits were responsible for most of the destruction to the global environment, having one child was the most ethical choice. "And of course," his father said, "you get every bit of our love and devotion. You are all the kid we'll ever want or need."

As he stared at his admirable, moral, loving mother on that summer morning (the car windows open; no AC to eat away the ozone layer), he wondered something else: Had his father known about the abortion, and when was it? When Robert was two, or six, or ten? He realized, with a visceral sting, that even though he was almost an adult, his mother was still young enough to get pregnant. She could have had the abortion that very summer. . . . The more he thought about this chain of logic, the more painful and creepy it was.

But Trudy Barnes had been so wrapped up in her morning thoughts, or so focused on the aggressive driving of the other commuters, that she had not asked why Robert was staring. And he had asked nothing in return.

4

The day on which Robert, his pal Arturo, and the pixieish but undeniably talented teacher began to build the tree house was likewise the day on which Mistress Lorelei chose to flourish an olive branch and the day on which I met Sarah: for the second time, if one is literal-minded, but for the first if, like me, you believe that you have not truly met someone until you have looked him or her in the eye as a soul with a place in your future.

Jolted from a dreamless, fogbound sleep, I nevertheless recognized at once the percussive clatter of lumber beneath my bedroom window. My heart sank. This was a disruption that, with the final transformative batterings on my barn, I had hoped not to hear again at such close range. I'd fallen asleep deep in the brutal Australian outback with Patrick White's explorer Voss, and as I sat up, the splayed volume hit the floor. I staggered to the window and was about to yell some what-in-tarnation expletive when I spotted my grandson.

"Good Lord, Robert. Did I forget to expect this?"

He looked up, along with the teacher fellow whose name I had yet again forgotten. They smiled and waved. Arturo came around the corner of the house and waved as well.

"Hey, Granddad. Aunt Clo didn't warn you?"

The teacher called out, "Did we wake you?" Talented, yes, but not too observant. (Irving? Ernest? The name began with a vowel. . . .)

It was nine o'clock. I groaned at the notion of my run, usually over and done by that hour. "Are you about to execute my tree?" I called through the screen.

"*Negativo,* Granddad." Robert grinned. "I know all about creating domiciles that harmonize with nature."

He had a point. Robert had spent the summer after high school helping build a hotel in Costa Rica. An "eco-lodge." Halfway through that summer, he'd threatened to stay on for another year. Alarmed that he might dismiss college altogether, I asked if he was having doubts. He replied, "Who in their right mind doesn't?" So true! His parents seemed, as always, unruffled. (Back then, I harbored a secret yen to see Douglas Barnes, my son-in-law, suffer from an episode of indecisiveness, impatience, or ire. I had waited in vain for two decades.)

I changed into my running clothes and stretched out my cantankerous limbs. In the kitchen, I drank my glass of orange juice and forced down the large capsules Clover had cajoled me into taking. Fish oil and a lurid green pill whose name I could never remember. Something like spartina. (Ira: that was the teacher's name!)

As I stood in the kitchen giving myself a pep talk, shaking out my shoulders, pulling my knees toward my chest, I saw a pink envelope peeking coyly from under the door.

An out-of-season valentine? When had I last received one of those, even on the proper day?

My dear Percy,

First off, I have to tell you that despite my initial misgivings, I am so pleased to see that Elves and Faeries has found such a perfect new home!! The voices of little children at play in the morning are, I am surprised to confess, nearly as lovely as the birdsong with which they mingle. How wise you were, as well as generous.

Perhaps the spirit of youthful enthusiasm is contagious, for I find myself eager to have you over for tea or cocktails, the sooner the better, not just to discuss a plan I have to benefit the Historical Forum but to make neighborly amends. You have been correct about many things regarding our shared environment here, and I wish to offer you my humble apologies for calling in Hal last spring when we could have settled our differences without the interference of outside agencies!

Is tomorrow or perhaps even this very afternoon too sudden? 4:00? 6:00? You name the time. I am wide open!! (Do you like smoked salmon? Edgar just expressed me this very special treat, wild-caught in Alaska, and I am longing to share it.)

Please do call!

Warmest regards,
Laurel

Wide open? I had to laugh at that: a frightening vision indeed. Little wonder that her son, Edgar, had fled to the farthest corner of the country as soon as he could make his own living. His father had fled long before. Whenever I felt myself pitying Mistress Lorelei, so rich but so lonely, I had only to remember (would that I could forget!) the way she'd literally flung herself at me after her divorce. At the last Christmas party I gave, more than ten years ago, she had lured me upstairs to my own bedroom, insisting she had good reason to suspect the existence of a secret compartment or passage near the chimney. Since our houses were built in the same year, by the same housewright, I assumed she was looking for the twin to some feature in hers. She had knocked and pressed her ear to the walls for ten or fifteen minutes—very convincing, this ruse—and then she had pounced.

I cut off that conduit of memory, but I would answer her note. With the arrival of E & F, the diplomat's role was part of my new, godfatherly persona. (I shook free a fleeting vision of Condi Rice in one of her twee Barbie suits.)

I picked up the phone before I could change my mind. Thank heaven: her machine. "Percy Darling here. Why not this afternoon? I'll cross the Rubicon at five or so. Salmon sounds splendid."

Tossing aside the cotton-candy missive, out the door I ran, the vigor returned to my legs. As I passed and hailed the tree-house builders (pleased to have remembered Ira's name), I noticed, over the wall and through the line of maples along the driveway, Mistress Lorelei's Mayan gardener watching them intently. I waved to him as well. "Hello there, Celestino!" I called out. *His* name I could recall, though I had not laid eyes on him in a month.

I ran toward town and circled the green. As always when I passed the library, I felt a frisson of despair. On the front door was a poster, hand-lettered in Magic Marker, urging passers-by to stop in for a workshop—FREE! CHILD CARE AVAILABLE!—on building your own Web site.

This propelled me into a sprint.

The profession I chose, like the woman I chose, belongs to the past except in the minds of those who truly loved it and mourn its tragic demise. Even the educational path upon which it is based has become all but unrecognizable. What was once called library science now has a trend-driven hocus-pocus name, something like "informational studies." A library that is respectably up to date is no longer a temple dedicated to the guardianship of books or a sanctuary for the hallowed art of reading.

No.

A library is a zone of cyberkinetic values, a brain as viewed by the cold, lizardly pathologist: a numbingly gray place, of systems and wiring, of knowledge-related transactions that may or may not (preferably not, to many of my grandson's peers) require the use of books. A library is now far more like a bank than like a church or a museum—cause for rejoicing in the minds of the Orwellian clerks who service its needs. Ten years ago, Matlock's public library—a cathedralesque Victorian structure, built of red brick, its front door crowned with a stained-glass window depicting the warrior-scholar Athena—endured a so-called renovation. Perversely, all books were permanently removed from the vaulted central room, the tall shelves replaced by carrels containing Internet Access Stations and bins displaying movie DVDs. The information desk is now manned (womaned) by someone whose main job is to help you reserve time slots for the computers or guide you through the arduous process of "logging on." If you do not watch your feet as you pass through this room, you are sure to trip on the electrical cords that creep everywhere like kudzu.

Once, I blamed these changes on the computers themselves. (Through my decades at Widener, we classified and reclassified volumes again and again, enduring a series of achingly absurd systemic quakes, each christened with yet another acronym from MARC through OCLC to HOLLIS. Walls were ripped open to accommodate more cabling. Throughout our reading rooms, the bitter glow of screens began to clash with lamplight.) But such blame is naïve, merely another form of condemning the messenger. In retrospect, I am forced to accept that an atheistic passion for the abstract nature of existence, a leaning toward the mathematical, would have led sooner or later to an antireverence toward all things bibliographical, a sort of baby-with-the-bathwater ethos. It is no coincidence that the first books were religious in nature. Word of God and all that. Since I stand firmly in the God-is-for-sissies camp, I follow the logic of this evolution with more sorrow than outrage.

You will assume that my house was filled to the rafters with books. Well, yes, there were quite a lot of books throughout, underfoot and overhead, tumbling out of my haphazardly placed bookshelves, stacked beneath chairs, beside beds, even in the bottoms of a closet or two. But I was never a "collector." My love of books is a love of what they contain; they hold knowledge as a pitcher holds water, as a dress contains the mystery of a woman's exquisite body. Their physicality *matters*—do not speak to me of storing books as bytes!—but they should not inspire fetishistic devotion. I kept no preciously glass-fronted cases, did not assign a room of my home to be an officially designated library, nor did I collude with antiquarian book dealers, haunt trading fairs, or participate in any bibliographic commerce other than spending too much money at the bookseller I have always favored in Ledgely. It was and still is called the Narwhal, a play on the name of its longtime proprietor, my dear friend and onetime colleague Norval Sorenson, who can still get me nearly any volume my heart desires and whose wife, Helena, became one of Poppy's closest friends.

Why did I, a robust red-blooded man born before World War II, become a librarian . . . a profession that, in the mid–twentieth century, was scorned as the refuge of timid, bookish women and a handful of homosexual, sandal-wearing fops? I loved to read, and both of my parents were teachers. Mother English, father history. Really, it was as simple as that. In our house, in Montclair, New Jersey, there were bookshelves in every room, and every room's collection of books fell within a designated subject. All wars up to and including the Civil War occupied the living room; twentieth-century wars dominated the foyer and downstairs hallway. (My father, a fellow of pacifist temperament, taught history through teaching wars.) British fiction, my mother's first love, encircled the dining room table. There were cookbooks in the kitchen, of course, but European literature in translation crammed the breakfast nook, and up in my parents' bedroom lived biographies and memoirs. In the guest room slumbered science and the visual arts; a dozen gardening volumes held court in the downstairs bathroom. In my room, however, books toppled this way and that, as I pleased; my mother, wisely, relinquished her control beyond my door.

It was straightforward, then, the path I followed; I see it as proof of a happy childhood. Take that, Dr. Freud (Philip Larkin, too). And like so many people who find their calling early, I found my spouse early as well. I met Poppy at a party in Cambridge, the year I started working as a stacks page at Widener. I had been invited to one of those cattle-call cocktail gatherings at the home of the curator of rare books. There, nearly *all* books were housed in glittering glass-fronted shelves, where keys in the locks left one assuming that to open the cases without permission might trigger an alarm.

Knowing no one, I gripped my gin and tonic (too strong for me back in those innocent days) and pretended great interest in a case of leather volumes in languages I did not speak or read.

"Boo," said a girl from close behind me. "You are just pretending, aren't you?"

Genuinely startled, I said, "Pretending what?"

"To give a hoot about those books." She peered into the case. "I mean, Chaucer? Who really enjoys Chaucer?"

She was extremely pretty, the cheeky girl, and she knew it.

"As it happens, I love books. And Chaucer."

"Of course you love books. You're here at Rupert's. Which means you're at Harvard. So of course you do."

I was confused. "Well, then you're at Harvard, too."

She laughed. "I'm the daughter of people who used to be."

"Used to be?"

"Mm. Used to teach here. Now they teach in France. It's not so cruel there."

"Cruel?"

She laughed again.

"My father says Harvard is a difficult mistress, ready to betray you at the slightest lapse in protocol or devotion. If you make it here, you can't relax. Not for a minute. The peak of a mountain, he says, is always a perilous place to stand, no matter how sweeping the view."

Articulate though her speech might have been, I found it irritating, but at least someone was talking to me. I took a sip of my gin and felt its sting deep in my sinuses. I sneezed. "Well," I said, "in principle, I see what you mean. But I'm very happy here."

"Yes, that's because you're young. You're grateful to be here. And that's fine! That's exactly as it should be. For now. If you're smart, though, you'll see it as a stepping-stone, not a destination."

My eyes watered from the impact of my drink. "Who are you? Are you always this impertinent?"

She did not answer my second question. She introduced herself as Penelope Goodwin. "I'll let you call me Poppy if you tell me your name."

"I don't care what you let me call you, but I'm Percy," I told her. "Percy Darling."

She looked at me, wide-eyed for a moment, as if I'd shocked her. I braced myself for some predictably dog-eared jest about my surname. "Percy *Darling,*" she said, "are you from Vigil Harbor?"

I'd begun to find her less attractive than strange. I glanced about, to see if any of my new coworkers stood nearby, anyone to rescue me from this peculiar interrogation. "Where's that?"

"Darling," she said, "is an old name in Vigil Harbor. You've never been to Vigil Harbor, up near Gloucester?"

"Never heard of it."

She looked skeptical. "Very old, very romantic. That's where my father's family landed. A place for seduction, my mother says. So. The very first lighthouse keeper was Ezekiel Darling. We're probably distant cousins." She took my drink out of my hand and set it on top of the bookcase. "You're not enjoying this—the drink or the party. Come to my house for something better than Chaucer and pretzels." She started away from me but stopped when she sensed I wasn't following.

"Come on, cousin. I live next door. You can always change your mind and come back. I'm taking care of my parents' house. Let's go make ourselves some supper, what do you think of that?"

"Do you even know the Smithsons?" I said as we crossed our host's backyard and passed through a hedge. "Did you simply barge in?"

"I used to babysit for their kids. The kids grew up, so now I take care of their plants and their dog. They invite me to everything. They think I'm lonely."

Why she had approached me in that crowd of strangers, I did not ask for months. I did not want to press my luck. When I finally did, she told me that she had been attracted first by the color of my shirt ("It was such a celestial blue, I mean like *actual sky*") and then by the earnest look on my face as I pretended to scrutinize those books.

"My heart went out to you," she said, "for being so over your head. And then I found out you were a Darling. And you are."

We married the next year. We were twenty-four years old.

~

When I returned from my run, I saw that Robert and Arturo were up in the tree, straddling limbs on opposite sides of the trunk, while Ira was—with the help of Celestino—handing up a long board. Robert and Ira were bare-chested. It was early October, yet the heat had returned for what was sure to be the last bold parry of summer.

I stopped at the tree. "Hello, young craftsmen," I said, striving not to sound winded. "Please do take care not to kill yourselves."

"Granddad," said Robert, "this part is a cinch. And hey—Mrs. Connaughton's loaned us the help of this very able-bodied guy."

Celestino nodded at me, his smile aloof or shy, I couldn't tell which.

"Now let me get this right," I said. "I thought the idea was that the precocious little architects of the—the Nightshades? the Toadstools?—were to build this masterpiece."

"We build the platforms, ladders, and guardrails, the basic structure," said Ira, "and then we bring the kids in to do the fun stuff. The embellishments. The interior details. They're like the decorators."

"Ah! Well, carry on." As if my permission were the least bit germane.

I struggled with the recurrent sensation I'd been having for over a month, that I was not the lord of the manor here but, rather, a favored guest at an eccentric country estate where children called the shots. A sort of toffee-coated *Lord of the Flies*. If Julie Andrews or Suzanne Pleshette had appeared on the lawn and broken into song, it wouldn't have fazed me one bit.

Ordinarily, I got in my postmarathon swim before the kiddies' first recess, but that day, my late start meant that—unless I wanted to run the gauntlet of their impish stares on my way to the pond—I had to wait until after lunch, after "first dismissal." Most of the children were picked up, swallowed by the maws of their parents' lumbering minivans, at twelve-thirty, though a small group stayed on for Lunch Bunch, a nosh-and-nap session that lasted another hour. And then, except for the teachers who lingered to clean up the day's bedlam, I had the place to myself.

I paid bills in my study, pausing to watch Robert and his crew balance and hoist boards, hammering in stereo. That poor tree. I could feel its anguished gaze through the window: its arboreal *Et tu, Brute?* I sighed.

Poppy had once called herself my leavener; she had known how to tease me out of my possessive, pessimistic anxieties. If she had been there beside me, she would have said, "Percy, it's a tree. A divine majesty of a tree, but your grandson knows just what he's doing. And please think of the delight he is building with that hammer. Think of it!"

The years I spent with Poppy amount to less than half—even closer to a third—of the time I have known our daughters, and yet the truth is that Poppy abides with me still, inside my head, speaking to me, far more than do Trudy or Clover. If I had a nickel for all the times I have uttered, alone with myself, "Oh, Poppy"—in sorrow, in exasperation, in pleasure or relief or physical pain—I would have amassed a bank balance large enough to buy the entire town of Matlock and to rule the place as I damn well pleased, from firing the idiotically plugged-in librarian to knocking down the hideous addition on the Harris Homestead and replanting Jonathan Newcomb's three-acre turfiganza with nothing but milkweed. Ah, but that was not to be my destiny. Far from it.

I waited until the last civilian tank had slid past the window. I grabbed a towel from the mudroom and set off for the pond. Passing the barn, I could hear Ira as he led the Lunch Bunch in a song comparing love to a magic penny. He played the guitar and sang the sappy lyrics without the slightest inhibition. Actually, he had a rather nice singing voice, and I chastised myself for regarding his choice of employment as any more odd, in these times, than mine had been in a stodgier era. As I had done for my entire working life, he was holding his own in a profession ruled by women. Good for him, I thought as I backstroked my way across the pond, from under one shore's canopy of yellow leaves across the open stretch of sky to another.

You give the magic penny away and, poof, you possess another, and another and another and another. *Lend it, spend it, and you'll have so many, they'll roll all over the floor!* Whether she'd been sincere or not, Mistress Lorelei had a point about the children's voices. They had a tranquilizing, even mesmerizing effect. "Oh, Poppy," I said for the five trillion ninety-ninth time.

At last I pulled myself from the water, wading through the soft sandy mud. I wasn't squeamish about the mud, as most people were; I loved the feel of it between my toes. Our neighbors had always thought us vaguely mad to swim in the pond—someone had seen a snapping turtle more than once—but Poppy and I scoffed at their timidity. For years, until it finally rotted, I put out a raft from May to October. Perhaps, I thought idly that day, I could bribe Robert into building a replacement.

I wrapped the towel around my shoulders and walked up to the house, to the outdoor shower. Members of the Lunch Bunch were making their exit, receiving their hugs and kisses, relinquishing their tiny satchels.

I stayed in the shower a long time, staring up at the sky through the trees. I would swim at least through the end of the month, but this would be one of the last balmy days of no goosebumps, no gasps from the cold air against my wet skin. The morning paper decreed a sharp downturn in the temperature that night. Very soon, for a brief time, the water would be warmer than the air.

I came out onto the pathway singing snatches of the magic penny song. I was still in my swimsuit, toweling my hair, when I practically collided with a mother leading her child by the hand.

"Greetings!" I barked in sudden alarm.

"I'm sorry!" said the mother.

Startled speechless, we faced each other, six inches apart. I glanced at the boy to be sure I hadn't knocked him down. He stepped off the path, scowling at me. When I focused on the mother, she was staring at my midsection. She actually laughed.

I was poised to express my territorial indignation when she said, "Why, if it isn't the pink pineapples."

I had definitely seen this woman before, but then, all these fit, generically charmed mommies had been passing by my windows for a month. I'd surely seen them all.

She said, "Do you remember me from the store? I helped you pick out this suit. I must say, it does make a positive statement."

Oh heavens: my sartorial handmaid at The Great Outdoorsman was a mother at Elves & Fairies.

I bowed. "How kind of you to follow up on customer satisfaction. You see that I have put the garment to good use. I have definitely got my money's worth!"

We laughed together.

"Then you're Percival Darling," she said.

"In the flesh. A bit too much of it on view right now."

"I'm Sarah Straight. My son, Rico."

I held my hand toward the boy, but he did not oblige me with his. I noticed that he did not look a thing like his mother. Where she was fair-skinned, he was quite dark, with a broad face where hers was narrow and angled.

"Well, Sarah Straight, it's good to see that real people with real jobs and real manners are among the parents at this institution."

Her smile stiffened. "Manners don't seem lacking around here."

"True enough," I said. "On the surface."

"That's what manners are about, though, wouldn't you say? A smooth surface."

Rico tugged on his mother's arm. "Patience, honey," she said gently.

"Do you live in Matlock?" I said, at a loss.

"Oh hardly. We live in Packard. I was lucky to get a scholarship for Rico. Do you know the arts building, on the river?"

"The old mill."

"I have a loft there. I do stained glass. That's what I think of as my real job."

"Stained glass! Intriguing. Wonderful!" I longed for an exit. Aside from feeling like a social ape, I was cold.

"Come by on a Sunday," she said. "The studios are open, noon to five. Not just mine."

"Yes. Yes, I've heard about that. We need all the local culture we can get."

Rico saw his opening; he launched a plea of thirst and fatigue.

"Next time we meet," I said, "may I be fully clothed."

As I walked toward my back door, I heard her call back, "Hot pink becomes you, Percival Darling."

"Who would have guessed?" I called in return.

After dressing, I went in search of Robert, but his car was gone. Feeling deprived, I decided to inspect what he had accomplished. The lower part of the beech tree looked as if it had been cunningly entrapped, yet as I circled the tree and examined the handiwork, I could not find a single nail that penetrated the trunk or branches. All the boards were nailed to one another. Nor could I find evidence of a single amputation.

I wondered what Trudy would say if I called her that evening to praise her son's extracurricular talents. Not, I reminded myself, that I needed a reason to call my daughter.

"It's such a shame that we must begin to lock our cars and our houses."

"Must?" I scoffed. "Paranoia is certainly infectious."

"Are you really going to take such chances, Percy?" said Laurel Connaughton, Mistress Lorelei to a tee. "I've just spent a fortune to alarm the house, but I won't bat a lash if it lets me sleep soundly."

"If some jokester wants to stuff my dishwasher with regimental neckties or my underwear drawer with brussels sprouts, well boolah-boolah to him."

"Or her. You know, the police haven't been able to pin down a bit of evidence. This person is clearly sophisticated and wily."

"Or our police department is out of its depth."

"Percy, dear, it's not just Matlock. Ledgely just had an incident."

I helped myself to a fifth cucumber sandwich from a platter perched on a leather ottoman between us. Cucumber sandwiches are a weakness of mine, even if Laurel did not make them as well as Poppy had (with garlic and anchovy rather than dill). The promised salmon had not appeared, but I was holding a Tanqueray tonic in my free hand. I was not exactly suffering.

My hostess pulled her skirt down over her knees and laughed shrilly. She was, as always, meticulously dressed, though I noticed—sitting this close to her for the first time since our showdown over the bats—that she was beginning to look her sixtyish age. A bit heavier through the hips (though who was I to smirk?), and she'd pulled her bottle-blond hair back tightly enough to create the same effect as plastic surgery. At least she hadn't overdone the makeup. I tried to expunge the unpleasant memory of her red mouth, a small, garish sea anemone looming toward my face as I knelt by my bedroom fireplace. . . .

"Well, Laurel," I said briskly, "if you're inviting me to join a vigilante group, the answer is no thank you."

"Now there's a bold idea," she said brightly. "But no, no. What I invited you over to discuss is the possibility of a Christmas house tour to benefit the Forum. Do you realize, Percy, that our houses—yours and mine—turn two hundred and fifty years old this year? The Fisk brothers hired a housewright who knew what he was doing. I was thinking of throwing a birthday bash for my house and then I said to myself, 'Use it, Laurel!' One of our younger members—of whom we have far too few— has a terrific idea to fund a series of historical field trips for local public schools. As Barack Obama is showing us all these days, it's time to inspire patriotism in our youngest citizens! And why not start with local history? Right around the corner, we have the Midnight Ride, the Old North Bridge, the Battle Road. . . . We'd love to have something ready to go by next Patriots' Day."

"Admirable." I sat back and savored my drink. For once, I couldn't disagree with anything she'd said.

"Our houses would be absolute gems to include on the tour, and if we start the ball rolling, I know I can convince others to open their doors as well. It's always dicey until people see that it's going to be a feather in their cap to be on a really *first-rate* tour."

I certainly hadn't expected this. I hadn't, actually, expected much more than free smoked salmon and nicey-nicey talk that might earn me enough points with Clover to make her ease up on the subject of my cholesterol intake.

Laurel leaned forward and put a manicured hand on my naked knee.

"Well!" I said, shifting my leg. I looked around her living room: at its carefully oiled original paneling; at the exposed beams and corner posts, the skeletal timbers of the house, gnarled yet aesthetically prized; at the antiques Laurel had selected to dovetail with the architectural vintage. Periodically, a tumbleweed that passed for a cat would dart behind a doorway, pausing briefly to glare at me. Were I to inquire about this creature, I'm sure I would have heard that its particular breed had been imported to Salem via Asia during an era roughly congruent with the building of our houses. What else might justify its snub-nosed appearance and sociopathic behavior?

Our houses had been built in 1757 by Azor and Hosmer Fisk. Hosmer, "my" brother, had been the younger and poorer, the one who chose to farm while his older brother ran a flourishing cabinetry business. Though Hosmer was the one who married first—and who, with his bride, Truthful, bore so many children—his was the slightly smaller, simpler dwelling. It shared many details with this one, features that

Poppy and I had restored, but Laurel's house was the grander of the two. Though my parlor was paneled, it lacked Big Brother's dentation along the wainscoting and the broad bolection framing the larger hearth. I had also neglected to primp and pamper such details after Poppy's death. Much of the wood was now stained and parched; some of my floors were worn bare; and in two rooms where I could no longer cope with the horsehair plaster, dropped ceilings obscured the beams.

While my house faced the road (through trees that had colonized the fields once farmed), Laurel's house faced mine—as if Big Brother had intended to keep a permanent eye on Junior. Whenever Laurel and I were at odds, I would look out a side window and, glimpsing her house through the trees, project her face, in full-flush disapproval, across its symmetrical façade.

Now, thinking of my inferior home as a "gem" in any context, I laughed.

Laurel looked wounded. "I don't see anything amusing about this idea."

"Laurel, you misconstrue my mirth. What amuses me is that our houses were practically twins at birth—mine the runt, of course—yet here you are in a veritable museum, while I live in, shall we say, flagrant bachelor mayhem."

She touched her throat as she laughed. "You mean your place is a mess."

"A pigsty, my younger daughter calls it when she thinks I'm out of earshot."

"Oh, hahaha," trilled Laurel. "But Percy, my dear, I can put together an honest, eager crew of young girls who will tidy the whole place up, give it a good polish. And Tom Loud sends me this top-notch Guatemalan fellow, who I'm sure could weed-whack your front yard right into shape. You do have some rather stately hostas under all that bittersweet. . . . The important thing is that yours is one of the houses that remains unravaged."

"Unlike the Harris house."

"Exactly." She drew the word into a groan. "That was *such* a tragedy."

She took my empty glass and, without asking, went to refill it from the bottles in the Revere tray on the McIntyre sideboard. Like a cuckoo in a clock, the feline tumbleweed popped into view on the threshold nearest its mistress. It took two steps into the room and hissed at me.

"Oh, *Horace*," said Laurel, leaning down to extend a hand. "Quit your drama and come on in for a snuggle." The cat fled.

"You must be a covert cat lover, Percy. Only if you're truly phobic will he insist on claiming your lap!"

I looked at my feet, at the hole in my right sock (having been compelled to surrender my shoes at the door, a custom I find pretentious in the extreme). Was I already drunk? How was it that I had not made my excuses to leave?

Over our second drink, she told me how the occupants of the Harris Homestead had outweaseled the Forum with a game of bait and switch on the alleged "restoration" plans—going so far as to find out when Laurel and the other members of the Forum took their August vacations in Maine and Martha's Vineyard. That's when the building took place.

"Technically, we have a right to put a lien on the house for violations within public view, but we've never done such a thing, and frankly, should they choose to meet us in court, they have more money than God—which the Forum most certainly does not." All of a sudden, she gasped. "My goodness! I completely forgot the salmon, Percy!"

"Indeed you did."

And thus did I find myself, over salmon on pumpernickel toast, along with microwaved quiche Lorraine from the best gourmet shop in Ledgely, drawn into planning a house tour; into making lists and pledging that I would telephone old friends I rarely saw, couples who had once come to Poppy's wonderful parties, whose children had played with ours, who had sung "Jerusalem" beside us at local weddings. And who, of course, lived in some of Matlock's most treasured antique houses.

Were Matlock not a town that cherished antiquity, Poppy and I would never have bought our house, since it would have been condemned long before we saw it. For fifty-some years, it had been in the hands of a family with declining fortunes and the consequent variety of listlessness that blinds one to the conditions of one's surroundings. It had been on the market for several seasons, and Matlock's real estate agents had given up on showing it to clients, unable to convince the seller that his price was absurd. But all this we learned much later.

We had just begun to look at houses closer to the city: in Belmont, Arlington, Watertown. These were the towns for newlyweds, we'd heard, yet their suburban monotony dismayed us. We decided to take a weekend off from our house hunt and headed to Matlock to attend what Norval had told me was the secret best book sale in the world: the town's bohemian elite would donate tattered yet still exquisite volumes of fine art and architecture, which would sell for bargain prices to bene-fit the public library.

We parked on the green but found that we had arrived an hour early and decided to explore. Following a lane that descended through a tunnel of tall flourishing trees, we were charmed by the English feel of the wanton greenery—wild roses swooning over crumbled stone walls, fusillades of daylilies aquiver with bees and butterflies—and by the glimpses we had of houses built in a time when these woods had surely been open fields.

Just as we were about to turn back toward the green, Poppy pointed and laughed. "Now *there's* a house we could afford."

On first impression, set back in deep, distant shadows, it was a con-cise, steadfast structure, shamelessly plain in shape, its many-paned win-dows unshuttered, its roofline forbiddingly steep. I knew enough about architecture to see that its narrow front porch was a later addition and that its twin chimneys meant it would be the kind of house that feels big-ger inside than out.

Ordinarily, houses of this era were built within a few feet of passing traffic, for easy access during the winter; this one, however, stood well off the road. "A farmhouse," I said. Behind it, I saw the bowed summit of the barn. And then, in glittering patches through a stand of birch trees, I spotted the pond.

We exclaimed in unison.

That was also when I saw, to one side of the driveway, a stubby wooden FOR SALE sign entangled in poison ivy, as if it, too, were a relic of the past. An old man—sixty or eighty; we were so young and glib that any degree of old was simply *old*—sat on the front porch, reading. He must have seen us at the same moment we saw him, for almost instantly he waved. His wave looked like a beckoning. That moment—the sighting of the water, the old man, the sign, together as in a collage—is one I am certain I will carry to my deathbed.

Poppy, before I could stop her, started up the drive. "Hello!" she called out. "Hello there!"

Back in those early days, her ability, even proclivity, to strike up conversations anywhere with strangers—even though it had brought her into my life—still made me nervous. I suppose I couldn't quite suppress the adolescent anxiety that one of these many strangers might usurp me.

"We're in search of the book sale," she said as she approached the porch.

"Ah," said the man, "the library. Just up the road. Follow it left and you'll hit the town common. Can't miss it."

"I see you love books, too."

"I do." The man raised the volume in his lap, a novel by Elizabeth Spencer.

"Oh I am crazy about her," said Poppy. "Have you read *The Voice at the Back Door*? Do you know that it was *denied* a Pulitzer prize?"

"Never heard of her before this one," he said. "I like to check out what's new. That way, I don't read the same book twice and fall into a time warp."

With her customary ease, Poppy began to tell this elderly stranger about her favorite recent novels. She took a small pad of paper out of her purse and started making a list. I lurked on the lawn, pretending to examine what remained of a once-classic flower garden.

I looked up when I heard Poppy tear off the page and hand it to her newest friend. She was leaning back, gazing up at the face of the house (its paint puckering away from the clapboards in blisters the size of cocktail coasters). "Can I tell you," she said, "how rare and wonderful it is to see an old house preserved like this?"

The old man's laugh was harsh. "Poverty is a powerful preservative."

I wanted to flee. Poppy had gone too far. I was glaring at her by then, but she kept her attention on the old man.

"My father fell in love with this place," he said to Poppy. "Little did he know what it costs to romance the past."

Scanning the second story, I could see that a number of the quaintly diminutive lights in the windows had been replaced with squares of cardboard. Moss grew on the shingles. A wooden gutter had cracked from end to end.

"It's a brave thing, staying faithful to the past," Poppy said. "I dream of caring for a house like this one day. When you take on a house this old, you're reminded that you're only passing through. Humbling, isn't it?"

The old man squinted at Poppy, who had taken the liberty of stepping onto the porch and sitting in the only other chair. I couldn't tell if he thought she was full of baloney or if he was simply trying to see her more clearly.

She told him the story of her own childhood in an antique house in Vigil Harbor, a house that had belonged to a mariner, then a sailmaker, then a cordwainer, then a teacher, and, finally, to Poppy's professorial parents. "But they decamped to the city, to lead a life of high acadee-me-ah," she said. "And now they're in France, happy exiles." She sighed. "They sold the house where I grew up, the one I used to dream I'd raise my children in. It wasn't quite as old as this, but almost."

I looked at my watch. The book sale would start in ten minutes; I pictured a line of shrewd bibliophiles waiting there already, our chance at the best bargains gone up in smoke. I tried to catch Poppy's eye. Still she ignored me.

Over the next hour, we drank hideously sweet powdered iced tea (tepid to boot; no ice in the old man's frostbound freezer), and we toured through the house: up and down its steep staircases, front and back, beneath its undulating ceilings, through its batten doors sloping this way and that, according to the will of gravity and the settling of earth over two hundred years. Most of the windows—those panes that remained intact—contained the original glazing, which bestowed a rippling, underwater texture on the world beyond, a world of fathomless greenery and avian flutterings. Upstairs, three bedrooms held up the vertiginous roof, their ceilings giddily sloped. I felt like a giant in this house, yet comfortingly so. In the kitchen, when Poppy saw the robust utilitarian hearth, so tall that she could stand inside it (and she did), she gasped.

"Would you ever sell it?" she said, her two arms stretched out to touch the rough walls of the fireplace. "We're going to have a baby, and we're looking for a house just like this one."

He laughed harshly again. "Madam, you didn't see the sign?"

Later, she swore to me that she hadn't. And when I asked her if we were, de facto, "going to have a baby," she said, "Well, ipso facto. It's early to put stamps on the announcements, but I say we should waste no time getting ready."

"Wouldn't you say that buying a house whose roof is about to cave in is a curious way of getting ready?" I said.

"Percy. A house with a barn by the water. Think of it."

I did. And in truth, I was smitten, too.

Before we shook hands and promised to be in touch, Poppy pointed out the back window. "What's the name of that pond?"

His laugh was long and sawtoothed. "The things people bicker about," he said. "History-minded folks call it Azor's Hole. After the first property owner." He swept a hand vaguely toward the house that Laurel and her husband would purchase and polish a few years later. "Newcomers petitioned for Painted Turtle Pond. Cute. Those of us right here? The pond. Too small to name on a map."

"Name or no name, it's beautiful," said Poppy.

Poppy's father, who finally gave up renting the Cambridge house and sold it at an eye-popping profit, generously provided our down payment. We had enough savings to make the smallest down payment ourselves, but then we'd have been left with nothing to throw at the house's numerous (shockingly numerous) geriatric needs, many invisible to the beholder: new furnace, new septic tank, the installation of chimney crickets and attic vents, replacement of two supporting beams devoured by modern-day termites.

Yet Poppy's optimism kept us giddy. Her charm brought us friends, her growing belly (for she would indeed be pregnant within a year) many extra sets of hands—to paint, plaster, paper, and then populate the interior.

A few years later, my parents retired, decided to sell their house full of books and move to an apartment. There was a signed first edition of *Finnegans Wake* that my father had always known could bring in some cash, yet there were other pleasant surprises. The greatest was that the collection of gardening books sequestered in the downstairs bathroom happened to include a rare set of illustrated horticultural guides personally annotated by a garden designer whose work apparently graces many of the most distinguished estates in Scotland, Balmoral among them. My father made the magnanimous decision to give us the proceeds of the entire sale. Both girls were small at the time, and I suppose he saw it as seed money for their education. Fortunately, he did not specify, so it went to shore up the crumbling barn and to build a modest, historically respectful extension on the kitchen at the rear of the house.

When I look back on life as we lived it in our much-trafficked, much-cherished home, my happiest memories are of the parties Poppy loved to give. At one time or another, every room contained and magnified festivity, celebration, from friends' book launches to the girls' slumber parties. Poppy's parties were the ones our friends and neighbors looked forward to the most. There were her traditional celebrations (Fourth of July, Christmas, New Year's Day, and a Winter Doldrums party she threw every year about a week after Valentine's Day), but more numerous and selective were the cocktail soirées and intimate dinner gatherings whose dramatis personae she strategized with military cunning. I loved watching her sit at the kitchen table with a notepad, a pencil, and a goblet of wine, poring through our address books and the local directory, rarely assembling the same group twice.

One night, I sat across from her, stealing sips from her wine as she quizzed me about my library colleagues. It was that delectable moment in early fall when the girls had just returned to school. Perhaps they were in second and third grades, their first art projects already taped to the cupboard doors (rubbed leaves, brutishly charming self-portraits). Both girls were thrilled with their new teachers, thrilled to be back with their friends all day long, falling asleep early and abruptly, as if drugged, so that the evenings we parents shared in private were just that much longer.

There was a pot of pasta cooking on the stove. The lid muttered above the boiling water.

"I am so longing to find someone for Bettina," said Poppy, referring to a friend of hers who'd been divorced for a couple of years. The split had seemed sudden and baffling to all their friends. "Surely you know someone agreeable, civilized and smart enough for Bets."

"As you know," I said, "the male pickings are slim at Widener."

Poppy gave me a sly smile. "Percy, I'm not entirely certain that Bettina is looking to meet a man."

It took me a moment to comprehend. "Well," I said prudishly. "Well then."

"Oh Percy, be modern for a change." Poppy reached over to tickle me under an arm.

"I wouldn't have the faintest notion which women I work with . . . which ones . . ."

"Are lesbians?"

I asked her if she was sure about Bettina.

"I don't even know if Bettina is sure about Bettina," she said. "But it can't hurt to test the waters, and at a table of a dozen friends . . . no harm, no foul."

This bit of speculation led us to wonder about the intimate secrets of a few other people we knew, to recast alliances we'd never quite under-stood, and by the time the pasta was done, we were laughing ourselves silly. As Poppy poured out the pot into the colander, I stood behind her, leaning into her back, and said, "What would all our friends do without your machinations?"

"They would end up lonely and bitter."

"Then you'll have to live forever," I joked, and as I did, we both looked up at our conjoined reflections in the window above the sink, crisp against the encroaching dark. At that instant, steam rose from the colander and fogged the glass. Our faces vanished.

"Actually, they'd get along fine without me," said Poppy. "Me, you—none of us are indispensable."

"*Is* indispensable," I said, piqued by a vague sense of gloom. I did not protest that I wouldn't have the faintest notion how to survive without Poppy. We served ourselves dinner and went back to planning the party.

After all these years, it stands to reason that all these parties, in my memory, would have blurred together—or vanished, like our faces in the kitchen window that evening. Yet many of them remain distinct, pre-ciously so, when I set aside time to remember. They are like the cards in an old-fashioned library catalog. Many are brittle and yellowed, dark-ened at the edges, typed imperfectly, even altered by hand, but there they are to flip through at will. The one turned to most often would be the last.

It was a midsummer gathering of our closest friends in Matlock, with the addition of a couple who'd just moved in across the street. Poppy had met the wife while waiting for the P.O. to open its doors one morn-ing. "Percy, you'll love her. A consummate book hound, this woman."

I would grill lamb chops. Poppy, who'd just discovered Middle East-ern cooking, had made a couscous salad. Back in 1975, no one had heard of couscous; that night our guests would rave about the odd combination of fruits, nuts, and exotic vegetables (Swiss chard!). On a recent visit to Harvard Square, Poppy had bought a Moroccan dress embroidered with flowers, white on white, its neckline loose and low. How she sparkled in that new dress, the snowy cotton setting off her youthful skin, brown as butterscotch.

I would have felt passionately in love with her that perfect summer evening—hot but alluringly breezy—if we had not quarreled in the kitchen before the guests came.

Clover was just shy of fourteen, about to start high school. She'd been spending a good deal of time that summer with a group of youngsters whom even I, the librarian nerd, could spot a mile away as the popular crowd. It was clear that she and one of the boys had paired off, were "going together," in the parlance of the day. Two or three times, I'd seen them holding hands and giggling—I'd take a deep breath and tell myself this was normal—but a few days before, one of Poppy's friends had called to report that while jogging along the nature trails behind the Old Artillery, she'd seen Clover and this boy engaged in "some rather heated kissing."

Poppy had asked me several times already what I felt we should do about this, and I had so far managed to evade any true discussion of the subject.

"I think it's time to take Clover for a visit to my gynecologist," Poppy declared, out of the blue, as she sliced oranges for sangria. "Just to have a talk with a grown-up who isn't one of us. Who can talk straight without making her fall through the floor in mortification."

I'd been tasting the mint sauce for the lamb chops and nearly choked. "Good God, Poppy, what are you suggesting? That we gift wrap a prescription for the birth-control pill? She is still a child!"

"Percy." Poppy regarded me with a sardonic sort of pity. "I am suggesting nothing of the kind. Quite the contrary."

"I wouldn't say sending her to a sex doctor will help her . . . abstain."

" 'Sex doctor'? Percy, you've been hanging out too much with that Nathaniel Hawthorne guy. And I suppose you think just letting her loiter about with boys in the woods *will* help her 'abstain.' "

"We should speak with her directly. Specify limits. Make it clear there will be consequences if she ignores those limits."

Poppy had laughed. "Now that's sure to work. And I presume you mean that I should speak with her. Would you have the nerve? Or do you mean we should give her a list of anatomically specific rules and then, when she breaks them, lock her in a tower? Hmm. Last I looked, we don't actually *have* a tower."

"Shall we talk about anatomical specificity? I warned you not to leave that granola book on women's bodies lying around the living room."

"Oh for Pete's sake, Percy. If anything, that book will help our daughters make smarter decisions when it comes to boys."

"I rather doubt it," I muttered, crumbling dried rosemary over the meat.

Poppy made a faint noise of disgust.

"Listen, darling," I said, abandoning the lamb to put my arms around her, "isn't it your job as her mother to give her that . . . straight talk? If we had boys, well . . . but we don't."

Poppy freed herself and turned to look me sternly in the eye. "My job as her mother, right now, is to accept that I'm the last person whose authority she respects. I am not a fool."

"Don't be silly. Clover only pretends to see you as a square."

"Well, as it happens, I've already made the appointment."

I took a deep breath. The guests were to arrive in twenty minutes. "We will take up this discussion tomorrow," I said. "But let me tell you, I believe your plan to be rash, incendiary, and devoid of common sense." Before she could reply, I marched upstairs to change my clothes.

We were careful that evening not to mingle our disagreements, for another dispute lurked beneath all the talk of gynecologists and female maturation and—a foolish remark on my part—our not having boys. Earlier that summer, to my alarmed surprise, Poppy had begun to petition for a third child. Still shy of forty, she was feeling what I perceived as nostalgia pure and simple. Bluntly, I told her so, but she would have none of it. She suggested that we might have a son. Didn't I yearn for a son? (I did not.) "We'd name him after your dad," she persisted. She'd raised her eyebrows coyly and pointed to her belly. "Perhaps a tiny Alva is growing here already. . . ." On seeing my stunned expression, she told me she was joking, but I became nervous, even reticent, when we were together in bed. I do not mind disclosing that during the fifteen years of our amorous relations, I cannot recall a dry spell of longer than a week.

That night's meal, which we served on the outdoor table, was one of our best. It was lovely to see some of our friends—like Norval and Helena Sorenson, who had been away in Vermont—for the first time in many weeks. We were tanned, ripe with contentment, rested. Over cocktails, the Sorensons announced that they were thinking of buying a pair of goats so they could make their own cheese. The rest of us, even Helena, shared a good laugh at the vision of scholarly Norval milking a goat.

Clover and Trudy were swimming; I let my glance stray from the guests to watch them dive from the raft, first Trudy, then Clover. My little mermaids, I thought with pride. As they made their way up the sloping lawn, I motioned them over. Some of these friends had known them since they were babies, yet they were both reserved with the grown-ups: polite but clearly eager to head indoors, become separate again. I realized that in a few months I'd be the father of not one but two teenage girls. Only fourteen months apart, my mermaids, but Clover had, just that year, shot far ahead of her sister in growth. As they stood close to me in their wet swimsuits, towels draped about their necks, Trudy's body still had the boyish lines of a kouros, while Clover, in a red bikini I'd never seen before, had crossed a delicate but obvious line. As they went into the house, Norval nodded toward Clover and said to me, "I think you're going to be in big trouble soon. That one just became a genuine beauty." His smile was more wistful than wolfish.

I glanced at Poppy; she'd heard him and would, I knew, use his words as ammunition when we resumed our debate.

The conversation was lively and smart—until, over dessert, we arrived at politics. In Matlock, back then, this was generally safe ground: we saw ourselves not as smug and cocooned in our moderate wealth but as enlightened, even embattled. Had we been religious, in need of a patron saint, small plaster statues of Eugene McCarthy would have adorned our sprawling lawns.

Talk had turned to the fiasco of our exit from Saigon that spring. There we were, privileged liberals going through the worn ritual of savaging Nixon and his cronies, the intertwining travesties of Watergate and Vietnam. These twin wellsprings of national shame still fueled our outrage; though nearly everyone was trying to quit, the cigarette smoke twined thick with smoke from the citronella candles.

I had just noted the long silence of our new neighbor, husband of the consummate book hound, when he made this declaration: "We'd have seen none of this infernal mess if we hadn't elected that Mafia puppet Jack Kennedy to the White House."

Had this remark been made earlier in the evening, when we'd all been sober, perhaps even if Poppy and I had been more complicit, I'm certain we would have steered the conversation down safer byways—but before we could rescue our guests from themselves, three of our dear friends were excoriating the new neighbor, who resisted the ambush at first with conviction and then with scorn.

Kip Lightman, who taught poli sci at Harvard, said to the neighbor, "So where did you move from again—Oklahoma? Let's talk about oil, shall we?"

"I was warned about people like you when we moved here," said the neighbor. "From Nebraska." He stood up from the table and almost physically lifted his wife from her chair. "It's clear we've entered a hotbed of radical righteousness," he said to her. She looked as if she wanted to cry.

Poppy tried to soothe the man, to assure him that we'd all had too much sangria, to let us please enjoy the grasshopper pie and change the subject. He stepped back from her conciliatory reach and said, "Thank you for dinner. It was delicious." He put his arm around his wife. "And we, by the way, have not had too much to drink at all." As he led her away, his wife turned toward Poppy and mouthed, *I'm sorry.* By then the poor woman was indeed crying.

The party broke up, moments later, with a sense of resignation and vague repentance. After we waved off the Sorensons, the only ones who had to drive, Poppy and I carried the dishes into the house without speaking. I was in the midst of loading the dishwasher when she announced that she needed to take a walk around the pond, to work off her "radical righteousness."

Ordinarily, I would have joined her, but I was tired and dismayed. I abandoned the cleanup and went upstairs. I turned on the fan in our bedroom and was about to take a cold shower when I heard Trudy calling me from down the hall.

She was sitting up in her bed, leaning toward an open window. "Dad, I think somebody's calling out there."

"Calling? What do you mean?"

"I don't know," said Trudy. "Just . . . a voice."

The breeze had risen, and the leaves of the many surrounding trees made a clamorous shushing. Perhaps I heard what I thought was the call of a nocturnal creature, a fox or an owl; the woods of Matlock are, to this day, a wild kingdom by night, and the pond magnified its feral sounds. I listened, then whispered, "Perhaps it's your sister's young Romeo, hoping to spirit her away. Little does he know that she sleeps like a fossil."

In the half dark, I could see Trudy glaring at me. "Very funny, Dad."

The crickets were in full voice as well as the trees. I realized, as one does from time to time, how very loud the country can be in high summer.

"A cat, I'll bet you, sweetie. Go back to sleep. You have tennis tomorrow," I said. "I tell you what. I'll go check it out."

I made her lie down. I returned to the kitchen and listened at the screen door. Crickets, leaves, and the wind chimes at the entrance to the barn. I stepped outside and down the back steps. I saw the beautiful moon, reflected on the pond. I tried to listen harder. I heard a fox call: There we go, I thought.

I saw a light on in the barn loft. Perhaps Poppy had gone up there to avoid me. Well, I thought peevishly, irritated anew at the memory of our argument, let her dance the night away on her own. As for me, I felt as if I could sleep for a week. I sighed and returned to the house, pondering the question of how we would ever make amends with our new, conservative neighbors.

I took a cool shower and put on a clean pair of boxers. I aimed the fan at the bed and slipped between the sheets.

In the morning, I was awakened by Clover's insistent shaking. She and Trudy were in their tennis clothes, ready to be driven to their lessons in Ledgely. It was Saturday, and this was my responsibility, since Poppy ferried them to their various obligations throughout the week. She rose early on weekend mornings to spend a few hours alone in her studio. It was odd, though, that she hadn't been the one to wake me. Perhaps, suffering as I was from a colossal hangover, I had returned to sleep and did not recall that she had.

I rushed into my clothes and out the front door with my daughters. My head pounded as I made the drive to Ledgely without coffee, so after leaving Trudy and Clover at the courts, I drove to the Narwhal and begged a cup from Norval. In lulls between customers, we talked about the disastrous end to the dinner party. Perhaps we *were* a righteous lot. But then of course we rehashed our indignation over national affairs. We debated the pros and cons of Jimmy Carter. Poppy did not like the way he mentioned God so much. "Church. State," she'd say, making a vertical slash with one hand between the two words. "He's a good man, genuinely pious, but he's opening the door to a world of trouble."

I stayed with Norval long enough to pick up the girls at the end of their lessons without having gone back to Matlock.

When the three of us entered the house, I noticed that dishes from the party still lay about the kitchen, exactly as I'd left them the night before.

"Hey, Mom!" Clover yelled as she tossed her tennis racket onto the table. Normally, Poppy would have been making them lunch. "Hey, Mom, where are you? We're starving here!"

I was about to reprimand Clover for not putting her racket away when Trudy said, "Look, Dad, is that a swan?"

I followed her gaze out the window and, for the briefest moment, laughed. Trudy might need glasses, I was thinking as I saw quite clearly, with my excellent vision, that the white mass at the edge of the pond was Poppy's new Moroccan dress.

Perhaps at that very moment, the Minkoffs, who lived in one of the Three Greeks on the other side of the pond, were watching a policeman cover Poppy's body with a sheet. I did not witness this horrendous scene myself, but my imagination has had so much time to construct it that sometimes I'm convinced I was the one to find her.

Simultaneously, a police car was turning down my driveway. From the kitchen, I could not see this, either, but when I heard the doorbell, already I knew that something was urgently wrong. I forced the girls to go to their rooms before I answered the door. I remember saying to them, "Go! Now! Please!" They must have thought I'd gone mad.

I did not admit the young policeman but walked swiftly from the house and led him halfway across the lawn, nearly dragging him by an arm. That he allowed me to do so was, I knew before he spoke, a very bad sign.

In short order, I returned inside and called upstairs that Clover and Trudy should stay there until I came back.

"Jesus, Dad, what's going on?" Clover called down.

"Just stay," I called back. Two words—two *syllables*—that I knew, even then, would have made all the difference in the world had I spoken them to Poppy, twelve hours earlier, instead.

The policeman drove the circuitous looping of country lanes that took us to the opposite side of the pond. We did not speak.

An ambulance was parked in the middle of the Minkoffs' lawn. This was an absurd sight. Beside it stood two men in white uniforms, facing the pond. Their arms were folded. Why did they look so relaxed? Beyond them, men in darker uniforms walked back and forth by the water.

Saul and Linda Minkoff stood on their porch, watching the various men on the lawn as if they were actors in a play. When I got out of the police car, they went inside. They were neighbors I did not know well, because the pond, like a small ocean, kept us apart. I recognized them from town meetings and the grocery store.

Poppy's naked body had lodged in the cattails. Like me, the Minkoffs respected the pond's varied wildlife and did not mow to the water's edge.

What flashed in my head was an illustration in a collection of fairy tales I had bought for Clover and Trudy, years ago, at the Narwhal. In the tale "Binnorie," a treacherous girl drowns her sister in order to marry the sister's sweetheart, and a traveling minstrel makes a harp of the dead girl's breastbone and hair. He travels by happenstance to the castle of the evil sister, where the harp, laid aside on a shelf, sings a ballad about the betrayal. Both girls found this story too frightening, so I would page past it. Yet my eyes sometimes lingered on the painting of the maiden lying drowned on the banks of the milldam, golden tresses wound through stalks of grass.

Half covered with a sheet, Poppy lay before me like a flesh-and-blood forgery of that illustration.

"That's my wife," I said stupidly as I joined the men who already knew this fact. As I have said, ours was such a small town. These young policemen had waved to Poppy when she rode her bike along our safe, pretty roads. Perhaps one or two of them had been among those who had given her warnings, never tickets, about the speed at which she drove.

One of these fellows asked if I wanted them to call someone. I asked them to call Helena. Understandably, but idiotically, I did not want to leave Poppy, so it was Helena who went to the house and told my daughters their mother was dead. As if hypnotized, I spent the afternoon dealing, almost calmly, with the police and their meek, provincial inquiries. By the time I arrived at home, several cars lined the driveway. I found Clover and Trudy at the kitchen table, Norval and Helena sitting close beside them. Helena—or someone, I never asked who—had cleaned and put away every dish from the party.

I was in Packard already that Sunday, at my favorite hardware store, throwback to one of those charming Robert McCloskey books I read to the girls when they were small. The warped wood floor wears a scatter of sawdust, ancient dusty tools and coils of rope hang from the rafters, and a freckled blond boy leaps to attention when you enter. He even calls you sir. (I like to believe that it will remain exactly so until the glaciers have melted away.)

I'd bought a special kind of oil I use for my rotary mower and picked up a few rolls of tape. On the way out, I bought an Eskimo Pie from the freezer (a clever source of bribes for impatient children, sheer indulgence for me). I was heading for my car when I saw the orange banner on the old mill, gussied up and spared from collapse, that now houses artists and a few craft boutiques. OPEN STUDIOS.

Well why not? I placed my purchases on the backseat of my car. I didn't even have to feed the meter.

The cavernous halls of the brick building were chilly as I wandered past the open doorways, each leading to a cornucopia of chandeliers, charm bracelets, tapestries, or some other form of elaborately creative effulgence. I tried to fool myself into believing that I was there to browse. I waved awkwardly at lonely artisans hoping for someone, anyone, to look at their frivolous wares. On the third floor, I found her.

I saw a plaque with her name, *Sarah Straight,* before I was able to look through the open door. Too late, I panicked at the thought that her work might be trivial, tacky, or downright ugly. What would I say? I've never been good at pretending I like what I most emphatically do not.

A slim shaft of violet light crossed the threshold, like a stray laser beam. I stepped into it and was, for a moment, blinded. Stepping aside,

I saw the source of the purple ray: a large fan window that depicted, in brilliant, varicolored, varitextured fragments of glass, a landscape. A seascape, to be precise: marbled rough-hewn slabs of rock against a wide blue turmoil of sea, a stormy sky. The low afternoon sun was shining right through it.

"Percival Darling!" She'd spotted me before I spotted her.

Two other people stood nearby, Sunday strangers admiring Sarah's work.

She crossed the space between us, her hand held out. As I shook it, I realized that my own hand was sticky. "Oh dear," I said. "Eskimo Pie."

"Sticky hands I'm used to," said Sarah. As if on cue, Rico streaked past, riding a tricycle across the concrete floor.

"Please don't go anywhere," she said. "I mean it. Look around, or sit, help yourself to food over there. Just give me a few minutes with these people." She whispered, "I think they might give me a commission."

So I looked while Sarah had a quiet conversation with one of the strangers. Her windows were landscapes, all devoutly New England in their images and tone: autumnal hay fields, snow-laden pines, islands off the coast of Maine. I saw her writing in a notebook, giving a card to the man, shaking his hand. When he left, she returned to me.

"How nice to see you."

I laughed inanely. "I was across the street, at Conley's. I've been going there since . . ." I skidded to a halt. It was clear to me that I did not want to tell her how many years I'd been shopping in Packard—shopping anywhere at all.

"Isn't Packard fabulous?" she said. "Last year one of my friends got a loft in this building and we came for a visit."

I found *fabulous* a curious word to apply to this rundown corner of the world, but I hastened to agree.

A bell, like a school bell, rang from below. "Is that a fire alarm?"

"No. Studios close in fifteen minutes," Sarah explained. "But stay; would you stay for a bit? The fruit and cheese shouldn't go to waste." She pointed to an arrangement of plates on a table, next to a pair of wine bottles, both empty.

"What if I were to say I'd rather have the wine?" I cringed to hear myself sounding so coy.

Sarah laughed. (How readily this woman laughed!) She said quietly,

"I have a much nicer bottle in the back that I'd never share with just anyone."

"Thank you!" called out the straggler. "Your work is amazing!"

"Come back anytime," Sarah said. She crossed the loft and locked the door behind him. She closed her eyes and leaned against it. "These afternoons take a lot out of me."

"But you must enjoy sharing your work." I looked around. "Your quite impressive work." *Your breathtaking work*, I wasn't brave enough to say.

Sarah had stepped behind a curtain at the end of the wide-open studio space. She emerged carrying a bottle of wine and two colorful hand-made glasses. "I'm glad you like it. Rumor has it your praise isn't easy to earn."

She set down the glasses and started to open the bottle.

"Oh dear. I was joking about the wine," I said.

Rico shot past us again, imitating a police siren.

"No!" I exclaimed when I saw that I'd embarrassed her. "What I mean is that I'd love to linger a bit—and I'll help myself to that Brie, since my daughter's not here to take it away—but I can't drive home if I drink. I'm very careful that way." She stood still, listening to me. Was she waiting for something?

"And surely you'll want to get back to your husband soon," I said.

"There is no husband. Thank heaven. As for 'getting back,' we live right here, Rico and I." She pointed at the curtain. "That's our lair. I'd show it to you, but it's all topsy-turvy right now."

"Topsy-turvy," I echoed vaguely.

Rico dismounted his make-believe cruiser and marched up to the table. He grabbed the largest bunch of grapes he could engulf in a fist and, while stuffing his small face, declared loudly and redundantly that he was hungry.

"Oh bunny, you didn't get lunch, did you?" His mother looked at her watch. I was prepared to be dismissed when she said, "How would you feel about an unfashionably early dinner at an unfashionably kid-friendly restaurant, Percy? May I call you Percy?"

"Of course!" I said. There were times when I embraced my elder status. This was not one of those times.

The next two hours, which the three of us spent in Packard's oldest eating establishment, a diner whose charming exterior belies its leaden, rather Paleolithic offerings, felt utterly bizarre yet utterly thrilling to me. Sarah, I learned in the harsh light of Mama Jo's, was neither as young as I had guessed nor as saintly as she seemed. She was fifty-one; had been married, young and briefly; had fled to France for several years, where she'd studied glass with "the masters"; had returned to the States and "run wild." (I asked for details about the masters but not the running wild.) Four years ago, on her own, she had adopted Rico in Guatemala. "I made a lot of mistakes," she said, "and then this little boy just up and saved my life. Tied me down. Which I used to think would kill me. And was I wrong." She mussed his hair, and I could tell he had heard this speech before, since it did not disrupt his confounding enjoyment of a hamburger that looked like a disk of macadam between two slabs of toasted Styrofoam.

The two of them shared an enormous hot-fudge sundae—a dessert that's hard to ruin.

"Tell Mr. Darling what you're going to be for Halloween," she said when they had finished sparring for the last glob of fudge at the bottom of the dish.

"I am going to be the Grim Reaper," said Rico.

"Oh my," I said. "With a scythe and a great black hood?"

"Yes, a scythe. Mom knows how to make one."

"A homemade scythe," I said, honestly impressed. "Well, please do not darken *my* door, young fellow."

Rico looked at his mother. She said, "Can we promise him that, Rico? I don't think so. The Grim Reaper visits *everyone*." She looked at me and began to chuckle maniacally. Rico looked confused.

I walked them back. I insisted on seeing them to the door of the loft.

"That was fun, Percy."

"Yes, it was." I'd meant to direct this remark at Rico, but he had run off already. I said good night.

In the dark, I drove to Matlock feeling as if I'd drunk that wine after all, the entire bottle, though all I'd imbibed was a glass of water and a cup of coffee that tasted as if it had been brewed sometime during the Reagan administration.

A few days later, I found myself furtively watching for Sarah as the Lunch Bunch spilled out of the barn. When I saw her leaving with Rico,

I stepped outside, pretending to inspect the tree house. It wasn't quite finished, but Ira had hung from the lower framework a string of orange lights for Halloween. The visible parts of the tree house were being constructed with limbs pillaged—or pruned—from other trees: I recognized birch and sycamore among them. (Ira had made a habit of checking in with me after every sprint of progress on his project. He was never the least bit obsequious, and I had the feeling that if I'd told him I wished it would resemble a mosque or a burlesque hall, he'd have done his best to comply. I had also noticed, from glances out my back windows and remarks dropped into Clover's cheerful chitchat, that he and my daughter were becoming friends. Oh please not more than that, I begged the parental gods. Nothing personal against the talented pixie.)

I hailed Rico and asked him if he was in one of the groups entrusted with decorating the tree house. As luck would have it, he was; I drew him out about the furnishings he and his classmates were hammering together in the wood shop.

And then, as clumsily as one can possibly imagine, I turned to Sarah and said, "Would the two of you like to come for dinner sometime?"

Rico, whom I'd managed to interrupt, was still talking about the table they were making with Mr. Ira, how it would be painted in all the colors of the rainbow. Sarah stared at me so fixedly that I knew she must be struggling with how to decline my invitation.

"Excuse me for just a second," she said to Rico. To me, she said, "Yes. When?"

"Oh." I hadn't planned what to say if she accepted.

The day before Poppy's funeral, I kicked everyone out of the house: her parents, who'd flown in from France and were staying at the Ledgely Inn; my widowed mother, whom I banished to the Sorensons; and even Helena, who'd spent three nights on the fold-out couch in my study to be with the girls while I made arrangements. I had come downstairs that morning to find the two older women and Helena cleaning my kitchen and murmuring sadly among themselves. Poppy had been dead for four days. I heard our daughters' names on these women's lips.

When the three women looked up at me in unison, I was struck with a manic vertigo, the specific fear that someone, somehow, would take Clover and Trudy away from me, too. Before my eyes, my mother,

mother-in-law, and wife's best friend became my adversaries. Their presence felt not the least bit consoling; it was stifling, suffocating, cunning, a covert invasion. I was on the verge of hysteria. My voice shook as I said, without greeting them, "By lunchtime, I require you all to leave. I wish to be alone with my daughters. Please."

None of them had argued. After breakfast, they made a rich, nurturing lunch (I remember Helena's ice-cold watercress soup) and set the table for three. They hugged the girls, one by one, as if in a reception line, and they drove away.

We shared lunch in perfect, heartbroken silence. Trudy and I ate almost nothing; Clover ate two bowls of soup, much of the cheese, and devoured the entire loaf of bread. I had meant it when I said that I wanted to be with my daughters, unchaperoned, but after lunch they went upstairs, into Clover's room, and closed the door. It seemed clear they did not want my company, so I lay down on my bed, on Poppy's bed, feeling no purpose, no sense of time. I could hear Clover and Trudy together at their end of the second floor, speaking in low voices. The phone rang only a few times; every time, Clover ran downstairs to answer it. The first time, she came to the door of the bedroom, which I had left ajar. I'm sure she could see that I'd been crying, though she did not offer to enter the room or comfort me. I told her that unless the funeral director or the minister called, I wasn't available. Although we'd made a will, Poppy had left no directions about rituals in the event of her death. I buckled, without protest, when her parents requested a service in Matlock's Episcopal church, though we agreed on cremation. Her ashes would be buried an hour north, in Vigil Harbor, in the graveyard where her father's ancestors lay and her parents intended to wind up their days.

I must have fallen asleep before dinnertime; I slept until the following morning.

What a beautiful day it was: dry, almost cool, the birds singing their tiny lungs out in the trees around the house. I awoke without so much as a single merciful moment of amnesia. My eyes were still swollen, and I was fiercely thirsty. In the kitchen, I was stunned to find Trudy and Clover, sitting at the table eating breakfast, both dressed in black, hair studiously combed. Clover wore lipstick. Towering above their heads, in the center of the table, was one of the many flower arrangements that would not stop arriving.

Their eyes, like mine, were red, but they were composed. "Hi,

Daddy," said Clover. She sounded years younger than the teenage daughter who'd begun to speak to me that summer with thinly veiled condescension.

I uttered the only word my mouth could form. "Daughters." This word meant everything to me in that moment: sun, moon, stars, blood, water (oh curse the water!), meat, potatoes, wine, shoes, books, the floor beneath my feet, the roof above my head.

I moved the tastelessly magnificent effusion of flowers from the table to a counter. I stared bleakly out the windows toward the pond. I knew that I needed to speak, to be reassuring, loving, protective, but no words came to my aid.

Clover made me a bowl of Cheerios. She sliced strawberries on top, slicing them the way her mother had taught her, between her hands with a small sharp knife. "You have to eat something, Daddy," she said. "Or you'll faint in the church."

I did as she asked. I sat at the table, a slovenly mess, not caring if milk dribbled on my robe. The slate floor felt like ice beneath my feet. "This is going to be terrible," I said at last.

"I know," said Clover.

"Do you really want to go to Aunt Helena's after? You don't have to."

"I think I do. I think we both do." I could see, and yet another part of my heart began to crumble, that Clover was trying on the voice and manner of a little mother.

I looked at Trudy, who hadn't spoken. "How about you, sweetie?"

"Yeah," she said, her voice dull.

"You want to go?"

"Yeah. I'll go." She stared into her empty bowl. The room became silent again.

I finished my cereal. Clover cleared away the bowl. Without guidance, she had made me coffee, too—ghastly, muddy coffee, but I was profoundly grateful.

Then Trudy stood up from the table and walked across the room. Beneath a very short black skirt, she wore fishnet stockings. They, too, were black, but they startled me.

"Sweetheart," I said, "I haven't seen those stockings before."

"They're Clover's." She stood facing me, her arms stiff at her sides. She had my fine, sand-colored hair, my large forehead and ears. Anyone would look at her features and suspect, without having met me, that she was a girl who resembled her father.

"I don't know if fishnets are the wisest choice for a funeral, sweetie." Why did I say this? What did I know? Why should I care?

"Well, maybe Mom didn't make the wisest choice, either," she said.

Clover stood by the kitchen sink, staring at each of us in turn.

"Oh Trudy, honey, your mother didn't choose to die. It was a terrible, terrible accident. Is that what you think, that she killed herself?"

"No," she said. "Of course I don't think that. I think she was totally drunk after your party where everybody got into that big stupid argument. She was drunk and she went swimming. Is that smart? What do *you* think?"

Both of my daughters seemed to have changed overnight, their behavior bewildering, alarming, dismaying. I felt as if I were having one of those dreams in which your most tender friends reprimand you or long-vanished traitors show up on your doorstep to tell you how wrong they were, how they want your love after all these years. None of it feels right or good. The world is widdershins.

"Daughters," I said for the second time that morning. I held out my arms. "I love you both like nothing else under the sun. Let's say whatever we want to say to one another, whatever we need to say, if that's what it takes to hold ourselves together."

Clover came over and hugged me. Trudy went upstairs. For the next several days, I was afraid to be alone with my younger daughter. I knew she had not forgotten the night of her mother's death, her certainty that someone outside had been calling. And yet I could never find the courage, despite what I'd told the girls about speaking from our hearts, to mention that night to Trudy. That she had been lying awake, listening to a group of adults attack one another like petulant children, made me doubly ashamed. She never mentioned it, either.

After Trudy went upstairs that morning, after Clover went back to putting bowls and plates in the dishwasher, the phone rang. For the first time in days, I answered.

It was the secretary in the office of Poppy's gynecologist, calling to confirm Clover's appointment the following day.

"No," I said, "she will not be there. . . . No, there's no need to reschedule. Thank you." I hung up.

Clover turned from the sink. "What was that?"

"It's unimportant," I said. A lie, but also the truth. Poppy's death did for Clover what nothing else could have accomplished so well. It took the allure out of boys and sex—out of everything—for many months to come. Years later, she would make up for that loss, but in the short run, Clover lived as if someone had, after all, locked her up in a tower.

A few nights after my visit to Packard, Sarah and Rico came over for dinner. I promised burgers far superior to those at Mama Jo's. Sarah arrived with a pie for dessert and a DVD for Rico to watch.

We ate in the kitchen, and then I set Rico up with his movie—starring an animated sponge (good Lord)—in Poppy's dressing room. In the living room, I lit a fire. This time it was Sarah who did not drink. So when she flirted with me, I knew it had to be deliberate, and I was unnerved. She sat next to me on the couch, rather than in the wing chair by the hearth.

"I suppose this is our chance for grown-up conversation," I said.

"It's a place to start." One of Sarah's knees touched one of mine.

This agitated me so much that I got up, poked at the fire, then took the wing chair myself. We talked about the candidates, the upcoming primaries, and we talked about her stained glass, how she'd arrived at this medium through sculpture.

During a pause, she looked around the room. (I hoped the dust wouldn't show in the firelight.) Her eyes came to rest on the pastel portrait of Poppy that sits on top of a bookcase. It shows her, full figure in black leotard and red tights, arms raised to form a steeple, fingertips touching. It's not terribly good, but it was done by Helena, who took a few art classes at a nearby museum.

"Is that your wife?"

"Yes."

Before I could fret much about what I'd say next, Sarah said, "I know about how she died. How awful."

"Does Clover tell everyone?" Irrationally, I felt angry.

"Everyone seems to know anyway."

"One of the town's sordid evergreens."

"I wouldn't say that. Apparently everyone loved her. What I heard is that you're not the only one who still misses her."

What could I say to this? Was it a test to see just how much I *did* still miss her? Finally, I said, "I'm sure you don't intend to, but you make it sound as if there's a competition."

Sarah frowned.

"I'm sorry," I said.

"I'm sorry, too. For you and your daughters."

"Oh, we've done all right, despite their being raised by me. They taught me that you don't pack sandwiches with mayonnaise in a brown-bag lunch. That Charlie Rose is better than Ted Koppel, because of the guests, not the hair. And that girls are smarter than boys. About everything. I taught them that you can survive having your sheets changed once a month or less. And that being able to drive a stick shift is not just useful but cool."

Sarah did me the courtesy of laughing. I told her all about Trudy, how she'd been a moody, secretive teenager yet a brilliant, driven student. I bragged about her recent promotion. I did not tell her Clover's history.

When she and Rico left—at eight-thirty, because it was a school night—Sarah kissed me on the cheek, but she held her lips there for several seconds.

I stayed up well past midnight. I felt as if my breathing wouldn't slow down enough for me to sleep. I spent a long time looking at myself in the mirror over my bathroom sink, in the harshest light. I wasn't ugly, not yet. I had a full head of silverish hair; my complexion hadn't burst into a doily of varicose veins. Since starting my retirement fitness program, I had lost ten pounds. I fancied that strangers might now describe me as solid rather than portly. My shoulders were broad, my posture decent. Perhaps I looked young for my age? At my last checkup, Dr. Fields had joked that I looked much better in person than on paper. . . . But really.

What was it, after all these years of casual, unforced monkery, that made me want to take this woman into my arms, to see her naked—no, to be naked with her? Had I become, at last, the quintessential dirty old man? Was I deluded, pathetic, about to fall off a precipice of mortification? My earlier confidence in her attraction to me began to look as absurd as it was. I went to bed a self-appointed fool.

Yet the next day she called and asked if I would like to accompany her and Rico into Boston the following weekend, spend an afternoon at the Fine Arts Museum. We drove together in her car, listening to a tape of Peter, Paul and Mary that Rico loved. Was this nothing but children's music now, the songs that were sung in Cambridge coffee shops when I had courted Poppy, songs meant to rouse a rabble? Had Pete Seeger evolved into a banjo-plinking Captain Kangaroo?

At the museum, when we entered the galleries devoted to antiquities, Sarah let Rico run farther ahead of us than I would have allowed.

"He knows this place by heart. And he won't go far," she said. "He even knows some of the guards by name."

In ancient Egypt, where the lighting was grim and the mummies held Rico's young, ghoulish attention, Sarah took my hand. I gasped so loudly that a nearby stranger glanced at me, concerned. She squeezed my hand harder.

"Are you all right?" she whispered.

"I would describe myself," I said, after the stranger turned away, "as febrile with apprehension. No, anticipation."

She positioned herself in front of me, so that she could look me in the face. "Me too."

"Tell me what this writing says!" called Rico, sparing me from cardiac arrest. We gathered around an elaborately graffiti'd mummy while Sarah read the captions aloud.

In the car, driving back, it was all I could do not to take her hand between the seats. We talked about Elves & Fairies, soliciting Rico's opinions on the tree house, Mr. Ira, the sing-alongs. He wasn't the most talkative child (how Clover could fill the world with words at that age!), but he described the tree-house furnishings in almost scholarly detail.

When we reached Matlock, Sarah dropped me off without coming into the house. I was exhausted, yet equally disappointed to see her drive away.

I called her that night, when I felt sure Rico would be in bed.

"I'm so glad to hear your voice," she said. "I'm sorry we left you off like that. I didn't trust myself."

"I'm no scoundrel."

"I can't say the same for myself," said Sarah. She told me that she had a cousin who lived in Ledgely and sometimes helped out with Rico; he'd take the boy for an overnight visit almost any weekend.

"Week*end*?" I groaned.

"I'm afraid so. And I have a lot of work right now. Which is good." She laughed. "Anticipation. Remember?"

Somehow, I made it across the desert that stretched toward Friday. And then she was there, on my front porch, wearing a long blue dress, carrying a bottle of wine. She wasn't inside my house ten minutes before we fumbled our way upstairs, already enmeshed. I had made the bed up with excruciating care. I had swept and dusted for the first time in weeks, instigating a fit of sneezing. I had neatened the stacks of books on the window seat. Yet none of this order mattered in the least.

As we became gradually naked, under the covers, in the mercifully early dark of late October, I felt Sarah's strength, so surprising, so oddly comforting, as we solved the urgent puzzle of fitting ourselves together for the very first time. I forced myself to remain silent, not to make the pathetic excuses that older men do in movies with scenes like this one; she would understand or she wouldn't. Yet I was trembling, too. I could feel exactly how my body had aged since it had last engaged in a naked embrace. I could feel the appalling looseness of my flesh, from my throat to my thighs.

I opened my eyes at one point, unable to believe that Sarah felt such ardor. Sensing my hesitation, she opened her eyes as well. "I know what you're thinking," she whispered. "And you're dead wrong." She did not, thank heaven, tell me that I was handsome or virile or sexy. She just closed her eyes again and wrapped herself more tightly around me.

In the middle of the night, I woke abruptly at the sound of the toilet flushing. Terrified, I sat up and must have cried out. Framed in the bathroom door, in the instant before the light snapped off, I saw the silhouette of a woman.

"It's me," said the silhouette. I remembered who she was only when she sat on the edge of the bed and put a hand on my shoulder. She said in a rough, sleepy voice, "Are you hungry? We never had dinner." She offered to make us grilled cheese sandwiches or a salad or French toast: whatever I had on hand. I remembered the preparations I'd made for our dinner, the food still waiting on the kitchen counter.

"Steaks?" I said.

"Absolutely anything," said Sarah.

After dressing, making dinner, eating it together at the kitchen table, we returned to bed. Naked again, this time I became aware of her body more than mine. She was indisputably younger, but I felt, too, how much older she was than Poppy had been when we last shared this bed.

I did not know it yet, but already that night my physical memories of Poppy—her fingers, breasts, tongue, and feet; her frazzled hair against my face—had begun to fade. Perhaps, I realized later, I stopped guarding them so closely.

In the beginning, Sarah was firm about keeping Rico ignorant of our involvement. This meant that we made love at the oddest of times: mostly in the morning, on Mondays and Wednesdays, when she did not have to report at TGO. After she dropped Rico off at the barn, she would park out on the street, walk through my front door, and head upstairs. I would be waiting, having showered after an early run.

I don't know why it felt risky and illicit, but I worried that someone would notice the change in my running schedule or the frequent loitering of Sarah's car on the street. We did not speak, at first, of whether we cared if the adults around us knew we were lovers. We were doing nothing "wrong," were we?

I knew that Poppy would have liked Sarah, but did this matter? Did I feel, against all logic, an adulterer's guilt? Elsewhere in my addled psyche, I wondered just how much of a fool I'd been to spend the prime decades of my life so blandly as a monogamist and then a monk in an era of merrily fulfilled concupiscence. Poppy would have been amused to see me loosening up just as the rest of the world clamped down. "Neither a leader nor a follower be, sometimes I think that's your motto," she teased me once.

One evening in early November, as I read alone at the kitchen table, my dinner plate pushed aside, I was startled by the sound of my front door opening. Certain it must be Sarah, I closed my book and stood, a wide smile on my face.

But it was Clover who entered the room. Since the start of school, I rarely saw her after she finished her afternoon duties. Sometimes I would ask her to stay for supper, or she would invite me out, but ordinarily she went home to her apartment. Now she stood in the kitchen, looking decidedly unhappy.

So she had found out. Could she have the nerve to be distressed about my relationship with Sarah? (Was she jealous?) In haste, I began to cobble together my defense and was about to preempt her when she sat down at the table, across from me, and said, "Daddy, I need your help."

I closed my book. I waited.

"Daddy," she said, "I want them back. Filo and Lee. I need to ask if you'll help me hire a really, really good lawyer."

I saw her repressing the tears. I thought of her breakdown, the tornado of emotions it had unleashed. "Sweetheart," I said, "is this the best time to think about that? I know you feel well established here now, but it's only been a few months since you started this new enterprise. And it's not as if . . ." I fought my desire to protect her from the truth. I spoke softly. "Todd's a good father to them, and New York is the home they know best."

"Daddy," she said, "Todd's found someone new. He said she loves the children. She loves *my* children. My *children*! And she . . . *She*." Now the tears fell.

Into my mind came the duplicitous thought that Todd, after all he'd been through with Clover, would have made a wise choice in her replacement. Clover had no idea how often Todd and I had spoken in the first weeks after she'd fled. I liked Todd, and I was certain that if he said this woman cared for Filo and Lee, it was true. I was also certain that Clover hadn't a prayer of winning a renewed battle for custody. I thought of the lawyers I knew best—all retired.

That I did not answer her at once was cruel, however unintentionally. What remained of her composure collapsed. She began to sob. "Daddy, it's a *woman*."

Would his newly chosen mate have been a polar bear? A sailboat? All I could say was "Yes, well . . ."

"Oh Daddy, there's so much I didn't tell you. I'm sorry. You must think I'm such a loser." I could barely make out her words.

I got up and went to her at once. "When you need my help, daughter, that's what I'm here for."

Oh, Poppy.

5

So what do you think, everybody? Is this the coolest thing or what?" Ira stood, along with his assistant, Heidi, and ten four-year-olds, at the foot of the beech tree. They stared up into its branches, marveling at the wide structure that looked like a ship lodged snugly beneath a canopy of glistening burgundy leaves. Ira marveled, too, at how the tree appeared both gracious and omnipotent in the way it held the tree house so securely. Though he was being given the credit for this achievement, he wondered now how he'd ever believed it would actually, practically come into existence. He was a poor carpenter at best, and he'd copied his drawings from books. Robert's manual ingenuity and Celestino's brawn: those were the secret, essential keys to Ira's success, and they had been little more than serendipity. What would have happened if that grandson hadn't shown up the day Ira stood by the tree, gazing into the branches with total *What now?* bewilderment?

The children began talking all at once. Ira clapped rhythmically to ask for silence. *Clap-clap, clap-clap-clap.* Obediently, they echoed the cadence precisely. Often now, Ira was newly astonished by the authority he could exert without words. There was so much he no longer took for granted, and this was not entirely good.

"Now!" he said. "We are going to be taking our wood-shop skills and our safety rules up this ladder with us when we go up to decorate the inside of our tree house. We are going to split into two teams, the way we do for the sand table. Heidi's team will go in first, then my team."

The kids began jumping up and down, shouting that they wanted to be on Heidi's team. Again, Ira clapped. Again, obedience; silence.

Robert and his grandfather emerged from the house. Robert waved a camera. "Yo, Ira! We have to document the inauguration!"

So as Heidi helped her five team members up the ladder through the trapdoor to the first level, Robert moved around the tree with his camera.

"Where's your Man Friday on this important occasion?" said Percy.

Robert lowered the camera and gave Percy a scolding look. "Grand-dad, I did not hear you say that."

Celestino had helped them out just twice, with encouragement from the woman whose garden he tended next door, but his strength had been crucial in lifting and bracing the largest, longest timbers, those support-ing the three different levels. The levels diminished in size as they rose, each one safely walled on all sides. Celestino had also supplied a load of branches he'd been about to cart off for mulching at the dump. They gave the tree house its fabulous chameleon aspect. When the tree fell into shadow at the end of the day, the structure nearly vanished from sight.

Clover and Evelyn came running up the hill. "Wait, Ira, wait!" Clover flourished a camera of her own. She gave Ira a rough hug with her free arm. "Moment of architectural truth!"

Truth! Now there's a concept.

It seemed there was nothing Ira could do these days to banish this sour, ironic voice from his head. It did not matter that he felt welcomed here, that he liked Evelyn, Heidi, Clover, and the rest of his colleagues as well as (if not better than) the women he'd worked with back at The Very Beginning.

As Clover posed Ira's team in front of the tree and Heidi lined hers up along the rail of the tree house above their heads, Evelyn approached Ira.

"Maurice and I are having a cocktail party next Saturday, mostly for the school's new neighbors. We'd love it if you could come—and please feel welcome to bring a date. Clover tells me you have a housemate? I know just how intimidating this town can seem to newcomers."

"Oh dear. I'm afraid I already have plans," said Ira. Instantly, that inner voice piped up. *Plans? We have plans? What plans might those be? To, oh let's see, order tandoori takeout and rent a good movie to watch with our "housemate"?*

Evelyn looked honestly disappointed. "Maurice is dying to meet the mastermind behind the tree house. I think he's feeling a tiny bit up-staged. He's built an opera house, but never a tree house!"

"I would love that." This was true, though Anthony would kill him if he went to that cocktail party alone.

When Clover finished taking pictures, the children ran to Ira like well-trained puppies.

"Back to the room," he said. "Our turn comes after block time."

"Can we please roll down the hill?" asked Marguerite.

The grassy slope leading to the barn was irresistible. Ira looked at the five faces before him, all exhilarated, all (except for Rico's) white as Easter lilies, white as the adorable spotless Austrian jacket that Marguerite wore.

Roll to your aristocratic little heart's content.

"Why not?" said Ira. The children squealed.

"But one at a time, okay?" He helped them line up. "And when we get to the bottom, let's put on our walking feet."

Ira watched Marguerite's imported jacket as it became a blur descending the hillside.

Oh now please, sniped Inner Ira. *Parents are instructed to send their children to school in clothes that are ready to play, play, play!*

At last, five small faces beamed up at him. "You, too, Mr. Ira!" called Jesse.

Ira hadn't rolled down a hill in at least twenty years. What the hell. He lay on the grass, raised his arms, and propelled himself down. As the world tumbled fiercely around him, he let the vertigo take hold. "Banzaaaaiiiii!" he called out.

At the bottom, he faced the sky, laughing uncontrollably, the world still spinning, his ears buzzing. He pulled grass from his mouth. Five faces clustered above him. All were amused, laughing along with him, except for Rico. Perhaps Rico had X-ray vision and could see right through Ira's laughter to the vertigo that had nothing to do with rolling down a hill.

He sat up, but he had to wait a few moments for the dizziness to pass. Then he got up and brushed himself off. "Okay then. Who's for building a zoo?" As he followed his followers into the barn, he heard Clover's voice behind him.

"Bravo, Mr. Ira! That was awesome. I know five sets of parents who will hear about this at the dinner table tonight!"

Ira liked Clover, but it made him nervous that she had so obviously decided, from the start, to make him her friend. They were the two newcomers here, yet in a way everyone was new because the setting was new. Ira had had an equal share in deciding just how they would make the most efficient use of the space. And from a certain perspective, Clover was the least new. She had grown up in this place—this extraordinary place. Ira's heart had quickened at his first sight of that pond from the top of the hill; but to end up back here in your forties?

During Ira's break period, when his kids were in movement class or having a science stroll outdoors with Miss Ruth, Clover sometimes invited him to have coffee at the edge of the pond. More than once, she'd brought along homemade scones or muffins; Ira had the feeling that she'd made them with *him* in mind. Early on, she'd shown him pictures of her children, who lived mostly with their dad in New York. This led to the "what we love and miss most about the city" conversation. Clover was thrilled when she found out that Ira had grown up in Forest Hills. But a week or so later, as Ira consumed a ginger-cranberry scone, savoring every bite yet trying to banish from his mind the disturbing suspicion that it was a bribe, Clover had brought up her ex-husband again and said, out of the blue, "He's in the process of coming out of the closet. If you want to know the truth, that's why we split up."

Actually, Ira did not want to know this truth—not this Ira, the newly paranoid Ira—yet she'd looked right at him as if she expected some specific reaction. Did it mean that she simply *assumed* he was gay; that, contrary to his best efforts, he could set even a middle-aged, middle-class woman's gaydiation detector bleeping off the end of the dial?

"Well that is a tough place to be," he'd said to Clover, "especially with kids. And wow, I guess it's good that you're clearly not bothered by it." What did he mean by that? Of course she was bothered by it!

"I'm trying to be . . . civilized about it, if that's what you mean. Though maybe at this point it's foolish for me not to be there. I kind of ran away. No. I ran away. 'Prune the hedges,' as my therapist likes to say. It looks terrible, I know, but I wasn't emotionally prepared to . . . be a full-time mother while having my heart whacked slowly into little bits."

Maybe the best approach was to pretend he was in a parent-teacher conference. He asked how she thought the kids were doing without her constant presence. She laughed, self-deprecating, and said that she thought they were doing remarkably well. He asked if she wanted to return to the city, children aside.

Her smile vanished. "Ira, there is no 'children aside.' That's my lesson. But I know what you mean. And I can tell you this much: there's no way I could afford a place of my own in the city."

"Your ex wouldn't help? Wouldn't he rather have you there for convenience of . . . visitation?" God how he hated that word.

Clover was silent for a time, looking at the water. "Todd was pretty mad when I left. He told me I really screwed up. So I can't imagine how I could ask for something like that."

"If he's a good father, he'll be more circumspect by now," said Ira.

"Circumspect," she said, sounding amused. "How can parents ever be *circumspect*? How often have you seen that, Ira?"

Exactly then, to Ira's relief, Evelyn had called his name from the barn. He had not been alone with Clover since; come to think of it, he had not seen as much of her as he usually did. A few days before, when he'd greeted her outside her office, she looked as if she'd been crying. Should he ask her what was going on? Only a year ago, of course he'd have held out a hand. No question. But that was then. He no longer presumed that because you were likable and smart, you were also to be trusted.

"How are the little Trumps and Trumpettes of tomorrow?" asked Anthony. He kissed Ira on the mouth. When he stood back, he feigned a look of horror. "Good grief, could this be *dirt* in your ear? Don't tell me there's actual, real-live dirt in Matlock."

"Oh stop," said Ira, though he leaned in to second the kiss. "Your jokes are growing tiresome, you know that?"

Anthony was browsing through the cupboards and fridge. He still wore his tie but had abandoned his jacket in the living room. "How's perciatelli with feta, mint, and olives? I bought rosemary bread at Ooh La La."

"Skip the feta; I could eat the goat." Ira held up his paint-stained hands. "We've entered the decorating phase. It's looking practically palatial."

"No more slumming it for you," said Anthony. "Like, do these kids know what a tire swing is?"

"You have got to stop. Really." He had been looking forward all day to telling Anthony about taking the children up into the tree house for the very first time. Anthony had been impressed when Ira told him about Robert Barnes, how he'd helped build an actual hotel in a tree, and about Arturo, who had grown up in three different countries and spoke all three languages well. But when Ira had mentioned Celestino, how he'd briefly joined their team and had made such a difference, Anthony had interrupted with "Noblesse oblige, Matlock style. Migrant workers as flesh-and-blood people!"

"Anthony."

Since starting at Elves & Fairies, Ira felt he had to censor himself whenever he talked to Anthony about his work. Anthony was a high-end divorce attorney in Boston, and it was certainly easy to make fun of the capitalist pigs with whom he schmoozed on a daily basis, but he also did pro bono work in Lothian's family court, representing mothers who'd once been prostitutes and crackheads, children who'd been beaten and maliciously starved. Anthony despised the citizens of the much wealthier nearby towns who, as he put it, wouldn't know juvy from the juice-box aisle at Whole Foods.

"Did you catch this?" Anthony pushed a copy of the *Globe* across the counter. It was folded open to the West Suburban section. The largest headline read, *ECO-VANDALS STRIKE AGAIN: Four Towns Coordinating Search*.

The dateline was Matlock. Ira sighed and picked up the paper.

It looked at first like a series of elaborate practical jokes, but apparently it's war. "Today's incident is the third to hit Matlock, and it is downright weird," commented Capt. "Cap" McCord, the bucolic town's police chief, as he described the latest act of sabotage. Early this morning, a 46-year-old female citizen of Matlock who wishes to remain anonymous walked out of her house to discover that seven bicycles had been locked tightly together around the body of her car. According to Capt. McCord, "The vehicle's windshield had a big sign glued onto it. The sign said, PEDALS, NOT PETROL. The bikes were junk—rusty, some without tires. We are investigating whether they were taken from the local transfer station. That might give us a lead."

Almost simultaneously, in neighboring towns Ledgely and Weston, citizens awoke to similar displays of blatantly "green" bravura. In Ledgely, a homeowner who had not locked his residence returned from work to find every lightbulb within the premises replaced with a compact fluorescent. LET THERE BE FUTURE, read the sign affixed to his front door. . . .

"Can you believe it?" said Anthony. "I thought my lunch would come out my nose."

"It's not so uproarious if you're in Matlock," said Ira. "Some of the parents want to hire independent detectives. People are pretty pissed off."

"Did you get to the part about the letter? They may be lunatics, but these guys have got balls."

Ira skimmed a few paragraphs till he read, *The police departments of all four towns in which these pranks have been perpetrated received the same letter. Reporters have not been shown the full text, but Capt. McCord revealed a key message: "The DOGS have been unleashed." The acronym of this previously unknown organization stands for Denounce Our Greedy Society. Some are claiming it's terrorism; others are saying, "It's about time!"*

Unable to help himself, Ira burst out laughing. "The DOGS? Oh my God."

"Isn't this just too fabulously in their face? And I'll bet the bozo cops who get paid top salaries to work in these towns are bumbling around like a bunch of Inspector Clouseaus. Can you honestly feel sorry for any of those people?"

Ira said, "I do admit it's a challenge," but he knew how prim he sounded.

Before his new job in Matlock, Ira's contempt would have been no less vehement than Anthony's, but now he clammed up at dinner parties where their friends threw stones at the wealthy—the landed liberals, Anthony called them. After all, *they* were wealthy liberals, too. Ira and Anthony might live in a frontier neighborhood in Lothian, where the closest thing to a grocery store was a deli with stale sandwiches, canned beans, and a pit bull in the back room, but they had two cars and could shop with abandon at the Fresh Pond Whole Foods and the uppity food boutiques of Faneuil Hall. Unlike many of the rich suburbanites Anthony scoffed at, *they* would never face the cost of putting kids through college. As Ira had recently learned, making smug, class-based assumptions was more than foolish; it was hypocritical.

Back at The Very Beginning, a signature end-of-year tradition had been the teachers' assembly of a keepsake book for each of their little students. In mid-May, teachers from all four classrooms spent a week of late nights together, sorting through snapshots, photocopying Raffi song lyrics, three-hole-punching sheafs of construction paper and binding them together with yarn, to produce *Our Amelia* and *Our Zach* and *Our Keesha*—each one a story, in pictures, poems, ballads, and handprints, of that child's year in the Red, Blue, Yellow, or Green Room. Ira had been through three years of this tradition; in retrospect, he was amazed by how respectfully, even lovingly, the teachers went about this laborious task. Even if Amelia or Keesha or Zach had been a whiner, an instigator, or a know-it-all, Ira and his colleagues regarded each child as just that: a child, still very much in the making, faults eminently forgivable, character embryonic at best.

That's why Ira had embraced early education in the first place, despite the lousy pay. Small children made mistakes. They bragged and bullied. They were sloppy. They cried and yelled at the least provocation. They were exhausting and often stunningly rude (on purpose or not). But there was still a decent chance that you could help guide them toward a future free of the xenophobia, self-righteousness, and cowardly inhibitions that afflicted many of their parents.

Yet it was this sweet tradition—it was, to be precise, the celebration of *Our Ramsey*—that ultimately drove Ira from a job he loved and at which he was damn good. From this unjustified disgrace, Ira had learned a grave and bitter lesson about what you should and should not share about your personal life.

Lothian was a town with a surprisingly broad social spectrum—something else that Ira had treasured about The Very Beginning. After he'd landed the job, he and Anthony had decided that they should leave the city and fully embrace a community that could use their skills. Over three years, Ira's classroom included the four-year-old children of cops and cashiers, university professors and aspiring sculptors, accountants and bankers, waitresses and sanitation workers. There were children to match every color in the Crayola Multicultural Markers box, children whose parents owned two houses trading Legos with children who shared a bedroom with two siblings and whose parents' preferred language was definitely not English. Since the abolition of rent control in

Boston, Lothian was a town where Ph.D.'s lived beside auto mechanics. Ira used to call it a "true cultural crossroads." Now he tried not to talk about it at all.

Ira had believed that most of the parents who sent their preschoolers to The Very Beginning shared his pride in its diversity (a word that now left a bitter taste in his mouth). When Betty, the director, had hired him fresh out of his master's program, Ira had been secretly certain that being not just a man but a gay man gave him a double edge over all the eager single white women, even those who'd put in a few years of teaching already.

Anthony had joined him for the staff party at the start of his first year, had even helped him give the Green Room a fresh coat of paint in a new, more stylish shade, a bright urbane kiwi to replace the tired old kelly green of poster paint and Playskool toys. The two of them socialized with some of Ira's fellow teachers (all straight) and even, by the third year, with a few couples whose children he'd taught in the Green Room. It was typical for the little girls to have their first crush on Ira, and the mothers with whom he was most familiar (those who came in to read stories or serve snacks) would make jokes to Ira like "Now please let her down easy!" and "Oh if poor Alexa only *knew*." One mom, standing next to Ira on the playground at recess, had actually told him, "I know this sounds perverse, but sometimes I wish Chloe could grow up and marry a gay man. You understand women so much better than the guys we get to choose from!" Ira had forced a congenial laugh.

It was a foregone conclusion that the adults who were the most comfortable with knowing he was gay were the educated, wealthier ones. Around the others, especially those from more conservative cultures, he tried not to be self-conscious. He had reasoned that people like the Sanchezes, the Ngs, and the Wozniaks were too busy making a living to think about such things anyway, let alone stand around flirting with their children's nice, cute gay teacher from New York. Still, when Ira talked with hard-hat dads like Victor Wozniak, he found that, instinctively, he turned his natural effusiveness down a notch.

So when it happened—when the bigoted shit hit the fan—he was stunned to see the blow come from one of the families he had seen as social allies. In the fall of that year, Ramsey's parents had hosted a cocktail party for new parents at their renovated double row house. Ramsey's father, a man who made money from money, could have bought a house in Charlestown if he'd chosen to stay in the city, but it wouldn't have been so large. Willard Caldwell liked to brag that a team of wild horses couldn't drag him to the "snootier" suburbs; he wanted his five children to grow up with people "of all kinds."

Anthony had happily attended the party with Ira. Toward the end, they found themselves chatting about marriage equality with a few of the mothers. They'd all had a bit too much Merlot when one mom said to them, so loudly that it turned heads, "Isn't it so great that we live in this fabulous state, especially now that Mitt's on his way back to Utah? Can you believe the rest of this country and its puritanical stupidity? Only *here* could you guys actually tie the knot. And why *shouldn't* you?"

After that, Ira saw Ramsey's dad only two or three times in school. His wife made all the drop-offs and pickups, always rushing to buckle Ramsey into his car seat at the end of the day so she could make it to Cambridge in time to pick up the older kids at their private school. At midyear, Betty mentioned to Ira that Ramsey's family had requested a switch to the Blue Room, supposedly because he wanted to be with a playmate there. But the Blue Room had been full, so Ramsey had stayed with Ira.

Two other little boys were pulled from the Green Room that winter— one because the family was moving, the second because he got into a magnet program for special-needs children.

At the school auction that spring, Ira noticed a clutch of dads in one corner, looking at him repeatedly as they drank and gossiped. Anthony said, "Oh sweetheart, they're just speculating about our sex life. Straights have such pathetic fantasies sometimes. They can't help themselves, poor things." Ira had smiled, knowing that Anthony was one of the best-looking men in the room.

And then came the end of the year: the good-bye parties with the tearful moms, the cubbies emptied, the children's keepsake books passed out, the homely homemade teachers' gifts accepted in return. Over the next week, Ira and his colleagues scrubbed their classrooms, waxed floors, tallied craft supplies and packed them away for the summer in Rubbermaid boxes.

On the final day, after most of the teachers had left, Betty had called him into her office and shut the door. On her desk sat *Our Ramsey,* its cover a splashy apple red that Ira had picked to match the boy's bold, physical nature.

"Ira," Betty said, "we have a very difficult situation on our hands."

"We do? Oh dear." He assumed that the *we* referred to an alliance including him.

Betty turned Ramsey's book to face Ira. She opened it to a photo of Ramsey blowing out the candle on his birthday cupcake. The picture had been taken by Ira's assistant, Heather. Ira knelt beside Ramsey's tiny chair, laughing gaily (yes, gaily), one arm around the boy's shoulders. Betty turned to a later spread. On the left was glued a sheet of simple music entitled "The Mammal Song." *Ramsey's favorite mammal is the camel,* Ira had written below. On the right was a snapshot of Tunes Time. There was Ira, leading them all, and in his lap sat Ramsey. Sitting in the teacher's lap was an honor that all the children vied for; Ira was careful not to play favorites.

Ira looked at Betty, smiling, clueless.

"Ira." She sounded mournful. "Willard Caldwell believes that you have established an inappropriate closeness with his son."

Ira had burst out laughing, remaining, for one more second, baffled.

"You understand what's going on here."

By then he did. "Absolutely nothing. That's what."

Betty reminded him that Willard had recently joined the school's board of directors. "I'm afraid he's been having conversations with other parents, and he's made suggestions about the children who left the school—your room—in the middle of the year. I wish I had been aware of all this talk sooner, because I would have put a stop to it, Ira."

Oh would you? Ira could remember thinking in that moment, feeling the bile rise in his throat. Betty was a woman who'd come of age in the scrappy sixties yet seemed averse to confrontation of any kind. "This is outrageous," said Ira, "and it's absurd, and it's . . . insulting."

"I agree with you," Betty said, yet still she spoke in that funereal tone. "But the cat is out of the bag, and I—"

"And you're too much of a wimp to stare it in the face."

Betty was silent. She did not look angry, only embarrassed.

"I am one of the favorite teachers here, and you know it," Ira had said. "How could you even listen to that man for one second?"

She shook her head, still unable to speak.

"Oh," said Ira. "Because he has money. And two more children—those perfect little Aryan *twins*—yet to add their aid-free tuitions to the coffers. Let's see. Has he agreed to finance a new set of play equipment? A minivan for field trips to the science museum?"

"This is so painful, Ira. Because as you know, people like the Caldwells are the ones who make it possible for the Sanchezes and the Wozniaks—"

"People *like the Caldwells*," Ira said slowly, his voice quivering, "ought to be publicly shamed. As should the people who condone their behavior."

Ira watched Betty fight back tears.

"I deserve that," she said quietly. "But I am going to lay out the options here. One, we do the so-called right thing and we stand up to Willard Caldwell. Either he takes his child out of The Very Beginning—along with his money and probably a few of the other families in his tax bracket—or he decides to take you, and us, to court. He's already got Ramsey seeing a therapist—"

"A therapist?" Ira bolted up from his chair, his rage kinetic, but found himself penned in by the tiny office and its shelves overflowing with the director's "special situation" books on how to talk to a child when a parent is ill, when a pet dies, when Grammy loses her mind, when sex rears its head a little sooner than convenient. Nothing about when a rich parent blackmails you into firing your goddamn best teacher.

"Well, sorry, Betty, but I'll see that bastard in court." Anthony would get him the best possible defense attorney. Willard Caldwell wouldn't know what had hit him. This story would make the front page of the *New York Times*.

Betty had stood as well. She walked up to Ira and took him by the shoulders. She forced him to accept her embrace, close and strong. After a moment during which neither one moved a muscle, she stepped away and took her chair. "Sit down," she said calmly. She waited to see if Ira would follow her command, which he did, and if he would unleash further venom, which he didn't. He was breathing fast, but he decided to listen, not to flee.

"One of the reasons you're a favorite teacher here is that you are dedicated to this school. You are not a transient. You are not some starry-eyed girl waiting to find a man and go have children she can call her own. You are rare." She stared at him for a long moment and then said simply, lovingly, "Ira."

He began to breathe more easily.

"Ira, if you say so, we—I and two of the board members who know paranoia and bigotry when they see it—we will go to the mat for you. I'm afraid there would be an investigation of some kind . . . of you, no matter what I say. If you want to go through that, we'll do it together. But I want you to stop and think about The Very Beginning. What would happen to the school. The media alone."

"Right," said Ira. "Not me. I'm not supposed to think about what would happen to me."

"Ira, I've spent this entire week—day *and* night—thinking about almost nothing *but* you." She smiled, briefly. "I've made a lot of telephone calls. Some of which I am not proud to have made. But here's something good. I hope you see it that way, because I do. A professional friend of mine runs the nursery school of everybody's dreams," she said. "And she has an opening. Which, by the way, pays more than what you make here. And I've already told her about you."

"The whole story."

Betty had laughed, sardonically, heartily. "Oh no, Ira. No. I have met enough families in my career, heard enough unsavory stories, to know that you never tell more than necessary. If you want to stay honest. And out of trouble."

The two of them had walked, in silence, down the hall to the Green Room. Ira had looked around the classroom—musty, too brightly lit, its carpet inescapably dingy; the cinder-block walls, despite their vibrant color, a little depressing—and the emotions that filled him felt liquid. First came grief, then fear, and last of all fury. He faced Betty.

"Can I ask you something?"

"Please." She gave him her first genuine smile.

"Did you know I was queer when you hired me?"

Her face fell. "Ira, do you think that would have mattered? Of course not."

"It will certainly matter from now on, won't it, Betty?"

"Ira, let's not have this conversation."

"Right. Let's not," he said. "Please leave me alone here, would you?"

Ira had walked out of The Very Beginning for the very last time that afternoon. And for the first time in his life with Anthony, he had kept to himself the events of the day. He had pleaded end-of-year exhaustion and gone straight to bed. He had slept late the next morning.

When he got up, he went out and walked, walked, walked. He walked himself into a rage, into a determination that, fuck The Very Beginning, he would go to court. If Anthony had not worked late that night, or if he had called Ira before Betty did, before she gave him the number of her counterpart at Elves & Fairies, who knows what might have happened?

He made the phone call. A phone call wouldn't hurt. Evelyn answered the phone and, when he mentioned Betty, became effusive. Oh, she told him, Betty was her idol. What a crusader that woman had been when she started The Very Beginning in the late 1970s. "You're too young to know this," said Evelyn, "but back then Lothian was a town where passing motorists closed their windows and locked their doors. People like Betty weren't scared by that."

The children in Ira's room, the Birches, were smart, well mannered, and eager to please their teacher. Whatever bitterness he harbored, it was hard not to feel fortunate to be in this place. Every afternoon, once the Lunch Bunch departed, Ira would walk to the back of the long hall and just stand at the great window overlooking the pond, taking in the miracle of so much wild, verdant nature so close to the city. The surface of the pond was silver in places, scattered with scarlet leaves in others. Nearly all the trees were naked now, so the sun seemed actually brighter, nearer, as winter approached. On afternoons like this one, its radiance on the unshaded roof of the barn made some of the rooms uncomfortably warm.

He enjoyed the view for a few minutes as he sipped his tea. This had become a ritual now. As he gazed out, a canoe appeared, gliding from the hidden corner of the pond. Robert and his friend Arturo paddled toward shore.

They came out to Matlock once or twice a week, even now that their work on the tree house was finished. Ira wondered how they found the time. He remembered how completely enmeshed he'd been back in college and grad school. He could hardly believe he'd actually written all those papers, aced all those tests. Now, his evenings were spent watching TV, talking current affairs with Anthony, or going to parties. That night they were going to yet another black-tie benefit, invited as usual by one of Anthony's brahmin-wannabe clients. What was tonight's cause? Inner-city poetry programs? Battered spouses? Autistic children? Ira had once loved these parties, but now that he'd drunk champagne in every hotel ballroom within twenty miles of the Pru, they had begun to seem as phony as their charities were deserving.

He returned to his classroom to tidy up. Heidi had left early, for a dentist appointment. Because their room faced west, it was stifling by late afternoon. Ira cranked open a window.

As he removed paintings from the clothesline where the children had hung them to dry, he heard the young men outside, pulling the canoe to shore.

"Turo, you're insane," said Robert.

Ira heard the canoe being dragged through the reeds, the oars rattling against the aluminum shell.

Turo said, "You have to decide what matters."

Robert laughed. "That's a pretty complex question, man. Like, isn't that part of why we're in school to begin with?"

Turo laughed. "To fiddle while Rome burns."

"I really can't let you use my car anymore. This whole thing is— I don't know . . ."

"Creeping you out? You want me to move? Would you feel safer?"

"Jesus, no, dude. No way."

"Think about what's urgent. You have my total, rock-bottom respect, whatever you decide."

"I'm just . . . oh Jesus, look at the time. Clara's got tickets to that symposium on torture."

"Did you tell Clara?"

"WTF, Turo, you think I'm off the deep end?"

"I'd understand it. If you did. But you have to let me know. I have to look after the interests of the group as a whole, not just mine."

Robert laughed harshly. "Are we friends or what? You don't judge my life, I don't judge yours."

"Word," said Turo. "Thanks, man."

By this time, Ira was standing with his ear against the screen.

"Ira?"

He jumped and turned toward the door. "Oh, Evelyn!" He veered away from the window. "Eavesdropping," he said. "I fully admit it. Idle ears and all that."

"On whom?" Evelyn seemed, thank heaven, amused.

"Robert Barnes. But anthropologically, if you know what I mean. Aren't college students fascinating, their culture and language? Can you believe we were ever that young?"

"Well, you were that young far more recently than I," said Evelyn.

Ira busied himself stacking the children's paintings. "Will you look at this one?" He held up Marguerite's painting of seals basking on rocks. Though her rendering was crude—a row of blue-gray lumps, etched with linear smiles and crooked whiskers—it did capture a certain modest joy one associated with these animals, at least in the wild. Which was where Marguerite was used to seeing them, off the porch of her family's home on some northern isle whose name Ira had never even heard. The kind of obscure that denoted elite.

Evelyn stood beside him, expressing her admiration. She studied the pictures still hanging on the line.

"Everyone painted the animal they'd most like to be," said Ira.

"These are wonderful," said Evelyn. "But you could have a Freudian field day, couldn't you? Which of the Birches would like to be a—what does this say?"

"Anaconda," said Ira. "That's Rico."

Evelyn smiled mischievously. "A boy with a single mother wants to be the largest snake on earth."

"Not to nitpick, but I think the largest snake is a python of some kind." He added quickly, "Look at this one, look at Neve's incredible peacock—can you believe this tail?" Back at The Very Beginning, Betty would never have made a salty remark about a child's artwork. Ira liked Evelyn, but sometimes he felt uncomfortable with her wit, as if it might be a test of his dedication. Which of course it wasn't.

"Maybe this would be a good start for your class auction project," said Evelyn. "Maybe a folding screen laminated with paintings like this. It's not too soon to start getting organized." Ira was relieved that the subject had turned a corner. Until she added, "Can you imagine what some of these parents would pay to own an object like that for their child's room?"

About what they'd pay for a fourth car, no sweat.

They spoke about Ira's kids for a few more minutes, and then Evelyn left, telling him not to stay too late. As always when she left after one of these drop-ins, Ira had to sit down and wait for his equilibrium to return. He couldn't shake the memory of his last day at The Very Beginning, when Betty had appeared in the door of the Green Room and asked him to come to her office.

I should be in therapy, thought Ira. This is pathetic.

Inner Ira chipped in, *Oh listen, honey, buck up.* Everybody *ought to be in therapy. But everybody isn't.*

In five years together, they'd never had such a fight. The worst part was that Ira had seen it coming for three days, ever since his first conversation with Evelyn Fougère. Waiting for Anthony to come home, he'd sat in the living room, a bottle of wine on the coffee table, watching the clock on the kitchen wall, just waiting. He hadn't been able to bear the thought of music, certainly not TV or uppity NPR, so he drank. That he wasn't much of a drinker only made it worse.

At 7:41, Anthony had walked in the door. Right away, he'd seen Ira's face and the bottle of wine (containing very little) on the table before him.

"Ira? Sweetie? What is it?"

"Well." Ira prepared himself for the line he'd decided on hours before, after getting Evelyn's call with the offer (providing his background check was clean; thank God that schmuck Willard Caldwell wasn't in the FBI). "So the good news is, it looks like I'm getting a new job with a bigger paycheck."

Anthony sat down on the chair across the table from Ira. He looked predictably stunned. He said, "So . . . I think I need to hear the bad news first. Hazard of my profession." He reached for Ira's glass, filled it with the last wine in the bottle, and took a sip. He waited.

Ira tried not to cry, but he failed. "I got the ax." This was not the second line he'd rehearsed.

Barely five minutes later, having skimmed as quickly as possible through the essential part of the story, Ira was telling Anthony about Elves & Fairies. He spoke in a manic rush. He had made himself stop crying. He described Evelyn as if she were his new best friend. "Her husband is *Maurice* Fougère, that amazing architect who designed the children's museum we went to with your niece. Do you remember those windows in the ceiling?"

"I don't care if her husband is Mark Fucking Wahlberg." Anthony wore a look of contempt at the brink of violence. He had finished the wine. He stared for a moment at the empty glass. When he got up and went to the kitchen, Ira assumed he would fetch another bottle of wine. Or water. That would be wise; his head already ached. Ira heard water running, but he also heard what he knew was the sound of Anthony's briefcase, the clips snapping open.

When Anthony returned, he placed a glass of water before Ira, but he was also carrying a tape recorder, a legal pad, and a fountain pen. "I'm going to forget that you waited three days to let me know you were fired. Just tell me every detail of your conversation with Betty."

"Forget it, Anthony. It's too late."

Anthony leaned toward Ira. "We are going to flay them, Ira. This is never going to happen again. Willard Caldwell is going to wish he'd been given the option of very slow castration."

"Do you really want to see the school go down? That's what will happen, you know."

"The answer to that is yes, Ira, if those are the cards they choose to play."

"It's not a game."

"Ira, you've just let yourself be bought out, for fuck's sake! I have to ask myself why you'd cave in so fast. Are you really that spineless?"

"I am not spineless. And, unlike you, I am not heartless. Can you see that I'm doing everything I can not to crack into a trillion pieces?"

"Yes. I can." But Anthony's voice was a hiss. He threw the pad of paper down on the table. The empty bottle toppled, barely missing Ira's glass of water as it rolled off. The rug muffled its fall.

"I have to go out," said Anthony. "I will be back later."

Ira lay down on the couch and stared at the boring, pitiless ceiling, tears sliding down the sides of his face. On top of his professional misery, he was confronted yet again with the reasons that he and

Anthony probably wouldn't marry—wouldn't join the several couples they knew who'd thrown jubilant, socially rebellious yet often profoundly romantic nuptials over the past few years. At these celebrations, he and Anthony sat side by side, hands in their laps, never looking at each other as their friends made vows not just to be true and loving to each other for the rest of their lives but to show the Willard Caldwells of the world that they were wrong, wrong, wrong. What a coward Ira was.

The phone rang. Ira's former self announced his unavailability. He was answered by Maryjane, whose fiefdom was the Yellow Room.

"Ira? Ira, are you there?" She was waiting for him to pick up. "Ira, are you okay? I hope you're okay. Please call me the minute you get this message, I don't care how late it is. . . . Please."

So they knew. Well, that was fast, thought Ira. And then, like a pool of ink, a cold revelation spread through his sodden, defeated being.

Betty had spoken with them, with the rest of the staff—of course she had, she must have *quizzed* them about Ira—before she had called him into her office. They had known all week long, or longer; there had been just enough doubt in Betty's mind that she had asked his colleagues if the evil allegations could possibly be true. They had *known*, the colleagues he thought of as friends, yet they hadn't said a thing to warn him.

6

If he were to look back on this night sometime in the future—Jesus, Robert's heart was beating so fast that he was having a hard time believing there *could* be a future—would he blame it all on the stupid ring? Or no, the stupid argument he'd had with Clara about the ring. The ring was blameless; maybe the ring had been a necessary catalyst in the destiny of their relationship.

The three of them walked single file through the woods, wearing black from head to foot. It was so cold that the leaves beneath their boots were brittle with ice, but Robert's nerves worked overtime, producing so much heat that he sweltered inside his down vest. He wished he could stop to take it off. The bucket at his side, which he'd been carrying for fifteen minutes, felt like it was filled with bricks. Turo had refused to tell him what it contained.

At the head of the line, Turo stopped abruptly; Robert bumped into Tamara. When he started to laugh, she turned and put a hand over his mouth.

Beyond Turo's silhouette, Robert could make out three lit windows in the imperious house behind the even more imperious lawn. (Was that shrub a topiary horse?) Turo had assured them these people were away; his local contact had studied the house for days and determined that the lights were on a timer. Motion detectors triggering two outdoor spots hovered beneath the eaves of the garage and the portico, but they would venture nowhere near those areas. They would not be entering the house. Pretty minor consolation, thought Robert.

The night was moonless—a factor taken into consideration as well—so the three of them had to press close together to see the hand signals Turo had taught them. *Ten minutes, the bucket. Two minutes later, the banner and stakes.*

Like all the most desirable houses in Ledgely (in Matlock, too), this one was ostentatiously private: screened from the road by a towering hedgerow and from the adjacent properties by expanses of landscaped lawn and clusters of mature maple trees.

Robert looked again at the luminous face of his watch. Was it ten minutes yet? How could he not know? *Oh God oh God what the HELL am I doing?* he thought as Tamara silently urged him away from the trees.

The pool looked black, fathomless; a slick, dark cover stretched across its surface, effusing faint clouds of steam. The water was heated for swimming through the fall. According to Turo, it was cheaper to leave the heater on during a few days' absence than to turn it off and risk a freeze.

Turo stood by the side of the pool, beckoning. Robert set down the bucket and, as Turo had described in the car, helped him remove the cover from the pool, folding it back in measured pleats, then lifting it up and away to place it, gently, on the grass. As if what they were about to do was an act of reverence. Now thicker, more pungently chlorinated plumes of heat rose toward the sky.

Turo pried the lid off the bucket. He carried it to the diving board. Standing almost at the lip of the board, in a slingshot motion that made Robert cringe with fear, he hurled the contents of the bucket into the center of the pool.

Robert heard a series of muffled splashes and watched several dozen irregular forms bob sluggishly along the surface, a few sinking toward the bottom. He wanted to see what they were, but Turo poked him and gestured toward Tamara, who had joined them. She held out the furled banner.

Yet again as he'd been instructed, Robert took the free end and pulled the banner away from Tamara's arms. It had been rolled around a dowel, to unfurl quickly and smoothly. The white cotton canvas glowed alarmingly. Glancing toward the neighboring house, Robert noticed that its flanking trees were almost bare. From the distant (or maybe not so distant) porch, a harsh spotlight lit up their spidery branches. Had it been on all this time, or had someone, just now, seen or heard something?

Oh God oh God even if we aren't caught, I am NEVER doing this or anything like it ever ever EVER again. I am MOVING to the library tomorrow.

Turo seemed alert yet calm. He moved methodically, and when he faced the distant light, Robert could see his steady smile.

Once in position, the banner obscured the entire length and nearly the entire width of the swimming pool; at one end it had been split to wrap around the base of the diving board. (*No detail unexamined,* Turo bragged about the work of his "organization.") Tamara and Robert held it taut, end to end, while Turo pinned it securely to the lawn with tent stakes. It was huge—though the surrounding prairies of darkened grass and night sky made it look puny all of a sudden. It read, in painted crimson letters four feet tall, H 2 OVERKILL.

Robert retrieved the bucket. It smelled indescribably foul. As Tamara and Turo walked swiftly—not too swiftly—back toward the woods, Robert paused to lean over the edge of the pool, where one of the cryptic dark forms still floated.

It was, unless his eyes were playing grotesque hallucinatory tricks on his psyche (and why not?), the carcass of a squirrel. A bucketful of roadkill? His stomach clenched. He felt Turo's hand on his arm, pulling him away.

They returned, walking as fast as they could without running, along the trail that linked the parking lot of the bird sanctuary to the imperious lawn of the imperious house. They did not speak until they were on Route 2, one anonymous car among many, headed back to Cambridge.

Turo whooped like a Hollywood cowboy. "You are now a made man, amigo!" He slapped Robert's shoulder.

"I am about to frigging drive off the road," said Robert. "Do not touch me."

"I'll drive," offered Turo.

"No you won't."

In the backseat, Tamara laughed coolly. "Relax. We got away with it, Bob."

"Unless they have video surveillance. That kind of money, they would."

"Even if they do," she said defiantly. "Even then, they'd never know who we were."

"But they don't," said Turo. "We have good sources."

Robert decided not to speak again, not to argue. He let Turo and Tamara gloat over the apparent success of their sabotage. Robert had not laid eyes on Tamara since the evening of her freegan spiel; was she the one who'd drawn Turo into this business? The DOGS. Jesus.

Gone to the dogs, thought Robert.

They would get back to Cambridge, Robert would make sure they shed Tamara, and he would give Turo a piece of his whacked-out mind. For a moment, Robert felt embarrassed for his friend; how could he hope to accomplish anything constructive this way? And who were these sketchy "sources"?

"Tell me you don't love the rush of sticking it to the warlords," Turo said as they began the steep descent toward the city, Boston a sprawl of indifferent roads and towers, grubby and dim but for the space-age sweep of the Zakim Bridge, its cables gilded like the strings of a massive harp.

"What makes you so sure they're 'warlords'? What does that mean?"

"Oh don't get all mince-minded, dude. That kind of wealth? No good can come of it."

"Yeah?" said Robert. "Like, how about Bono's money, or the Gates Foundation? Some rock star from the seventies saved the woods around Walden Pond, and he's probably got a mansion three times that size. You're assuming a lot, Turo."

Turo and Tamara laughed in unison. He leaned toward the backseat. "Oh man, do we have some deprogramming on our hands or what."

Robert went silent again. They were passing the cineplex, the discount liquor store, the pasta franchise, everything closed up tight yet beckoning with brilliant signage, the pointless wattage like squandered hope.

"My friend," said Turo, "my good, smart friend, don't be so fearful. You've grown up so protected. You've grown up so—"

"Soft?" barked Robert. "Ignorant? Go ahead, dogmatize me, Turo." *Dog*ma. The pun he hadn't intended to make was almost funny. But not.

Turo let Robert's sarcasm ring through the car. "No," he said quietly. "I was going to say, so insulated from corruption. Which is no insult. You know what I think about your family, man. You know how envious I am. But your family, it's not the world most people live in. Your family is Disney compared to most people out there."

"While you," said Robert, "you grew up in a peasant village in the mountains, exploited by fatcat landowners, slaving away at menial harvesting tasks. . . . Oh but wait!" Robert slapped the steering wheel. "Gosh how could I *forget,* your father *was* the fatcat landowner!"

"Go ahead and mock me," said Turo. "At least I'm facing down the guilt of my inheritance. Just think what the world would be like if we all gave it a try."

"Wow, chill, you guys," said Tamara. "It's not like we signed the Kyoto Protocol here."

"This is the adrenaline talking. No big deal," said Turo. He turned on the radio. "Coltrane. Bingo."

Robert slowed the car when at last they approached their neighborhood. He started searching for a space; this late at night, they'd be lucky to park within ten blocks of their building. Here, night was undermined, darkness trumped by streetlamps. As they drove past the mansions of Avon Hill, their fancy façades oozing hauteur yet separated one from the next by little more than a pebbled driveway or trellised path, Robert wondered if the DOGS would ever dare launch an attack on one of these places. They wouldn't have the guts.

Two blocks from Linnaean, Robert squeezed the car into a nearly impossible gap, turning the wheel so many times that his shoulders cramped. The walk to their building was mercifully short.

Tamara unlocked her bike from the street sign and waved. "Make peace, you two," she said before riding off toward Mass. Ave. She raised one hand over a shoulder to flash them an old-fashioned peace sign.

Robert rolled his eyes.

"We should've offered to drive her home," said Turo. "That's a long ride. Long and cold."

Robert walked ahead, up the stairwell and into the apartment.

Once they were both inside, Turo said, "So you're really that flipped out."

"I am really that flipped out, and I am going to bed, so I can flip out in my dreams, too. I have two labs and a lecture tomorrow—excuse me, today. In like three and half hours. Jesus."

"Have dinner with me tonight, will you? Back here?"

"Yeah. Fine." Robert shut his bedroom door, practically in Turo's face.

He went to his desk, turned on the computer. He groaned. Three e-mails from Clara. He read the last one first.

Oh sweet cat, I don't know where you are, and I'm going out of my mind. I've tried your cell a jillion times and you're not picking up. Please, please forgive me. I acted like a lunatic, a crazy-jealous-hysterical GIRL. I want us to be strong, Robert. I can't go to bed till you call. PLEASE call; I don't care how late. I love you I love you I love you I love you.

Clara wrote e-mails like she wrote her papers, everything tidy and grammatical. The torrent of *I love you*'s was something akin to radical.

Turo, Robert, and Tamara had left their phones behind when they went on their "mission." According to Turo, this was part of the preordained M.O. Robert picked up the phone from his night table. He flipped it open. Thirteen messages. Clara Clara Clara Clara . . .

Robert's freshman-year roommate had been a jock Neanderthal, straight from central casting. Huge and blond, a true golden boy, a virtual Viking, Sam was a lacrosse player from northern Minnesota who aspired to become "an economic player in D.C." Robert had liked the guy at first—different was good, right?—but the farm-country charm wore thin when he'd sampled the sexual wares of a dozen girls by Christmas break, most of the merchandise poked and prodded in their way-too-small room at all hours of the day and night. Sam saw himself as a genius stud and loved to spout advice to Robert, whom he saw, by contrast, as hopelessly challenged on the mating frontier. Robert came to think of Sam as the Pillager, and while he could have blamed the guy's hyperactive sex life for inhibiting his own, he actually found it perversely distracting—a guilty form of entertainment. That spring, Robert finally hooked up with a few girls, including a classmate from Newton South, but no one sparked him until Clara, whom he met in statistics the fall of sophomore year. By then, he was rooming with Turo, and the Pillager was just another dorm mate he'd greet with a "Hey, how's it hanging?" as they lined up for lunch.

But now, as sleep refused to bless Robert with a respite from his bifurcated guilt, a stray bon mot from Sam flashed past: "The minute they offer to do your laundry, it is definitely severance time."

Not that Clara had never done Robert's laundry before. A washer-dryer combo in the kitchen was one of the perks in his apartment; since Clara still lived in a dorm, Robert was happy to let her use it, and if his dirty stuff filled out a wash or two, then so much the better for him.

But Wednesday (just yesterday?) was the first time she'd put his clothes away, which she did without asking him—and which, really, shouldn't have been a big deal. She decided to surprise him by "neatening up" the contents of his dresser, emptying out and rearranging everything from his tennis socks to the cummerbund and tie Granddad had given him to wear to his prom.

What happened was this. Robert came back from the library to find Clara reading on his bed. She gave him a secretive smile. "*Hey*, bobcat," she said. "I think I found something I wasn't supposed to find."

"Yeah? Well, then probably I wasn't supposed to find it, either." He thought of Turo, who by then had begun to disclose the details of his midnight escapades.

Clara was straightforward—she was practically a guy in this respect, which was cool—so instead of going through some big, coy guessing game, she just reached over to the side table and held out a small red box. Robert didn't recognize it, not at first.

"Okay," he said. "So I'm still in the dark, Clara."

She opened the box and held up the ring. "It fits perfectly . . . here." She slipped it onto her left pinkie.

"Oh that! That's the ring Aunt Clo gave me. *Years* ago. I had this major crush on her when I was a kid. She gave it to me as a consolation prize. I guess the only reason I haven't lost it is that I never really wore it."

"Oh." Clara's smile dimmed a bit. "That's so sweet."

"Yes. It was." Robert remained standing. Why was he pissed that she'd put on the ring? "So. You just happened to be, like, rifling through my drawers?"

Clara explained about the laundry. "Wait till you see your T-shirt drawer," she said proudly.

"Color coded?" he joked. "Wouldn't want the reds to compromise the blues. Too much at stake." Still, he did not sit beside her on the bed. Pointedly, he emptied books from his backpack onto his desk. He turned around and said, "I'm hungry. Want some soup?"

"You," she said. "That's what I want. You."

"Food first." Robert leaned over to kiss her, but quickly. He left the room to go to the kitchen. He wasn't really hungry. He wanted her to put back the ring without having to ask her. But in the kitchen, there she was again, sitting at the table, wearing the ring, polishing the stone with a corner of a sleeve. When had he last even looked at it, taken it out of the box? It was silver, the traditional clasped hands (Amish or something, Clover had told him), but between them nestled a small triangular garnet rather than a heart. It hadn't occurred to the lovelorn young Robert, when he accepted the ring, that it was meant for a girl. For a week or two, he'd carried it on a key chain, deep in a pocket, because it was too large for his fingers, but he'd put it away when he decided that he didn't want to risk losing it. He had also feared that his mother would find it, that she might tease him about it, that she might learn his secret.

He pulled a wax carton of soup from the fridge and poured some into a saucepan. He put it on the stove to heat. When he turned around, there was Clara, twirling the ring on her finger, her smile self-conscious and bland.

"So," she said. "What if I wear it? Would you let me wear it? Just to borrow? Or am I being presumptuous?"

"Well, yeah, if you want the truth, sort of." He laughed, a pose.

"Sort of what?"

"Presumptuous. Your word, Clara. I mean, it's this irrationally sentimental thing, okay?"

"This is new. Your sentimental side."

"Well there you have it." He turned around to stir the soup. "We should still be capable of surprising each other, right?"

"It bothers you. That I found this ring and thought it was for me. Like I assume something about us you don't."

Tiny bubbles encircled the soup where it met the edge of the pan. Robert stirred again.

"Answer me, bobcat."

Robert looked at his girlfriend. It was one of those rare moments when, alone with her, he didn't like what he was looking at. "This is so weird," he said. "Like you find this old ring in my drawer and you think I've got some kind of . . . proposal in mind?"

She gasped. "That is so unfair. I did not think anything of the kind."

"But so, then what? Like, if you wore this ring, we'd be . . . going steady? Like that?"

Clara removed the ring, slow motion, meticulous, and set it down in the center of the kitchen table. "Wow, do you ever sound slippery right now." She grimaced dramatically and folded her slender arms.

As if to upstage her gesture, Robert spread his arms wide—but not with the intention of wrapping them around her. He ignored the soup that dripped from the wooden spoon in his right hand onto the linoleum floor. "I am yours, Clara. I'm not hooking up with random people. I'm not prowling online, friending the universe on frigging Facebook. I'm— wow, I'm defending myself! Why is that? I'm defending myself because you did an inventory of the stuff in my dresser? Does this make sense to you?"

" 'Inventory'?" She whistled. "Okay, let's inventory this. How you've spent so much of your free time out at your grandfather's place building a tree house for a nursery school. I mean, you never even asked if I might like to help."

"You wanted to help? Come on, Clara." But she had his number, in a way. The truth was, he'd enjoyed the time with Turo and Celestino— whom he was going to interview for his immigration paper—and even Ira, with his queeny wit. The four of them had laughed a lot, and they'd built this phenomenal thing together. The work, the energy, even the exhaustion—all of it had rocked. Clara hadn't really crossed his mind while he was up that tree.

And of course, if she *had* been with him, Robert would have had to deal with Granddad's bizarre, inexplicable aversion to her, the way he acted like she was practically invisible.

She said, "You've stood me up for that lecture series three times now."

"I didn't stand you up. I called and said I couldn't make it."

"Oh. Right. For*give* me."

Robert heard the hiss of soup boiling onto the stovetop. He turned around quickly and took the pot off the burner. He stirred it and poured some into a bowl. Joining Clara at the table, he knew he ought to reach across and take her hand, but he picked up his spoon and ate. Why didn't he feel like making peace?

The door had opened just then. Turo carried a large black plastic bucket, not books. He looked startled. "*Hola,*" he said, which was what he said by way of greeting whenever something or someone made him nervous.

He took the bucket into his room and then joined them. Clara and

Robert were silent. Turo went to the stove and asked if he could have the rest of the soup. Only when he sat down at the table did he catch their vibe.

"Uh oh," he said. "Have I landed in the dead zone?"

"That's not funny, Turo," said Clara.

Before Robert could remove it from the table, Turo saw the ring and picked it up. "Now this is a juicy clue."

Clara stood and stared at Robert, ignoring Turo. Robert only felt her stare; he focused on his soup, blowing on spoonfuls, drinking them down one by one.

"You are such an asshole," she said. But still she waited.

"Hey, I'm sorry about what I said," said Turo. He, too, stood.

Clara told Turo to sit. Robert looked at neither of them. He continued eating his soup. He was a robotic consumer of soup. He thought, weirdly, of that saying *Cat got your tongue?* No, he thought, cat got nothing of mine.

He heard her sob of dismay as she slammed the apartment door behind her.

Turo said, "You going after her, man?"

"No," said Robert.

"Story?"

"Not now."

Turo drank his soup, set down the bowl, and went to the refrigerator. He pulled out containers of this and that. Did Robert want to share a salad? Fine, said Robert. He would now become a robotic consumer of salad. On top of being an asshole. She was right. But sometimes being an asshole had a kind of inevitability. He felt relieved of something. Guilty but relieved.

Turo made their dinner with an antsy hip-hop glee. He left Robert to himself, reading at the table. After setting down bowls of salad and a plate of sliced bread, he pulled a copy of the *Crimson* from the recycling bin. They ate, and they read. Robert found childish comfort in the sound of their forks, their chewing and swallowing, the clunk of their glasses on the table, even the whisper of pages turning. But once Turo finished his food, he shoved the paper aside. "You are tied up in knots, my friend." He waved a hand in front of Robert's face. Robert looked up from his textbook. "And I have got just the solution."

How Robert had let himself be talked into driving out to Ledgely that night was, and wasn't, a mystery to him. Mostly it had to do with the way he saw Turo, the way Turo's passions drove him crazy yet held him in awe.

Turo's mother, unlike Robert's, lived on the other side of the planet. Robert had never met her—or any of Turo's four half siblings, all much older, also living distant lives unconnected to his. The story Turo had told, matter-of-factly, was this: His dad had owned several coffee plantations in Guatemala and Honduras. Turo confessed that there had once been rumors his father was involved in the drug trade as well; but if so, he'd never been caught. At seventy-four, the man had slipped silently away as he slept beside Turo's mother, his second wife.

Turo's four half-siblings were the offspring of his father's long, contentious marriage to a wealthy Guatemalan woman who had died of ovarian cancer when her husband was in his sixties. He had apparently mourned very little, said Turo, since he'd promptly set about to marry a good, pretty, docile woman, one who would say very little and never oppose his wishes. By this point, he traveled a great deal—between his properties for work, to Europe and South America for pleasure—and had no need for a wife with demands on his time or person. "Dude, you are looking at the son of a mail-order bride," Turo had said over coffee (fair trade) at the Gato.

Turo was nine when his mostly benevolent but mostly absent father had died. For all those years plus one, his mother had done her good, pretty, docile duty, as expected, yet she had also learned the language she was not to speak too often and, not incidentally, had secured the friendship of an excellent lawyer who spoke it far better than she and knew, furthermore, how to use it in matters of delicate family finance. So Turo's mom, Maria Doria, did not need to be greedy (i.e., piss off the adult heirs from *matrimonio numero uno*) to claim a sizable settlement and leave the plantations behind her. She joined her sister, who'd married in similar fashion, way up north in Chicago. There, Maria Doria found a job selling jewelry in a store that catered to wealthy Latinas. She proved herself indispensable to the business while studying (and paying) her way to legal citizenship. She and Turo lived in a two-bedroom apartment overlooking Lake Michigan. Turo did well in school and won a scholarship to Exeter. Every Christmas, Maria Doria took her son and her sister to Manila, where she paid for her parents and siblings to share part of a very nice hotel.

When Turo left Chicago for his final year of school in New Hampshire, his mother felt confident enough in her son's future to sell the apartment and return to her country for good. According to Turo, she had a kindly older boyfriend and played a lot of golf. In the Philippines, she could live like a queen yet soothe her conscience by spreading the wealth. Her share of his father's coffee fortune went a long way toward supporting relatives who hadn't made a canny bargain like hers.

"What a saga, you must be saying, right?" Turo had concluded, draining his coffee with a flourish and smiling like a man who'd won a prize. "Son of mail-order bride did good, huh?"

After their sophomore year, while Robert worked in Maine, Turo had spent the summer in Manila, living with his mother and working for an American businessman who exported rattan furniture to European resorts. For three months, Robert had pictured his friend relaxing every evening on a high porch, a true veranda, surrounded by rattling palms, swooping parrots, the air electric with insects. Costa Rica: that's what he was picturing.

They'd e-mailed back and forth, but Turo said little about his job. He wrote about politics—American, the Hillary-Obama stuff—and sports. (Could they nail tickets at Fenway? Wasn't there some influential family friend in Matlock who had a corporate box?) Nothing about school or girls; nothing about his mom or how weird it was to be halfway across the world. Maybe, for Turo, it wasn't weird. Robert's fairy-tale images of his friend, his privileged life abroad, never morphed into anything fixed or real. And Robert didn't push it, the stuff he wished he understood better. Because he did know this: adamantly, defensively even, Turo saw himself as American. "I love my mom," he once said, "but in terms of who or what I am, I might as well be an orphan. In a good way, an unencumbered way, don't get me wrong. No pity. No way." At such moments, so beguilingly, pugnaciously sure of himself, Turo flashed a smile that could have powered a small city.

That was the smile with which he greeted Robert the evening after the insane outing to Ledgely. Through a long day's agony of scientific drudgery, of prepping slides and peering through a microscope, of struggling mightily just to focus, Robert had suffered flashbacks of the dark woods, the steaming pool, the dead squirrel bobbing in the water. They had only deepened his anger and bewilderment at Turo—though maybe they'd also kept him awake.

Yet all his resolve to blow Turo's ego out of the water simply crumbled when he entered their apartment and felt his roommate's charismatic glee. Without a word, he let Turo trade him a glass of purple wine for his backpack, then lead him, brotherly hand on shoulder, to the kitchen. The table was set for two. Candles flanked a pot of auburn chrysanthemums wrapped in orange foil.

"What, is this a date?" said Robert. He had a sudden vision of Turo engineering a reconciliation with Clara. Would she jump out of the bathroom now, surprise him with apologetic kisses? He'd left his phone in his room that morning, refusing to deal with her panic. His own panic, over the surreal night before, was plenty. So now, if she were to emerge (he glanced at the door to the pantry), would that be better or worse than the face-off with Turo that he'd been rehearsing as he pushed his way against the wind across the Common and up Mass. Ave., weighed down by chemistry tomes.

"A culinary peace offering, friend," said Turo. "Off with that coat."

Robert set down the wine, took off his coat, and went to the bathroom to wash his hands and muster his will. Maybe this wasn't a date, but it was clearly a seduction. Was that Astrud Gilberto?

He sat on the side of the tub and said to the towel rack, "Jesus. Astrud Gilberto." His brain was so fried that he felt like, if he didn't state the realities here, literally announce them one by one, they just might turn out to be illusions. But he couldn't beg off.

So he entered the kitchen on the offensive. He picked up his wineglass, took a dramatic slug—Dutch courage, right? why Dutch, for God's sake?—and said, "Dead squirrels, Turo? Dead squirrels? WTF, man, are we back in junior high? What next, you plan to fill a hangar at Logan with fart cushions and Limburger cheese?"

"Sit," said Turo, unfazed, "and we'll talk."

Robert sat. Turo stood over a dish, hot from the oven. It smelled incredible. Somewhere along the colorful paths of his youth, Turo had learned to cook. Really cook. Robert had assumed that the impromptu gatherings their room had attracted throughout their year in Kirkland House would turn into kickass dinner parties once they had their own kitchen. But Turo claimed he no longer had time to hang around so much. No more long coffee jags at the Gato, pool games in common rooms, tossing or kicking balls by the river—at least not with Turo.

This meal was a seduction all right: a spicy squash strudel with quinoa and jicama salad, spinach sautéed with garlic and lemon.

"Here's what you need to know," Turo said when he finally sat down. "My life is completely serious now. I think yours could be, too. I'm not saying ditch your studies, man, although"—he paused to laugh—"in a way it wouldn't matter. Believe me. You can make a joke of what we're doing. The newspapers try, though would they bother to cover our actions if they didn't know we're dead on target? Forget the meek stuff. Recycling's great, group showering, local eating, yeah yeah, all good. But it's not dramatic enough to make a dent."

"Okay," said Robert, "I get it, but what's wrong with working from inside out, the bottom up? Did you hear about the organic lawn care they're starting on campus? 'Start small and grow it'—isn't that what you've always said?"

Turo shrugged. "I've outgrown small."

Robert watched Turo eat, his slim dark face flattered by the candle-light. If Robert were a girl, he'd have fallen hard for the guy long ago. Had he, in a warped way, chosen Turo over Clara? Or maybe he'd out-grown something, too: the playfulness of easier passions. Maybe he longed to trade up for something hard core, like Hemingway and all those ordinary guys who ran off to fight in that Spanish war.

For dessert, Turo set two plates on the table: two perfect creamy flans, each shaped like a miniature fez, surrounded by a pool of amber syrup. "My mother taught me this," he said. He lit a match and, one plate at a time, set the liquid gold on fire. The heat smelled richly, briefly, of sun-baked oranges. "Now eat," he said when the flames died down.

7

≈

Celestino took a long shower, devoting extra care to the soil beneath his nails, the dust around his ears, the sweat trapped in the creases at the base of his throat. His hair seemed to be graying quickly now, and the skin beneath his jaw, sunburnt too many times, was beginning to resemble the hide of an iguana. The shower in his tiny bathroom was made of flimsy tin; toward the bottom, a hole had rusted through, long before he was the tenant. In summer, mildew gathered like moss around the gap. By late fall, because the bathroom was unheated, a cold draft poured through onto his ankles. No roaches, though; in New York, he'd never lived in a place without bugs.

When he stepped out, he could see his breath. The steam had retreated to the ceiling, where it hovered like a miniature cloud.

He dressed fast, in jeans and a plaid wool shirt he saved for special occasions—of which there were next to none. Make that none.

To Celestino's surprise, Robert seemed to know Lothian well. Well enough to suggest they meet at a place not far from where he lived. Celestino had passed the Big Oven many times; it served pizza that was cooked in a much bigger version of the oven in which his mother had baked tortillas and roasted chicken when he was a boy. People stood outside the window just to watch the cooks with their long wooden paddles, as if they were watching a play. Looking at the menu, you could see that people paid extra to have their pizza cooked like this.

The air was cold enough for snow, yet so far the snow had held off. And so far, he had escaped leaf detail. The blowing, gathering, raking, and shredding of leaves was much of Loud's business now. In Matlock, so thick with woods, the trees old and massive, leaves blew down in blizzards even if the snow did not.

Loud had given Celestino the job of staking and wrapping, one by one, the hundreds of roses and shrubs in the walled garden behind Matlock's oldest church. Celestino had helped care for this place in the summer. According to Loud, people paid a lot of money to be married there. The garden was shaped like a funnel, four terraces descending toward a ring of slender pillars and a fountain. In the center of the fountain, a naked woman made of marble poured water from an urn. A bronze plaque outside the wall told passers-by that this garden, called Rose Retreat, was a hundred and fifty years old. It had been abandoned, grown over with weeds, for nearly half of that time. Only a few years ago had Matlock's history-minded citizens cleaned it up and replanted it just the way it had been designed. It made Celestino think of the dig, wonder if the garden had been buried under the earth. Had archaeologists worked here? The smooth skin of the marble woman bore the ghostly tracings of ivy. She had been wrapped tight in those vines, both smothered and protected. Her features had worn to a blurry version of whatever beauty she'd once possessed.

"Putting the garden to bed," as Loud called it, took Celestino nearly a week. And then yesterday morning, assuming that he'd end up on the truck at last, manning the blowers and mulchers—so loud they left your ears ringing for hours—he'd been surprised when his boss met him at the train, alone and on foot.

"*Hombre!* Come to the office with me," he said. This was odd. Most of Loud's workers were picked up in Packard at the start of the day, returned there in the evening; no one, to Celestino's knowledge, ever set foot in the office.

It was a single room above the row of shops next to the Matlock train station. An older woman stood up from a desk and beamed at Celestino.

Loud leaned across the desk and kissed her on the cheek. "Meet my mom. The true brains behind the operation."

"The one who knows where everything is, and where he's supposed to be when. That's what he means." She squeezed Celestino's hand with conviction. Like his own mother, she was short and plump.

"Mrs. Loud."

"Happy." She laughed. "My name! Call me Happy."

"This way." Loud beckoned Celestino to the far wall, where he opened a closet. Inside the closet was a huge pegboard covered with clusters of keys, each cluster hanging on a hook above a number.

"Mrs. Bullard—you remember her? Mrs. Havahart-and-Pass-the-Rodents-On? She needs someone to care for her orchids and suck-youlents while she's in San Francisco for the next few weeks," said Loud. "Her usual sitter's away and she called me to ask for *you, hombre.*" He reached for the set of keys over the number 29, then hesitated. "Mother, is Bullard twenty-nine or thirty-nine? I'm losing my mojo."

Loud's mother looked at her computer screen and hit a few keys. "Twenty-nine. Yes indeed."

"She'll show you what's what when you head over there this morning," said Loud as he handed Celestino a ring of keys. "And she thinks you've caught that groundhog, but she's afraid to look at the trap.

"Oh—and the keys come back here each night. Mother is the keeper of the keys—and the codes. Not even the cops are this plugged in. She's like the warden of Matlock, only nobody knows it." They laughed together, mother and son, as if this were a grand joke.

When they stopped laughing, Loud said to Celestino, "The ladies seem to trust you, I've noticed." He shook his head. "Women run the show in this town, so who knows? Maybe you'll steal my business, huh?"

Loud spoke loosely, as if he were still joking around, but his eyes were like the eyes of the stone head that Dr. Lartigue had kept on his desk.

Robert was waiting for him outside the restaurant. He smiled eagerly. "Hey!"

They went to a booth at the back. "Wow, it's noisy," said Robert when they sat down. "I was going to record this, but . . ." Out of a backpack, he removed a tape recorder and a thin silver computer.

"You want to record?" said Celestino.

"Are you cool with that? I mean, is that okay with you?"

Celestino paused. Was it okay? Was there any kind of risk? He liked this boy—surprisingly strong for someone so skinny, also surprisingly good with tools and wood. A boy with practical skills in a world of people whose lives seemed absurdly impractical—or enviably so. A boy with the privilege to live in the world of Dr. Lartigue. Robert's company gave Celestino the illusion—he knew it was an illusion, but still it was pleasant—that he was once again within reach of that world.

"Hey, I don't have to record. I can just type. That's cool, right?"

"That's cool, yes," said Celestino, relieved. While Robert fussed with a notebook and opened his computer, Celestino looked around the restaurant. It was made to look primitive on purpose: artificially crooked beams on the ceiling, rough plaster slapped on the walls. Posters of Italy: the Colosseum, a gondolier, a narrow street with walls overtaken by flowering bougainvillea.

As he was taking this in, someone else joined them. Celestino felt a tremor of panic, his legs ready to run, until he saw that it was the other boy, Arturo. Now both of them sat across from him.

"*Hola,*" said Arturo. "Sorry I'm late," he said to Robert.

Robert looked at Celestino. "I thought that since you and Turo speak the same language, it would be good if . . . I mean, I know you're cool with English, but just in case this makes it easier for us to talk." The boy was terrified of insulting him.

Feeling sorry for Robert, Celestino laughed. "No, it is not quite the same language your friend and I speak. He is coming from a very different part of my country. Life is not the same; language is not the same, either."

"But you understood each other."

"Oh yes, the words, that much. Yes."

Now it was Arturo who looked nervous. Celestino felt a small satisfaction; oddly, this boy was less clear to him. He wished that Arturo had not come along. But this was Celestino's fault, for hiding his fluency even as he had enjoyed the hours of working on the tree house.

"Okay. Well then, let's roll!" said Robert. He looked at his notebook. "So I have a list of questions, and if some of them make you uncomfortable"—edgy laughter—"well, just tell me to back off, okay? But like I said, I promise this is only for a class paper, and I'm not going to use your name. I'll call you . . . Diego or Juan or something anonymous like that. Okay?"

Celestino nodded.

"Oh—but food!" Robert waved at a waitress. "You want a beer or something? Have anything. On me, of course." In a place like this, a place so popular, the staff did not have to be efficient. In New York, Celestino had washed dishes for a few months in the kitchen of such a place, a taqueria in the touristy part of Greenwich Village, where the waitresses came into the kitchen and bad-mouthed the customers loudly, not caring if anyone heard.

Robert asked about Celestino's village, his part of Guatemala, how and when he had come to leave. Had he left because of the civil war? Celestino had contemplated inventing a story, making it more like the sad, hard-luck story of his lawn-work *compañeros*. But he liked Robert. And it had occurred to him that Robert might even know about the Lartigues. Señora Lartigue had taught at Harvard, too, though she had not been the esteemed professor her husband had been. She had been a French-language teacher.

"Wow, an archaeological dig," said Robert when Celestino got to that part of his story, "and from Harvard! That is wild."

"Yes, it was a . . . radical change to our lives. My father saw his opportunity there, sooner than others, and he took it."

Arturo raised his eyebrows. He had said nothing so far, sitting on the sidelines, no translations needed.

Robert said, "Radical. I bet." Did it surprise him—both of them— that Celestino spoke English this well? Of course it would.

"So this—the dig—that's what got you to the States?"

"My father saw a chance for all of us in me. I was the quiet child, the one who takes things in. *Una pequeña esponja,* he called me. But my father knew how to make himself important. Important to the professor who was the *patrón* of the dig. Dr. Lartigue was a man who paid attention to children. A lot of Americans do not. Children are bothering them often—the children of other people."

Robert typed as Celestino spoke. "This is a fascinating story. Not what I expected. Okay, I need to shut up. So tell me about the archaeologists. Did they take your dad back to Cambridge, like as an assistant?"

Celestino shook his head. "Not my father."

He told Robert about the Lartigues—the professor and his wife, not Isabelle, not her brother. He realized that he had not spoken out loud about these people for years, and as he did, he felt the terrible, wonderful lure of longing for the past when the past is a place of safety, a place of choice. In actual words, he described his childhood beginning even before his earliest memories: how his father gained responsibility, learned to speak simple English, supervised a team of workers, many of them relatives and friends. Then he described how he had joined those workers when he was old enough, how his father had taken him along to Dr. Lartigue's tent in the evenings. He described the artifacts they had found. But behind these stories, other memories began to unfold and gleam.

He remembered his first meals with the Lartigues in their house. He remembered sitting on the couch in the study, reading his first compositions out loud to Dr. Lartigue. He remembered going to a Christmas play in a shockingly plain white church: no saints, no Virgin, no crucifixion. He sat between Isabelle and her mother, the three of them so close together that the skirts of the mother's and daughter's stiff red dresses had spilled across his narrow lap, his unfamiliar woolen pants.

Without ceremony, the waitress placed on their table a pizza as big as a bicycle tire, turned, and hurried away. The pizza was covered with sausage and many kinds of vegetables. It smelled heavenly.

"Take a break and dig in," said Robert. "But let me ask—when exactly was this? Wasn't this like when Guatemala was on the State Department list? Weren't there guerrillas kidnapping American nuns and Peace Corps workers? Wasn't it dangerous for Americans to run projects like that in the jungle?"

Celestino chewed his pizza. He had never tasted sausage like this.

"Let the dude eat, for God's sake," said Arturo. "I can answer that one. The civil war put just about everybody at risk for thirty years—but life was worst for Indians of any kind." He nodded at Celestino. "But if you were rich and privileged, or if you were some archaeologist from Hotshot U, you paid for protection." Arturo glanced at Celestino and asked him, in Spanish, if Dr. Lartigue's expedition came with protection.

Celestino looked at Robert. He answered in English. "Sometimes they had men from the capital with them, Ladino archaeologists. For this, I think they would not have been bothered. Also, we were near where the tourists came, to see ruins and temples. The famous one is Tikal."

"Tikal," said Robert. "Wow. You've seen Tikal?"

Celestino shook his head.

"Nor have I, if you can believe it," Arturo said to Celestino.

"Hey!" Robert said. "Am I writing a travelogue here?"

Arturo raised his hands. "I'll shut up! I think I'm superfluous."

Celestino told them about going to live with the Lartigues, about the Spanish program in the school, to which he took a bus each day. The classrooms were shiny and new: tile floors, large windows, sleek furniture in colorful plastics. He had loved all the light, the open green playground where the pupils played soccer. None of the other pupils, however, had come from Guatemala, so he had not made any close friends.

Celestino had not thought ahead of time how he would tell Robert what happened later, after he came back for college—how stupid he had been, how cowardly. His mother had told him it was never meant to be, his love of Isabelle becoming a match. She had urged him to return to Guatemala, join her and his sisters in the city, use what he'd learned to get a good job and a Ladino wife. Marry up, this he could do: rise to the top of a mountain, but to the moon? What had he expected?

"I quit my studies. They were too hard for me. But I did not want to go back to my country." One lie, one truth. Not that they balanced. Celestino was quiet by nature partly because he hated telling lies.

Robert typed quickly. Arturo ate, but he rarely took his eyes off Celestino, as if waiting for a particular detail in the story, as if he had heard it before—or as if he could recognize the lies.

"So you came here?" said Robert.

"I went to New York, to where I have family. I had never met them before, but there is . . . a network. I had cousins. Some of them have papers, some have children born here. There is legal work for some, not for others."

To Celestino's relief, Robert wanted to know more about the "network," how it worked, whether it crossed what he called "cultural borders." He did not ask more about what happened before New York.

It was easy to talk about the many short jobs he'd had, some abandoned when better ones came along, others when it looked as if someone might want to see papers, identification. Some of the *indigenas* he met had false cards they had bought when they came into the country. Celestino had asked about the cards and was shocked to hear what they cost, for a deception that looked so flimsy.

For a long time, Celestino had found that there were always jobs he could get without showing papers. New York was a place where what kept him safe were the crowds of people like him. He was just another tree in the jungle. But things were changing fast, even there. And in a town like Matlock, Loud might decide at any moment that the money he saved by hiring and keeping these men wasn't worth the risk. Any minute, it might not matter how much Celestino pleased his boss.

He did not raise these worries to Robert as he answered questions about the lives of the workers who lived in Packard—what he knew of their lives. He could tell that Robert was disappointed to find out Celestino wasn't one of those men, part of their strange bubble of existence, a life lived parallel to the lives they'd left behind. They led what Celestino thought of as "instead" lives, substitutes for reality. Because of money, despite money.

Yet the boys who sat across from him, chewing on the last bits of crust from the pizza, were not stupid. As if guessing at some of Celestino's fears, Robert said, "Well, I'm sure you've figured out by now that Matlock doesn't live by most people's rules. Like, I'd love to see the INS march in and deprive Laurel Connaughton, who's the heiress to some bath towel fortune, deprive her of"—his voice went singsong in excellent mimicry of Mrs. Connaughton—" 'the very finest of all the gardeners who've ever tended my little patch of pah-rah-dize.' "

Celestino laughed freely for the first time in front of these boys. Robert had ordered him a second beer, and he felt relaxed—perhaps relieved, simply, that he had done what he'd promised. He said, "I have been curious to see Mr. Connaughton. He is never at home."

Robert snorted. "Oh please, that dude tucked tail and ran, somewhere back around the invention of the catapult."

Arturo said, "She lives in that place all on her own? Three stories?"

"Did you see inside? It's like the bigger, richer cousin of Granddad's house. They were actually built by brothers. Our brother was a farmer who couldn't keep up with supporting all his kids. Hers was like this bachelor who had a successful carpentry business and kept making his house larger. She keeps that place like it's a wing of the MFA. She wears ballet slippers and makes guests take off their shoes. She claims some important British general stayed there before the Revolution. Now she's getting it even more duded up so they can stage a big house tour. And she's roped in Granddad, too."

"What the F for?" said Arturo. "Show off your house to the world so you can attract future thieves?"

"It's to raise money for some architectural cause," said Robert.

"Oh, like supporting impoverished architects? Right."

Celestino sipped his beer and watched the boys banter. Their friendship was fascinating to him. They were from different but harmonious worlds. Money spoke louder than blood, language, religion—everything.

Suddenly, Robert turned back to him. "So the last question I wanted to ask is, What now? I mean, what happens next for you? Are you going to go for citizenship?"

Arturo frowned at his friend. " 'Go for citizenship'? Do you read the papers?"

"Well, if you get trained in some special skill, you can justify it to the authorities, that's what I mean."

"The *authorities*," Arturo said scornfully. "Please. As if, since nine-eleven, since the whole flight-school fiasco, they have much sympathy for foreigners trained to do useful, productive tasks that could help them get ahead." He glanced at Celestino. "No offense."

Celestino had heard Gilberto, in the truck one morning, talk about an uncle who'd become a certified arborist, how this had earned him a legitimate green card. "I've heard it can happen," he said.

"You're just a knee-jerk cynic," Robert said to Arturo.

"I am many things, man, but not a cynic. As you know by now."

Robert turned back to Celestino. "Tell me what you do for Tom Loud. Nobody seems to know how he suddenly started hiring all these Hispanic guys. According to my mother, one day it was locals—in the summer, kids off from school—and then, wham, one day everybody's from Brazil. Or, I guess, Guatemala? What does he pay you guys?"

Celestino felt a completely unfamiliar urge to defend his boss. It was true that Loud paid better than the bosses who had picked up his *compañeros* from city streets. He paid better than the fish factory. But the wages were still meager, and they came with no guarantees, no promises of any kind.

"I am paid better than many others," said Celestino.

"Because you speak English."

"No." Celestino laughed. "Because I know more than he does about gardens and trees. I know the answers to questions he does not." He began to tell Robert about the job he would have caring for Mrs. Bullard's orchids—though of course this would take just a fraction of his time—but suddenly Robert looked at his watch.

"Oh shit." He punched a key and abruptly closed his computer. "Granddad. I told him I'd help move furniture. His floors are being sanded."

"For the indigent architects' charity ball."

"Hey, it's all relative," said Robert. "It's not a McCain fund-raiser, right?" He stood and waved at their waitress. "I'm getting this. Sorry I have to split." He packed up his computer and notebook, pulled on his puffy orange coat.

Robert thanked Celestino and asked if they could get together again. "Are you staying on the same schedule at Mrs. Connaughton's?"

Celestino said he would leave a message with Robert's grandfather if anything changed. Awkwardly, they shook hands.

He finished his beer and reached for his coat.

"One more for the road?" said Arturo. "On me."

Celestino was quiet, still. If the next words to emerge from his mouth were in Spanish, they would mean one thing; in English, another. Or perhaps he was wrong. Maybe, as his mother believed, everything was written by God in some great gilded book. Maybe the choices he made were futile.

"You don't want to go with your friend?" Celestino said.

"I like it here, where it's warm. Don't you?" Arturo wore a knowing smile. The girls must go wild for this one. He had a rich boy's teeth: white and evenly spaced. His eyes were the deep brown of the coffee beans that had paid his way through life, his black hair slick as a bird's wing.

Arturo signaled the waitress. As if reading Celestino's mind, she came to their table at once. The boy ordered two beers.

"Why does your friend call you a cynic?" asked Celestino.

"Because I don't take yes for an answer." Arturo smirked. "Something like that."

Oh, a clever one, thought Celestino. Young, naïve, and trying to be anything else. As the waitress set the beers on their table, he realized that she had not asked to see the boys' cards, to check their age.

Arturo pulled a glass toward his side of the table but did not drink right away. "So. Your connection with Harvard. That's bizarre, man."

Celestino felt his heart quicken. "The widow—Señora Lartigue—she taught there, too. French."

"Not my subject. Never heard of her. But in the Fogg, there's a collection named for her husband. Pre-Columbian. Some of it must come from that dig."

"They had two children who are grown up now. Etienne the son, Isabelle the daughter. They were kind to me."

"But you lost touch, huh?"

"I wonder where they are." Celestino felt as if the boy's gaze would puncture his armor at any moment. Did it matter?

"So Google them," said Arturo. Almost at once, he laughed. "Yeah, like you've got free computer access. Sorry. But hey." He reached down and squirmed around until he pulled out a cell phone. It was a bright metallic red and, like Loud's phone, had a full screen without keys. Turo punched at the screen with his thumbs. "So. Isabelle with two *l*'s— or . . . well, bingo. Isn't the Web like something just plain unholy?"

Arturo held the phone toward Celestino. "This her?"

Her name stood out on the screen, in clear celestial blue. *"The Stigma of Parental Renown: Growing Up in the Shadow of an Esteemed or Notorious Parent." Panel Discussion with Ph.D. candidates . . . Dept. of Psychology, William James Hall 765, Harvard University. December 3, 4:00 p.m.*

"Apple fallen not far from the tree," said Arturo. "What do you *know.*" He withdrew his phone and tapped its surface a few more times, absorbing information he did not share. Then he turned his sly gaze on Celestino. "Dude, from the look on your face, you've done more than wonder about this woman."

If Celestino had met Isabelle in his village rather than her city, his little sisters, or younger cousins, would have gone with them to the movie they saw the first time they went out together alone. But of course, there were no movie theaters in his village: a handful of televisions by the time he left for good, but nothing so grand as a cinema.

It was two months after Celestino had arrived in Cambridge the second time, to begin college. Isabelle, who was in her last year of high school, had suggested they walk into Harvard Square to see *The Perfect Storm.* Afterward, they went to Brigham's for ice cream.

"Gosh, this is so old-fashioned," Isabelle had said, licking chocolate sauce off the stem of her spoon. "I feel like I'm living in the nineteen-fifties. A picture show and a hot-fudge sundae. I always have fun with you, Celestino. A kind of fun I have with no one else. You don't have any 'attitude.' "

"Attitude?"

"You know what I mean. Like you're going to own the world one day; that's how almost everyone I know behaves. Though you—maybe you will, and not all those Brooks Brothers princelings I'm stuck with all day at school. I freak out when I realize that I'm expected to end up with one of those guys."

"You will end up with someone like your father."

"Don't bet on it," she'd said. "You know just a sliver of my father. God, if egos were houses, he'd be Versailles."

Celestino did not acknowledge this remark. She apologized and put her hand on his. "My father must be a saint to you, and I guess he should be. He's just so"—she'd laughed in her birdlike, carefree fashion—"French."

"Your mother, she is French also."

"And *how*. But me—I mean, more than Etienne—I've been raised here. So the French stuff—the twisted xenophobic-but-totally-magnanimous thing? Like they're cultural ambassadors at large. Know what I mean? It is such a façade."

He asked her what *xenophobic* meant. She paused before answering. "It means that you're threatened by things or people that are foreign." The look on her face was a challenge; what did he think of *that*?

He decided that she meant her parents were rich people who fought their own prejudice against the poor. Could you hold the prejudice against them if they were trying to change it?

Before he could find the words, Isabelle began talking about the movie again. "I am going to have nightmares about drowning," she said. "Someone told me the book describes exactly what it's like to drown." She shuddered. "I'll happily miss out on *that*."

Celestino had confessed to her, then, that he did not know how to swim.

"Oh my God, I am so going to teach you!" she'd said, and she'd grabbed his hand. "My parents have friends with the most outrageously awesome pool, right here in Cambridge."

In a way, Celestino and Isabelle had known each other for three years already. The first time he had come to live with her family, when he was fifteen, they had not spent much time alone together. For one thing, he had been overwhelmed by schoolwork. And back then, she had seemed like a creature of another species. He had seen her as an ocelot or a puma cub, moving deftly through her world, free to be playful, fearful of nothing. Celestino, by contrast, had felt his way through that world too cautiously for play, confident of nothing. Three years later, he still felt the weight of her worldliness, but now he was taller (if only by an inch), more fluent in the customs of his wildcat companion, more aware of how she used those customs to hold his attention.

Isabelle had gone to a private school a few blocks from her house. On many afternoons, other girls followed her home, draping themselves around the green table in that huge, lovely kitchen. If Celestino was upstairs at work, he would hear them enter the house like a flight of raucous parrots. He might go quietly downstairs to the kitchen on the pretense of getting a drink or a few crackers—but he would leave quickly, wanting only to catch a glimpse of these girls from around the edge of a cupboard door. They moved as if their bodies were entirely liquid, limbs curled impossibly around the furniture, their silky sweaters and scarves flung here and there, even their big furry boots in the winter. Their toenails were painted, black or green or midnight purple, never red or pink.

When they shut themselves in Isabelle's room, he could hear their conversation through the wall, almost always about the boys they wanted to stalk—or elude. They sounded predatory, sly—again, cats at home in a jungle—and he did not seek to know them (though he heard them ask questions about him, tease Isabelle about her "live-in stud"). But when he had Isabelle to himself, she was . . . easy to be with. And then, more quickly than he had ever dreamed, too easy—though it would be fairer to say that they had been equally easy. No one had been the seducer, no one the seduced.

Once they had discovered that they enjoyed each other's bodies as much as they enjoyed going to movies, walking by the Charles and talking (of course, Isabelle did by far most of the talking), it wasn't hard to be together for the long velvet hours of the night. That she did teach him to swim, as she'd promised, in that outrageously awesome pool, gave an even greater logic to the need for their physical closeness.

Isabelle would wait for the light to go out under her parents' bedroom door. Celestino became so alert that, from Etienne's old room at the far end of the hall, he would hear the tiny snap of Señora Lartigue turning off her lamp. In a few minutes, he would see his bedroom door open, in the dark. . . .

But they did not risk using either of their beds, since their rooms were on the same floor where Isabelle's parents slept. They would creep to the third floor, up the carpeted stairs to the room where Celestino had stayed during his first visit there. It was now a cold, sparsely furnished guest room. They kept a large beach towel rolled tightly beneath the small bed. Isabelle would spread it across the bed and they would fall there, or throw each other down, holding in their laughter like breath underwater, nearly drowning under the necessity for quiet, but happier than they'd ever been before. So they told each other often, in the hours they had to be careful to stay awake before slipping downstairs again, to their respective beds, shivering in the cold sheets.

At breakfast, in the hectic rush to get out the door to their different schools, Isabelle and Celestino would play a secret game. The first to break down and catch the other's eye would be the submissive one, at least to begin with, when they returned, hours and hours later, to the small bed in the small room just under the roof of the house, the room where Celestino had first felt the yearning to live forever in *this* place, not the place where he had been born and once assumed he would always stay.

8

~

In early November, true to her Vassar-inflected word, Mistress Lorelei deployed a squadron of surprisingly efficient teenage girls to strafe my house with dust cloths, sponge mops, tubes of polish, and aerosol cans of cleaning fluids so potent as to drive me off to the Narwhal every day for a solid week. (Norval grew weary of my whining.)

One afternoon, arriving home just before dark, I beheld quite the apparition: out on the frozen lawn, four of these girls, each grasping a corner of my living room rug, vigorously snapping it up and down. In my headlights, the cloud of dust rising into the air looking positively atomic. The girls, unimpressed, chewed their gum placidly, wires twisting from their ears to the music pods tucked in the pockets of their very tight jeans. One of the more unsettling side effects of my resurrected sexuality was a sudden, inappropriately visceral appreciation for female anatomy even in its early bloom.

I had allowed Laurel into my house with extreme reluctance; she, in turn, suppressed her disapproval. ("Percy, are those exquisite black sconces by any chance brass?") We decided that the tour, in my house, would be restricted to the first floor. Chez Lorelei, visitors would be able to follow a path—restricted by velvet ropes—reaching even up the ladderlike stairs to her third floor, where they might ogle and coo at the quaint furnishings of an ersatz nursery and stroke the original brickwork of a well-built colonial chimney.

Sarah watched me endure the scrub-down with devilish amusement. She was drinking tea in my kitchen the afternoon two oil paintings were carted away for cleaning. (This I had agreed to pay for, and it would not be cheap.) "Percy, you look like someone just stripped off all your clothes and shoved you onstage with Larry King."

"Who's he?" I asked.

She laughed her laugh of astonishment. "A lion trainer with Barnum and Bailey."

"Some media character I'm supposed to worship."

"Worship? Depends on your religion."

I recalled a song, from a musical, that for a time Poppy would sing to herself in idle moments. It's a song about what happens when you marry: how everything's different yet nothing's changed. I told her the song was incorrect; that my life, had we not married, would be to the life we shared as any one continent is to another. A world apart.

This song, or what I vaguely remembered of it, came back to me often last fall. For as much as everything around me was shifting shape, from the barn to the beech tree to the placement of my furniture, the further these alterations progressed, the more I felt like myself, *this* man in *this* body in *this* time. Strangely, it was Sarah, more than anyone or anything else, who underscored this feeling.

Sarah made me feel younger—the lovemaking, yes, but in equal part the conversations and jests that we shared, the increase in laughter alone—and at the same time so much older. I found myself aching and cramping in anatomical niches and gullies that my running and swimming routines had never explored. I cramped up in less definable ways as well. After staying overnight in Packard twice, I had to inform Sarah that I wasn't comfortable there and knew I never would be. The sheer space of the loft, its very loftiness, confounded me when I awoke in the middle of the night. I remained forcefully alert with an unfamiliar agoraphobia, perturbed by the shadows cast on the industrial ceiling, far too high above me. I felt like a child who worries that goblins lurk in his closet. En route to the bathroom in the middle of that second night, groping about for the switch, I tripped over Rico's tricycle. Sarah, a hearty (and often noisy) sleeper, was not roused by the commotion. I sat on the cold concrete floor in my undershorts, wincing and gasping as I clutched my battered shin, unsure whether or not I wished she would come to my aid.

So the younger, randier Percy and the older, ossifying Percy were constantly forced to meet in the middle, so deliberate in their dance that I knew, as I'd never known before (or had refused to know), exactly where I stood on the meandering road of my life. Does this sound pompous? Too bad. It was true. I looked upon my daughters and grandchildren from a new, more precisely calibrated angle, as if I could literally see them in distinct generations following mine, as if we stood on a tiered stage.

In this scheme, Poppy now stood so much farther behind me, genuinely lost to me once and for all, out of sight beyond a dozen bends in the road. To be alone with myself whenever I faced this loss was nigh unbearable. At such moments, I welcomed the incursion of the cleaning squads or the mothers babbling beneath my back porch or the teachers emptying the tree house for winter, waving coyly through the window in my study as they relayed little chairs and tables down the ladder and off to the barn.

"I dreamed that I married a Muslim cabdriver. He had very bad teeth but a beautiful smile. He told me he could make a wonderful lamb stew. And then we were in his house, and he was making it, and it was in fact amazing. I can almost remember the taste."

"Please tell me this qualifies as a nightmare," I said.

We were sharing a shower, as we always did after a rare overnight visit. I stood behind Sarah, soaping her lovely back. Her wet hair enveloped her shoulders like a slippery pelt. It smelled of grapefruit, the scent of the shampoo she kept in my bathroom.

"No, not at all. I had this generalized happy feeling about the guy, even though I was also thinking that maybe he wasn't too literate—that did worry me, vaguely—and there was this nagging sense I had about a complication I couldn't put my finger on."

"Which would be me."

"No. Rico."

The sun angling through the bathroom window had spotlit the line of mildew where the edge of the tub met the tile wall. The disadvantage to having my first floor stripped and polished to a fare-thee-well was that the second floor now looked horrendously grimy. A well-greased slope, this business of renewal. I was thinking idly and self-righteously about the parallels to plastic surgery as I slipped my arms beneath Sarah's and began to soap her breasts. She giggled and bent slightly forward, but she did not turn around or pull my hands away.

How I loved, even obsessed over, Sarah's breasts. Poppy, against the prevailing trend of our time, had nursed both daughters. I'd suffered no anxieties—no "hang-ups" as we liked to say back then—about sharing, though one male friend, after a few drinks, confided that I would feel differently if my babies had been boys. Indeed, I loved Poppy's breasts more than ever after she weaned Clover. I loved the purple veins newly and sharply etched on her fair skin and would trace them with the tip of my tongue. Her breasts seemed fuller to me, more welcoming, as if they were live beings that took their own pleasures separately from those I wanted to lavish on my wife. But the second round of nursing, Trudy's turn (so soon after Clover's), left them depleted. They felt, to my hands and mouth, as if they'd been hollowed out, paid their biological dues.

Sarah's breasts, like the rest of her body, felt unvanquished, almost virginal in their resilience. Privately, I thought of her breasts as warrior breasts. I was careful never to hint at any comparisons, though I wonder if she knew how inevitable they were, even as they began to obscure my memories of Poppy.

As I savored them there in the shower, she was silent for a moment. Then she said, "It must be the residue of a cab ride I had in Boston yesterday." She pressed her bottom into the alcove beneath my stubborn belly. "Sometimes I think dreams come from a place in your brain like that filter in the dryer. Fuzz from your day accumulates there. Because now I remember looking at this guy's mug shot on his license. He was handsome in this wind-beaten way, but he must've been twenty years younger, because when I looked in the rearview mirror, the face I saw was so much more . . . collapsed. His hair gone gray. Oh my God, I thought, he's been doing this job for his whole adult life, probably for his kids. I tried to guess his nationality from his name. Lots of consonants, *z*'s and *y*'s." She knew she was teasing me with her casual monologue, that the more words she doled out as she pressed against me, the fewer I'd have at my service.

I was speechless, but not because of my desire. As my left hand kneaded and stroked the corresponding side of her marvelous chest, I felt a distinct knot, separate from her nipple. A small, discrete . . . what? A stray bit of cartilage?

I was about to search for a parallel form in her other breast when she turned around, still in my arms. "I have to pick up Rico in an hour," she said, "but if we're quick . . ." She turned off the water and, looking me square in the eye, pulled me close. Noticing that I was no longer aroused, she kissed me, more tender than amorous, and stepped through the shower curtain. This was one of her many virtues: that she changed course as necessary, sensed the faintest alteration in the mood or impulse of those around her.

As she dried herself, she talked about the remainder of her weekend. She was—and she blamed me—falling behind on the commission she'd received to render a willow tree in a large panel that would fill a window at the turn of a grand staircase. The client was a radio host on Boston's NPR station; Sarah had heard that he entertained a great deal, that she could hope this window would win her admirers with money to burn. She dreamed of the day she could give up her job at The Great Outdoorsman, spend a normal workday preoccupied by art alone. I did not share with her my view that such a life is rare indeed, especially if there are children to support.

As for my Saturday, I would face the tricky, less creative task of sitting down with Clover and telling her about the counsel I'd received— hardly encouraging—from an old affiliate at the law school, a professor for whom I'd once researched the topic of divorce as represented in nineteenth-century British fiction. Yet divorce and stained-glass willows and gadabout NPR celebrities were relegated to the virtual lint filter of my consciousness as I focused on the lump I'd felt in Sarah's breast.

Sarah hurried about my bedroom, pulling on her skirt, searching the floor for her socks, buckling the wristband of her watch.

"Please stop a minute," I said, fearing she would dash downstairs and out the door. In our reunions and partings, we no longer stood on ceremony. Often, she was running late.

"Percy?" She stood still, smiling sweetly. "I can stop for two seconds, but not a minute."

"Sarah, your breast. Your left breast."

Her right hand reached for it, as if she were about to say the pledge of allegiance. "My breast?"

"I felt something there."

"That would be my heart. Which is yours." But ever so slightly, she frowned.

"What I felt was . . ." How difficult can one word be? I pushed it forward. "A lump." I felt as if I'd shoved a knuckle in her eye.

Yet she was smiling when she crossed the room. She touched my cheek with the hand that had occupied her breast. "Percy, I have . . . well, I'm lumpy by nature. I have cystic breasts. It's nothing to worry about."

I watched her return to the bed and pull her thick sweater over her head, retrieve her damp hair from inside the cabled collar, smooth it with her fingers.

"Oh," I said. "Well, good then. Good to know." From my experience, admittedly scant, women take a superior attitude not just toward knowing their bodies but even, sometimes, toward knowing ours. By default, we men are biological dolts.

She paused to squeeze my arm as she passed me to leave the room. She whispered, close to my ear, "I'll see you Monday morning."

I stood there, still clad in nothing but my towel, shivering.

I offered her my handkerchief. This was what I had feared.

"I can't believe what a mess this is," she said, wiping her eyes. She hadn't touched her tuna sandwich. I had polished off mine, ravenous after my night with Sarah, and had to resist the urge to reach across and help myself to Clover's.

"Daughter," I said. "Sweetheart. I'm afraid that you would only squander thousands of dollars"—in all likelihood mine, I did not add—"to put yourself in an even more antagonistic position with Todd. Gerald told me that you would have to move back to New York, realistically, to approach winning even a shared custody arrangement."

Gerald had quizzed me over lunch at the Faculty Club, plates laden with the obscene bounty of the daily buffet, and the more I disclosed to him about Clover's situation, the harder it became for him to remain his sanguine self.

"Well, Percy," he said at last, "is there any reason to believe the children would *choose* to be with their mother instead?"

I felt myself redden as I told him that I had a feeling they would not. But how would I know the answer to this? I felt ashamed of myself. Clover had recently blurted out to me that part of what drove her away was a conversation in which Todd had told her he might be *gay*. Having subsequently forced Trudy's hand on the subject, I now believe Clover's story may have been true, but my knee-jerk reaction to her confession had been one of despair more than empathy: that this was a childish delusion, a ruse of her fragile unconscious. I did not share this part of the saga with Gerald. (Should I have done so? Was there some dirty-pool legal precedent by which a husband's admission to a different so-called orientation might justify spousal breakdown or even render him unfit to father?)

"Daddy, I can't leave this job. It's the best one I've ever had. Evelyn and I are a team."

"That's heartening news," I said.

"But this just isn't a fair choice!"

How many times had I, like the next parent, told my children about the dearth of justice in this world? Cornered, I said, "What does your therapist say?"

Clover sighed. "That I have got to stop fighting everything. That I have got to take a deep breath and be more . . . humble." She covered her face with my handkerchief. I couldn't tell if she was crying or hiding.

She sat up straight and bared her face. She leveled at me a look of urgency. "Thanksgiving," she said. "When they're here for Thanksgiving, maybe you could talk with them. Or just Lee. He's old enough. Maybe you could . . ." Her lips clamped shut. I had a feeling she wanted to issue the verb *persuade* or *uncover* or even *convince*.

"You've spoken to Douglas, haven't you?" I said. That I had a son-in-law who made a living sitting in a room with couples who'd already decided that nothing could induce them to remain together—or, rather, that he had gamely *chosen* this livelihood—never ceased to astonish me. At first I had wondered whether this vocation masked ulterior motives (to harvest material for novels, perhaps?), but eventually I realized that Trudy's husband was simply that rare male who loves constructing a peaceful compromise the way a painter loves filling a canvas or an athlete loves winning a game.

"Daddy, I don't want to lean on Douglas. Trudy just isn't . . ."

"Isn't what?"

"She isn't really on my side these days."

"That's absurd. She's your sister. She's . . . I admit she's a little intimidating, even to me," I said, "but for God's *sake* she loves you."

"Yes, she does, I believe that. But she has her own ideas about what that love means. Like, keeping me aware of what's 'good for me.' From her perspective as somebody totally worshiped by about a million women whose lives she's saved. Or that's how *they* see it."

I sighed. "That's a bit harsh."

A daunting silence ensued. "Ira," Clover said at last.

"Sweetheart?"

"Ira, the teacher, the wonderful teacher who built the tree house."

"Have you invited him to Thanksgiving, too?"

"No, no, Daddy." She smiled weakly. "He has a roommate, a lawyer who handles divorces and custody and . . . that sort of thing."

A divorce lawyer with a roommate could hardly be a roaring success, I thought rather haughtily as I waited for her to unravel her next thoughts.

"I'm going to meet with him on Friday," Clover said. "Ira says he'll meet with me for nothing. Once, anyway. A consultation. I think I have to take this dilemma by the horns. Myself. That's part of the problem, right? That I didn't face up to my responsibilities on my own. That I ran back here, without stopping to think."

Amen crossed my mind. I waited to hear more.

"So I'm going to do that. And I'll go from there." She picked up half of her sandwich and took a bite, then set it down and stood. "But thank you, Daddy. Thanks for trying," she said. And then, as Sarah had done two hours before, she kissed me on the cheek and left the room.

I ate the rest of her sandwich in a few speedy bites. In addition to pangs of esophageal distress, I was beset by an uncomfortable conflict of hopes: that my part in this particular drama was finished and that it would be better for all concerned if it were not.

~

From: laurelc@matlockhistoricalforum.org
To: bookman37@econet.net
Subject: 28 days and counting!

Dear Percy,

I wager I'm as new to this technology as you are, but what a blessing it is as we approach the Big Day! Seven of the ten houses are ready to go—including mine, of course, but then I must be the shining example!—and the mailing has gone out as of Friday, not a moment too soon, so this is in part a warning shot across the bow that you may be approached at Wally's or the P.O. about your participation. I believe there's already quite a "buzz" in the autumn air. I've even had a call or two from people who feel slighted that they were not included; not entirely beneficial to the cause, but unavoidable. The *good* news is that tickets are selling briskly and we're already talking about the lineup for next year! We've got ourselves a town tradition in the making!!

What I'm wondering is if I could come by for a bit of a look-see sometime this week, to check if you need assistance with finishing touches. (How was Deirdre's work on those wonderful portraits? She really is the best!)

Any chance I could come tomorrow afternoon, once the E & F gridlock abates? Tuesday would work for me as well.

Fondly,
Laurel

From: Trudy Barnes, M.D. <tbarnes@mattmed.org>
To: Dad <bookman37@econet.net>
Subject: tgiving etc.

dad: let's talk re final plans. food etc. douglas wants to do brined turkey w oyster stuffing. 2 pies from me. robert bringing turo. will call tnt or tmw. need to catch up on other things too. sorry so brief.

xx
trudy

From: Robert <baobabbob@econet.net>
To: GD <bookman37@econet.net>
Subject: hey!

hey, g: sorry so out of touch—can't wait for txgvg! hope it's ok to bring turo; he loves hanging out with you and we may stay a night or 2, go hiking or if snow xc ski. ok? are mom's skis still in the bsmt? does tgo still rent stuff?

reading heavy now, 2 papers due early dec + lab demo. if this is minor cf. med school, not sure i'd cut it.

widener not the same, g. nj! miss you as my main excuse to slack off. in ref rm, looked thru porthole and saw this yng bald dude, clrly the NEW U. too weird.

yfg,
rb

The planets must have aligned in the house of communication, for rarely had I received more than two personal e-mails at a time, even checking my in-box every other day, as was my usual habit. Norval was the only person outside my family circle to whom I had given my address, so I was more than mildly annoyed to hear from Mistress Lorelei in this fashion.

I noted that Laurel's e-mail had been dispatched at 8:01 the previous evening—meaning that her "tomorrow" was in fact "today"—and that my daughter had sent hers at 2:24 a.m., Robert his at 4:07 a.m. Curious, these telltale time signatures, allowing me to deduce that my daughter was alarmingly overworked or suffering from insomnia—neither scenario heartening—while my grandson was keeping hours considered normal for an overachieving premed student at an Ivy League institution.

My tripartite inclination, unnecessarily grumpy, was to delete my neighbor's request without reply, to quiz my daughter about the hours she kept, and to wonder why my favorite grandson was so blatantly stroking my ego. His friend Arturo had certainly never "hung out" with me, though he did seem to enjoy the pastoral amenities of Matlock. I am, however, a great believer that "txgvg" is a holiday to be shared, especially with acquaintances orphaned by geography. The coward in me was also relieved that another outsider would be present when I introduced Sarah, formally, to my daughters. Had Clover not been so preoccupied with her quixotic assault on sensible family law, she would, I am sure, have been more inquisitive about my poorly camouflaged liaisons. I had a feeling that she knew and did not disapprove. As for Trudy, Clover's remarks about being estranged from her sister led me to believe that she was, as Robert would have said, cosmically clueless.

I took a deep breath. I glanced at my favorite tree, which, in its denuded wintry state, now looked like it was wearing a most unseemly wooden corset. "New me," I said to myself, "chill."

I replied to Laurel that she could come by between three and five that afternoon. I replied to Trudy that I needed to have lunch with her any day that week; that I would meet her in town, wherever she chose. To Robert, I replied that his friend was welcome, that skis were in the basement but hadn't been waxed in a decade, that TGO was probably a better bet, and that studying mattered a great deal more than keeping tabs on my well-occupied self.

"New me," I said as I clicked my computer to sleep (the screen blackening in instant obeisance, showing me my own bejowled, woolly-haired, stunned-looking visage), "keep up the good work."

~

Once through the vast, stubbornly autonomous revolving door, I felt as if I had entered a spaceship. Before me sprawled and soared an undeniably wasteful largesse of light and air—fashionably known as an atrium—sprouting in every direction a Seussian array of elevators, balconies, catwalks, stairways, and beckoning trajectories of patterned carpet. Here and there, cunningly artificial plants proffered false assurance that I hadn't left the planet.

I stood in the center of this space, looking up and around me, the hem of my raincoat and the tip of my umbrella dripping onto the marble floor. I had walked from the T.

I saw the information desk, but several fellow earthlings were huddled there already. Male pride propelled me onward, willy-nilly, as once again I pictured Trudy's directions sitting on the kitchen table back in Matlock.

This was to be my very first visit to my daughter's office. On the rare occasions when we met in town, always for dinner, she would name the time and choose the restaurant. Typically, Douglas would be waiting when I arrived. We would converse politely until Trudy arrived, late by half an hour or more. The advent of cell phones had given her license to be later than ever. From the moment I shook hands with Douglas, I'd simply wait for his pocket to ring.

So that day's appointment was a first, resulting from my flat refusal to let her put me off another week. Thanksgiving would not do, I'd said: I needed to see her in private.

I had not been inside a big-city hospital for decades, not since the stroke that killed my father when the girls were small. I saw my own doctor in Ledgely, in a storefront office suite that shared a parking lot with the Narwhal and three other local merchants. To submit to the occasional X-ray or colonoscopy, and, most recently, as an escort to Norval when he endured a bit of surgery whose delicate nature I shall not disclose, I had visited the hospital in Packard of which Trudy so firmly disapproves. ("Dad, if you die of pneumonia one day in that ICU, I'm not sure which will upset me more: my certainty that you would not have died like that at St. Matt's or my frustration that you won't be around for me to say I told you so.")

I made my way toward a corridor that clearly spanned our galaxy.

THE MAX STENHOUSE ARTERY, bellowed a row of chrome letters affixed to the wall. Along this curved thoroughfare hastened people of many colors and dimensions, most of them young, uniformed, and radiant with importance. Signs bearing dozens of arrows showed the way to every medical specialty known to humankind (including, my favorite, the Swallow and Speech Clinic) except for the one I sought. What would happen, I mused, if the Max Stenhouse Artery were to hemorrhage?

"May I help you?" A sharp-looking gal who sported a stethoscope, a blond ponytail, and oblong purple eyeglasses had noticed my inertia.

"Oncology," I said. "I am searching for oncology."

"Well, that depends," she said cheerfully. "Here for a procedure or a checkup?"

"I am here to see Dr. Trudy Barnes."

"Oh! Breast! Meeting a wife or daughter?"

"Daughter."

She nodded. "Down there. See the drinking fountains? Take a right after the men's room and you're at the main elevator bank. If you hit Neurology, you've gone too far. Go to three and take the Rabbi Newman Bridge."

"Not to be mistaken for the Cardinal Law Aqueduct."

She paused. "Excuse me?"

"Or the Phil Rizzuto Wind Tunnel."

Her expression froze. I thought of asking her where I could find Captain Kirk, but instead I patted her on the shoulder. "Thank you very much, young woman."

The elevator was posted with admonitions warning me that latex balloons and conversations about patients were, along with smoking, forbidden. I began to wonder if someone would demand to see my passport.

The so-called bridge was nothing more than a passageway to an older building that must have been cannibalized by the mothership. The ceilings became lower, the lighting harsh, the signs few and far between. I took two compulsory lefts and found myself facing a doorway fashioned of dark, expensive-looking wood.

THE GRAZIELLA MURCHISON GOLD ONCOLOGY SUITES
RING BUZZER AND ENTER

One rabbit hole after another. Starship *Enterprise,* via Dr. Seuss and Lewis Carroll. Whoville with a dash of Borges.

My destination proved to be an elegant but chilly, windowless room furnished with saffron velvet couches and large watercolor paintings of birds in flight. Linen-shaded lamps affixed to the walls cast a soft, cheddary glow over half a dozen women who waited in silence, reading magazines or dozing. Two of them looked up and registered my arrival without a hint of surprise. I tried to seem equally blasé at the sight of a woman completely and effervescently bald.

The sound of a cello, both soothing and sad, seeped from hidden speakers overhead.

Three more women sat behind an elliptical counter, each facing a computer. My entrance had made no impression on them; I felt as if I were seeking approach to the Oracle at Delphi. After I'd stood at the counter for a few seconds, one of the women glanced up and said, "Sir?" She was large and firm, her skin gleaming with good health, her hair plaited flat to her skull.

I leaned over the counter and whispered, "I have a lunch date with my daughter. Dr. Barnes. I'm a few minutes early." I tapped my watch.

Now she smiled. She whispered back, "Nice to meet you, sir. Let me tell her you've arrived." She reached for the phone, addressing me at normal volume. "Have a seat. Dr. B lives in a time zone all her own. But when you get her, honey, you have *got* her. As the ladies here will testify."

A few of the women on the golden couches met my eyes and smiled. Having turned my attention from the three receptionists—all black—I noticed that all the waiting women were white. I tried not to see any meaning in this observation.

I found a couch of my own. The only magazines within reach were called *Real Simple* and *Self.* A rack of pamphlets presented further choices: the warning signs of ovarian cancer, the best foods to eat while undergoing chemotherapy, how to care for a mediport, a list of support groups.

I had not brought along my current book; like Trudy's directions, it remained behind on my kitchen table. Nor had I taken the time to figure out exactly what I would say to Trudy, once I had her attention.

I contemplated the watercolors visible from my seat: a hawk, a cardinal, an oriole. The artist's pencil lines were visible through the paint in a way that struck me as false, ostentatiously casual.

I returned to my receptionist. I noticed her name tag: CHANTAL.

"Now don't go holding your breath," she said cheerfully. "You want coffee or tea?" She gestured down the hall that was guarded by her desk.

Pretending this was just the remedy for my impatience, I followed her gesture. Other corridors branched off left and right, down which I could see curtained alcoves and doors. I arrived at a counter offering a range of unappealing snacks (I hadn't seen Lorna Doones in decades) and studied the directions to prepare a cup of coffee I did not want.

"I'll do my best to be right there with you, I promise. The first time, I always try to do that." Trudy's voice. "Absolutely. You bet."

I saw her standing some distance along an adjacent hallway, one arm around the shoulders of a much older woman. Older and smaller. Trudy gave the woman a hug and pointed her down the hall in my direction, then turned and walked the opposite way. Had she seen me?

My paper cup had filled, so I took it out from under the spigot. It was so hot, I nearly dropped it.

I left it on the counter and went into the nearest restroom to wash spilled coffee off my hands. Above the paper towel dispenser, a framed notice read, ARE YOU AFRAID OF SOMEONE YOU LOVE? TALK TO YOUR HEALTH CARE PROVIDER. WE CAN HELP.

What sort of a place was this? No wonder my younger daughter had grown into such a serious woman. I had to remind myself that I was there *because* of Trudy's seriousness.

Sarah had been in a buoyant mood when she'd walked into the house that Monday morning. "I have something to show you," she said.

She'd pulled a camera out of her satchel and led me to the living room couch. She did not seem to notice that the slipcovers had returned from the cleaner in a startlingly different blue.

We bent together over the camera. "Look at this shade of gold. I've been saving this glass for years, for just the right project. I got it in France. I love the way it looks green, that perfect new-leaf green, when the light strikes from an angle." We were looking at her willow window, still in progress.

After a few images, Sarah turned to me. "What, Percy?"

"What?"

"That's what *I* said. What's making you antsy?"

"I'm antsy?" I told her this wasn't an easy way to look at pictures; whatever happened to snapshots?

"Adaptation, Percy."

We bantered a bit about my resistance to change, a subject with which we collided too often.

"Oh hell. Let's look at these later." Sarah turned the camera off and laid it on the coffee table (polished; denuded of books and papers).

An hour later, we lay in my bed. Down the hill, we could hear the start of first recess, the children's riotous voices as they rushed from the barn. I heard Ira shouting, "Yes! You! Now! Go!" A cannonade of happy, athletic exhortations.

"Sarah." My voice was rusty after the silence between us. "Your breast—"

She sat up quickly. She looked down at me. "Percy, I'm *all right*. I'm perfectly healthy. I know my own body, believe me."

"You do go for checkups, for . . . mammograms."

"Percy, you need to stop worrying. Really. You sound like an ad campaign." She told me to look after my health and she'd look after hers. She said this sweetly, but the sweetness took effort, I could tell. She pulled herself to the edge of the bed and began to dress. I watched with regret as her back, flushed in patches shaped vaguely like my hands, vanished under a T-shirt.

"Are you leaving?" I asked morosely.

"After you make me some lunch." She stood beside the bed, hands on her hips. "Or tell you what. I'm a big girl. I'll make it." Downstairs she went, just like that, subject changed. Over the continuing sounds of playground fervor, soon I heard the radio, then Sarah singing along, opening cupboards, placing a pan on the stove. She'd learned her way around: around my kitchen, around my orneriness; and now, around my intrusive concern.

Forty-five minutes had elapsed since my arrival when Chantal stood up behind her desk and signaled me. I followed her down three corridors, until she knocked on an unmarked door. In the interim, a buxom woman in a garishly flowered smock had come to the waiting area, introduced herself as Angel, and given me a take-out menu from which to order my lunch ("Our treat").

"Oh, Dad, I'm sorry."

Trudy came around from behind her desk and hugged me more warmly than she had in years. She wore the requisite doctor coat, her plastic identification card pinned to a pocket.

"It's bad enough that you have to chase me down at work. I'm sorry I got hung up."

Chantal, as she set our lunch-in-a-bag on Trudy's desk, snorted. "Like that is something she just never, ever does, our Dr. Barnes. Gets herself *hung up*." She and Trudy exchanged wry smiles before she left the office.

I sat in one of two chairs facing the desk. While waiting for my precious turn with this popular woman, my daughter, I'd conjured a range of smart-aleck greetings ("Pray what do you have against balloons?" "Beam me up, Trudy!" "Since when did pain become a little army of moons?"). But now I found myself wanting only to absorb the details of her inner sanctum: a place far more modest than I had imagined all these years. The one window was miserly, offering a sullen glimpse of windows no more generous or revealing than hers in another building across the street. Behind Trudy's back, medical journals and reference volumes filled several rows of cheap, laminated shelving. I saw only two photographs of family, one of a thinner, shaggier Robert accepting his high school diploma, the other of herself and Douglas, in formal attire, faces pressed together, blanched by the flashbulb.

On a bulletin board dominating another wall, dozens of other photographs—the Christmas cards and bar mitzvah announcements of people I'd never met—curled away from thumbtacks. And everywhere I looked—on notepads and pamphlets; on a T-shirted teddy bear slumped in a corner; even on Trudy's lapel, rendered in rhinestones—lurked that pink loop of ribbon, that mealy-minded equivalent of blurting out to a total stranger, *Gosh it's so awful you have cancer, but we can fight it together, yay!*

Yet amid such tacky surroundings, I was smacked by a wave of nostalgia when I saw all the framed certificates: my daughter's college and medical degrees, for which I had remortgaged the house, along with a series of honors I did not know about. Had there been a presentation of the Geraldine and James Quigley Chair in Medical Oncology? If so, had she simply not bothered to invite me? Had she assumed I wouldn't want to go?

"Dad? Did you hear me?"

I looked at Trudy. "I'm sorry, daughter. I'm just . . . taking it all in."

"Such as it is." She laughed. "I can tell you're appalled at the squalor. Now you know why doctors will sell their souls to attend pharmaceutical conferences in Maui and Scottsdale. Fresh air!" She opened the bag and handed me two paper napkins. She pulled out our sandwiches, peeling back the paper.

"Roast beef, Dad?" She shook her head in mock disapproval.

"Special occasion."

"Listen. I hate to do this to you, but we have about twenty minutes and then I really have to get back to seeing patients. I see patients only two and a half days a week now. It's absurd. Chantal stacks them up like planes at Logan."

She was wedging me in, no special treatment, yet I could not recall when I had last seen Trudy—the adult Trudy—so relaxed or bouyant. Was this airless labyrinth her oyster, the place she felt most at home?

Her intent regard was now entirely mine. *When you get her, honey, you have* got *her!* She sat still, her forearms pinning to her desk a scatter of manila folders. She'd unwrapped her sandwich, but it rested on the deli paper, untouched.

"You said you had something urgent to discuss."

"Yes!" I said. "Well."

She waited. Of course, she would be used to this: facing people who couldn't utter the most important questions of their lives. *How bad is it? Has it spread? Can you cure me? How long do I have, doc?* Though no one, I was certain, addressed this woman as "doc."

I'd never heard her discuss this part of her work—the people, rather than the science—and why would she have offered? I had no more insight into such drama than the average viewer of daytime TV.

"Is this about Clover, Dad?"

"No. It's . . ." A light blinked on her phone, but she ignored it. "Trudy, what are cystic breasts?"

I had assumed she might laugh, but she didn't—though her surprise registered in a passing grimace. "Fibrocystic breast condition, that's what I assume you're referring to."

"So people who have them—this condition—they should be seeing a doctor about it, regularly, for, in order to . . ."

Trudy interrupted my muddle. "This *is* about Clover, isn't it."

"No," I said. "It's about the woman I . . . this friend of mine. Her name is Sarah." I exhaled forcefully; when had I taken in so much air?

Trudy's reaction was startling. She blushed and smiled. She raised her hands in surrender. "Confession, Dad. I've heard about Sarah. Clover told me, in an e-mail last week. Dad, it's great. We've wanted this for ages. For you." She expected me to speak again, but I couldn't. She leaned across the desk. "Clover says you've been acting sort of sneaky, as if there's something wrong. Did you think we'd be angry? We couldn't be *less* angry."

Had I been engaged in a normal conversation with my daughter that happened to concern my so-called love life—if such a conversation could ever be regarded as normal—would I have succumbed with relief to her joy on my behalf, happily disclosing details about Sarah that emphasized her maturity rather than her youth, painting her as "suitable" despite the two decades between us in age, despite her having a child barely out of diapers? Would I have been reassuring Trudy that I never planned to marry again? Until a week before, *that* was the conversation I'd tried to imagine. And to think it had seemed so difficult, that one!

"Trudy," I said, "I'm here because you're a doctor. Or the doctor that you are. I'm—I can't stop worrying about her. About Sarah."

"Dad, I assume she has a doctor of her own. The condition you're talking about is normal. Though if her doctor wants her to see a specialist—"

"She won't talk about it. But I have the distinct impression she's . . . not paying proper attention to certain . . . well, specific issues that . . ." As I spluttered into silence, I saw Trudy look furtively at her computer screen, which was turned away from me. She frowned. When she looked at me again, her features remained tense. She did not, thank heaven, ask me what the hell I was talking about. She asked, "Are you telling me that she's ignoring a symptom her doctor thinks she should worry about?"

"I don't know."

"Dad, there's a reason *you're* the one sitting in that chair." Trudy drank from a cup of coffee that looked hours old, its surface murky. She put it down and pushed it away. "Okay, Dad. It feels bizarre to be telling *you* this, but in a nutshell, most lumps turn out to be nothing of concern. Most biopsies, by far, yield a benign result. But all the same." She opened a drawer and pulled out a business card. She wrote on the back of the card. "I'm guessing she needs to see a surgeon. Have her call Chantal's direct line—here it is—and say that she's your friend. She has to use your name. Chantal can get her to the head of the list with one of the surgeons whose names I've written there. They're both excellent. Her doctor can take care of the referral."

"Surgeons?"

"That's the place to start," said Trudy. "They look at the films. She has mammograms, right? Don't look so alarmed, Dad. It doesn't mean anyone's going to pull out a scalpel."

I took the card. "I've invited Sarah and her boy for Thanksgiving. I was wondering, if the occasion . . . hoping you could . . . maybe . . ." Once again I plowed into a syntactical snowbank.

"Take her upstairs and ask her to disrobe?" Trudy took a large bite of her sandwich, chewed, and swallowed. "Dad, I'm really excited to meet her, I'm glad you're including her, but there's nothing I can do for her as a physician if she's in denial. Do you know any of her female friends?"

Someone knocked on the door. Trudy walked around me to answer it. She stepped out and closed the door behind her. I examined the card I held, the freight train of initials following my daughter's name. What were all these credentials? Did the average patient understand what they meant?

Like an obedient child, I stayed in my assigned seat, snooping with my eyes alone. Flattened against the back of the desk chair lay a girlish cardigan: fine wool in a yellow as timid as Trudy was not, to be fastened with a row of buttons resembling pearls. On a shelf behind the chair stood a photograph I hadn't seen while Trudy was seated: Poppy and me, in our late twenties, parents already but out on our own, dressed up for some festive occasion. I wore a white shirt and a large, almost clownish orange bow tie—an early present from Poppy. (Where was that tie?) She wore a scanty summer dress of which the picture showed only the shoulder straps, white with blue daisies.

I couldn't help myself: I stood up and walked around the desk to hold the picture in my hands. Did I have a copy of this image, in an album somewhere?

Norval and Helena's wedding. That was the occasion. Helena's parents' lawn in Ipswich, its view of tawny, luxuriant marshes receding toward the ocean. The mosquitoes had been frightful that evening. One had to stay in motion, on the dance floor, to escape them. Luckily, the band had been good and lively. Poppy had removed her shoes and misplaced them. At the end of the party, I carried her down the road to our car. Before we'd fallen into bed that night, tipsy, footsore, I'd rubbed calamine lotion across her back. The sheets were pink as bubble gum when we awoke.

The events of that day and night opened before me as if I were flipping through a favorite childhood book. Helena's wedding dress had been red, its color verging on scandal among guests from our parents' generation. Norval told me later that she'd believed she was pregnant that day, had hoped it. They never did have children, and I realized, as I looked at the picture of Poppy and me in Trudy's office, that I did not know precisely why. And should I have known? Should I have, at some point, asked them? Poppy would have known, and told me quite plainly, long ago.

"Dad?"

I faced Trudy. "Red-handed."

"No. I'm the culprit here. I've always loved that picture of you and Mom. I stole it from your study years ago. I decided that if you mentioned its absence, I'd put it back. Please take it home."

I handed the picture to Trudy. "It's yours, daughter. You keep it."

"I have to kick you out now. I'm sorry. I didn't get a chance to ask you about Robert. Do you hear from him? I feel as if he's disappeared this year."

"The lad is buried under books, as well he should be. Or so I gather from his latest e-mail."

"He tells you more than he tells me." Trudy paused. "Did you know he's broken up with Clara?"

"The girlfriend?"

"She called me last week. She's very upset. With him and about him." Trudy sighed. "It gets so complicated, when you like them."

"Whom?"

"Your child's . . . special friends. That's *whom*."

"I never faced such a dilemma with you or Clover," I said. "With Clover, the 'whom' changed a bit too often, and you—you snatched up the highly eligible Douglas on your first go-round."

"Dad, 'snatch' is not the most flattering word; and a college grad with a psych degree isn't exactly what I'd call 'highly eligible.' You might say I just followed in your footsteps, yours and Mom's." She still held the photograph from Norval's wedding. She looked at it, pointedly, and polished the glass on the inside of her white coat, then set it back on the shelf.

"One might say so, yes," I conceded. I did not see Trudy and Douglas as possessing the passion I'd shared with Poppy—but then, how could I? What did I know about their life when they were alone? Perhaps they stripped naked in their tasteful dove-gray living room, late at night with the curtains closed, and tangoed for hours, roses clenched between their teeth.

"Good-bye, Dad. I'll see you next week. I can't wait to meet Sarah." Trudy hugged me again, but she had changed back to the Trudy I knew: each gesture a preface to the next, her life a perpetual progress, a sailboat before a steady wind.

Ten minutes later, after retracing my journey through the hospital maze and stepping back onto the street (Trudy's voice, in my head, exclaiming "Fresh air!"), I realized that I had left my umbrella back in her waiting room—and, as I thrust my hands into my raincoat pockets, that I had neglected to give her the birthday present I'd picked out at Sarah's loft: a pendant made from a nugget of ruby-colored glass.

It was raining the next day, too—another day on which I'd chosen to venture into town. I parked my car in the Charles Hotel garage and walked across the Square toward the Yard. Mercifully, the rain let up just then, so I took the longer route through the phalanx of brick buildings, stopping briefly to regard and contemplate the only place of employment I had ever really known.

But for a drowning, this entire institution would not exist: a macabre fact that did not occur to me, or did not seize my full attention, until I returned to work following Poppy's death. For sixteen years of ascending and descending those thirty granite steps, I had felt an invigorating awe at the scale of the place, underscored by the justifiable grandiosity of the letters engraved across its masculine façade. I enjoyed a commensurate pride (though I knew it to be silly) that my job within the walls of this monument helped give it a living purpose. Yet the very public tragedy without which it would never have been endowed or built was something I had acknowledged only in a distant, muted way.

Credit Mrs. Widener with an aversion to melodrama. Another grieving mother might well have chosen to dramatize her son's untimely death with murals of violent despair (how easily one could picture a scene à la *Raft of the Medusa*) or lengthy narratives describing the ordeal and fate of Harry, his father, and their fellow unfortunates. But Mrs. Widener was not tempted by such bathos. What she wished to commemorate was her son's life—brief but precociously dedicated to a connoisseur's love of books. Enter the undistinguished vestibule of the library and you must deliberately face left to see the plain marble tablet informing you that Harry Elkins Widener, class of '07, "died at sea" after the "foundering of the steamship *Titanic*." (I had always regarded *foundering* as a meticulously chosen word, restrained yet potent.)

The day I returned to work after Poppy's death, I had walked directly to the Memorial Rooms, in part to put off my reunion with colleagues—who must have been equally apprehensive, sitting in their cubicles behind what we called the porthole (the window in the padded leather door that divided our offices from the reference room). Standing before Harry's Gutenberg—and, behind it, the ropes demurely forbidding entry—I surveyed with new eyes the small salon bordered by the cases containing his books. There was the same portrait of a pale, waxen-looking Harry, over the hearth laid for a birch fire that no one ever lit, and the same empty desk with a vase of live carnations whose scent few visitors could ever approach to enjoy.

This was back when the room still looked into the ashen depths of twin air shafts. To view the flowering trees that surrounded Widener, one had to visit an exterior space. (My own cubicle, for my last twenty years, was situated with such a vista.) Harry's room was, in every sense but the literal, a tomb.

From then on, I made a point of visiting Harry when I arrived at work. I didn't believe in heaven, of course, yet I wanted to believe that Harry and Poppy were somehow together, belonging to the same nether region of memory—a limbo exclusive to the drowned—just as dictionaries of Latin and Japanese will share the same shelves of any library in the world. This superstitious logic was a source of consolation for which I forgave my most primitive self.

Sarah would meet me there in an hour. I had decided to give myself the extra time to visit my old coworkers—or the two with whom I remained loosely in touch—on my own. I was not quite ready to introduce her to everyone in my life—and now, when I thought of Trudy's casual question (did I know any of Sarah's "female friends"?), I realized that she must feel equally cautious. I resisted the notion that she was in any way ashamed of me.

I'd asked Sarah if she might like a modest tour of Widener, after which we could share dinner out at a restaurant. She had been delighted. She told me she'd passed through the Yard countless times—as tourists and casual voyeurs were still, surprisingly, free to do in this newly paranoid age—yet never had she passed through the library's doors.

I spent a pleasant hour visiting with Suzannah and Earl. Crowded into Suzannah's cubicle, we drank tea, and I listened to the latest rounds of gossip. The new occupant of my former cubicle was away, and I tried hard not to linger too long at its entrance. At four-thirty, I said my goodbyes and told them to come out to Matlock anytime. They were unlikely to take me up on that invitation, yet I knew that they liked me still and were glad to have seen me. Following Norval's departure from Widener, I had never formed another true friendship at work.

So I was in a rare, nostalgic frame of mind when I greeted Sarah back on the front steps and pulled her in out of the cold. I kissed her quickly beside the marble tablet mentioning Harry's death at sea. For the second time, I swiped my library card and greeted the security attendant, a woman who'd started there just before my retirement.

We made our way up the central stairs, letting the architecture lead us deliberately to the Memorial Rooms. I described to Sarah how, during the renovations just a few years before, when the air shafts were transformed into reading rooms, I and my colleagues had worked in the rotunda, a false wood floor mounted over the marble tiles, our computer connections snaking beneath; how, as drills and power saws and nail guns had fired all around us, we had maintained our concentration, marveling that none of the marble acanthus and oak leaves high above had cracked off and fallen on our eggish heads.

Sarah looked at me fondly. "What a rarefied life. Lofty, even."

"Sometimes I felt like little more than a highly educated errand boy," I said. Though there had been times when I felt like an ace detective, too. At the end of my tenure, I had been the reference liaison to the literature and language departments. The library's bibliographers (Ph.D.'s all) had once looked down on my tribe as a menial lot, but the Internet changed all that. We became, like it or not, the "vanguard" when it came to showing Harvard's professor class how to navigate, how to stay afloat on, the Nile of information that flowed to the library from uncharted domains far beyond the continent comprising our stacks. I was hardly the best at this navigation—I leaned heavily (and somewhat furtively) on a series of work-study students assigned to me over my final years— but navigate I did. Each day when I returned to Matlock, I sank gratefully into a life rooted in the past. The only electrical gadget I relied upon daily at home was my toaster.

I told all this to Sarah as we perused the glass cases showing Harry's days as a thespian, his secret code for recording transactions on books, and the building of the library itself.

"My God," she said, "I knew I'd fallen for a weenie, but a Luddite?"

"Not quite. For which you may thank my grandson Robert." I'd half hoped we might run into him. In the two years during which we'd overlapped, he had favored studying here, rather than in Lamont, where most undergraduates gathered. I loved it when I wandered out into Loker, the main reading room, and found him in one of the chairs near the dictionaries of proverbs and aphorisms.

So I looked for him that day, too, but no luck. From there, I took Sarah to the reference room. I indicated the porthole, the door behind which I'd worked. She peered through it, but she did not ask to enter.

Throughout our meanderings, Sarah looked up constantly, remarking in a fervent whisper on the ornate, pastel-colored ceilings, so far overhead that people who spent days or weeks in these rooms might never notice them at all.

When we left the library to head to the restaurant, Sarah took my arm and thanked me. "Extraordinary," she said. "I have just one critique of that place."

"Which is?"

"Needs stained glass. Like, *lots* of stained glass."

We were frivolously happy through cocktails and a shared bowl of soup. And then it came up on its own, because Sarah mentioned that her cousin (would I ever meet this cousin?) had just come through a series of tests with good news: he did not have prostate cancer.

Perhaps she realized, too late, where she had led us.

"And you," I said before she could change the subject. "You've been checked out as well in recent months?"

"Last time I looked, Percy, I was not in possession of a prostate gland."

"Count me grateful for that," I said. "But I'm serious, and you're being cagey. What I am asking for is the assurance—from a bona fide physician, not your feminine intuition—that you are healthy. Now that you're on my list of people to worry about."

"Assurances are tricky things."

"Sarah." I put down my knife and fork. "Sarah, please. Make this easier for a man who was born in the era of the whalebone corset."

Her expression cooled. "Percy, I've always been healthy. I feel healthy. I think people obsess too much about the slightest symptoms."

"I'm not going to argue. Just tell me when you last went to the doctor and I'll leave you alone."

Sarah also set down her utensils. She sat back against the velvet upholstery of our booth and crossed her arms defiantly. She told me, clearly agitated by my persistence, that while Rico was insured through an assistance program, her own insurance had lapsed. It was from a job she'd held a few years back. "I cut no corners with Rico," she said. "And that's what counts. Okay?"

I sat back as well. "Sarah, that is not 'okay.' Not with me. Nor would it be with Rico, if he could understand such matters. You are his *one parent.*"

"You mean, I'm all that stands between him and an orphanage, is that it? I suppose you think that having been widowed gives you some authority on being a single parent, right?" Sarah wore contempt on her face with frightening conviction. But then she closed her eyes for a moment and sighed. When she opened them, she said, in a low, careful voice, "Percy, we are not married. You know how I feel about you, but you don't need to give me a roof or a bank account or a—"

"Sarah." I reached across the table for one of her hands, but she withheld them both. "Sarah, what do you mean, your insurance has 'lapsed'? You need to look into that. Meanwhile, I want to give you a checkup at my doctor. May I do that? *Just* that?"

She looked angrier, at me, than I had ever seen her. "And what if I told you to mind your own business?"

"Then I would have no choice." I astonished myself by adding, "And then my heart would break."

Her expression softened, and she leaned forward. I was relieved until she said, "Percy, is this about your wife? About Poppy? Because you couldn't save her, you want to save everyone else you possibly can? You're terrified that at any hint of mortality for someone you love, it's your job to be the crusader?"

"That is a cruel thing to say. Cruel and presumptuous."

"Well, then I apologize. But let's look at *your* presumptions, Percy."

"I presume nothing. That is why I am trying to make you see reason."

The waiter hovered, covetous of our plates. I waved him away. I said, "If you care about Rico, you'll do this for me."

She looked offended, but I had cornered her.

"Percy, not many people could speak to me like that."

"And how about me? Am I one of those not-many people?"

"Yes, you are," she said quickly. "We will talk about this in the car. I want dessert, and I don't want it soured by talk like this."

"Very well."

Later, as I drove her home, she said she would consider my request. I called Dr. Fields and made an appointment for myself, on a pretext. I was not going to lose this battle. Perhaps Sarah was right. Perhaps it was Poppy I was trying to save. But what harm could I do by simply being careful?

9

~

As Ira hustled the last child into coat, boots, and backpack, he saw Clover hovering, waiting, holding a long paper cone. "Scoot, girl!" he said to Marguerite, aiming her like a padded missile down the hall toward Heidi, who'd redirect her out the door, across the yard, and into her mother's car.

He beckoned to Clover, who followed him into his classroom. She spoke in effusive bursts, as if winded. "Thank. You. From the bottom. Of. My. Heart." She handed him the flowers.

"Don't thank me. Thank Anthony." Ira unwrapped the bouquet—tiger lilies—and told her she shouldn't have. But he did not gush. He looked around until he spotted the one clunker of a vase they kept in the classroom.

After putting the flowers in water, he began the afternoon cleanup, mixing bleach solution to wipe down the tables, retrieving a putty knife he used to pry away globs of tempera and glue. Clover offered to help, but Ira told her he had his routine and would only be confused.

Clover sat on the reading couch by the window. "I'm sure I couldn't afford him," she said, "and he didn't give me any kind of slam-dunk scenario—I'm not stupid, I know this won't be easy—but he did say some hopeful things about my situation. If I could be more flexible."

"Hopeful is good. Flexible's good, too." *So is realistic,* put in Ira's unkind alter ego.

He scrubbed at a fuchsia stain where Lily had been painting. Lily refused to wear or make art with anything but pink.

Since Clover had confided every gory detail about her split-up, Ira had developed the sickening sense that to encourage further intimacy would be to put himself in the path of a potentially mammoth breakdown. Back in college, he'd had a couple of female friends who were smart and fun but equally needy—like his friend Sadie, who thought that just because he was gay, he was also a port in the dating typhoon. After graduating, they'd taken a summer share together in Hampton Bays—a perfect arrangement until the weekend she'd swallowed two bottles of pills (one of them his!).

He knew now that he would rather be holed up alone with a dozen uncontrollably sobbing three-year-olds than sit beside the hospital bed of a woman who'd nearly thrown her life away over a married cad and saw Ira as her "last true friend in the world." He still felt guilty about losing touch with her. He had never deleted Sadie's last e-mail—awkwardly cheerful, the tone of their entire correspondence after she left town—and sometimes, late at night, he wondered if he should cast a line her way. But he never did, reasoning (feebly) that no doubt her address had changed several times since then and his words would scatter in the ether of undeliverable bytes.

"The thing that upsets me so much," Clover was saying, "is how soon he's planning to marry this woman. You'd think, especially if he sees himself as having married a screw-up the first time around"—she laughed bitterly—"well, you'd think he'd be extremely cautious."

Ira put the bleach and the spritz bottle back on their high shelf. He looked at Clover briefly. "People are inexplicable, aren't they?" he said before going to the closet to get out the broom. *Love is irrational,* he might have said, but this would have been hurtful—and, in this case, probably not even true. You didn't have to be a genius to know why the man might want to remarry quickly. He probably wanted someone to take on full-time sharing of his kids' lives, all those responsibilites and chores, as soon as possible. And there was always a good chance that the second wife wanted to have a child or two of her own.

"I should have brought the kids with me," said Clover.

"No. They were old enough to be rooted where they are. You did the better, less selfish thing by leaving them with their dad."

How sincere was this consolation? The story he'd heard from Clover was surely skewed in her favor, no matter how self-deprecating she was; and that story gave him no reason to think her husband and the new wife *shouldn't* be raising those kids. What would he think if he heard the ex's version?

Ira tried to imagine returning to his own parents if his life were to crash and burn. What if, six months before, he'd simply lost his job at

The Very Beginning, without the safety net of Elves & Fairies, and had fallen into a deep depression, leading Anthony to dump him? What then?

He pictured himself arriving, suitcase in hand, on the doorstep of his parents' Tudor house in Forest Hills, retrieving the key from under the stone hedgehog that lurked beneath a bush of bleeding-hearts.

Ira's father and mother did everything in tandem: ran his father's chiropractic office, took out garbage, cooked dinners, had sent Ira and his sisters off to school every morning—a clockwork pas de deux. The harmony of it—the perfect "dividing and sharing," as they called it—would have been caviar for some women's magazine if his parents had wanted to be famous for those fifteen minutes, but nothing could be further from their humble intentions.

So say Ira had shown up, unannounced, sometime before 5:22, the usual time his mom arrived home from the office. She'd come in the door and maybe, despite the empty nest, a matter of habit, call out, "Anybody home?" He'd startle her by calling out that yes, here he was—"Just me!"—exactly as he'd replied in the old days. (Ruthie and Joanna, his sisters, were the sporty ones, so Ira had often been the only one home when his mother arrived.)

"Darling, do you want a little nosh?"

"Thanks, Mom!"

She'd fill the dishes in the lazy Susan on the kitchen table: cottage cheese sprinkled with Lawry's salt, Wheat Thins, black olives from a can, cherry tomatoes. While he ate and answered questions about his day, she'd do the "prep work" for dinner, finishing almost precisely as his dad walked in the door at 6:30. She would hand Ira's dad his sole drink of the day (a vodka collins), and when he said, "Son! What brings you home?"—with genuine pleasure—Ira would tell them everything: how he'd lost his job, how his boyfriend thought he was a coward and a loser, how he had no choice but to move out, how he had almost no savings and wasn't sure he still wanted to teach. . . .

But where had this morbid fantasy come from? He didn't have to go home. He didn't have to watch his parents remind themselves (through glances they'd exchange, thinking he didn't notice) that they were liberal-minded, modern-day folks and felt not a mote of shame or disappointment that their only son was gay, and thank heaven he didn't have

AIDS! He was in a stable relationship with the kind of man they'd have killed to see one of Ira's sisters marry. (Ruthie had married a dentist—not bad—while Joanna had become a financial analyst but couldn't hang on to a guy for longer than a couple of months.)

Now Clover was saying, "Do you think I should just go ahead and ask Filo and Lee what *they* think about everything? And about this . . . stepmother? Risk hearing the worst so we can just go forward, so I can ask their forgiveness if I have to?"

Ira leaned the broom against a bookshelf. He sat next to Clover on the reading couch. "I don't know," he said. "That sounds pretty scary."

"You're right. I'd be terrified."

Ira put a hand on her knee and sighed. He'd meant that it would be pretty scary to her children, but all he said was "I know."

Saturdays, they worked out together at the fancy gym Anthony paid for. Or Ira swam while Anthony did his weights, and they joined up in the sauna. Usually, they sat side by side on the bench, sweating in silence. Ira loved this silence, especially when they had the sauna to themselves. They hardly touched, yet it felt wonderfully intimate. He imagined the week's anxieties seeping from their pores, soaked away by the club's enormous plush blue towels.

But that day, Anthony spoke. "Your pal Clover."

"Mm."

"So I saw her."

"I know. She's incredibly grateful."

"That's what I was afraid of."

"Afraid of?"

"Ira, she's living in a dream. Is anyone treating this woman like a grown-up? Telling her what's what?"

Leave it to Anthony to ask the glaringly obvious question.

"You know, it's not like she's my best friend. And she has a therapist."

Anthony laughed. "A therapist. Well. Therapists come in many flavors."

Ira made a noise of amusement. He thought, No talk, please.

Anthony, no mind reader, continued, "Though it's water way the hell under the bridge, I wanted to ask her why she hadn't tried to reconcile.

And I had to wonder why nobody else had pushed her in that direction. Or maybe they did. But the story she told—God, it involved one of those horrible conversations you have with a mate that linger between you like a cloud of poisonous gas. The kind you'd pay a fortune to take back. The kind that sits in a closet like a time bomb, just waiting to blow you up."

Ira looked sideways at Anthony. Was he alluding to something about them? As Ira did too often, never voluntarily, he remembered the night he'd told Anthony about being fired; the night Anthony had called him spineless—and he, rather than turn the other cheek, had called his partner heartless.

Was that one of those "horrible conversations"?

"There are cases," said Anthony, "where against the odds, some clever attorney convinces a judge that a mother's place as the chief source of nurture is essential, that so long as she has a stable home and a means of support, she deserves primary custody. But the kids are usually little, and"—he laughed—"the judge is almost always a much older man, like the kind who got out of law school before the Beav was a glimmer in June Cleaver's eye."

Ira echoed Anthony's laugh.

Anthony punched him playfully. "Hey. This is your friend."

"She's been extremely nice to me, but I hardly know her. For God's sake, Anthony, I've been at that place less than three months." Ira stood and secured his towel. "Let's go to a museum. Want to have lunch in Cambridge? Let's walk around and ogle the baby best-and-brightests, then grab a little culture."

In the shower, he found himself thinking of Sadie for the second time in two days. Had his conscience hardened—or was it softening again? He realized that the children now in his care concerned him less, when they weren't with him, than the kids he'd looked after in Lothian. His class was smaller, yes, but the main difference was that he had far fewer worries about these children. Marguerite was a little pushy, Rico tended to brood, and Lucian had been sent home with lice. And thanks to Lily, they used up twice as many art supplies in every shade of pink.

So had part of his brain opened up, posted a vacancy, into which a new batch of tenants (questions about friendships, old and new; questions about himself and Anthony) had moved?

Ira felt as if he'd contracted an all-over emotional itch, as if he'd put on a sweater made of spiritually abrasive wool—but to take it off would leave him dreadfully cold.

"This is definitely not fun," he muttered as he took the shortcut through the local playground that Sunday, hunching into his collar as he passed the swings. If his arms hadn't ached from the weight of the groceries, Ira would have skirted the park. He should have taken the car—but who knew there'd be a sale on OJ *and* the canned nuts Anthony loved so much?

How much nicer Lothian had seemed—and, face it, how much cooler Ira had felt—when he had walked to work at The Very Beginning, proud to be a full-time member of a community both real and colorful, struggling but on the rise. Once, he'd even had wispy notions of running for the local school board. He'd loved strolling the residential streets lined with working-class houses, plain clapboard or aluminum siding, painted white or gray or yellow. A few had been embellished with sun porches or ready-made arbors from Home Depot.

But there were still areas of town where a single culture asserted itself, where Ukrainians, Brazilians, or Italians held fast against the yuppie tide. In the four square blocks of Lothian called Little Palermo, the postage-stamp yards filled with grapevines each summer. In cast-off bathtubs, fruit trees blossomed as willingly as they would have done on a terraced Sicilian hillside. And from house to house, laundry lines criss-crossed these tiny vineyards and orchards, bedsheets snapping and luffing like sunlit sails. At Christmas, this was the neighborhood decked most sumptuously in blinking lights, inflatable Santas, and glowing Wise Men with extension cords trailing from the hems of their plastic raiments. "Ethnic snow globes," Anthony called such pockets of charm.

But now, if Ira did venture out for a long walk or the occasional run, he shunned these folksy streets. Of the families he'd known through work, he still remembered which ones lived where, and he did not relish the idea of running into the parents (who *knew* what tale they'd been told about his departure?) or even the innocent children he'd taught (who would make him sad whether or not they recognized him on the street). Though he was ashamed of it, more than once Ira had turned away from walking into a store, or had crossed a street, when he'd seen such a run-in about to occur. (I'm sparing them too, he reasoned.)

Anthony had scolded him last month when he'd hesitated at the suggestion of going to Courgette, the one upscale bistro within walking distance of their apartment. Ira had tried to pretend he wasn't in the mood for French, but Anthony had seen through him in a flash.

"You are worried about meeting up with that perv dad, I know it," said Anthony. "But me, I'm just raring to confront the bastard. Bring him on."

"Oh really? And what would you say?"

"It would come to me," Anthony said. "I work best off the cuff. That's how I win my cases, darling. I'm a pro at handling hypocrites. Rich ones? Fish in a California Chardonnay barrel."

So they had gone, and of course they'd seen no one familiar at all. Yet every time the door to the restaurant had opened to admit someone new, Ira's pulse had soared.

So here he was, passing a simple playground as if he were a fugitive, keeping his eyes on the asphalt path, moving as fast as the overloaded canvas bags allowed, when he did, after all, run smack into someone he knew—though not from The Very Beginning.

The shoes—severely worn work boots—had halted, facing him. Quickly, Ira looked up at the face that went with the shoes.

"Oh! Goodness. Hi!" he exclaimed. He set down the groceries. To his embarrassment, he was panting, even perspiring.

"Hello. You need help?" Celestino smiled. He held out a hand.

"What are you doing here?" said Ira, then realized how rude this sounded. "I mean, this isn't—do you live around here?"

"I am walking home from Mass."

"Goodness, are we neighbors?"

"I live several blocks that way." Celestino pointed in the direction of the grocery store, the less gentrified side of the park. "You could use help with those," he offered again.

Ira sighed. "Shows, huh? I am so totally out of shape these days."

Celestino picked up the groceries.

"Oh no." Ira took back one of the bags. "And I'll only let you help if you have a bite with us. Really. At least a cup of coffee." He'd done it before catching himself. Acted as if the world were this friendly, open-arms, homo-accepting place, the place he had naïvely believed it to be in the not-so-distant past.

Celestino seemed unsure, and for a moment Ira hoped he would refuse—but how could he? And Ira wondered how much of his eager invitation had sprung from the same place those dreams did: twice, he'd had a dream in which he was alone with Celestino in the tree house, alone and naked. The only impediment to their wild-horse passion (which was mutual—oh the wishes of dreams!) had been the presence of the Birches and Cattails milling about below, waiting to come up the ladder.

"Coffee, yes, thank you," said Celestino.

Awkwardly, Ira stepped ahead, leading the way. For the next two blocks, they walked in silence, single file.

Please let Anthony be dressed, thought Ira. He might have phoned ahead, but he hadn't felt like stopping again. As a compromise, he rang the bell. He waved at the video cam. "I've picked up a guest!"

Anthony had showered and dressed. Sections of the Sunday *Times* lay scattered across the kitchen counter, the *Boston Globe* untouched.

"Do you remember my mentioning this incredibly strong—talented guy who helped build the tree house? Turns out he's our neighbor!" Ira explained.

Anthony shook Celestino's hand. "Pleasure."

As Ira hung Celestino's coat in the closet, he noticed that the lining was torn in several places. He had a strange, squeamish sensation as he heard Anthony offer this man a cappuccino and then, as he probed the groceries, ask Ira, "Did you get Scotch or Novy? Oh look—nuts to last me all winter long! No foraging in the bushes this year!"

Celestino stood by the counter drinking from his tiny cup with care.

"Please say you'll stay for a bagel," said Ira.

Celestino smiled that smile again: was it shy, or simply aloof, maybe even contemptuous? "If you have enough, thank you."

Ira set the table for three while Anthony cut bagels in half and asked Celestino to tell him about the tree house.

"You've seen photos," said Ira. "For heaven's sake, it has to be the most photographed tree house on the planet."

Anthony shot him a furtive, halting look. Oh—the opening to small talk. The setting your guest at ease with the topic you hold in common. By example, Anthony was constantly reminding Ira about the art of conversing with *adults*. Adults who didn't spend the majority of their time with four-year-olds.

"Juice?" Ira reached for the cupboard that held the glasses. He could have offered a mimosa, but this seemed too much somehow. *What,* chided Inner Ira, *you don't offer champagne to a guy who works as an itinerant gardener? What does that say about you, sweetheart?*

But who said the guy was itinerant? He'd been working next door to Elves & Fairies as long as Ira had been around. Maybe *Ira* would become the itinerant worker, moving from job to job.

To make a place for the glasses on the counter, Ira moved the *Globe.* The front page showcased a color photo of a huge suburban house. Another story on the real estate market? He looked closer. The photograph had been taken from an aerial perspective. Across the vast lawn stretched an equally vast shape—a footprint. The footprint . . . sparkled. Ira picked up the paper and held it toward the light. He read the caption. The footprint had been constructed with hundreds upon hundreds of glass bottles. *Prankster DOGS return to Ledgely,* read the caption, directing readers to a story deep inside the paper.

"How do they know it's not art?" he mused aloud.

Anthony and Celestino, whose conversation had not taken fire, turned to Ira. He held up the paper.

"Those people are getting tedious," Anthony said.

"No lack of imagination, though. In fact," said Ira, "they'd make great preschool teachers. I mean, wow, this took a lot of focus and creativity."

"Which is leading to the waste of more investigative man-hours than you will ever know. A K A, our tax dollars. This is actually no laughing matter."

"At least they haven't hit Lothian."

"Lothian, my dear, is not the home of people like that guy"—he pointed at the paper—"who happens to be the CEO of the biggest beer distillery in New England."

Ira glanced at Celestino. He was watching them. He had finished his cappuccino. When their eyes met, Ira looked away and blushed.

"Sit. Sit!" he said, carrying the basket of bagels to the table.

Once they were seated, Anthony began to pass the various plates: bagels, salmon, sliced pineapple, tomato, cheeses. "So from what I hear," he said, "you get to see all the best gardens of Matlock."

Ira couldn't have thought of a more tactful way to ask about

Celestino's work. Sometimes Anthony really did trump him in manners as well as intellect.

"Yes." Celestino looked as if he wanted to say more, but he didn't.

"You work for that guy with the red trucks all over town?" asked Ira.

"Thomas Loud."

"I hear he has quite the monopoly."

Celestino was eating. He did not nod or indicate that he agreed with this. When he'd finished chewing, he said, "He works hard. He makes us work hard, too. With some men like him, there is work in only the warm seasons. He keeps a lot of workers all year round."

"So it's a trade-off," said Ira. "Work all year but work your butts off."

For the first time, Celestino laughed. "You have it."

Ira began to understand that Celestino might not be legal. There had been two families at The Very Beginning whose immigration status was, as Betty had put it, "in the gray area." She'd been apprehensive when the annual inspections took place, the checking of children's birth certificates and medical records.

Did Celestino have to worry whether any new people he met might denounce him in some fashion?

Now he was talking about the possibility of studying to be an arborist.

Anthony was the one who asked him questions: polite, never prying. It struck Ira, watching Celestino relax, just a little, that for all the things he shared with Anthony, he was unlikely ever to watch his lover do what he did best: make a case in court. For a brief time, Ira had been addicted to that Boston-based TV show *The Practice*. He loved the opening and closing arguments in court. Anthony (often prowling through the apartment as he worked on legal challenges all his own) would pass through the living room and snort at whatever scene was unfolding. "Ain't fiction grand," he might say, or, addressing the lead actor, "Dylan McDorable, exonerate that dude!"

Celestino left within the hour, thanking them warmly. Ira protested that it was his place to say thank you; he'd have had a premature heart attack carrying those groceries if Celestino hadn't happened along.

As soon as Ira heard the downstairs door close, he said to Anthony, "You're a million times better at talking to people than I am."

"What do you mean?"

"I have all these hang-ups about people, ideas based on who I expect them to be."

"We all do, darling. I just deal with more strangers than you do. More surprises, many of them rude. You work in a family, a family that's meant to be nice and cozy. I work in a social wasteland, an emotional war zone."

That they did such different work was sometimes a blessing, sometimes a source of friction. Ira worried when they talked too much about their jobs.

Their friends Mark and Charles, mavericks who'd been determined to have children since their twenties (and had managed to make it happen with some costly, byzantine arrangement involving sperm shipped on dry ice, donor eggs, a surrogate mom, and legal papers up the wazoo), had told them that one of the best things about raising a family was how it took your focus off work.

"I don't care how much you love your jobs, I don't care if you're the Dalai Lama *and* the head of the UN," Mark had said. "It's going to get stale, trading tales from the workplace."

"Even diaper talk gets your mind off how much you'd love to poison that secretary who spends half the morning admiring her tacky nails," said Charles, a partner at Anthony's firm.

"To a *point,*" added Mark. "Charles, in case you didn't notice, people are *eating* here." Everyone laughed.

The classroom auction project was so quintessentially Matlock that Ira could hardly keep a straight face when Tristan's mother, the self-appointed Class Parent, explained it to him.

There remained in Matlock one working dairy farm—or, more accurately, a dormant dairy farm had been revived by a couple who made their fortune young, the husband having designed a suite of video games combining medieval warfare with intergalactic travel. He was now retired from the virtual mass-murder business and, with his wife, had rebuilt the derelict house and barn, sent himself to "farm school" in Vermont, and purchased a small herd of picture-perfect, Ben & Jerry's–style Holsteins. They sold their premium products at a handful of boutique grocers, but their true claim to fame was their clandestine supply of raw milk, available to a select group of Matlock families sworn to secrecy (or relative discretion) in exchange for the assurance that their children would have the very best, bacterially robust immune systems imaginable.

There was a waiting list for this coterie, but Kendra's mother had nobly donated her membership to E & F's fund-raising efforts, sending herself back to the bottom of the list. She had procured from Farmer Xbox ten empty glass milk bottles, onto which she and two other crafty moms would decoupage self-portraits painted by the children. These bottles would be placed in a wooden carrying crate to be fashioned by Kendra's dad, a weekend woodworker. This creation, along with the coveted dairy co-op membership, was expected to fetch a price higher even than the quartet of season tickets at Fenway or, possibly, the Fourth of July weekend at a seaside house-for-eight in Chilmark.

The mom committee had just left Ira's classroom after delivering this wonderful news. And in fact, if all the children had to do was create oblong self-portraits suited to fit on an old-fashioned milk bottle (though associations with the milk-carton portraits of the missing gave him a momentary chill), Ira was getting off lucky. Joyce, who taught the Oak Leaves, had been roped into helping make a quilt. Each child's square would be rendered in ikat, a technique that one of the Oak Leaf dads would be teaching the kids. It sounded complex and messy to Ira, who preferred simple art projects like hunting down autumn leaves and collaging them between waxed paper.

These were the projects he had stayed late to trim and pin on the wall that afternoon, following the auction project meeting. After he'd finished, he wandered outside to one of those flawless autumn afternoons when a low sun casts prismatic rays through naked trees. He walked down to the pond and sat on a log that functioned as a rustic bench. As he sat there, he heard noises in the undercarriage of the barn, the floor beneath the nursery school that still served as storage, which Percy Darling now shared with E & F.

He turned to see Arturo, Robert's friend, emerging. They were mutually startled.

"*Hola!*" exclaimed Turo. "You're a stealthy one."

"Look who's talking," said Ira.

"Stowing the canoe. End of the boating season."

Ira expected Robert to emerge from the storage space as well, but he didn't.

After a gaping silence, Ira said, "So how's life at Center of the Cosmos U?"

Turo laughed politely. He sat down beside Ira. "The intellectual navel of the world. I sometimes forget to sit back in awe of myself."

"Well, that's a relief."

"And you, how are you faring with your little ones?"

Ira wondered at the boy's formal diction, but he supposed it was a subtle reminder that however fluent he was, English wasn't his first language.

"When I sit here," said Ira, "I think I've arrived prematurely, and undeservedly, in heaven." *Only not so secure,* sniped Inner Ira. *Hardly.*

"A complex heaven, this place," said Turo.

"All lasting pleasures are complex, wouldn't you say?"

This amused Turo. "No, I wouldn't say that, but I'm no philosopher. And what do I know at my age, right?"

Ira felt his butt growing cold on the log. He stood. "Probably more than you realize," he said. "But humility is always the wiser approach." He looked at his watch, though he had nowhere pressing to go. Anthony wouldn't be home for hours. Maybe he'd go the gym, pick up ingredients for crab cakes.

"Say hey to that roommate of yours," said Ira.

"I shall, I shall," said Turo. "See you round, man." He remained seated on the log while Ira returned to his classroom. *Well now* that *was peculiar,* the unwelcome voice in his head declared.

10

W here's the iron maiden, dude!"

"I told you to stay upstairs," said Robert. "You're going to wind up with a colonial nail in your skull."

Turo had followed him into Granddad's cellar. Just as Robert had hoped, snow fell on the last day of classes before the break. How perfect was that? Back in October, searching for a can of stain, he'd seen a stash of skis down here.

Hunched low, they moved carefully through the underbelly of the house, barely more than a cave. The floor was packed dirt, rocks protruding like the spines of primordial subterranean creatures. When Robert was little, he'd peer down the basement stairs in wonder and terror. Like Turo, he'd thought of dungeons: manacled prisoners and colonies of bats.

He switched on the fluorescent strip over a workbench cluttered with tools. At the opposite end of the cellar, chinks of lamplight pierced the floor of the living room, between the old planks not covered by rugs. Granddad had never installed insulation down there—one of too many trivial things, thought Robert, that irritated his mom.

Robert groped behind the wide stone arch that anchored the kitchen hearth. "Jesus." He coughed and spat, brushing at cobwebs now glued to his face. He pulled out two pairs of cross-country skis, one at a time. Hanging on a nail was a plastic shopping bag. Yes: boots.

Turo toyed with a couple of the tools lying on the bench, then wiped his hands on his jeans. "Does anybody ever *do* anything down here?"

Robert handed Turo Clover's skis. They were sticky with years of residue, heating oil fused with dust. He hadn't thought about boots for Turo. Robert's mother had huge feet, so he could wear hers, but Clover's would be way too small for Turo.

When they hauled the skis into the kitchen, Robert's dad was whipping cream. "Please take those outside! No spiders in my tiramisu!"

"Great title for a memoir, Dad."

"Outside!" Flecks of cream covered his navy-blue sweater.

It was the afternoon before Thanksgiving. Every surface in Granddad's kitchen was occupied by bowls, cutting boards, heavy knives perched at perilous angles, cartons of eggs, loaves of bread, vegetables, cheese. Robert's dad was making pumpkin tiramisu, vegetable terrine, and stuffing. It looked like he was planning to feed Afghanistan.

Other dads had midlife crises involving cars or boats or the totally tawdry affair with some desperate younger woman, but Douglas Barnes had smothered his fear of old age in an avalanche of butter. Or that's how Robert saw it. For the past year, whenever he went home to Newton, Dad got all tangled up in three or four complicated recipes at once, usually French. If he was rebelling against the "heart healthy" diet of Robert's childhood, it didn't seem to bug his mom too much. She joked that the cooking posed a greater danger than the food. More often than not, the smoke alarm went off, something got burned, and Mom had to stay up half the night washing every dish they owned. One time, a stray towel caught fire, and as Robert's dad jumped up and down on it to extinguish the flames, three fancy wineglasses fell off the counter and broke.

Robert paused at the door to the porch. "Has Granddad seen this mess?"

"He's in Packard, with his ladyfriend. When I finish this stage of the—oh God!" Something was boiling over on the stove.

Robert stepped outside.

To clean the skis, the two friends ran them back and forth through the snow. According to Robert's father, Granddad's "ladyfriend"—how weird was that!—worked at The Great Outdoorsman and had promised to pick up wax for the skis. Robert thought about the irony that he was now, in Turospeak, *senza ragazza,* while Granddad had apparently scored.

The barn—the nursery school—was a dark void against the sky, though Robert could see, through a window, a red sensor blinking, technology on the alert even in the land of Play-Doh. Behind the barn glowed the pond. It had frozen just enough to hold the snow, the ice but a delicate skin on the water, like eggshell. Robert had hoped that he and Turo could go skiing by moonlight, if only to avoid the predictable awkwardness of the total family reunion. Once the wine was open and all the stiff, prickly feelings were squelched (like the "Oh that's right, no more Todd" sensation), the danger was past. People acted happy, even if they weren't.

Robert groaned. "Oh man. Poles!"

This time, he took a flashlight to the basement, sweeping its beam around the area where he'd found the skis. He tripped on a rock and fell into the space between the chimney arch and the rough mortared wall.

He remained wedged in the space for a moment, cursing, waiting for the pain in his arm to subside. When he pushed himself up, his elbow made an impossibly hollow sound against the wall. A wooden cupboard door. Out of simple curiosity, he tried to open it, but it had no handle and wouldn't budge. Probably a long-forgotten root cellar, an antediluvian fridge.

When his foot struck something loose, he redirected the light. The ski poles had tumbled into the crevice between chimney and wall.

"Robert? Can I get your help up here? Now, please?"

Clutching the poles with one hand, the ladderlike stairs with the other, Robert climbed to the kitchen. His father stood at the stove, where three pots simmered. He looked like a lobster, his face aflame with the heat, his hands in red oven mitts raised, like claws, as if in defense.

"The asparagus! In the colander, the sink! Can you please run cold water on it? So it won't turn gray?"

Robert tossed the ski poles under the table and saluted. "Asparagus SWAT team reporting." Funny how Dad's freak-outs were confined to the kitchen; even then, he hardly raised his voice.

As Robert turned on the water, Granddad entered from the living room, behind him a bright-faced woman with thick, youthful hair, behind her a small boy carrying a small truck. Granddad surveyed the kitchen and said, "Am I hosting the latest cooking show? How grand of me."

The woman laughed as if she'd been tickled. She put one hand around Granddad's waist; with the other she held her kid's hand.

Robert couldn't help staring. The woman wasn't precisely hot—she was too old for hot—but she was dressed like his way-cool freshman-year English professor (long swishy skirt, long swishy earrings, blue cowboy boots), and he could see that she got off on Granddad's imperious humor.

Robert waved from the sink. "Hey!"

"Hail to your hey, young stranger." Granddad crossed the kitchen and surprised Robert by kissing him on the cheek.

Robert blushed. At the stove, the ladyfriend was introducing herself to his dad. The little boy stood by the back door, looking through the glass.

Was Turo still out there?

Now Robert was shaking the woman's hand as he continued to hose down the asparagus (which looked sort of gray, despite the dousing). "Nice to meet you, Mrs. Straight."

"Please. I'm Sarah to everyone here and a 'Mrs.' to no one," she said. "I'd make a terrible matron."

Robert nodded and smiled, unsure what to say. He turned off the water and searched for a towel to dry his hands. (When Dad cooked, all the towels wound up on the floor.)

The little boy turned from the door, looking worried. "My school is all dark," he said to his mother.

"It's vacation, Rico!" She lifted him onto her hip. "I'll bet we can build a snowman tomorrow. We couldn't do that at our house, could we?"

Robert went back outside. Darkness had fallen fast, as it always did in November, but he could see the skis lying in the snow. The porch light illuminated Turo's footprints; they looked like blue notes on a musical score, a melody curving round the back of the barn.

Turo stood beside the pond, arms crossed against the cold. He stared at the houses on the opposite shore. The Three Greeks were lit from top to bottom, every window ablaze. "Cue the holiday kilowatts. Carnivorous excess and buckets of booze."

"It's Thanks*giving*," said Robert. "Every house in this town is jammed with relatives. If you lived here, you'd have a million guests, too. Everybody wants to be here, nowhere else. It's like a blender drink of Norman Rockwell and Andrew Wyeth, spiked with a few rich potheads and off-the-grid entrepreneurs."

Turo's lazy smile caught the light refracted by the snow-covered pond.

Without a jacket, Robert was shivering. "Hey. Come inside and be civil for a minute. We'll figure out the boot thing, make our escape later on."

They climbed the hill. Robert saw headlights approach from the road, sweep through the tangle of branches surrounding the house. For an instant, the tree house was captured in silhouette, a black shape that mirrored the barn.

His mom or Clover: either prospect made him uneasy. Only a month ago, he'd had nothing to hide from anyone.

In the kitchen, Robert's dad had turned on the radio and sang along—a sign that he was temporarily out of trouble, possibly because he'd recruited the ladyfriend as sous-chef.

Robert paused beside her. "You cool with this?"

"I am more than cool with this," she said. "Years ago I worked in a kitchen. Just to make money, but I liked it. Oh—and I have your wax, whenever you need it. I can't believe I remembered."

Robert wondered if she felt, on some level, like she was auditioning—as if she had to pass a family test, make them all like her. If so, she didn't know Granddad that well.

In the dining room, the table had been set—but not by Granddad. The grandmother Robert would never know had collected Mexican everything, and out it all came at the big, fancy dinners: the thick flowered plates, the cockeyed blue ceramic goblets, the napkins with sunfaded stripes. But there were flowers in actual vases—Granddad never did flowers—and the striped napkins had been folded into the goblets so they looked like origami birds.

Through the door to the living room, Robert saw his mother, still in her coat, holding her hands toward the fire. Granddad knelt beside her, prodding the logs. When she saw Robert, she came toward him so quickly that he took a few steps back.

"Honey, I have *missed* you." She hugged him tight and then, to his surprise, held him. Her coat was cold against his neck.

"Hello there, Arturo," she said when she let Robert go.

"A pleasure to see you again, Dr. Barnes." Arturo dipped his head in that ass-kissy, Ricardo Montalban way. He was incapable of being himself around parents. Or maybe it was a cultural thing, but Robert found it sort of skeevy.

"Turo and I might go skiing," he announced. "We have to get boots for him. Like, when does TGO close?"

"You're too late," said Granddad. "Stick around and socialize. Let your mother in on where those tuition dollars are going, hm?" He winked. "We'll find you a team of sled dogs tomorrow, whatever you require for manly exertion. Of which I do approve and shall partake, but not until the morning. Now I plan to drink and eat and lounge about like an emir in his palace."

"Dad, your palace looks amazing," said Robert's mom. "Look at Mom's bowl." She examined a silver bowl on the mantel as if she'd never seen it before.

"Please do not elaborate on *how* amazing. After this infernal house tour, I do not plan on making spotlessness a habit. Or polishing silver. Take heed."

Granddad had opened a bottle of red. He poured it out into six glasses and offered them around. After he carried the remaining two glasses to the kitchen, he returned and sat on the couch next to Robert's mom. She was clearly startled when he put an arm around her shoulders. He leaned toward Robert.

"Talk of palaces brings to mind something remarkable I must share with you," he said. "I have just, for the very first time, visited your mother's kingdom in the hallowed halls of St. Matthew's Ecumenical Synagogue for the Faint of Heart and Weary of Womb."

Turo laughed loudest.

Robert's mother rolled her eyes. "Dad."

Granddad continued to focus on Robert. "But seriously, now, I had no concept of your mother's power. Benevolent in the extreme, I hasten to add."

"Dad, don't make jokes. Hospitals are crazy places, nobody's denying that. But we've got a pretty good operation, all things considered."

"I do not tease, daughter. I was genuinely impressed. You have a staff who think the world of you, patients willing to wait all day long for your care—"

"*Dad.*"

"Do not interrupt me. I had never honestly considered before how challenging your work must be, how much courage and steadiness it takes. Not the medicine, but the vulnerability of all those people who depend on you, daughter. How you hold them all together."

"Well, that's a rosy picture, Dad."

Robert saw tears forming in his grandfather's eyes. He wasn't sure his mom could see this, because Granddad still had her pinned to his side. There was usually a jagged edge between them, so the emotions of the moment, or his Granddad's, felt strange.

"She's dedicated," Robert said quickly. "She doesn't even see that anymore. She just is." He laughed nervously.

His mother regarded him with a bemused frown. "And I am being buttered up because . . . ?"

"Because you better not have forgotten those pies," said Robert. "Like, you got the apple with the custard, right?" Other people's mothers made kickass pies; his knew exactly where to buy them.

She sent Robert to her car. When he returned with the shopping bags, Turo was excusing himself, saying that he had to go upstairs to work. "Unlike Roberto, I've been having a little too much fun this semester."

"Well, don't miss dinner. Sarah's made a vegetable curry," said Granddad. "People may help themselves and eat in the kitchen. I've had a call from Clover, who's stuck in traffic coming up from Connecticut. She'll take the children straight to her apartment and join us first thing tomorrow."

Robert heard these logistics as he carried the pies to the culinary war zone. His father now stood over half a dozen bowls of puree in different shades of green, red, and orange. Decorating the wall behind the food processor (which the Midlife Chef had brought along) was an exuberant flare of . . . beet juice? Cranberry goo? "Yo," said Robert, "are you really in charge of the main show tomorrow?"

"I'll have it all under control before we turn in tonight. O ye of little faith."

Sarah turned from the sink to smile at Robert. She was washing dishes. If approval did matter, Mom would give the ladyfriend an A plus.

After finding space for the pies in Granddad's fridge, he climbed the back stairs, ducking at the top where the roof began its steepest plunge. The second floor of Granddad's house was warm and nestlike, the kind of place children loved because it harbored so many spaces impassable to adults. On a clear day, the heat of the sun penetrated the shingles and the plaster just beneath. At the top of the stairs, you could place a palm against the ceiling, or even one of the hefty beams, and feel that heat. On a summer afternoon, it was punishing; in the winter, it was a balm. The entire house needed better insulation, but Granddad had long ago made it clear to everyone that he would die in this house "as is."

In Clover's room, the roof slanted sharply to meet the low frames of the windows. Beneath them, a pair of brass beds flanked the wall, foot to foot. Turo had closed the purple velvet curtains—legacy of Clover's high school days—and claimed one bed, burrowing under the quilt. He was curled around his laptop, his face rapt and glowing. As Robert crossed the room, he closed it.

"Working hard now, are we?"

"We are. We are," said Turo.

"For the record, you continue to freak me out."

Turo smiled abruptly, as if friendliness were a patch on his thoughts. "In that case, dude, pay me no heed. As your erudite granddad might say."

From under the quilt, Turo's phone rang. He pulled it out and flipped it open. "My mom." He answered warmly, lovingly, launching into the strange language they shared.

Robert sat on his bed and opened his backpack. He had work of his own, a paper on the blood-brain barrier. It wasn't due for another ten days, but if he didn't finish it by Monday, he'd be up against a wall in two other subjects. He had hoped that, by bringing Turo along for the weekend, he could keep an eye on his friend, put him under behavioral quarantine.

After the "swimming pool action," as Turo called it, Robert had gone along on two other MnMs. This was DOGS shorthand for Midnight Missions. The DOGS were big on jargon. Though Robert had begun to feel the exhilaration of acting out and getting away with the carefully choreographed mayhem, he was only semipersuaded that wreaking havoc on rich assholes' lives would make a constructive difference in the way other rich assholes spent their money. Turo spoke of shame as a powerful and worthy political weapon, used everywhere from the civil rights movement to demonstrations against the wearing of fur, and that was just in the tame, pampered United States. He talked about Paris, Argentina, Chile. And now, every time one of the MnMs hit the pages of the *Globe,* there were letters from people cheering them on. *Sometimes you have to break the law to shake the law,* wrote an ecology student at Columbia who had helped revive SDS. A letter from a popular poli sci professor at Harvard, one of those gurus whose courses were like secret societies, had filled a whole column, concluding, *To challenge complacency in the face of new technology is essential to our continued survival. Perhaps the methods of these activists aren't entirely wise or their positions uniformly defensible, but they cry out in demand of a new, global patriotism we must all embrace. It is literally a matter of life or death.* That letter got published in boldface. Turo had practically danced in the middle of Mass. Ave.

He had never invited Robert to attend meetings of the "inner circle," and frankly, Robert was relieved. Apparently, at one of these meetings someone had suggested a new target community in New Hampshire— but someone else had shot her down, pointing out that to cross state borders would call in the FBI. So long as their adversaries were suburban cops in fatcat Boston suburbs, they could keep up their work— though eventually, someone would be caught and go to jail. Probably soon. And that's when they'd go big-time. They were already talking New York, forming a chain, ready to act on a larger stage. DOGS would become the new Greenpeace.

"Quit if it makes you too nervous," Turo had said, "but tell me this, friend. When you go off to med school, to pursue the healing arts, you'll cut up a corpse first thing, am I right? So how do you think the work of saving anything begins? With work that breaks down the structure of things, calls corruption by its name, disembowels the status quo. That's how."

"Great. Fine," said Robert, "but then what are you wasting your time in school for? Why don't you just tell the dean you're taking a year off to fix our busted society?"

Turo had snapped, "The one thing I am not doing is wasting my time. Any of it."

Robert didn't really buy Turo's corpse analogy, but maybe in the bigger picture he was right. Turo had something Robert thought he'd had but was maybe losing: doubt-free dedication. You couldn't help craving a share. And sometimes, when Robert met someone new at a party or a political meeting on campus, he could see how impressed that person was to learn that *he* was Arturo Cabrera's roommate. Awesome.

~

Once Turo got off the phone with his mom, they spent a quiet, companionable hour clacking away at their laptops. Like Siamese twins joined at the soles of their feet, they lay full length beneath Aunt Clover's comforters (turquoise with big purple daisies), scrunched low against the cold air seeping through the curtains. Turo muttered from time to time in Spanish, a scowl on his face. He told Robert he was being tortured by some bonehead economist who predicted a never-ending ascent in the stock market. Robert, meanwhile, tried to explain the mechanism by which new chemotherapy agents could scale the parapets of the human brain to hunt down malignant growths that had already done so. The human body was a miracle machine, no doubt about that—but sometimes, like certain individuals, it was stubbornly, blindly counterproductive. At one point, Robert stole a glance over his screen at Turo, who looked too unhappy to be doing anything other than schoolwork.

But then Turo looked up. "Dude, I am famished. You smell that?"

Someone was heating up the ladyfriend's curry.

They threw off their quilts and went downstairs.

The kitchen had returned almost to normal. The dishwasher was mumbling away, and all that remained of Dad's chaos was a stack of bowls soaking in the sink. Sarah was setting the kitchen table. Without a moment's uncertainty, she opened drawers and cupboards, knew where to find forks and plates. Robert offered to help.

"Fill water glasses?" she said. "Find another bottle of wine?"

Granddad sat in front of the fire, playing a game with the little boy. It looked like vertical tic-tac-toe.

"Hey," said Robert.

"Is for scarecrows and livestock, as I am constantly reminding you." Granddad did not look away from the game, but the boy looked up, startled.

"I'm Robert," said Robert. "That game looks cool."

The boy stared at him. "Connect Four," he said shyly.

"This is my friend Rico," said Granddad, "and he is whupping my prominent derriere." He leaned forward and slapped his own backside.

Rico laughed.

"That's good," Robert told Rico, "because he needs whupping. Not just anybody can whup my granddad."

"He beat me once," said Rico. "I'm beating him the fourth time."

"You go, dude." Robert turned to Granddad. "The wine cupboard's empty, except for some dusty bottle from Greece that looks hugely suspicious. You have a stash somewhere else?"

Granddad thought for a moment, then sighed. "I left the wine at Sarah's. A whole case."

"Hey, dry is good. Milk is good." As Robert started back toward the kitchen, his mother emerged from Granddad's study.

"I'll make a run to Ledgely," she said. "Keep me company, Robert."

He stood still, excuses firing in the stubborn fortress of his brain. Why did he want to avoid this errand?

"Get your coat." She spoke in her doctor-knows-best voice. "Could you go warm up the car? I'll ask your father if he has everything he needs. He's always short a pint of cream. Keys are in my purse up front."

The surface of the snow twinkled like mica. The moon, nearly full, leaned close through the branches of the pines that partitioned the house from the road. It was, mourned Robert, a perfect night to go skiing.

He adjusted the driver's seat and started the engine. His mother's radio blared forth trumpets, something high-minded, baroque. Robert found a station with a live concert, blues from a club in New Orleans. Katrina, Katrina, and more Katrina. Now there was an outrage at which to aim your passions. He could do that instead; one group of students at Harvard had pledged all their vacation time to rebuilding homes in New Orleans. Maybe Robert would look into that, after exams in January. No way he could do anything over Christmas but work his tail off. Yet somehow those other students did it.

He watched the house, waiting. The one lit window framed his grandfather's face in profile, against the roaring fire. His white hair stood up, all haywire. He was mussing it dramatically, probably bemoaning another defeat by Rico. Robert could barely remember being that young, but he could recall playing games with his grandfather: old-fashioned tic-tac-toe, on paper, or cards, Old Maid and War. Life, Monopoly—though board games came later. How old had he been when he began to suspect that sometimes—not always, but sometimes—Granddad was letting him win? Robert smiled at the thought of Granddad's having a lover. Of his *being* a lover. *Dude.* He laughed.

His mother was laughing, too, when she got in the car. "You drive."

"That's funny?"

"Your father is fussing with his turkey on the back porch, and I startled him so badly when I opened the door that he dropped it down the stairs. So he runs after it, grabs it up in his arms, looks at me, and says, in his awful Julia Child voice, 'The guests will never know.' He is the eternal optimist."

"Yeah, but this haute cuisine thing? Mom, he's a maniac."

"Oh Robert, he's having fun with it. And now I *never* have to cook. He seems happy even when he flubs a meal. He sees it like a domestic Everest, I think. Men, the eternal mystery."

Where the driveway met the road, Robert accelerated carefully in case there was ice (salt was verboten in Matlock). He felt his mother's penetrating gaze. That "men" remark had been aimed in part at him.

"So," he said, "Granddad showed up at your office."

"It was odd, I have to say. I'm not sure either of us realized he'd never been there. Of course, why would he?"

"Did he say lots of embarrassing things to Chantal and the nurses? I love his totally incorrect nickname for the hospital." The true name of his mother's hospital was the sum of an alliance joining three hospitals, each of which refused to surrender its identity. The new, collective name was like a freeway pileup: St. Matthew Sinai Mothers of Mercy— known to those who revered it as St. Matt's, to those who did not as Matt's Moms.

"Actually, he behaved himself. I think he was mildly terrified. It's a very different experience to hang around a cancer ward when you're seventy than when you're twenty. Especially when you're healthy."

"Is he?" said Robert. "I hope so."

"He sees his doctors. Which is something for a single man his age. But listen, Robert. I don't want to talk about Granddad. Granddad's doing fine."

Christ, here it came. If he drove at the speed limit, and didn't spin out on black ice, it would still take ten minutes to reach the wineshop in Ledgely.

She turned off the radio. "Robert, Clara called me."

He groaned.

"Can you tell me what's been going on? I know you are studying hard, but I thought we had . . . I thought you'd let me in on anything important."

"I totally do," said Robert.

"Breaking up with Clara isn't important? You've been together a year."

He turned on to the main road. A dark furry creature, raccoon or cat, bolted through the headlights. His entire body tensed.

"Mom, I don't want to talk about Clara."

"Well, sweetie, I do. Clara's heart is broken. And you sound pretty emotional yourself. I liked her—I *like* her very much. She was devoted to you. For God's sake, she came to our home for special occasions over the past year, stayed with us on the Cape that weekend before you went to Maine. . . . If nothing else, I'm going to miss her."

"I'm sorry about that, Mom. But you don't know the whole story, do you?" He knew he sounded angry. What was the whole story? Was there a whole story? It was true that Clara had given up on texting and calling him after he told her he needed "some distance," but if you could call this rupture a breakup, it was less than a month old. Who could say it was final?

"What I am asking for *is* the whole story. Your side as well as hers."

Jesus, did she have to be so rational? Could he say it was none of her business? Not really, when he'd brought Clara into their life as a family. A lot of Robert's friends complained about how out of it their parents were, how twisted their priorities. Robert felt sorry for them. Were his parents really that much cooler? If so, he was lucky. But now he saw the advantage of keeping up a wall, your life a separate thing from theirs.

"Look, Mom, we're twenty. Nobody hooks up for life at our age. Or nobody we know. Not to say we won't get back together. I mean, Clara's being dramatic. We could be taking a break. That happens."

"I wouldn't call it a break if you do not respond to her leaving your belongings in front of your apartment door in a garbage bag."

Okay, that had been major. That was, what, not even two weeks ago? Robert had intended to sit down and write her an e-mail that night, but Turo had lured him out again, on that MnM with the firewood. Part of the problem was that Clara suddenly felt so . . . far away. And he missed her less (her company, her wit) than he'd thought he might. What he missed most was getting laid. Cruel but true. The ratcheting up of their relationship that came out with the stupid ring scene—that had freaked him out. And now—calling his mom? A spasm of rage at Clara registered in his chest. What the *fuck*.

His mother was talking about how she'd met Robert's dad by the time she was his age. They had been freshman sweethearts in college. Such prehistoric news. "We were apart for a couple of summers, and maybe we dated other people just to test ourselves, but we knew that we had each found a good friend and soul mate. If we'd broken up, we'd have gone on to find other partners, maybe never looked back. But we knew that making the commitment to each other would accelerate our lives in other ways, make our path so much clearer. And it did."

"So this is like, what, the bird-in-hand approach to marriage? Or marriage is like, what, an HOV lane? Why would you want me to get married so soon? Oh, I get it. You can't wait to be a grandma. Is that it?"

"I did not say I wanted to see you get married soon. I am simply wondering if you've done something rash." His mother spoke calmly, which only pushed him closer to the edge of fury.

"Some guys in my shoes would say this is none of your frigging business."

"Don't speak to me like that, Robert. As mothers go, I've always given you a lot of space, wouldn't you say?"

They had entered downtown Ledgely, where it looked as if every second and third cousin of every resident in a ten-mile radius had decided it was time to go shopping. The lot by the wineshop would be full, so Robert turned down a residential street.

"Wouldn't you?" she persisted.

"That's your stated M.O. Though it's always made me wonder, Mom, whether it's related to your never having more kids than me. Like, it's easy to give a kid space when one turned out to be more than enough."

His mother gasped quietly.

"Yeah, see what it feels like, Mom? That's not *my* business, right? Or maybe it is." Three blocks from the main drag, he found a spot in a dark lane of fancified colonial houses. He parked and turned off the engine.

"Robert. Are you telling me you've felt unloved?"

"Jeez, Mom, of course not." His voice cracked, as if he were still an adolescent. He opened his door.

"Do not get out. I have something to say to you."

Robert forced himself to look at her.

"I love and have always loved being your mother. Fiercely. Your dad would say the same about being your father—though that would be more obvious, right? My classmates at med school thought I was insane to willfully have a baby in the midst of it all, but I knew that if I delayed, if I thought a better time would come after endless residencies and studying for boards, and all that it takes to get where I am, then I would probably end up deciding to get pregnant when I no longer could."

The car was quickly growing cold, and Robert had left the house without gloves or a hat. He started to get out again, but his mom clutched his arm.

"Wait." She kept her hand on his sleeve. "I want to tell you what I see all too often in my practice. Women in their thirties, even forties, who thought they had all the time in the world to have a family. Even without cancer, they were probably fooling themselves. By the time they get to me, the grief they face is like a hurricane. A few go on to have babies, a few more to adopt, but a lot of these women are alone. They've passed up chances to settle down, and the regret I watch them battle, *while* they go through treatment . . . Robert, it's ghastly. People ask how I can bear to deal with so many people I know are going to die from their disease, but sometimes that's not the worst part of what I deal with. Regret— regret that devours people worse than a tumor—that's the hardest thing for me to see in my patients."

Robert couldn't look at her. What the hell was she talking about! "Mom, don't project those scenarios onto my life. Or, Jesus, Clara's life either."

"Fine." She got out and, without hesitating, walked toward Maple Street, toward the lights and the circling cars. He followed her at a short distance. The sound of her well-heeled boots on the pavement was loud and terse, an audible *fuck-you fuck-you fuck-you*. Except she would never have said that.

Vini, Viti, Vine was crowded, the rows of protruding bottles just begging to be toppled by the jostle of puffy coats and shopping bags. Robert's mother handed him a basket and told him to find a bottle of Harveys Bristol Cream sherry and four bottles of cabernet priced between twelve and fifteen dollars. She would meet him at the register.

He found the California aisle with its absurd range of choices. Turo was right about that. What might take down civilization was the sheer frivolity of choice. Who needed more than, say, a dozen red wines to choose from if it meant conserving resources, devoting land to more practical crops? After choosing two bottles of one cabernet and two of another, he cruised through a section called WINE ADVENTURES! Someone had lettered a bunch of cutesy little signs bragging about new combinations of varietals, new places in the world where viniculture had only just begun.

As he approached the counter, he saw his mother chatting with Granddad's friend Norval Sorenson. Robert walked up and said hello, murmured politely in response to the usual grown-up crowings about how much older he seemed, the questions (not meant to be answered, really) about school, courses, friends.

"Listen," said his mother. "You should drop by the house tomorrow. I haven't seen Helena in ages. You could even join us for the meal. Please."

Mr. Sorenson hesitated. "We're used to our holiday two-step, Trudy."

"Please come. Douglas bought a turkey the size of an ostrich."

Robert was unnerved by his mother's casual cheer, not five minutes after that grim infertility speech.

"I'm going to have Dad call you tonight, okay?" she said.

Mr. Sorenson seemed pleased by this idea, or maybe just let off the hook. He said good-bye and left the store.

Without conversing, Robert and his mother waited in line with their shopping baskets. When they reached the register, she told him to bring the car around so they wouldn't have to carry all the bottles so far. Efficient as ever.

They drove out of Ledgely in silence. Robert was not even tempted to turn on the radio. He still felt the burn of his anger, at both women, at their collusion. He turned up the heater.

He was startled when his mother pulled out her cell phone and made a call. "Dad?" she said. "Dad, we ran into Uncle Norval. They're alone for Thanksgiving, did you know that? Will you call and invite them? I'd love that. Clover would, too. . . . Oh good. We'll see you in ten."

Oh good. What gave her the nerve to give him a big Life Lesson Lecture, then gush over dinner plans? Never mind that being a good doctor meant being a good actor, too.

They crossed the town line into Matlock; by habit, he clicked on the high beams. At night, because of the sudden, dense woodsiness and the equally sudden dearth of streetlights, Robert the little boy had often felt as if he were entering a fairy-tale forest. In Matlock, the dark became darker, while the stars, filling the narrow rivers of sky that flowed between the treetops, shone much brighter. In winter, the snow in the occasional field seemed deeper, whiter, colder than anywhere else.

"So," he said into the silence, "is it true, Mom, that you had an abortion?"

She cried out, briefly, as if he'd struck her, yet he felt not even a splinter of guilt.

"Who told you that?"

"A couple years ago, at home, I overheard it."

"Overheard it how? What are you talking about?"

"When Aunt Clo stayed with us. When she flipped out over Uncle Todd."

His mother said nothing, all the way down Quarry Road. They were half a mile from Granddad's house.

"Pull over," she said. "Pull. Over."

The road had only a narrow shoulder, made narrower still by the swath of plowed snow. "I can't."

"Then pull the car into the driveway and stop there." Her voice was thick, almost menacing.

"Okay."

So they drove in silence for a few seconds more. Robert turned in at the mailbox and stopped.

"Turn off the engine. The headlights. Off."

Robert did as she asked.

"The answer is yes. Your father and I made that decision together. You were seven. Because yes, Robert, I did love being a mother enough to want you to have a sibling. Absolutely. If your father had had his way, we'd have had three or four. So I was pregnant. And when I was through the first trimester, your father wanted to tell you. But we had a blood test that didn't look good. And then I had an amnio. Do you know what that is, Robert? I assume you do."

Robert looked at her, certain she must be crying, but she wasn't. Her jaw was set—maybe in defiance of tears. She was waiting for an answer. Tentatively, he said, "So the baby was, like, deformed?"

"Down syndrome," said his mother. "And I did, we did, consider going to term with that baby. But it wasn't so. . . . Back then . . ."

"I'm sorry," said Robert. "Wow. I'm really sorry."

"Your Aunt Clover has caused me a lot of grief over the years, Robert. I have covered up for her, I have lied for her—your grandfather has *no idea* about some of the stunts she's pulled. The drugs in college. The . . . Well. I'll stop there. *Some* members of this family are discreet. And on top of everything else, I have graciously let her refuse *shitloads* of good advice. Chalk this up as just one more gift from my hopeless loser of a sister. It's a damn good thing she's not in that house tonight." She sighed aggressively. "Okay, turn the car on. Go."

Robert asked, as calmly as he could, "Would you never have told me?"

"Why, Robert, would there be any reason you *should* know? Why would you *want* to know?" Her voice was raised, as if his question had been idiotic, but then she put a hand on his arm and stroked it for a moment.

When they pulled up at the front door, she said, "Because you are bound to wonder, and I don't want you to ask me later, the baby was a girl. You would have had a sister."

She got out, slammed the car door, and went straight into the house. She did not wait to hold the door for him when he carried in the box of wine.

Turo was playing Connect Four with Rico. Robert's dad read a magazine, his stocking feet pointed toward the fire. For one shell-shocked moment, Robert stared at his dad's socks, which never varied: black, ribbed, that thin orange stripe across the toes. Dependable. A metaphor. Snapping out of his trance, Robert looked toward the dining room. There, almost but not quite hidden from view, Granddad was kissing Sarah (and boy was she kissing him back). Mom had gone to the kitchen or straight upstairs; though she had tossed her coat on the bench by the closet, she was nowhere in sight.

It was a done deal that he would lie awake that night, neither calm enough to sleep nor sharp enough to work on his biology paper.

Dinner had been a roving affair. People ate where and when they wanted: Sarah, Granddad, and Robert's father in the kitchen; Turo and Robert on the coffee table by the fire. Claiming she had to deal with e-mail, Mom took her plate into Granddad's study. Rico had been tucked in, much earlier, on a couch in the upstairs alcove that everyone still called Poppy's dressing room.

First Turo, then Dad, and finally Robert made their way upstairs. He hadn't seen Granddad and Sarah retire, yet now he saw the light under Granddad's door and heard them whispering, heard her laugh in her ticklish way. Through another closed door, the one that led to his mom's old bedroom, he heard his father snoring.

Turo, thank God, rarely snored. He'd fallen asleep the minute he climbed into bed. Robert kept his lamp turned low and tried to absorb an article on American immigration policies in the 1990s, jam-packed with graphs.

But all he could think about was his phantom sister, the daughter his mother had thought she would have and then didn't. Decided not to have. What was Down syndrome anyway, other than a certain appearance, the combination of ungainly head, flat face, and startled doe eyes that he could spot, and name, in an instant? How long did you live? Did you deteriorate, or stay the same forever? Did pain go along with the mental—what, deficiency? His mother had to be reminded of that daughter, that decision, every time she saw someone like that on the street, in the hospital. And not just then. How often? Every day, every few hours—or not so often at all? Did it ever come up with Dad? Jesus, did Granddad know?

Seven. Robert tried to remember his life when he was seven—his mom when he was seven. He could remember his first-grade teacher, the classroom, his best friends. Mrs. Kilgore read *Stuart Little* out loud at rest time. The kids lay down on plaid blankets to listen, after lunch. His dad packed bologna sandwiches. God, *baloney*. Who ate bologna anymore?

His mother was right; this was something he didn't need to know, shouldn't have known. It did not complete a puzzle or give any comfort to anyone. What you didn't know *could* hurt you.

Perversely, Turo's gimmicky little catchphrase came to mind: *senza ragazza*. Without girl. Over the past year, Turo had developed the philosophy that to resist the pull of a woman's emotions gave you that much more strength and purpose. Like some ancient warrior ethos. This was no excuse for a lack of attraction. Turo had juggled at least *due* if not *tre ragazze* toward the end of their year in Kirkland House. He wasn't tall or handsome in that oh-so-Ivy J.Crew way; Robert thought he was too skinny. But according to Clara, Turo had a "jive Latino impishness." Maybe other guys dismissed him as scrawny, but women saw him as wiry and supple—a certain essential sexiness if you were repulsed by the football physique. "Fred Astaire meets John Leguizamo," she said, at which point Robert had heard enough. As if he hadn't been the one to ponder Turo's appeal in the first place. Not that he'd been jealous, not with Clara.

And now here he was, *senza* Clara. This hadn't struck him so clearly until that awful, queasy conversation with his mother. Until then, he'd had this general feeling that it was more like he was . . . rebelling against the notion of some pathetically outmoded going-steady kind of relationship. At Clara's urging, they'd even celebrated a "first anniversary" on a particular day in early October. When he asked her what made that day an anniversary, she'd lowered her voice to say, "Like you don't know, bobcat."

That made it pretty obvious she'd committed to memory—or, what, recorded in some girlish diary?—the first night she'd invited him to her dorm room (her roommate gone for the weekend). Sweet, the way she'd made note of the date . . . but maybe a little creepy, too.

Had he resented that celebration more than he knew? They'd gone to Harvest, the totally overpriced restaurant where you were likely to see half your professors with their spouses (which was sort of like seeing them in their underwear, no matter how curious you thought you were). The food was pretty great—even if you couldn't have wine because places like that would have carded the pope—and he and Clara had split the check without any weirdness. Clara looked incredibly pretty in the candlelight. They'd gone back to the apartment and drunk champagne in his bedroom, naked.

Turo had knocked on the door at 2:00 a.m., wanting to borrow the car. Robert had said no, not at that hour. Turo hadn't seemed pissed, but the next day he teased Robert mercilessly about his "little wife."

"Been there, done that, right?" Robert teased back.

"On the contrary, my friend. *That* scene I reserve for the future."

"Your mail-order bride, once you secure the hacienda?"

"Ouch, man."

Robert had grinned at Turo across their kitchen table. "You started it."

"Hey. Clara is a catch. You know it."

"So come on. You have to be shagging that eco-babe. Miss OTF?"

Turo had looked puzzled for a moment, then whistled, long and low. "Robert, my friend, I thought you knew me better than that. Miss Tats and Manifestos? I do not mix business with sex. NFW. *Negativo*. Nyetzka."

They cracked up. Though he couldn't say exactly why, Robert was secretly relieved that Tamara was just a colleague to Turo.

As if guessing at, and misinterpreting, Robert's relief, Turo leaned across the table and kissed him on the forehead. "You, you are the closest thing I have to a wife these days. Perhaps I lie in wait for the end of your cozy duet with the estimable Clara. One day perhaps she'll wake up beside you and think you're not good enough for her."

Turo had rolled a joint; against his better instincts, Robert had shared it. By nine o'clock, he'd eaten a bag of cashews that were meant for a stir-fry later that week and fallen dead asleep. Clara had been hurt—just a little, she said in the e-mail he found next morning—that he'd forgotten to call her. Hadn't they had a wonderful anniversary?

"It was perfect, totally sweet," he'd said, calling her as soon as he got the e-mail. But maybe that had been the beginning of the end.

And maybe the end of the end had also passed without his fully knowing.

As so often throughout his childhood, Robert heard his mother downstairs, switching off the lights. She was almost always the last to go to bed.

Staring at the ceiling, he marveled at the radiance cast by the snow surrounding Granddad's house. He began to consider that maybe his mother had never recovered, deep down, from her own mother's sudden, premature death. Maybe her amazing efficiency, her professional cool, was like loneliness turned inside out. This grandmother Robert had never known was remembered by everyone as a colorful, universally loved, almost heroic figure, her death extra-tragic because her life had been so *special*. They'd talk about all the plans she had yet to fulfill. The tragedy to Mom—and Clover—nobody said too much about that.

Jesus, he thought now, to have lost your mother way too early—and then a daughter before she was even your daughter? What the hell could Robert know about living through stuff like that?

~

Granddad and Robert's father sat at the heads of the table. Robert sat between Sarah and his cousin Filo; across the table sat Mom, between Lee and Turo. Clover was between his dad and Norval Sorenson, Mrs. Sorenson on the other side of Sarah (Rico wedged between them).

Robert figured they had Sarah to thank for his father's failure to stage a conflagration. She'd organized a buffet in the kitchen so everyone could fill a plate and proceed to the dining room, where the table was a traffic jam of goblets, water glasses, candlesticks, flowers, and dishes of relish.

Once they were all in their places (was this Sarah's elegant script on these tiny red cards?), Granddad stood. He always dressed up for holidays, but this time he looked downright flashy: his shirt green like the inside of a dinner mint, his orange bow tie so huge it resembled an explosion. He waited till everyone was looking at him and said, "Thankful yet again. We do this over and over, don't we? Year after year. And isn't that *something*." He laughed. He glanced at Sarah.

The tradition was for each person to stand, starting with Granddad, and name something he or she was thankful for that year. Ordinarily, Granddad issued thanks for a "not" (not living in a nursing home, not having a child in Iraq, not being senile or not knowing if he was). This set the tone for a David Letterman kind of list from everyone else.

This year, however, Granddad said, "Everything. With a codicil here and a caveat there, I am thankful for everything." He sat down.

Robert's mother and Clover looked stunned, almost alarmed. Filo and Lee giggled. Lee was up next.

"Um, that I got onto A-squad soccer." ("Stand up," whispered Clover. Belatedly, he stood and then sat.)

Robert's mother was thankful for his father. Turo was (obsequiously) grateful for the invitation to dinner. Mr. Sorenson was glad to have a bookstore in the black, Clover to be loved by "both of my wonderful families" (never mind the dark expression on her sister's face).

Robert's dad sprang to his feet and held both arms out, like a conductor. "Call me unimaginative, but I'm just going to echo my sister-in-law. As my son might say, I am one righteously fortunate dude."

Mrs. Sorenson was thankful for a year of good health and prosperity in a world where so few people enjoyed either. Rico, after his mother whispered something in his ear, said, "I love turkey!" Laughter, agreement, fond gazes.

Then Sarah stood. "I am a woman who counts her blessings daily, yet I did not know how blessed I could be until this fall: until this enchanted place came into my son's life and, because of it, Percy came into mine."

"Yowza," Robert whispered. Then he was on his feet. "Yeah, well, Granddad, she's right. You're the man. This is the place. To you." He raised his goblet, though the thanks weren't meant to be toasts.

Arms rose. Robert's dad said, "Hear, hear." Glasses clinked.

And then everyone began talking all at once, lifting knives and forks, and like a symphony, the feast began.

Robert turned to his forgotten cousin, Filo, and whispered, "I sorta screwed up there. You want your turn?"

"Jeez no," she whispered back.

"But tell me what you're thankful for. You have to tell someone or it's bad luck."

She put her mouth close to his ear. "That my dad's getting married again."

Robert leaned forward to see her expression. She was serious. "You would not have said that."

"Duh," she said. "I'd have said I was thankful for getting to go to horseback-riding camp last summer. Which was here, with Mom. And it was really great. I'm going to do it again next summer. After the wedding."

Robert had actually forgotten the Todd news, which he'd heard from his mom. He glanced at Aunt Clover. She looked happy as could be; Turo was flirting with her in a courtly way (Fred Astaire ascendant) while Mr. Sorenson looked on, bemused. They were talking about the pros and cons of woodstoves. Was Turo capable of thinking about anything other than carbon emissions?

Granddad was teasing Filo about her newly pierced ears. She kept reaching up to touch them. "Do people mistake you for a gypsy?" he was saying. "Many people think they long to be gypsies, without the slightest notion of what that actually means. Let me tell you a thing or two about gypsies."

And then, to Robert's left, Sarah spoke. "Are you really on the path to becoming a doctor? Because I've looked at that tree house and I'm skeptical. I think you're a born artisan."

This close, she had shockingly fantastic eyes: blue but also gray. Atlantic Ocean eyes. She had a lot of lines around those eyes, half worry, half laughter. Wild, wiry hair, like Clover's but dark. A big, Carrie Bradshaw nose.

"You think so," said Robert.

"Know so," said Sarah.

"Tell it to my parents, who probably expect a return on their investment. And for the record, I was the contractor, not the designer."

She looked at him steadily, smiling.

"You're giving me that 'oh to be young again' look," he said.

"You're right," said Sarah. "Because I started out sure of becoming a lawyer. Change the world by changing the rules. But I had a smart, intrusive mentor, this sculpture teacher in college. He convinced me that, in the end, the rules—those kinds of rules—don't budge. Or not much. Most of the time, the rules change the lawmakers more than vice versa."

"So I've heard." Robert glanced at Turo. He was debating something, intently, with Dad and Mr. Sorenson. "But with medicine, the diseases don't treat the physicians. And physicians work with actual people, not words meant to, like, regulate those people's lives. People, sooner or later, they do budge."

"Or die." Sarah had a great laugh. She laughed from deep inside, the way a singer would laugh.

"There's a business to medicine, but that's something else." He sensed that his mother was listening in. Except when she'd asked him to fetch a load of firewood that morning, they hadn't spoken since the trip to Ledgely. He couldn't tell if she was avoiding him, but boy was she avoiding her sister. (Would everything feel different now if Granddad hadn't forgotten the wine?)

Next to his mother, Lee looked completely bored. He was trailing his fork through the gingered yams and humming Coldplay. Robert leaned across. "So hey. Want to go cross-country skiing with me and Turo? Tonight?" To Robert's surprise, Granddad had mentioned the ski-and-boots dilemma to Mr. Sorenson, and he'd brought along three pairs of skis and boots.

"Never done that," said Lee.

"Piece of cake," said Robert. "The trail out back is mostly flat."

"Cool." He resumed sculpting his yams.

Robert said, "That's great about the soccer team."

"Yeah."

"You still doing the soup kitchen thing with your dad?"

"Yeah. Building my character." He smirked.

"Seconds, anyone?" Robert's dad announced. "No one's holding *me* back." One by one, people stood, holding their plates. They groaned and went through that ritual of saying they shouldn't but it was all just too good. . . .

As Robert stood, his mother called to him. She'd gone to the living room to put a log on the fire. "Robert, could you help me out a minute?"

She was using the tongs, trying to maneuver the log into place. As she handed the tongs to Robert, the brief look she gave him was sad. She said quietly, "I was harsh with you last night. I'm sorry."

"Mom, forget it. You were right about a lot of stuff."

"Sometimes I think I'm too right for my own good."

He lowered his voice. "So give Aunt Clover a break, will you?"

She stood up and looked at him. "That is not a matter for negotiation between us. Between you and me."

Robert's dad entered the room and said, "Hey, you two. I made enough for everyone to eat themselves into a stupor. Get with the program!"

Obedient, they took their plates to the kitchen.

And somehow, through dessert and coffee, and more dessert, and the sky going dark, and a dozen more logs thrown on the fire, no one got into a fight.

The only tension, possibly experienced by Robert alone, was when his dad brought up the latest story related to the DOGS. Another suburban home, but this one out near Northampton. The entire façade of a very large house had been papered, seamlessly, with pages from the *New York Times* (allegedly taken from stacks in the garage). One by one, the sheets had been staple-gunned to the clapboards and window frames. Across the vast expanse of newsprint, someone had painted, in lime green, ALL THE NEWS THAT'S FIT TO PULP A FOREST.

Granddad laughed wickedly. "The crusaders appear to be migrating west."

Robert's mother sighed. "The crusaders appear to be getting redundant."

"A bit sophomoric, that one," said Mrs. Sorenson.

"They might have had an easier time wrapping the house in toilet paper. Same message, less effort," said Mom. "And really, newsprint these days is largely postconsumer, isn't it?"

Robert made every effort not to look at Turo, but then Turo spoke. "You're forgetting about the inks and their by-products—and have you ever seen a plant that creates 'recycled' paper? Or smelled it?" Turo's smile was arch. "You'd be deluding yourself to think it's a process low on energy or pollutants."

Robert felt a pulsating heat in his cheeks and forehead.

"One more incident like that in Matlock," said Clover, "and Katy bar the door. I hear the selectpersons have started a fund to hire an investigative team."

"Ooh, *CSI* in Matlock! Way cool, dudes," said Robert's father.

To Robert's horror, Dad actually winked at him. The smile Robert returned made his face feel like a rubber Halloween mask.

He knew there was no way Turo had been involved in that particular mission, at least not in terms of his presence. This made the whole DOGS operation suddenly more real to Robert. At one point, he had entertained the notion that Turo was it, the whole shebang. Like one of those circus musicians who plays a dozen instruments at once.

Now, if the "it" was something major—a countercultural machine in which he, Robert, had been a cog—the whole thing felt more frightening than thrilling. The truth was, Robert didn't have the stomach to be a guerrilla. On the other hand—and this was verified by a single glance down the table at his friend's glowing face—Turo so totally did. Totally.

"Yo," said Robert, "who's up for skiing off even one bite of that wicked fine tiramisu?"

The moon stood out from the sky like a medal. It cruised along beside them, calm and vigilant, passing behind tree after tree as their skis hissed through snow on the path that skirted the pond and then branched away into acres of trails winding through Matlock's fairy-tale forest.

Robert knew these paths in every shading of every season. Clover was the one who'd taken him on walks when he was too young to go on his own (the only danger that he might lose his bearings). Once he could wander the woods alone, he had loved the solitude. You could walk an hour out, an hour back, with only a distant, parenthetical flash of house or barn. You might run into a jogger or someone walking a dog. Everyone smiled, spoke a word of greeting, but no one stopped you to talk. That was the unspoken rule.

As if sensing this protocol, Turo followed Robert in virtual silence. Lee brought up the rear. Robert could have left them both in a wake of powder, but he moved along slowly, to make it easy for them. After twenty minutes, he could hear the two novices breathing more quickly. He slowed his pace further.

"Go," said Turo. "Don't let the city dudes hold you back. If we give up, we can retrace our tracks."

Robert stopped and turned. "Sure?"

"Vamoose," said Turo. "Let the tourists tour."

"Yeah, cool by me," said Lee.

So Robert leaned forward and raced ahead on his own, leaving behind the merciless small talk of the long afternoon, pushing against the stupor of his overfed body. Where the path veered left, departing from its circuit of the pond, he struck off through the trees, to stay along the shore. Soon he broke out onto the great lawn shared by the Three Greeks. If anyone in these houses should see him, they wouldn't think twice. Even though they didn't know him, they might wave. This was safe, protected Matlock—or was it, now? How unnerved had people become by Turo and his fellow mischief makers?

Robert stopped to enjoy the view across the pond to Granddad's. How odd the barn looked, all those new modern windows. Just over its roof, he saw the kitchen window, the figures of his family, spending more effort to clean up the leavings of the meal than they had to sit down and consume it. What did you buy with all that effort? What was the cost/benefit ratio? Was there, behind all the courteous conversation, a mysterious way in which people really drew closer? Had all that sugar in half a dozen desserts sweetened his mother's anger toward Clover? God, he hoped so.

He continued his orbit of the pond. The return side was dense with brush, especially as he approached the barn. He stopped to release his bindings, carrying the skis as he picked through a tangle of juniper and bittersweet.

By the time he reached the lawn, the sweat between his shoulder blades had cooled. Yet the shivering was pleasant, and he didn't feel like going in. He could see the faces of his father, Sarah, and Clover through the kitchen window. Quietly, he leaned the skis against the porch.

He hadn't been up into the tree house since the day of the "inauguration." Wiping snow off the ladder, he climbed slowly, careful not to slip on the rungs in his stiff boots. He climbed all the way to the third tier, the very top. There was enough moonlight that he could see the bright shapes the children had applied to the interior, to the plywood fixed against the cleverly pieced branches that formed the outer walls. He could make out crude animals, striped and spotted in lollipop hues; the great happy faces of daisies: all the usual motifs of childhood art. Matlock children might be favored by fate, but they were ordinary, too.

What a revelation to see the vista from aloft now that the beech had dropped its leaves. Robert could see not only the Three Greeks but the low hills beyond them, the few houses tucked into the sumptuous woods. In another direction, he saw the roof of the Old Artillery, the steeples of the churches on the green. Clouds moved vaguely across the sky, glowing like the fur of a tabby cat whenever they crossed the moon.

Turo and Lee emerged from the woods, from the path they had taken on their way out. They skied slowly, sluggish on their tired legs. They were laughing and talking. Lee looked downright expressive. Leave it to Turo to draw out even a sullen, withholding adolescent kid. Robert's worries about his friend were probably a waste of time. Even if Turo failed to turn in papers or show up at an exam, how well Robert could imagine the guy aiming a blast of his persuasive charm at some professor's flimsy disapproval. Whammo. Failure? *Negativo*, dude.

Turo could talk to anyone. You could even say he liked talking to everyone. (Politician syndrome, Granddad called it.) Like that time he'd joined Robert for the interview with Celestino. The language bond was minor; Robert understood that, classwise, there was a huge divide between those guys. Robert hadn't seen Celestino since the interview (he got a B plus on the paper, the professor wishing for *more detail on family ties/hierarchy/obligations*), but Turo had mentioned sticking around at the pizza place for another hour or so. "A good man," Turo had said. "Ought to have a chip or two on his shoulder, but he doesn't. Or seems like he doesn't."

Had Turo stayed in touch with Celestino? Were they actually friends?

Robert had to wonder about himself. He was acting like he was married to Turo, as if he had to know what the guy did, who he hung out with, 24/7. And now, here he was practically spying on his friend, straining to hear the conversation between Turo and Lee.

"Hey," he called down when they stopped at the house to take off their skis. "Up here," he called again when they looked around, confused at the source of his voice. "You gotta come see this view."

11

~

You have reached the home of Sarah Straight, Halcyon Glassworks, and, last but never least, Rico. Leave a message and we'll be in touch.

I had listened to this recording at least twenty times in three days. I knew its every lilt and stress, from the breathy ascent in the single syllable of *home* to the lambent tenderness in *Rico* to the remorseful, and in my case unfulfilled, promise to *be in touch*.

I had stopped addressing the beep after my second message. I continued to telephone because I was a wishful fool, listening to the entire message because it was the only way to hear her voice. Was she there, listening to herself as well? (Add to my long list of modern vexations the invention of caller ID.) I knew she knew I wanted to speak with her—good God, to be with her! I contemplated driving to Packard, standing in the rain at the entrance to her building, abusing her buzzer until she came down. Though no doubt she'd hold out on me.

For five days, with little respite, we'd been enduring an onslaught of rain, sleet, mist, and slush; the miserly sky withheld even from charmed Matlock the consolation of snow. The house tour had taken place on day one of this deluge, a Sunday; Sarah's diagnosis the day after that. Rico hadn't missed a day of school since, yet my twice-daily vigil for Sarah's car was futile—for, as I found out at last from Ira, once desperation trumped my discretion, other moms were taking turns ferrying Rico to and from school.

I broke down on Thursday afternoon, heading down the hill once I was sure the last child had left. Ira was still in his classroom. "We know about the cancer," he said. "Our class parents are joining forces to help out with Rico while Sarah goes through this ghastly ordeal of testing. Once she's scheduled for surgery, we'll create a meal chain. Both of you must be going through hell. I'm so sorry." Apparently, my relationship with Sarah was now out in the open at Elves & Fairies; why this did not come as a relief, I would have to examine later.

Ira resumed sweeping. I was about to make my retreat when he stopped again. "Something else." He reached down to rub at a pink blemish on a small white tabletop.

"Yes?"

"The one person who doesn't know yet is Rico. I wonder if you might talk to her about how important it is to discuss this with him right away. He's very sensitive—and what he doesn't do in talking he makes up for in listening! I've sent her a note that I'm happy to help her figure out what to say—sadly, I've been through this before—but I can't really bug her further. . . ."

He was fishing for assurance that I, as the trusted companion, would persuade Sarah to chat about this catastrophe with her child. What he did not know, and what I was only beginning to discover, was that inside the otherwise outspoken, generous, free-spirited Sarah lurked another woman: obstinate, fortress building, and (though I knew she'd deny it till kingdom come) surreptitiously fearful.

"I'll do my Yankee best," I said, simply to end our exchange.

I held my raincoat over my head as I dashed from barn to house.

Oh my poor, sodden, enthusiastically trampled house. Had it come to life in human form that day, it would have been a bride as she wakes the morning after an intemperately festive wedding. Cast me as the bridegroom, Mistress Lorelei as the wedding planner, Clover as the maid of honor, and half the citizenry of the twelve surrounding towns as the celebrants, adoring and approving yet buffoonishly overindulgent.

Except that the groom, at the advice of the wedding planner, had decamped for the occasion itself. Imagine the bride's despair.

After reading the forecast on Saturday, Laurel (call that woman anything but unprepared!) had distributed throughout the chosen houses dozens of clear plastic runners, which she had reserved "just in case" at a local rental agency. Yet since these houses were not alarmed and guarded museums, the people who crooned their way through the rooms strayed onto carpets, jostled tables, knocked over lamps, ran their oily fingers across ancient paneling, and, on departing, carved muddy ruts across the yards. (At least Laurel had thought to transport the tourees in groups via shuttle bus from the public library.)

The fingerprints could be scrubbed away, as could the muddy footprints on my front-hall floorboards, but a framed watercolor knocked to the floor had suffered broken glass that nicked the painting itself, and a tiny crystal bud vase that belonged to my mother had vanished. On my desk in the study, a pile of books had fallen against a pitcher of flowers (courtesy of Laurel's "committee"), sending a cascade of water into a basket on the floor containing old photo albums put together by Poppy. I did not discover the mishap until Tuesday, by which time the album on the bottom, featuring those old-timey black-paper pages, had congealed into a mush of tarlike paste and disintegrating snapshots.

Though I would never call it a blessing, a significant distraction from this minor nightmare had been Sarah's scheduled biopsy on Monday, in the office of Trudy's surgical colleague Dr. Wang. The drama I had already endured to get Sarah to consent to mammograms, to get Trudy to pull the strings to get her slipped into the schedule the week after Thanksgiving—well, I deserved a Tony for persistence if nothing else.

"If it will get you to finally, once and for all, *change the subject,*" Sarah had said, "then I will do it. I know I'm fine, and I'll just have to prove it. Then we will figure out your penance." She'd said this to me while I cooked her a dinner to celebrate the completion of the willow window. I even cooked the meal at her loft, in part so I could see the window before it was taken away to its swanky home, yet also in part so I could (after Rico was sound asleep) broach the subject of her health in a setting she could not flee. That night, however, she was in a bright mood, thrilled at how the window had turned out, excited at the hope that it would bring her more commissions, possibly even institutional work.

I did not accompany her into town for the mammograms, nor did I ask if I might. For one thing, that appointment fell during the final week of preparation for the house tour, and Mistress Lorelei, clipboard in hand, girl sergeants in tow, was prone to showing up for surprise inspections.

The night after the mammograms, I called Sarah when I knew Rico would be in bed. She sounded tired and said she needed to get a good night's sleep.

"But how did it go?" I asked.

"They put my tits in a waffle iron. That was fun."

"And? You're fine?" I tried to ignore her crude language.

"Well, my tits have recovered."

I waited. "Don't they give you the results right then?" I said after a moment. I did not tell her that I had grilled Trudy about the protocol.

"Apparently, not always. I have to go in for . . . more."

"More waffle iron?"

Again, she held back.

"Sarah?"

"Oh," she said impatiently, "I have to have a biopsy. They did an ultrasound, too. It's all about malpractice, these endless tests. Ridiculous."

"You're going to have it, though—the biopsy?"

"Since you'd bug me about it till the end of time, Percy, I don't think I have a choice—but do you have any idea what I have to pay to get it? There goes at least half of what I'm making on this window."

"I'll pay for it, Sarah."

This particular silence was different from the ones that had come before.

"Percy, I always pay my way. I'm no charity case. In fact, I'm sorry I told you Rico's on scholarship. I've lived hand to mouth, and I'm past that stage. I don't need a rich boyfriend to come to my rescue. Okay?"

"I'm sorry, Sarah. I honestly didn't—"

"I know," she said hastily. "Just drop it, the money stuff. Please."

"Fine. But I'm going with you this time. To the biopsy." I waited for her to protest, but she sighed.

"Well, Percy, you're in luck. Somebody does have to go with me. They won't let me leave 'unaccompanied.' The mom I know best at school is taking care of Rico's pickup. So congratulations! You get to be my cancer clinic chaperone. You win the prize." A quick laugh took the bitter edge off her speech. "Percy, I'm exhausted. Can you just say good night? I'm doing that now. Good night."

"Sweet dreams," I said, as I used to say to my daughters.

"Same to you," she said.

I was hurt, of course, that she hadn't wanted me, above anyone else, to act as her chauffeur. What did this mean?

∼

Of the countless medical terms and procedures that I needed Trudy to explain or define to me over the ensuing months, I never bothered to ask about the nature of a *frozen section,* which conveyed to us the first bad news. To our surprise, the news was delivered swiftly, even matter-of-factly, half an hour after Sarah emerged from the biopsy, woozy from a tranquilizer, leaning protectively to her left, guarding the bandaged breast.

She drifted in and out of a hazy sleep as I sat beside her in the waiting room (fraternal twin to the waiting room in Trudy's suite; the couches olive rather than saffron, the paintings of trees rather than birds). We were summoned by a nurse in one of those Carmen Miranda smocks, who showed us to the surgeon's office. Dr. Wang was an acutely slim Oriental woman who appeared to be a disconcerting decade younger than Trudy. Her hair was arranged in a glossy chignon, its elegance on full display because she was bent over a pad of paper, writing diligently, as we entered.

When I introduced myself, her smile was formal. "Trudy's dad. An honor and a pleasure." She rose only partway from her chair to shake my hand. She told us to sit.

"Sarah," she said, "I'm afraid the tumor is malignant. We'll do more tests, and they'll take a couple of days, but that hard news, I can almost guarantee, won't change. I'm sorry."

I reached for Sarah's right hand, but it was clasped tightly in her left, in the folds of the big, loose shirt she'd been instructed to wear. She did not look away from the doctor. She did not make a sound.

"But," said Dr. Wang, "you are fortunate to have been diagnosed at a time when we've made enormous strides in treatment. The complicated part, but it's the good part, too, is that we regard breast cancer as a wide range of distinct diseases, each with a treatment more tailored to that disease than we could offer just a few years ago. So there's a lot to learn about the different factors involved here, but we'll be able to address each one precisely. If you want, I can give you some literature to look at now. Some people like to learn everything they can as soon as they can." She seemed to be asking Sarah if she was one of these people. Still, Sarah said nothing.

"The first thing you need to do is go home and rest. Lily will give you a scrip for a painkiller on your way out, though it shouldn't be too bad.

The incision was fairly shallow, and I have good reason to believe the margins were clean. I'll talk to you in a couple of days when we know more, and we'll discuss how to proceed."

"Proceed?" Sarah spoke sharply, but her voice was hushed.

"With whatever our next step may be. Probably surgery first, but again, let's wait and see what the path report tells us."

"But I can't."

"This is a lot to take in, I know." Briefly, pointedly, Dr. Wang caught my eye. Then she said to Sarah, "Are you all right?"

"No. Of course I'm not."

I laid a hand on Sarah's arm. Dr. Wang smiled sadly. "It's good to be truthful. You're upset, as anyone would be." Again, she looked at me before turning back to Sarah. "Do you have questions now, or do you want to save them till later?"

"Later," Sarah said. "Definitely later."

Dr. Wang rose. She was stunningly short as well as slim. She came around her desk and put a hand on Sarah's shoulder. Sarah flinched.

"So you'll call her as soon as you know more," I said.

"Absolutely," said Dr. Wang. "And both of you should feel free to call me or Lily. I do e-mail, too." She handed me a card. Like my daughter's name on her card, Dr. Wang's was followed by a fleet of esoteric abbreviations.

I thanked her. We went to the reception desk, received the promised prescription, and then I was guiding Sarah (or following her) back through the warren of corridors and arteries and bridges that would take us to the hospital's subterranean garage.

In the car, I fumbled about for the parking ticket. Sarah hadn't spoken a single word since our audience with the diminutive Dr. Wang.

I opened the glove compartment. "Of all the times to—"

Sarah reached into a small well between the seats and pulled the ticket from a nest of receipts and paper napkins. She handed it to me without comment. She looked calm, dry-eyed. I wondered if she could literally be in shock.

I asked if she was hungry. Did she want coffee or tea? A doughnut? A bagel? An early dinner? She stared out the windshield, toward the numbered concrete pillar bearing the sign KNOW YOUR LEVEL.

I had no earthly notion of my level at that moment. There was no ground beneath my feet, no sky above my head.

"Just take me home," she said.

By the time we hit Storrow Drive, the silence felt like an acidic hum. Yet what could I say? What wouldn't sound like *I told you so*? What proclamations of devotion would console? I wished, most of all, that Sarah would *cry*. It occurred to me that I hadn't seen this woman cry. Not once. Of course, I'd known her now for a scant three months.

When I pulled up in front of her building, she said only "Thank you."

"Take your hand off that door," I said. "Speak to me."

"Can we talk later, Percy? I'm dead tired."

"All right. I needn't ask to know that you want to go up alone. But humor me a little. Let me take you to your next appointment. Just start there. Or let me take Rico, pick him up from school, and show him my centerfold collection. Teach him to smoke. Play poker. How about it?"

I did earn a smile, but it was like a gratuity, impersonal and brief. "Percy, you're amazing. I can't make you mad, can I?"

"You can, and you have. But not today."

"There's too much to think about before I can make any plans."

"Let me think about it with you. Let me cook for you while you think by yourself." I sounded desperate. God, I sounded old. *Let her go, you coot,* I admonished my feeble self.

"Percy, there's a part of me that feels like you got me into this shit," she said. "Not fair, I know. But I have to get past that. I need a break."

"From me."

"From your pushing me so hard. Looking at me from too close up."

"Which led to your getting cancer."

She opened the car door. "This is why we can't talk now."

"I'll call you tonight," I said. "After Rico's asleep."

"Not tonight. I have to crash."

"Tomorrow."

"Tomorrow I'll be in town. I have to make adjustments to the window, the way it fits. I'm not going to blow that connection." She kissed me quickly before getting out. "I'll call you as soon as I can."

I started to get out, to walk her to the door.

"No," she said. "Go home, Percy. You need rest, too."

Because I'm such a codger, I thought, and codgers need their naps!

I had to wonder if her sudden collision with the notion of mortality made me appear even older; if it put me in the clubhouse of those most definitely closer to death than to birth.

Winter, with its ever-looming darkness, draws out anxiety and suspicion, rather in the way that salt draws out water. It will do so regardless of extenuating circumstances, such as the refusal by one's sweetheart to return calls for four solid days in the wake of a cancer diagnosis or the oddly ornery, jumpy behavior of one's grandson when asked, in the most harmless fashion, what he'd like to do with his Christmas vacation.

To distract myself from Sarah's retreat (I would give her till the weekend before arming my catapult), I volunteered to take Robert out for dinner that Wednesday night. I took him to Gabriella's Garden, a restaurant tucked into a clapboard house on one of the last unravaged lanes of Harvard Square.

The bread was exceptionally good at Gabriella's; alas, so was the butter I spread thickly on my second slice. "Now that you're a bachelor again," I said to Robert, "you're free to gad about as you please once classes let out for the year."

"Well yeah," he said, "except for studying. Exams are in January, Granddad."

"You can take a week off," I said. "A few days, for heaven's sake. Maybe you'd like to spend New Year's in Chicago, with your pal Turo."

Robert did not look happy at this suggestion.

"That's where his mother lives, do I remember correctly?"

"Used to, Granddad. Like, eons ago."

"Ah. That's right. His home is in the Philippines, yes?"

"His mother's. He doesn't really have a home. His home, right now, is our apartment." Robert tore small strips from the napkin that belonged in his lap.

"How about the two of you take off somewhere together? New York. Or you could go skiing in Vermont."

"Turo's going to hang here, and so am I," said Robert, sounding testy.

Our house salads arrived. I liked this place because you could order "house" this and "house" that, perhaps with an inquiry as to what the chef considered the best dish that day, and put together a fine meal without ever consulting a menu.

" 'Hanging' sounds a bit dull—or fatal, depending on your definition. Can't a grandfather offer to fund a modest vacation?"

"Granddad, that's generous, totally, and maybe in the spring? Like, I wouldn't mind heading to New York then. Maybe stay with Uncle Todd."

This suggestion alarmed me at first, but I suppose it wasn't out of line. Since when had Todd become the bad guy?

"See your cousins—excellent idea," I said. "But in the meantime, you could come out and stay at the house after Christmas. Come do your studying, your 'hanging,' on my utility bills."

"Could work," said Robert, but absentmindedly. He gazed out the nearby window, at the dark, hibernating garden. He chewed his lettuce methodically.

"Bring a bunch of your pals," I said, attempting to regain his attention.

Robert looked at me. "Are you okay, Granddad?"

"I am perfectly 'okay,' young man."

"Everything okay with Sarah? Who's totally cool, by the way." He smiled sincerely for the first time since we'd met at the maître d's station.

"I'm glad you like her," I said. "That is not unimportant to me." Of course I wasn't "okay." Of course everything wasn't "okay" with Sarah. And of course my grandson knew me well enough to see that I was off my game. As he seemed somehow off his.

"So, Granddad, even though I'm not taking you up on that way-cool vacation offer—which is really awesome of you, and I might regret that I'm turning it down—I was wondering if maybe, something else . . ."

The waitress took our salad plates and put down our entrees, then offered us pepper (as if we weren't old enough to apply it on our own).

"What are you wondering?" I asked once we'd been served and peppered.

"Okay, like, I should probably ask Mom, but I so don't want a lecture. I'm wondering if I could borrow some money for rent."

"Ah. You've been living it up on burgers and illicit beers?"

"Actually, it's not me. It's just that Turo's mom screwed up on his latest money transfer. Or the bank screwed up. We're okay for December, because I covered him there, but just in case he's not square by next month . . ."

"What are grandfathers for?" I said, slicing into a fat, succulent ravioli. What a relief: a problem I could solve.

"Thanks, Granddad. I promise to pay you back. With interest."

I waved my hand. "Don't be absurd. We'll tend to that now." I took a check from my wallet and filled in a sum that struck me as a bit excessive—but I'd been hearing for years that rents in Cambridge had gone sky-high.

During the remainder of our meal—including the gelati du jour, a heavenly pairing of mango and butter pecan—Robert told me about his next round of courses. I was pleased to hear that he would be taking a literature course. "Latin American magic realism" would not have been my first choice (and perhaps revealed a bit of undue influence from his roommate), but how I looked forward to catching a glimpse of my grandson with his nose in a book that was not filled with graphs, molecular diagrams, or chemical formulas. Over my decades at Widener, whenever I strolled through a reading room of brilliant children engaged in the mastery of science, I might wonder how many of them were destined to become engineers of weaponry or even widespread destruction via computer. When I saw them deep in a volume of Fielding or Cheever, I felt a naïve surge of comfort, as if this were proof that the world, whatever its troubles, was still protected by the human heart.

On Thursday, the *Grange* arrived late, due to the relentlessly nasty weather. I was grumpy, because I could not risk running when the roads were nothing but slick, wet ice. The milk intended for my cereal had gone sour. And I had just hung up from my latest attempt to reach Sarah.

I took the paper in, microwaved my last cup of coffee, and opened to the Opinions page. My eye traveled immediately to the Fence Sitter's column.

"Move Ye on Over, Goodwife Martha!" was the title of her offering that day.

A resounding "Thank ye" goes out here to our very own crack historienne, Laurel Connaughton, for bringing off the first-ever Historic Matlock House Tour last weekend, competing bravely with a bout of weather to rouse old Noah from his nautically appointed coffin. Kudos, Laurel! Her efforts have netted an as-yet-to-be-disclosed sum (reportedly in the low but respectable five-figure range) designated as seed money for a school program to be titled "Who Says History Is a Thing of the Past?" Cumbersome, maybe, but we get the idea, Laurel, and like it we do— those of us who care about the heritage of our fine, well-aged town. Let a rowdy round of *Huzzah! Huzzah! Huzzah!,* complete with seven-musket salute, ring forth in thy name this coming Fourth. (Captain Jim Cusak of the Regulars, are ye reading this?) Now, let me take a moment on my humble colonial soapbox to single out as well our longtime citizen Percival Darling, one of the generous folks who opened their wainscoted parlors to history mavens, architectural voyeurs, and those who just wanted some inspiration on primo bathroom fixtures and wall coverings (that would be you, Jessalyn Paine!). But how I do digress! Percival Darling (may we call you Percy after lo these many decades?) is someone I neglected to felicitate earlier this year when he saved the proverbial day for Elves & Fairies by opening the doors to his old barn . . . once the haven of his talented ballerina of a wife, Penelope (may she rest in peace, especially knowing that the smallest dancers are romping in her graceful footsteps). Some of you newbies might not know that Percival's daughter Trudy Barnes, the renowned oncologist at St. Matt's, grew up in that magnificently quirky old house into which you set foot last Sunday. Percy, a heartfelt thanks for returning to the fold after so many years during which we hardly knew ye. Welcome back, comrade!

And now, segue to the succotash chowder recipe I've been promising the chefs amongst my readers. . . .

There are those who wouldn't give a freight train's hoot to see themselves trotted out in the Cheez Whiz prose of a local bigmouth like Mandy Pinkerton. (*Felicitate* my derriere.) And God knows, some poor souls probably relish such attention. Not (as you can guess) I.

I threw down the paper and cursed, on the one hand, my generosity and, on the other, my gullibility. Together, they had landed me in a capacious cauldron of hot water (or lukewarm succotash chowder; imagine!). I knew precisely what lay in store for me after a star turn in the town gossip column. It meant an even greater loss of privacy and rounds of giggles for the next few weeks in every commercial establishment from Wally's Grocery Stop to the wine store in Ledgely. This, at this moment, I did not need.

To hell with the mannerly make-believe world of Matlock. To hell with my resolve, my respect for others' "boundaries" and "feelings."

I picked up the phone and dialed Sarah. When I heard the beep, I said,

"Sarah, if you don't call me today, I promise you that I will handcuff myself to Rico the next time he leaves the bloody preschool in my backyard, if that's the only way I get to see you. Enough of this duck-and-cover. Enough of—"

"Percy."

"Sarah." I nearly wept at the sound of her voice, my name in her voice.

I heard her sigh (and not romantically). "Oh *Percy.*"

Old heart hammering, I waited.

"Percy, here's the thing. I know you feel you've done what's best for me, and I know objectively that you're right. But I had been hoping . . ."

I waited again.

"Hoping for my situation to change with this commission. I know it's naïve, but I thought it might put me in line for a job, somehow, with benefits or . . . Because of Rico, I . . . Jesus. The more I say, the stupider I'll sound."

"Talk, Sarah. Talk. Tell me the time of day. Tell me about the weather. The mud on your shoes. Sound stupid. Just try."

She told me that she had heard from Dr. Wang the previous afternoon. The pathology of the tumor was complicated. There would be more surgery, but it might come later, after other treatments, with each treatment another doctor. All of them—procedures, doctors—would cost the moon.

"That's not important now."

"Of course it is. Of course it's *important.*" She paused. "Or are you richer than I think you are? Is money a footnote to you? Are you the tweedy professor with a closet full of Krugerrands? A well-aged trustafarian?"

"I wish I were. But I can certainly lend you money until we straighten out this business about your insurance." Oddly, her anger couldn't touch me. I liked that word, *trustafarian,* and was mildly tempted to ask where she'd heard it.

"Percy, we are talking thousands and thousands of dollars. Add a few more thousands. I'm already up a creek for not having insurance in the only state that punishes you if you don't."

"You will. I'll see to that."

"My situation is complicated—"

"Oh, Sarah, whose isn't?"

"There are reasons I might not be eligible for that state insurance everybody talks about."

I'd heard rumors about our newfangled state insurance system, but I'd paid no attention, skipped all the articles in the paper. What if Sarah couldn't be insured? I thought about my retirement account, the second mortgage (half of Trudy's medical training) on which I still had a few years to go. I began to wish that, like my father, I *had* fussed over rare books and put away a cache to sell at a moment like this.

"Percy, I have an appointment to see your daughter next week."

Trudy, I thought. Trudy would solve this conundrum. "I'm very glad to hear that," I said. "What day?"

"I'm going to this one alone. I'm driving myself in. Don't even begin to protest."

I was standing in the kitchen, barefoot. I realized that my feet were freezing. I looked down. Lord but they were ugly, too.

"All right," I said. "But let's see each other this weekend. Take Rico to . . . Did you know there's a museum dedicated to knights and armor, in Worcester? I'll drive us there on Saturday."

"Knights and armor? Oh Percy."

"That's what you need. Armaments. Chivalry! What do you say?"

In the following silence, I could hear her striving to push me away. I could also hear myself winning. I clenched the fist that wasn't holding the phone.

"I can't seem to figure out what I need," she said. "Except, okay, you."

Right after Poppy's death, at least for a year or two, my habits changed. I locked the doors at night. I stopped drinking. In town, I limited myself to one cheeseburger a week. I played a lunchtime game of squash, on Mondays and Wednesdays, with Earl, my colleague in reference who covered physical science. All I could think about was how much my daughters now needed me. Needed *me*. If necessary, I would live forever.

For the last few weeks of that summer, none of us went near the pond. Helena devoted herself to getting the girls out of Matlock as often as possible. She took them to museums, to Crane's Beach on the distant

North Shore, to the mall for clothing safaris. The sound of my daughters' laughter returned to the house, in small rare bursts, by the time they were back at school, back in the buffering, benevolently selfish company of their friends.

For a time, they seemed to really like, even treasure, each other. Rarer than the sound of their laughter was the sound of sibling strife. They spent more time together in their rooms. They did homework together, both at home and at the library. *Silver lining,* that filigreed cliché, ran like a tremor through my head. In the pleasure of their harmony, I found a new source of guilt.

One night that September, I came out of my bathroom to hear them talking, in earnest tones, through Clover's open door. I stood in the shadow of the hallway and listened.

"If we were religious," said Clover, "we would believe that Mom's spirit was still alive. That she was around us, maybe hovering over the pond or something like that. That we'd meet her in heaven."

"But we're not," said Trudy. "We don't believe in God."

"Well maybe I'm not so sure."

"What do you mean?"

"I mean, I think Mom and Dad just don't get the spiritual thing. It's like a kind of blindness."

"Didn't," said Trudy.

"Didn't what?"

"You mean, Mom *didn't* get the spiritual thing. She's not around to get anything now."

"Don't be so sure," said Clover. "I get these vibes sometimes, at night. Like, if I'm out by the pond. I go down there, sometimes, if I can't go to sleep."

Dear God, I thought—and caught the irony at once. But would I have forbidden Clover from trying to commune with her lost mother? I had noticed that her recent reading included Hermann Hesse and C. S. Lewis's *Screwtape Letters.* I'd held my tongue until I saw her carrying a paperback copy of *Waiting for God,* by Simone Weil. She told me that one of her teachers had recommended the book. She seemed defensive, so I asked nothing more.

"You don't, like, go in, do you?" asked Trudy.

"That would be too creepy."

"Is it scary?" asked Trudy. "Like, do you think she's a ghost?"

"I think she's a presence. A presence specific to *here*. Like, I don't know, a warmth. Is that a ghost? Define *ghost.*"

"Well, whatever they are, I don't believe in ghosts any more than God. Science would have proved their existence by now." But after a pause, she said, "Though I almost wish I did. I'm kind of jealous that you do."

This pierced me to the core (a pain I deserved for eavesdropping on my children). Even losing Poppy would not tempt me toward some warm and fuzzy notion of afterlife reunions or the wishful nonsense of ghostly apparitions. But if Clover saw her as "a presence specific to *here,*" then I must do all I could to remain *here*. I could see that Trudy, despite her defiantly practical nature, her faith in the empirical above all else, would also feel bereft if—as so many people had suggested by now—I moved my precious little family closer to the city.

Matlock, back then, was not the hothouse of affluence it has since become, yet Poppy and I together were barely able to afford our mortgage, taxes, and the never-ending maintenance of our Methusalean home. Poppy's income from her dance lessons had been smaller than mine, but it had mattered.

From that moment on, I watched every penny, kept a budget, and tried not to let the girls notice (though I'm sure they did) that I steered them toward less expensive hobbies and summer activities. They never went to sleepaway camps, and we took our vacations at the summer homes of friends. (Helena, bless her, took Clover and then Trudy for two weeks in Paris after each girl graduated from high school.) I swore that nothing would budge us from our house with a barn by the water.

For all my economies, however, I'd stubbornly hoarded that barn. What would have happened, I wondered now, if I had shared it long before Evelyn's call—if it had evolved, comfortably, perhaps shabbily, into a local dance school run by someone else, into the office of an architecture firm, a law practice, a dental clinic? What else, other than posses of noisy toddlers, jungle gyms, tree houses, and Sarah, would be different now about the life I led? What else would I have missed?

12

Snowbirds, Loud called them, the people who left their homes every winter to go somewhere warm: not Guatemala, nowhere so unpredictable or wild, but Florida, or the tamer islands in the Caribbean. They would leave their big, elegant houses in Matlock empty for months on end. (After dark, timers turned lights on and off, to give the illusion that bodies moved upstairs and down. Anyone who had criminal intentions would hardly be fooled by this.) After Celestino took care of Mrs. Bullard's plants while she went away for November, Loud got the idea that he would offer plant-sitting over the winter, maybe even tie it in with a "plowing package."

"You figure," said Loud, "that if they've got the greenhouse of orchids, or even the scrappy collection of geraniums and spider plants, they can't get someone to come in if the house is inaccessible due to snow. Right? And some of these people have somebody check the joint for frozen pipes, sudden leaks. . . . So if I'm plowing for the caretaker, why not *be* the friggin' caretaker, right? Mother, what do we think?"

"I'd say we have a new service to offer," said Mrs. Loud. "I'll have the flyers printed out this afternoon. How about that? Or how about an e-blast? I'm getting good at that." She winked at Celestino.

Celestino had grown to like Mrs. Loud, perhaps because she never addressed him as *hombre* or asked him anything about his personal life. He had shown up at the office every few days to fetch Mrs. Bullard's keys, then returned them on his way to the train. They would talk about the weather or stories in the news unconnected to politics or war (or ICE deportations, which were suddenly very much in the news). Still, he could not bring himself to call her Happy.

Celestino had just returned Mrs. Bullard's keys for the last time. Loud had accompanied him that day, to make sure everything was in its proper place for the woman's return. He had gone in with Celestino twice during her absence. "Just to make sure you're not hijacking the silver. No offense, *hombre*," he'd said. "I know I'd be tempted!"

Celestino's contempt for Loud had increased, along with his dependence on the man. Why did it feel somehow wrong, immoral, this relationship? If the man wanted to give him greater responsibility, wasn't that a good thing? As he stood awkwardly beside the mother's desk, Celestino wondered if he could dare hope that Loud's "new service" might mean he could avoid the foot-numbing, face-freezing days spent entirely outdoors clearing the endless snow from the long drives, the patios, the rooftops and gutters, the paths to hot tubs and garden sheds. Loud had added firewood delivery, too, this fall. After one too many splinters, Celestino had broken down and bought a pair of thick leather gloves.

Finally, Loud looked at him. "So are you up for this, *hombre*? Indoor gardening? How's that for a softer mode of employment, hey?"

"I am certainly willing," Celestino said stiffly. If he seemed too eager, would Loud refuse to give him more money? Did he dare ask for more money?

"You hear that, Mother?" Loud laughed. "He's 'willing,' our *compadre* here. But in the meantime, the Pellinis are having a conniption about their leaves. That monster oak does it every year: drops a buttload of leaves all at once, right after Thanksgiving. Biological clockwork. Just like a woman."

The word *woman* pulled Celestino back to Isabelle. Not that his mind or his dreams had let go of her since Arturo had reported that he'd seen her.

After the meal at the Big Oven, the day Celestino had let himself be interviewed by Robert, Arturo had walked him home. Celestino had told him about Isabelle. He had told him too much, he knew, but this young man, Arturo, whom he would have despised in another version of his own life, had a way of making people talk. (Perhaps that's why Robert had invited him along to the interview, not just because of the language they shared.)

One evening two weeks later, Arturo had dropped by Mrs. Karp's house. He'd startled the woman, since Celestino never had visitors, but she, too, had been charmed.

He'd invited Celestino for a late dinner at a nearby bar. Arturo chattered confidently yet aimlessly in Spanish, skipping from one thing to another: the neighborhoods of Lothian, the Democratic political race, the climate. (Chicago had never quite hardened him to northern weather; was it the same for Celestino?)

Silently, Celestino wondered why Arturo wanted his company. They'd found a table and ordered beers when Arturo confessed that he was homesick for a home he no longer had. He talked about his half siblings, who had taken over his father's coffee business. "I could show up down there and they wouldn't sic the dogs on me—and there are dogs, literal dogs, believe me! But it would be weird," he said. "Which is too bad. They still resent my mother. Not the money, I think, but that my father loved her more than their mother. I'm the reminder. The love child."

They'd been in the bar for an hour, finished their burgers, when Arturo mentioned Isabelle. He had gone to that seminar at Harvard, the psychology seminar that showed up on his fancy phone. He'd invited Celestino to go—but of course he'd been working, as he did nearly every day of every week save Sundays. It shocked him to find out that Arturo had gone on his own.

"I was curious, you know?" he said. "About what kind of a woman holds a guy's fascination for years on end. Was she a siren, was she a vixen, was she an angel?"

Celestino's sudden, fearful jealousy must have shown on his face.

"Wow, man, don't chop my balls off. I said I was curious," said Arturo. "That is all. I am an inquiring kind of guy, Celestino. A student, not a schemer." *No soy un maquinador.*

Celestino tried to relax. "You spoke with her."

"No, no. Nothing like that. I just checked her out—she had to be the one you remembered. The name, the context . . . You can't turn your back on a coincidence like that. And sure thing, she talked about having had this famous archaeologist as a father, how it influenced who she is now, more than if he'd been an ordinary guy. She talked about what it's like seeing people react when they find out who your dad was. How you're tempted to flee to the opposite side of the world, just because no one there would know his name, but that's still letting him steer your life." Arturo paused. He stared at Celestino for a moment. "You're the silent one, man. Aren't you burning with questions?"

Celestino could not imagine what to ask. But there was so much he had to know!

"She's very stylish, your Isabelle."

"Yes. In that way, she was like her mother."

"That French thing."

Celestino felt miserable when he should have felt elated. Shouldn't he? He had dreamed of finding her, *intended* to find her—had he actually thought he would?—but on his own. A private search, at the right time. *When the time is ripe,* as he'd heard Loud say about this or that enterprise. He had not meant to involve someone else. He was no *maquinador,* either.

Arturo played with his empty beer bottle, printing rings of moisture on the table, the links of a chain. "So I have to confess, I followed her. After the symposium broke up, she went off alone. I know where she lives." He looked gleeful in a way that made Celestino feel ill. "Don't you want to know where?"

Celestino wished he had not eaten the burger. It was too large, obscenely large, more than he generally ate for any meal. "Why do you tell me all this?"

"Why wouldn't I?" Arturo shot back. "I thought . . . Oh. You think I've condescended to help you. Is that it? Robert does this, too. Accuses me of acting like I'm some kind of benefactor." He made a noise of disgust.

Couldn't the boy's efforts be sincere? He was obviously a romantic. And what was Celestino if not a romantic? His mother told him so again and again. In her mouth, it was an accusation.

"I want to see her," he said. "But I thought it would come at a time when I was . . . ready."

"Ready how? Who's ever ready for anything this important? I mean sure, it's totally risky. But next week she could up and move to California. Right? Or meet some guy. I'll tell you this, too, for what it's worth." Arturo leaned toward Celestino and grinned. He raised his left hand and spread his fingers. "No wedding ring, man. And only *her* name on the buzzer at her building."

Aware that he was blushing, Celestino thought about the girl he'd known: old for her age, yes, but still a girl; not a full-grown woman with style and money and . . . advantages that were matched by nothing he had to show. Celestino laughed.

"What?" said Arturo. "What's so funny?"

"I am thinking of how my mother believes in destiny. Destiny over choices that you make. As if it doesn't matter what you plan for. In the end, it's all written. It always was."

"Excuse me, but that is crap," said Arturo. "All that Catholic, God's-will stuff? I outgrew that by age five." He looked at his watch. "Sorry, but I have to make the last train in. So here." He handed Celestino a piece of paper, folded. "Her address. Also, my phone number in case you lost it."

When the radio news carried stories about the raids and the deportations, they were almost always somewhere distant—Illinois or Oklahoma, maybe California. They were in communities where poor white people, "legal" people, hated Latinos for having jobs when they had none. Not that they would have wanted those other jobs, the jobs killing pigs or cleaning sewers or climbing trees to pick fruit. Though sometimes the people who were deported had businesses, modest businesses like tailor shops or souvenir stands. But always, these things went on in distant parts of the country.

Celestino knew his geography, better than some Americans, but he also knew it was dangerous to feel safe just because these people were being persecuted somewhere else.

After returning Mrs. Bullard's keys, he spent a day clearing and shredding a truckload of oak leaves from the Pellinis' lawn. After Gil dropped him off at the station, Celestino went directly to Loud's office.

Loud's mother looked up from the desk she never seemed to leave. "Celestino! Did you miss me already? How nice to see your face."

Her enthusiasm was daunting. He hoped his smile looked genuine. "Will Mr. Loud return soon?"

"My grandson has a basketball tryout, so no. Not this evening," she said. "I'm just staying late to catch up on the books."

Celestino tried to imagine his mother, who was a good deal younger than Happy Loud, putting such energy, such uncomplaining efforts, into the business of one of her children. (Or would she have done this, something like this, if Celestino went back? Then he remembered that she could not do sums, would never learn to use a computer.)

"I wished to speak with Mr. Loud about the idea he spoke of yesterday."

She thought for a moment before she remembered. She pointed to a stack of envelopes on the corner of her desk. "Yes! The flyers go into the mail tomorrow. *Let us tend your winter gardens. Leave home without a care!* Is that what I cooked up?"

"I would like to do that."

"Well, yes, I think Tommy assumes as much, dear." She winked.

"Yes," said Celestino. "Good."

She patted him on the back as she saw him out the door. His usual train was pulling away. He walked along the platform to the box that held free newspapers about the goings-on in Boston. It was empty.

He sat on the bench and thought about the only thing he could these days: Isabelle. Her ringless hands. Her address—an unfamiliar street in Cambridge. Irving. He could, if he wanted, take the train right past Lothian and all the way to Cambridge. He could find that street. He looked down at himself; a peppering of shredded leaves clung to everything he wore.

It had been dark for over an hour; the long cold nights of December felt like a penance you paid in order to celebrate Christmas. Of all the very different, American versions of rituals he knew from his childhood, those surrounding Christmas were his favorite ones. He liked the colored lights: outside against the snow, inside among the branches of an evergreen tree. He liked the sound of carols, the way the singers' voices ballooned in the crisp, dry air. But most of all, Celestino loved the churches: how people filled a tall chilly space with candlelight, with song, with clothing that was suddenly bright (the men in jackets of red or brilliant green, holly pinned to lapels or woolen caps). Children became important, too, reminding him of home. Children acted out the scenes of the Nativity; babies, with their restlessness and crying, were no longer a nuisance.

Christmas was less than two weeks away. Would he spend it alone this year as well, join Mrs. Karp for breakfast if, yet again, her son did not come home from California? (Yet how could Celestino think ill of the man, of any man who, like him, stayed away from his family on such holy days?)

Celestino had spent three Christmases with the Lartigues: the first when he was fifteen, the others when he returned for college. Christmas had been a very social time for the professor and his wife. Dr. Lartigue stood on a ladder to string white lights through the branches of two spruce trees separating their house from the sidewalk, and he moved the furniture in their living room to make way for an indoor tree as well. He put electric candles in every window facing the street, and Celestino had helped him drape garlands of pine and holly along banisters, mantels, and doorways. The house became a visual fiesta. Señora Lartigue spent several days cooking for two separate parties. One was for colleagues from Harvard, along with their families. The adults gathered for civilized conversation in the living room, while the children (who did not know one another well, if at all) wound up watching a Disney movie on the VCR machine, down in the basement room that was filled with games and puzzles.

The second party was smaller but livelier, the guests a dozen French families who, like the Lartigues, had chosen to live in the States (though anyone, even Celestino, could tell that they saw in this choice a significant sacrifice). At this party, the grown-ups laughed and shouted together in their first, preferred language while the youngest of their children ran happily up and down the stairs, easy and playful with one another. The older children went to the basement and took turns playing Ping-Pong. Those who waited their turns would gossip and flirt, in English as often as French. The TV was on, but they barely watched it. That first year, Isabelle's brother, Etienne, smuggled a bottle from the kitchen, pouring slugs of rum into glasses of ginger ale and "virgin" eggnog. That was also the year when Isabelle welcomed him into this group. ("Don't follow Georges outside if he lures you," she warned him. "The guy is barely in lycée and high as a cloud like ninety percent of his waking life. Put 'waking' in quotes.")

That year, Celestino had strained hard to follow their conversation. But they taught him to play Hearts, and Isabelle smiled at him across her hand of cards, so that even if he never spoke, he felt included.

Three years later, he was welcomed instantly. The "older children" were older still, half a dozen in their third or fourth year of college. The rum no longer required smuggling, certainly not the bottles of wine. Still they played Ping-Pong and Hearts, though four of the college boys now switched to poker, playing for money.

Isabelle put on a tape of what she declared to be her favorite French movie: *Les Enfants du Paradis,* a long black-and-white fantasy romance, a fairy tale from the look of it. Her efforts to get anyone to sit down and focus on the movie were futile. "Later," she said to Celestino, "I am forcing you to watch it with me. It is beyond awesome. These thugs just don't give a damn about art."

Celestino was careful not to drink too much of the spiked soda or wine. That Christmas, during his first year at the community college, he was still nearly paralyzed with gratitude to be there, to have returned to the magical life of the Lartigues. As he played Hearts with Isabelle and her girlfriends that night, he would glance at the TV screen, fascinated by the chalky, soulful faces of the hero and heroine in the movie. Their world looked strange, but no more strange to him than this world, in the basement of this richly decorated house.

The guests left after midnight. Dr. and Señora Lartigue went up to bed, leaving dishes, wineglasses, napkins where they lay. Etienne had gone into the Square with the other poker players.

Celestino was about to follow Isabelle's parents upstairs when she said, "I meant what I said. About the movie. So come on, you."

He was tired, but he let her lead him back downstairs. She rewound the tape and started it again. He sat down on the couch beside her.

The English subtitles were hard to follow, but the story, its fairy-tale essence, seemed familiar. He had just begun to sink into the characters' lives when he felt Isabelle's hand. Ever so gently, she laid it palm down on his thigh. She kept her eyes on the actors. Terrified, he did nothing in response. He froze. Perhaps fifteen minutes later, she removed her hand.

At the end of the movie, she turned to him and said, "Have you ever seen a greater love story? Isn't Jean-Louis Barrault the most haunting, soulful, *beautiful* man you've ever seen? Not to imply anything homo-erotic, but . . . What did you think, Celestino? Did you love it?"

Celestino said, "I did. It was . . . it kept me wide awake." He looked at the clock. It was three-thirty in the morning.

She laughed. "Kept you awake? I hope it was better than that."

That was the beginning—not literally, because he held out until the spring, when Isabelle, as she had promised, gave him swimming lessons—but that was when he might have made a different, more defi-nite choice: spoken to her, laid down rules. But Celestino had never been the one to lay down rules.

"We are the children of paradise, you from one paradise, I from another," she said the first time they took off their clothes together and found, with stunning ease, how to fit their young bodies together. "I will always think of us that way, no matter what happens. *Les enfants du paradis, c'est nous.*"

The next month, he returned to his family. Summer passed like a long, rainy dream. He worked with his father, at a logging site and at the archaeologists' depot, cleaning artifacts. Raul teased Celestino that he would soon grow soft and scholarly, but he did so with pride.

Isabelle wrote him two long, passionate letters, yet when he flew north again in September, he felt more fear than excitement—until Isabelle, running ahead of her father at the airport, whispered in his ear, "*Salut, enfant.*"

Two Sundays before Christmas, he took an early train from Lothian to Cambridge and went to their church—the church where they had taken him when Dr. Lartigue was alive. A sign told him the first service would start at nine, the second at eleven.

At eight, someone pushed open the front doors. Celestino went in, choosing a pew near the back. Nothing had changed. The place was white as a newly frosted cake, the pews lined with limp velvet cushions the color of dried blood. The windows rose to the height of full-grown trees, each filled with dozens of panes, glass that was clear yet rumpled. Above the altar, the wooden cross was a blunt, declarative shape, no suffering Christ, no ornamental carving, not even a touch of color to suggest the extraordinary drama surrounding the crucifixion. Sitting there did not bring on the strong emotions Celestino had imagined. He was disappointed yet relieved.

An invisible musician began to play the organ. A young woman in a black robe carried a large vase of red and white carnations to the front of the church and placed it on a ledge beside the pulpit. She did not seem to notice Celestino. If anyone did approach, he would pretend to pray. Or perhaps he really would.

Supposing she still went to church—and there was a good chance she didn't; her attitude had never been one of devotion—would she go early or late? Would she go alone?

He paged through the prayer book, then the hymnal.

At eight-thirty, the organist began to play more loudly, as if he'd been practicing and now he was performing. A few worshipers walked in and took seats in the front pews. One woman looked at Celestino and smiled.

People were talking and laughing at the entrance of the church, through the wall at his back. But once inside, they fell silent or continued their conversations in a whisper. A woman entered holding a baby in a long dress, followed by a man and an older couple. A christening. Celestino smiled.

She walked in at five to nine, heading quickly toward the front. She wore her hair in the same way—curled in against the back of her head, tight and smooth, a graceful helmet—though it had grayed quite a bit. Right behind Señora Lartigue, though he was clearly her companion, walked a tall thin man who looked every bit as professorial as Dr. Lartigue had looked.

They seated themselves far forward, to the right, so that Celestino could see her almost in profile.

This was the logical encounter, he realized: the mother, not the daughter. But it wasn't the one he wanted, not at all. In fact, though he had felt nothing profound when he entered the church, he trembled when he saw Señora Lartigue. That visceral fear came over him like a heavy, suffocating hood.

As the minister took his place in the pulpit and held out his hands, asking everyone to rise and sing, Celestino fled the church.

He hurried toward the center of Harvard Square. How stupid was he? What had he expected? What, for God's sake, had he even planned?

He stopped at the news kiosk, where newspapers in every conceivable language were sold. He searched for something in Spanish; there was a Mexican paper with headlines about a political scandal that might as well have been unfolding in China.

He walked into a bakery and bought himself a bagel and a cup of coffee. He took them back outside and sat on a bench in the brick plaza. It was uncomfortably cold, but he needed to be outside, to breathe fresh air.

Why was he here: in this city, in this country, in this life? Was it all because a group of strange men had shown up in his village before he was born? Was his life being lived as a thread spooling out from that day? Could he cut that thread and begin a new spool—or tie a great knot in it, defy the silken, seductive unreeling over which he seemed to have little control?

The air was bitterly cold, yet the coffee was too hot to drink. He set it down on the bench beside him and ate the bagel. Seeds stuck to his lips and fell to his lap. Angrily, he brushed them away—and as he did so, he struck the cup of coffee, which spilled onto the bench against his pants. He stood abruptly, cursing. He reached into the pocket of his coat, hoping to find a stray bit of napkin. What he pulled out was a small sheet of paper, torn from a notepad, with the telephone number of Arturo, the half Guatemalan, the boy who honestly *missed* his home in the jungle. He was, right then, the closest thing to a friend in Celestino's life. And what did this say about that life?

13

The groom and the groom were cutting the cake. Raucous masculine cheers filled the room as Joe and Jonathan, playfully indelicate, pushed wedges of devil's food into each other's mouths. They wore tuxedos, Joe's shirt canary yellow, Jonathan's blue-chip blue. Anthony's cheer was so loud that Ira felt a ringing in his left ear after the clamor died down and the music rose to encourage dancing.

A Christmas Eve wedding was pretty cheeky, thought Ira, but some two hundred friends of the couple had been willing—had been thrilled—to forgo whatever traditions they normally pursued in order to be there. And of course, there were the Jews, including the lapsed Jews like Ira, those who celebrated Christmas as stowaways. (Anthony's Catholic parents lived in Ohio; only once had they gone out there to do the big-family thing.)

Joe was a partner at Anthony's firm. He'd been with Jonathan for four years. They'd registered at Shreve, Crump & Low, exchanged vows at the wealthiest liberal Episcopal church downtown, and here they were now, celebrating at Locke-Ober, their reception an elegant yet decidedly queer in-your-face jab at the straight, cigar-smoking WASP clientele of yore. Oysters Rockefeller, white asparagus, lobster bisque, filet mignon with scalloped potatoes. Ira couldn't believe they were now about to consume cake.

"Smile. You look like you're attending a *funeral*," Anthony whispered as they carried their plates to an empty table. "I'd tickle you if I had a free hand."

"And I would burst," said Ira.

They sat down, facing the tiny makeshift dance floor. Joe and Jonathan were dancing, alone, to "They All Laughed." More cheers, though kinder and gentler this time. A small but conspicuous smear of chocolate frosting besmirched Joe's yellow shirt, but those two boys, arms entwined, moving gracefully to that jazzy, sexy trombone, were a modern icon of newlywed bliss.

Side by side, Ira and Anthony ate their cake in silence.

And now, Ira saw it coming. Associate Janine approached their table with that very specific smile. Before Ira could head her off at the pass, she leaned down and said, "Are you next, guys? Hm?"

Anthony had learned to behave as if this were more funny than awkward. He turned to Ira and cocked his head. "Now *how* many garters have we caught between us, darling? Those years with the Patriots trained you well."

"Okay, okay," said Janine. "I'll back off. It's just . . . I mean, this was the most romantic wedding I've ever attended. Counting the I can't even *remember* how many where I was a bridesmaid."

Ira resisted the cruel urge to say, *And how 'bout you, Janine?* Janine was forty and had never been married. Ira knew, though Anthony had sworn him to secrecy, that she was in a longtime entanglement with a senior partner who, according to Anthony, would never leave his wife, if only because she was the one who owned the house on Nantucket.

He said, instead, "No one's ever asked *me* to be a bridesmaid."

Janine laughed, and Ira was grateful when she moved on toward another table. He was also grateful that the senior partner who'd stolen her heart (and her childbearing potential) had been unable to attend the wedding.

Anthony had finished his cake and was gazing at Ira, still smiling. "I love you in that jacket."

Ira blushed. "Pass muster in public, do I?"

"In private, too. As you know. You can pass me that muster anytime."

Ira looked reflexively away. Several guests were crushed together on the dance floor, curbing the extravagant movements inspired by "In the Mood."

"I think this is the one."

"This what is the one? The one what?" Ira tried to sound flip.

"The wedding that finally makes us talk about whether we're going to take that plunge ourselves."

"Anthony, this isn't the place."

Anthony leaned close. "Where *is* the place? Tell me, and I'll be there.

On time, even." When Ira did not answer, he stood up. "Let's go outside. Let's walk through the Common."

"And get mugged? It is freezing out there. And consequently deserted." Without meeting Anthony's gaze, he could feel its accusation.

Anthony sat down. He put his hand on Ira's sleeve. "Can I just say that it's like you were paralyzed by what happened last spring? Like you were hit by a bus and you're still in the ICU, breathing tubes and all."

"In case you haven't noticed, I'm very happy in Matlock. Some things happen for the best. Crisis equals danger plus opportunity; isn't that what the Chinese say?"

Anthony groaned. "Why are you talking to me like this?"

"I could say the same to you." Ira started to cry. He took the linen napkin with which he'd wiped cake from his mouth and held it to his eyes. "I'm sorry," he said. "I'm sorry."

He felt Anthony's hand on his back. It moved up and down in a way that ought to have felt comforting. He realized what his apology might sound like, so he wiped his eyes quickly. "I am not breaking up with you. Please, not that."

"Well. That's something." Anthony looked weary.

"It's time to go home. We don't dance anyway, do we?" Ira scanned the room for the newlyweds. Joe was dancing, tenderly, with Jonathan's grandmother. Jonathan was surrounded by a group of friends who were drunkenly hugging him, one after the other. Or maybe they weren't drunk. Maybe they were sincerely moved, and they were unafraid to show it.

"Fine. Let's go." Anthony stood and, skirting the dancers, made straight for the coatroom.

Ira had no choice but to follow. He glanced at the grooms, hoping for a quick wave, a gesture of joy and gratitude, but both men were soundly cocooned—yes, that was the definitive word.

They waited in razorlike silence for their coats and then, on the street, for the valet to retrieve their car.

"At the risk of deepening this chasm," Anthony said suddenly, "I have one thing to say, and then I'm done. I think we need a big celebration. Of us. It's time. And you know what? I'm up for an act of defiance. I see so many divorces. I'm getting fed up that they pay our grocery bills."

"I know," Ira said gently. "That is discouraging. I, on the other hand, see lots of little boys and girls propose to each other, hold hands, and trade kisses. They treat true love like the lark it ought to be." *But so totally and tragically isn't,* he did not say. Yet how could he not admire Anthony's yearning for an "act of defiance"? What if marriage was just as noble when it meant *no* as when it meant *yes*?

Anthony, as promised, said nothing more. Their car arrived, and Anthony drove them home.

Unless they were invited to someone else's place, Christmas was a lazy, low-key holiday for Anthony and Ira. They decorated a small tree—the kind you could put on a table, like a flower arrangement—and they exchanged a few gifts, luxurious yet practical (the cashmere sweater, the stack of intelligent mysteries, the copper saucepan). No stockings, no gimmicky gadgets from Brookstone, no fruitcake or mince pie, no mistletoe or holly. And God, no endless CDs of "Jingle Bells" as tarted up by Ella, Elvis, and Bing.

This year, Clover had invited them to her apartment in Matlock for "afternoon cheer." Ira feared that she had some scheme up her sleeve, involving Anthony and the kids, but Anthony assured him that if they were socializing, this would put a damper on any custody-related business in the future.

"And hey," he said, "you're always telling me you like the people you work with there, but I never get to meet them!"

"That's because you're so busy."

Anthony turned away from the recycling bin, where he had just put the folded tissue paper from their gifts. "Ira, that's a crock."

Clover lived in the top floor of a converted carriage house. She'd lit dozens of red candles and put on the *Messiah.* They were the first to arrive.

"Welcome, troubadors!" she said when she opened the door.

"We forgot our lutes, I'm afraid," said Ira.

"My son's studying the Middle Ages," Clover said to Anthony. "So we were just talking about the arts back then. Such as they were, with all the ambient warfare and violence. *Not* a time I would choose to have led a former life!" She put their coats on a bench—a cast-off church pew—

against the wall. Glancing around the large, raftered living room, Ira wasn't surprised to see its scattershot collection of funky furniture: a fifties formica table, a vast rococo wall mirror whose glass was brindled with age; an old postcard carousel, its porcupine prongs painted cobalt blue and hung with hats for every season. It looked more like a Christmas tree—more festive and gaudy—than the actual tree set up for the occasion.

Clover's children sat on the couch, huddled together over a hand-held device of some kind. Clover made them put it down, stand up, and shake hands. Ira offered small talk about vacations as the highlight of the school year. The girl, Filo, was extremely pretty, a nymphlike vision of what her mother must have looked like at nine or ten. Lee was aloof, nodding for yes, lips clamped in that all-suffering *Take me back to my people* facial expression of boys at the cliff of puberty.

Clover took their bottle of champagne to the kitchen. When she returned, she offered sherry, eggnog (sober or sauced), hot cider, and Shirley Temples. "Seltzer's available for Scrooges," she said.

Anthony proclaimed himself a Scrooge. Ira accepted a glass of sherry, though the thought of anything rich and sweet made him feel vaguely depressed.

Anthony wandered toward a side table (formerly the wrought-iron pedestal for a sewing machine) displaying framed photos. This was his habit in any new home they visited. It used to annoy Ira, who claimed that it seemed too nosy—but Anthony argued that people put those pictures on display *wanting* them to be perused; *wanting* questions to be asked, stories about their lives brought forth. ("Who's this grande dame in the amazing flapper?" "Is this Provincetown?" "Don't tell me that's *you* in the Jim Morrison T-shirt!") With rare exceptions, said Anthony, people want to talk about family almost more than anything else. "If there's one thing my work has taught me," he liked to say, "it's that we're all tribal in the end."

As if on cue, the doorbell rang—and in walked Clover's dad.

"Percy! Merry Christmas!" Ira exclaimed.

"Greetings," Percy answered, crossing the room to shake hands. He looked around, frowning slightly at the candles burning on a nearby windowsill. "Where is everyone? I expect the sharing of 'cheer' to be a populous affair."

"Just family and the best of friends," said Clover. "I don't do cattle calls." She took her father's coat.

Percy examined Ira. "Which makes you a best friend, correct?"

Anthony walked over and introduced himself.

"Percy made the new school possible," said Ira, not that Anthony didn't know this. Ira had told him a number of "Mr. Darling" stories.

"I gave it a new skin, that's all. One might say that the school went through a molting process." He accepted a glass of eggnog from Clover. "Hail," he called out to his grandchildren, who'd reimmersed themselves in electronic play. "Set that gizmo down and practice being social. It will serve you well in life! Come tell these folks about the real world beyond our castle moat."

"I grew up in New York," Ira said to Lee.

"Yeah?"

"Well, Forest Hills. Which might as well be Fargo. But I got into the city a lot when I was your age."

Tight-lipped nod.

"Queens is cool," said Filo. "I have camp friends from there. And I mean, we live in Brooklyn, so it's not like we would dis the outer boroughs."

"Tell them about your camp," said Clover.

Which led to Filo's description of a horseback-riding summer camp an hour from Matlock, for which she was already signed up and counting the days.

"My daughters were deprived of such luxuries," Percy declared.

"Daddy, we had 4-h, remember? It was the old-time equivalent," said Clover. "You can stop doing this thing where you compare what you gave us to what parents give their children now. I'm sure we're overdoing it."

The doorbell rang and Robert entered, along with an older man who appeared to be his father. Yes, Ira noted, they had the same tawny brown eyes, the dad's framed by tortoiseshell glasses. The dad also wore a cornball tie with red-nosed reindeer leaping in diagonal rows.

Clover rushed over to hug them. "Where's your mom?" she said to Robert.

"On call. She dropped us off and said to say she's sorry."

"How can she be on call Christmas Day? She's the boss!" Clover laughed, but she was frowning. "She didn't mention that this morning."

"Somebody called in sick or something. You know Mom. Dr. Perfect."

The father did not back up this statement but made his way toward the other guests. Right away, he introduced himself to Ira and Anthony. He was a plain-looking man—perhaps he'd simply aged out of Robert's appealing lankiness, the bearish thatch of dark smooth hair—but he was admirably fit and had, Ira noticed with envy, beautiful teeth. His skin, though patchy from the cold, looked young, symptomatic of a life with few concerns, a temperament unclouded by neuroses.

Douglas shook Anthony's hand for an extra beat or two. "I know I've heard your name," he said. And then he laughed. "Ah, yes. The Python. I have clients who've been tempted by your services. Tempted to empty their bank accounts, I might add!"

Ira watched Anthony react. He chose to be amused. "Clearly we have a juicy conversation ahead of us."

"The Python?" said Percy. "Keeper of the fateful apple?"

Anthony seemed to be considering his answer when Douglas said, "He's been known to squeeze his opponents so hard—and so subtly— that they have no choice but to cough up their hidden assets."

Percy continued to look aggressively baffled.

"We're talking divorce court, Dad," said Douglas.

Anthony was now the center of attention—which he loved, no matter what the circumstances.

"So, you're an engineer to the splintering of society," Percy said cheerfully.

"I would rephrase that," said Anthony. "Restorer of the peace where atomic war was imminent."

Percy laughed loudly. Douglas joined in, though a minute too late to look like he found it all that funny. Filo and Lee stared at the older men as if they'd arrived at this party from another planet.

Robert came out of the bathroom and called to his cousins, "Want me to set up your Wii? I'm dying to give it a go."

Without a word, the children fled, vanishing with Robert into another room. Ira felt marooned, since Robert was the one person he'd genuinely hoped to see at this gathering.

Anthony and Douglas stood at the drinks table, deep into gossip or shop talk. Was Robert's father a divorce lawyer, too? The world was a pathetic place if two out of five adults were involved in that line of work.

"Ira," said Percy, shocking Ira by using his actual name, "don't you have a family demanding your presence on this sacred day?"

"My family's Jewish—though not in any meaningful way. They do a seder. Light the menorah. That's about it. Fourth of July gets the biggest party out of my mom." Even Ira's bar mitzvah had been a tepid affair: more time spent in recitation at the temple than partying at the hired room of the local JCC.

"You live here?"

"Here?"

"Matlock."

"Oh no," said Ira. "Are you kidding? Lothian's where we . . . live."

Cat out of the satchel, sweetheart. Oh when would that voice shut up?

Percy nodded toward Anthony. "Your roommate would be the Python."

"He would."

"Your karma must balance his out. For every trust fund he plunders, you nurture another young soul."

Ira heard his own laugh as verging on manic. "Well. That's a blunt way to put it."

Clover joined them. "Daddy, did I hear someone call you 'blunt' again? Do I have to ask you to behave?" She glanced at Ira. "What did you say?"

"I said," said Percy, "that young men who wrangle small children without losing their wits deserve citations of valor."

Ira laughed, again hysterically. He set down his sherry and reached for a cheese puff. Suddenly he was hungry. So much for the four-thousand-calorie nuptials.

Heidi, Evelyn (no Maurice), and Ruth happened to arrive all at once. Ira was relieved and made his way to greet them, though this meant that, rudely, he abandoned Percy. The man seemed brilliant, even likable, but fearsome. Ira felt too fragile for fearsome. He was afraid that if they spoke for another ten minutes, Percy would come right out and ask why Ira was dragging his feet on marrying the Python. (Was it perhaps *because* Anthony was the Python? Now there was a provocative question.)

The party grew no larger, and an hour later (once Clover had flushed her children out of the room with the TV), Ira looked around to see Anthony engaged in serious conversation with Robert, Lee at the fringes. Somewhat pathetically, Ira had stuck with the easy company of his coworkers, leaving Douglas paired with his father-in-law.

He heard Percy say, "Trudy isn't really on call, is she?"

Douglas hesitated. "She's exhausted. This time of year does her in."

"It does everyone in. Or is she baking cookies for all her patients?"

"Take it up with Dr. B. I have little influence when it comes to her physical movements in the world. And how about *your* other half? Where's Sarah?"

"Prior commitments," said Percy. "And let's not exaggerate, shall we? Last I looked, I was all here, a glorious whole."

Suddenly Robert was standing beside Ira. "Hey, big dude. How's life with all the micro-dudes?"

"Just fine, but taking a break is even finer." Ira wondered sometimes if what he enjoyed most about Robert was his youthful ease, his glib sweetness.

The boy shifted from one large foot to another, like a horse. "So," he said. "Turo and I were thinking we might decorate the tree house for the auction."

"How brilliant!" said Ira. "We even have our theme. Woodstock. The invitations will instruct everybody to 'dress countercultural.' "

"Aunt Clo's idea. Yeah. So how does a tree do counterculture?"

"Grows against the grain? Listens to Donovan; you know, 'Jennifer Juniper'?"

"Dude." Robert groaned with amusement.

"The mini-dudes will want to help," said Ira, trying to hide how pleased he was at his own pathetic jokes.

"Word," said Robert.

"Where is Turo? I thought we passed him on our way over."

Robert shook his head. "Turo's at a friend's place, in the Square, for Christmas. I think he'd rather hang here, but he said he couldn't mooch for two holidays in a row."

Ira nodded, though he was sure that as he and Anthony had turned onto Percy's lane, he'd seen Turo standing in the woods. He'd said nothing to Anthony, who was ranting about a case involving three children with two drug-addict parents. Ira had waved, but Turo probably hadn't seen him. Was he on skis? Though what did it matter? It hadn't been Turo after all.

The week in New York was, in a word, restorative—never mind that they ran themselves ragged dashing from one attraction to the next, as if desperate to take in every play on or off Broadway; every fashion sale, from Barneys to East Ninth Street; every newfangled work of art, from Dia to Williamsburg. They ate ridiculously well: Italian in Chelsea, Japanese in TriBeCa, French on Gansevoort, Thai in Queens (an accidental find the day they visited Ira's parents).

Perhaps they got along so well, and loved each other's company so much, because they were constantly in motion. And then they were in bed, in the dark, where any introspective conversation they shared— inevitably and deliciously weary—would be about Richard Serra or Stephen Sondheim or the beet-red suit by agnès b. that Anthony was almost but not quite brave enough to buy. ("Maybe if your nickname in court were the Rooster," said Ira when they left the store on Prince Street. "Cock of the Walk," Anthony suggested. "The perp walk," Ira said, and they laughed wantonly for the next two blocks, drawing the envious irritation of everyone they passed.)

Ira realized that while he often missed New York, he had lost the prickly need to behave, when he returned, as if he were anything other than a tourist. Likewise, he felt surprisingly tolerant of his parents' ingrained habits and tastes, once as tough as gristle for Ira to digest. It helped that Anthony accepted them as they were (his own parents were equally if differently bizarre), but for the first time, Ira accepted Anthony's acceptance, understanding what it really meant.

On the night of their visit, Ira's mother made a casserole of broccoli, chicken, and cheese—mixed with a can of Campbell's mushroom soup. This had been Ira's favorite meal as a child, and why should he tell her that the allure of such food had dimmed almost as soon as he left home? So of course she made it every single time he returned—and as everyone finished their salad (served first, American style, with salmon-colored tomato wedges and dressing from a bottle), she would ceremoniously remove the immortal Corningware dish from the oven and set it down on the familiar heart-shaped trivet.

She would smile proudly as she focused both love and caution on carrying the hot dish to the table. In the past, Ira had often looked away from her smile, embarrassed. But this time, he was touched by her faithfulness to this ritual, and an odd thought occurred to him. He'd had a happy childhood, as childhoods go. He, the child, might not have been happy all or even most of the time, but his surroundings had been remarkably serene and cheerful. That was the "hood" part of childhood, the context, the environment, ecosphere—call it what you like. Ira had taken a course in grad school dedicated to the nature-versus-nurture debate: what makes a child grow up with a particular accent or a bad temper; prone to depression or excess weight; alcoholic; sporty; religious?

Ira's parents beamed at Anthony, as if he already *were* their son-in-law. Wasn't this the very best you could ask of your parents, at this point in life? This and your favorite food from ages seven to seventeen?

It dawned on him, so abruptly that he nearly choked on his rice pilaf: Inner Ira, resident cynic, had not come along on this vacation.

"Memory lane, Mom," said Ira after swallowing the first salty bite of the casserole.

The first day back at school, Ira and Evelyn arrived before everyone else, so they were the ones to discover the damage wrought by a frozen pipe. Evelyn cajoled Matlock's only plumber into putting them at the head of the day's list. Even so, the children's bathroom would have to be closed for the morning.

Ira realized that the task of soaking up the small lake in the hall would require more than a mop. E & F's part-time custodian, who brought his own equipment, wouldn't show up until the end of the week.

Up at the house, once he'd climbed to the back porch, Ira could see that Percy Darling was awake, eating breakfast at the kitchen table.

"I am so sorry to disturb you, but we're in SOS mode, desperately seeking a Shop-Vac. Or a gigantic pile of rags."

"Well." Percy smiled sardonically. "Happy new year."

"Oh yes, to you too!"

Percy held the door open for Ira to enter. "Let me look in the basement. My grandson keeps track of these things, to the extent that anyone does."

"Let me go down," said Ira. "I've troubled you enough."

"Sit." Percy pointed to a chair at the table. "I wouldn't want you to trip on the bodies. We do not cater to the squeamish."

Ira laughed nervously. He sat where he was told. Beside a plate holding half an English muffin, the Matlock town paper was open to the police log. He scanned the week's misadventures: the greatest tragedy was that a dog had fallen through the ice on a local pond; the owner had been restrained from an attempted rescue. This snippet of news did not include the fate of the dog.

Ira heard clattering from the basement. He went to the open door. "Everything okay down there?" He made his way down the steep stairs and, at the bottom, had to stoop severely to avoid cracking his head on one of the jagged rafters. The place was primeval in the extreme.

Percy, bent over as well, pointed to a barrel-shaped appliance under a worktable. "Is this the contraption you seek? Either that or it's some gizmo pertaining to Norval's beer-making scheme. Which I knew to be ludicrous from the start. But guess who had the space for such an enterprise?"

Ira did not ask who Norval was. Stepping over a coiled hose, a milk crate filled with extension cords, and a cardboard box labeled WINTER MISC., he discovered that the machine in question was indeed a Shop-Vac. "Thank you *so much*," he said as he hauled it toward the stairs.

Ira carried the body of the vacuum; Percy brought along the tubular accessories. In the kitchen, both men sneezed from the dust. Together, they laughed. Percy offered Ira a cup of tea or coffee.

"I wish I could say yes," said Ira. "But the kids arrive in fifteen minutes and we have Niagara Falls on our hands."

Percy stood by the table, glancing down at the paper. "All quiet on the eco-terrorist front. Do we think these crusaders head south for the winter? These—what do they call themselves—DOGS?"

Ira hadn't thought about the pranks in a month; Percy was right. "Like geese," said Ira. "So maybe they're fouling up pools in Palm Beach for a change. Ha. No pun intended!"

Percy walked him to the door. "Pity. I rather enjoyed their shenanigans. Last town meeting was almost as good as a Woody Allen movie."

"Oh, I doubt we've seen the last of them," said Ira. "They're too crazy—or maybe too stylish—to simply fade away."

By the end of the day, Maurice Fougère's glistening floors, cherry and tile alike, were scored and scuffed with muddy footprints. The children had tracked water into every niche in every room. The place looked dismal.

Ira would have to stay extra late, not just to do his share of cleaning but because Rico's mother had asked to meet with him after the other children left. Rico would stay in the classroom with Heidi; Ira and Sarah would confer in the tiny teachers' room that overlooked the pond.

Sarah was waiting for him, standing at the window. She'd lost weight over the break, that was obvious. Since she was a far cry from your typical bird-boned Matlock mom, this ought to have made her more attractive, but when she faced Ira, her entire body seemed to broadcast her anxiety.

"Sarah, how are you?" He crossed the room to stand beside her.

"Enduring." She shrugged. "I dramatize. Maybe better than that."

Ira nodded and asked her to sit.

"How's Rico? That's the important question," she said.

"Sarah, this is his first day back after nearly a month away. He was maybe a little more quiet than usual, but then, we had the Chatty Cathy Club trading factoids on their brand-new dolls. Guys couldn't get a word in edgewise."

"He seems to get quieter all the time."

"All the time, or in the past few weeks? Can I suggest it might be because he's *listening*? He knows something dire is afoot. Do I guess you haven't told him what's about to happen to his mom?" Ira made an effort to sound gentle.

Ira had worried about Rico already, just a little, before this unkind stroke of fate. His chronic reticence seemed more withholding than shy. The other boys had formed a closer alliance since September, accentuating Rico's tendency toward solitude—though maternal Marguerite was forever trying to induct him into her circle of influence. She was the queen bee among the girls, directing all games involving theatrical roles. Rico was useful to her whenever she needed an Aladdin to her Jasmine, a Wilbur to her Charlotte. She didn't mind if she had all the lines, including his.

"My treatment starts next week."

"Evelyn told me." He waited to hear her say something else. "Do you want my help to tell him what's up? He doesn't need all the gory details, Mom."

"It's not the details about me, about how tired or sick I'll feel—that's not what I worry about explaining. That's sort of the easy part," said Sarah. "Right. Easy." She laughed. "So, Ira, you know about my relationship with Percy."

"Sure," he said. "I think it's great."

She frowned. "I don't mean to be rude, but I don't care who thinks it's great and who thinks it's . . . not. I'm not happy that he lives right here, at the school, but I guess I wouldn't have met him otherwise. Well, that's not quite true." She seemed to consider this briefly amusing. "But here's the thing. The guy who helps me look after Rico—just sometimes, like when I have to travel for work, which isn't often—is this ex-boyfriend of mine. He loves Rico. I met him right after the adoption. But things between us didn't work out. I had a hunch he wanted kids of his own, and I didn't think . . ." She sighed. "Not relevant here. Never mind. But Gus is going to be crucial now. He might even—well, you'll probably meet him."

"I'm glad you have someone to back you up," said Ira. He had questions—oh *boy* did he have questions—but he knew better than to ask them.

Sarah stared out the window. She laid her hands on the table, palms down. For a moment, Ira thought she would put her head down, too.

"Sarah?"

"Percy doesn't know about Gus." She shook her head. "Why am I telling *you* this?"

"Because I have to know what's going on with Rico."

"Gus and I might not even be in touch anymore if it weren't for Rico. They . . . I guess you could say they bonded. I hate that word. They're friends. And feminist though I may be, I do believe little boys should have big guys to look up to, who care about them." She looked fondly at Ira. "Like you. Right?"

"Goes without saying." He laughed, but carefully.

She stared at him for a moment, as if contemplating just how good a role model he really *was* for her son. "I have friends who tell me I was stupid to break up with Gus. He was nice. He was dependable. Had a great sense of humor. All these things are still true! He just . . . we didn't have enough in common."

Ira wondered if she thought she had more in common with Percy. Sarah seemed to him like a woman living a century or more ahead of Mr. Darling. But who knew? Then he thought about Anthony: nice . . . dependable . . . sense of humor . . .

Sarah stood. "Wow. TMI. Right? All I really want you to know is how grateful I am that you're here for Rico. He does look up to you."

Did he? Ira could point to the girls who adored him, the boys who watched his every move with an eye to imitation. Rico was obedient, even sweet, but he wasn't on Ira's roster of groupies.

"You can count on me, Sarah. I will let you know anything, anything at all, that worries me. But again, you have got to talk to him. As soon as possible."

"I will. I promise."

In the hall, he stopped at the sight of Evelyn mopping. Evelyn Fougère the washerwoman. Sensing Ira's amusement, she looked up through her disheveled hair and held out the mop. "Your turn, buster."

14

When forced to consider my age, I realized how curious it was that I had yet to watch someone I knew go through the idiosyncratic hell of chemotherapy. From outdated movies and a novel or two, I had visions of relentless projectile vomiting, physical diminishment, the shedding of hair. (Yes, conceded Trudy, hair would be shed.) You might guess that my naïveté on these matters meant I had few close friends; the more time I spent with Sarah, the more I began to see this might be so.

Both of us had been surprised to learn that she would start chemotherapy—along with some companionable "biotherapy"—before surgery or radiation. Based on no concrete experience, we had shared a notion of chemo as the glowing cherry—or bushel of cherries—on the sundae of cancer treatment.

Sarah had held firm on seeing Trudy for the first time without me. As even I had suspected, my one attempt to make an end run by calling Trudy at home took me nowhere but into a wall. ("Dad, does the term *patient confidentiality* ring a bell?")

But Sarah did give me the honor of escorting her to her first "infusion." She made it clear that she wanted to go through the nitty-gritty—the being hooked up and pumped full of poison—on her own, at least for the inaugural go-round. It might take several hours, she warned me, so I should find a way to occupy myself in the city until she was ready to go home.

I made her sit on one of the couches. I went to the reception desk. Next to the sign-in sheet sat a vase of pink roses out of which protruded a large heart-shaped card covered in glitter. LOVE IS ALL YOU NEED! it proclaimed.

"Oh is *that* all?" I said. "What a relief! I thought we were here for intravenous warfare."

Chantal allowed silence to linger a moment before she looked away from her computer screen. She offered me a scolding smile. "Perhaps you'd like to add a footnote. A petite little asterisk after that *all*. List the many exceptions."

"Literalists are boring, aren't they?" Already I was failing to follow Trudy's recent advice: to "behave like a normal human being," at least in this context. Trudy had informed me that my particular brand of humor might prove tiresome for someone with a compromised immune system.

Chantal turned to Sarah, who had joined me. "Honey, I can tell you're terrified. But we take *such* good care of you here. That is a promise. Now put your hand out." When Sarah obeyed, Chantal put something in her palm. "For later. Little pick-me-up."

In Sarah's hand lay three chocolate kisses.

"Best medicine I know of," said Chantal. She stood. "And so. We begin with bloods. Come meet our world-class phlebotomists."

Sarah handed the candy to me. I slipped it into a pocket of my raincoat. She gave me a look I did not need help to interpret. *Now is when you leave.*

"When will she . . . when do I pick her up?" I asked Chantal.

"Not staying, Mr. D?" Chantal looked at Sarah.

"He's not. That's my choice."

Chantal patted Sarah on the shoulder. "A go-it-aloner. Good for you. I see you have spunk, and spunk is a powerful weapon." She pointed Sarah toward the nether reaches of the suite, but turned to me before leading her away. "Come back between three and four. But hang tight for a minute. Dr. B wants to see you."

The three women waiting on the couches stared at me. No smiles today.

At least I'd remembered my book this time. Revisiting the greatest hits of Henry James, I was halfway through *The Spoils of Poynton*. But after reading the same paragraph several times over, I closed the book. The woman sitting across from me was whispering loudly into her cell phone, describing the sores in her mouth.

I closed my eyes.

"Mr. Darling?" A nurse I had not met before leaned over me.

"I am just fine!" I said, too loudly.

"I know you're fine. Dr. Barnes is ready to see you." She spoke so quietly that my outburst felt like a crime.

A new clutch of female patients took over the staring. This time, one of them did smile. She pointed at my feet. "Your book." I picked it up and thanked her.

"Good luck," she said.

I looked at a clock as we passed through the halls. I had been asleep for half an hour. Quite likely I'd been snoring.

This was only my second visit to Trudy's little kingdom; would there come a time when I'd been here so often I'd know these mazy hallways as if they were mine? How strange that this is what I hoped for. Sarah had told me the stunning news that she would be coming here at least every two or three weeks for a year.

As if to underscore my lack of orientation, I was shown into a strange room, not the one in which I'd seen Trudy the month before. An exam table stood center stage, while two chairs lurked against a wall. At the far end, Trudy sat on a rolling stool at a computer, her back to me. When she heard me enter, she pirouetted neatly, without rising, and pointed to one of the chairs.

"Dad, I'm about to go in and get Sarah started. She asked me to go over her treatment with you. The big picture."

"She's explained it to me. The pathology and whatnot. The heart tests she had. This 'her-two' business."

"Don't get all bristly, Dad. Sarah needs to know you got this information from me. She has enough on her plate without having to answer all your anxious questions. That's what I'm here for."

The next ten minutes felt like a flashback to high school science. Would there be a test demanding that I discriminate hormone receptors from monoclonal antibodies, adjuvant therapies from axillary nodes, neuropathy from neutropenia? (Was Trudy showing off?) The evil "her two" was, in simple terms, a protein that Sarah's tumor was "over-expressing."

I cut in. "Like a bad Shakespearean actor?"

"Cute, Dad. I'll keep that in mind for my show-business patients."

Trudy and Dr. Wang did not like the aggressive nature or the size of this cancer. (I pictured a fat playground bully: Lester McClintock from second grade.) Sarah would require a mastectomy, but first, they would attack the tumor systemically. "This means six months of chemo, plus antibody therapy that targets the her-two factor," said Trudy. "Then comes the surgery, and after that, probably radiation and hormone therapy. The bad news is that Sarah's cancer has spread to her lymph nodes. The good news—very good news—is that her scans show no metastis." Watching Trudy's face, I saw her change from doctor to daughter. "I'm summing it up for you, Dad. It's a long haul."

"I gather you doubt my stamina."

Trudy moved to the chair beside mine. "Sarah's a tough cookie, but she has a lot of things to face here. Personal as well as medical. You guys haven't been together that long; you're not her husband."

"She doesn't have one, in case you hadn't noticed."

Trudy stared at me tenderly. Did I read pity in her expression?

Finally I said, "Are you trying to tell me I should abandon her? 'Break up'? I'm not a catch-and-release type of fellow, in case you wondered."

"There's no need to get hostile, Dad. I just want you to know what you're up against. I'm thinking about her child, too. Her son. His life should be as consistent as possible now, around the margins of all these changes."

Norval had recently expressed the opinion that doctors, like lawyers, were well trained, sometimes unwittingly, as master practitioners of euphemism and obfuscation. "So," I said, "is this tumor going to kill her? Is that what you're preparing me for?"

"I am absolutely not saying that, Dad. There are factors we don't know yet, but I will tell you this: that tumor's not one I'd like to meet in a dark alley, even in broad daylight."

"Very funny." Lester McClintock morphed into the far more sinister Reggie Kosinski, captain of the high school ice-hockey team.

"Dad, you're the one who brought up the Shakespearean actor." She touched her pager, letting me know my time was up.

"Did she mention the insurance business to you?" I asked. "She's losing a lot of sleep over that." Sarah had told me that just one of her drugs, if you could run down and buy it at the CVS, would set you back forty thousand dollars for a year's supply.

Trudy shook her head. "Can't discuss that with you, Dad. She'll have to work it out with financial. I'm going to help her as much as I can. And that, by the way, is a favor to you."

"I want you to know that I'll pay for anything she can't. Anything."

"I'm not going to discuss the money stuff with you, Dad. And right now, I have to catch up with my patients. Including Sarah, who's getting hooked up as we speak."

When I stood, I had to steady myself with a hand on the wall. My legs tingled slightly.

"I had a dream about your mother while I was waiting. And you."

Trudy's formal smile faltered. "Mom?"

"I dreamed I was taking your mother out to dinner for Valentine's Day. We were at that Thai restaurant, where we had your sister's birthday dinner. We had our own table—I had so much to tell her, after all this time apart—but people all around us kept crowding in, interrupting. The waitress. That teacher Ira from Elves and Fairies. Norval and Helena—who said she wanted to paint your mother's portrait. I was very angry and lost my temper. I told everybody to get out, leave us alone. But your mother told them to stay. She acted as if it were any other day, as if she'd never left us. I wanted to ask if she was back for good, but I knew that would be a mistake. . . ."

"Like Orpheus." Trudy had turned away from the door and faced me fully, hands in her pockets.

"So then," I said, "along *you* came. You were wearing your doctor regalia"—I gestured at what she wore—"and you sat right down at our table without so much as greeting me, and you held your stethoscope to your mother's chest, and you said, 'Mom, your heart is still beating. Mom, please order something healthy and we'll split it.' So there I was, my reunion with my wife after all these years invaded right and left, when who should walk through the door but *my* mother. And she walked right up to me and said—"

"Dad?" Trudy put a hand on my shoulder. "Dad, would you sit back down for a second?"

I felt her fingers on my wrist, checking my pulse.

"Daughter, there's nothing wrong with me. I'm sharing a dream."

Having forced me to sit, she sat beside me again. "Okay, Dad. Finish the dream. You're looking a little pale, that's all."

"Your grandmother told me to calm down because she had something to tell us. She said, 'Trudy always passed her exams. She passed with flying colors. She was at the top of her class.' I hadn't seen my mother look so happy in ages."

Trudy sighed. "I don't have to be Dr. Freud to interpret this one," she said. "Let me tell you right now that Sarah is in the best possible hands."

"As if I thought otherwise." Hastily, I wiped my eyes.

"I'm not just bragging. I'm not the only one treating her. I'm sorry, Dad, but I really have to go. Chantal has paged me three times already. Where are you going now? I want you to take it easy."

"Meeting Norval at the museum. He said he's in the mood for Monet. Haystacks. Water lilies. France without the French."

"Good idea," said Trudy. She spread a hand against my back and urged me gently down the hall, up from the underworld, back toward the sunlit region of benignly, symmetrically flourishing cells.

"I suspect we married our wives for the same reason," I said, breaking our comfortable silence. "Or have I mentioned this theory before?"

Norval laughed. "Can't remember. Tell me again."

"Camouflage."

He frowned at me, taking mock offense. "We stand out too much when we're on our own? Now that's a good one."

"Quite the opposite," I said. "We risk invisibility without a colorful, earthy woman tethering us to the here and now. The practicalities and limitations."

We stood before a glass case displaying three exquisitely vibrant kimonos. We'd had our fill of Parisian nudes, blue cathedrals, and the bourgeois blossoms of Giverny. So we'd paused for lunch in the café (a glass of Burgundy each), then wandered on sleepy autopilot into the Far East. Long ago, Poppy and Helena had agreed on the kimonos as their favorite collection at the museum.

Norval leaned closer to the case to read the label describing the kimono swimming with koi, orange and gold on silvery, striated blue. I could imagine what he was thinking: that if this were so, what had kept me anchored all those years since Poppy's death?

"You know," I said, "for most of my life, I've fancied myself a passenger on a train as it moves along through various landscapes. Some are repeated, some are unique—some ugly, some magnificent. But now . . . now I feel as if I'm a fixed point in the landscape itself, the trains passing me by. Each one faster than the one before."

"That's rather maudlin. So what sort of landscape are you?"

"I haven't the faintest idea," I said. "A field. Overgrown and weedy."

"Or a very large, gnarled tree."

"Hollow and half rotted."

"Inhabited by wild creatures of a dozen species."

"A zoo."

"A healthy ecosystem."

I turned to my old friend. "Norval, we are sounding perilously gay."

He put a restraining hand on my shoulder. "You wish."

"We shouldn't have had that wine."

"Nonsense. We deserved it."

We left the kimonos behind. "Speaking of gnarled trees, where is that Chinese scholar's room?" I said. "Do you remember that exhibit?"

Norval led us onward, pretending to know the way.

When we met that morning, in the museum lobby, he had asked me just enough about Sarah's predicament to know that I needed a distraction, not a confidant. Helena would be annoyed, like all wives who want the most dire, intimate news, who can't imagine what else two friends would discuss in the middle of a crisis. As we meandered through hallways, across centuries and oceans, I put my hands in the pockets of my coat. The fingers of my right hand encountered the three foil-wrapped candies. I tumbled them gently, reminding myself to return them to Sarah when I picked her up.

Norval and I became friends during the temptestuous days in the spring of 1969. I was new to Reference; Norval, five years older than I, was already a seasoned, elite bibliographer. We'd crossed paths in the stacks, but we'd had no reason to converse. And then came the night of the bonfires and the chanting, the Yard filled with angry students clamoring for Afro-American studies—or using that cause as a colorful reason to voice their double discontent: that of any young person lusting for change in the stodgy status quo and that of Americans who'd had enough of the political malevolence that hung about us all like a dank, stifling fog. Partly out of devotion, partly out of curiosity and a sense of youthful sport—wanting to be part of whatever "action" might play out—Norval and I joined the tweedy, professorial group who decided to guard the library round the clock against the possible incursion of the youthful barbarians. They would not burn the books or deface the Sargent murals; we would protect these musty treasures with our very flesh!

Norval had a flask of some beastly fruited brandy that he shared with me and the one other staff member who stayed up that night. The professors formed their own vigil: a bow-tied brigade including a handful of liberal luminaries. That was also the spring when Norval met Helena, a graduate student in Slavic studies. Poppy and I loved her the moment she set foot in our kitchen.

So I felt a piercing sense of déjà vu when, the first time I saw Norval after Thanksgiving, he told me that Helena was "tickled pink" about Sarah. She couldn't wait for an occasion when the four of us might share a luxurious meal; maybe Sarah would drag me from my lair just long enough to get me up to Vermont for a weekend. Of course, her little boy was welcome, too.

But neither Helena nor her husband had seen Sarah in the two months since that holiday. Too much had happened. And too much, I could see, had yet to happen.

Rico referred to the cancer and the proliferating symptoms of its treatment as "Mommy's illness." He uttered this noun so fastidiously that I wondered if he knew what it actually meant. It might have been synonymous with *window* or *dog* or *automobile*. "Mommy's illness is making her stay home today." "Mommy has a doctor 'pointment for her illness." "I'm going to Gus's house tomorrow so Mommy can rest her illness."

I had yet to meet this cousin of Sarah's, and I had grown irritated that she did not seem to trust me alone with Rico. "For God's sake, I'm the retiree here, the one who's free to watch soaps or drink scotch all day without letting down a soul. Make me useful!" I ranted to Sarah the week after her first infusion.

"I don't farm Rico out to people just to help them feel useful, Percy," she said. "And it's not that I don't trust you. It's just that Rico's known Gus forever. And honestly, *you* without a purpose?" At least she smiled.

Sarah allowed me to drive her into the city and pick her up after each of her treatments, but still she would not let me keep her company inside what she called "the suite." (I kept forgetting to chide my daughter about the irony in that pun.) She did not even like me to linger in the waiting room and read. For several hours, sometimes most of a day, I would find diversion of one sort or another. I had now acquired one of those umbilical cell phones, simply so that Sarah could call me when she knew she was about to be released.

In keeping with the stubborn distance she now maintained, she turned down my offer to let her move in with me, at least for the first four cycles, during which she would, according to Trudy, suffer the worst side effects. I offered her Trudy's old bedroom. Rico could stay in Clover's room; why, he could roll out of bed right into his classroom. How perfect was that?

"You're so generous," she said, "but Rico needs to be at the home he knows. And so do I. Whenever I have the energy to work, I need to seize it." She had a few small commissions and no longer worked at TGO. I wondered how she was paying her bills, but I had learned not to ask about money. She was going to the doctors, and that's what mattered.

Another source of my selfish irritation was the "meal chain" arranged and executed by Perfect Teacher Ira and the mommies of Rico's Birch buddies. Every other day, in relays, they delivered prepared food and groceries to Packard. They ferried Rico to their homes for playdates, birthday parties, sledding expeditions, and numerous outings that always involved what Sarah deemed the "healing" company of other children. Sarah had once confessed to me that many of these other mothers, however "nice," made her feel uneasy, too unavoidably different. Now she referred to them as her "community" and even her "support system." I had a hard time suppressing my idiotic jealousy.

Once or twice a week, however, she would bring Rico to the house, and I would make us burgers or pea soup or macaroni and cheese, whatever Sarah's appetite allowed. She had a frequent craving for pasta with a sauce I made, on her orders, from canned tomatoes, chopped garlic, and fresh basil.

When I worried that it would be too acidic for her drug-pummeled digestive tract, she told me it was one of the few foods that erased the bitter aftertaste of the chemo. "It goes into my veins and comes out everywhere else," she said. "I can smell it when I sweat. Like burnt rubber doused with Dr Pepper. I'd much rather smell like garlic."

She smelled no different to me. I desired her as much as ever, even—perhaps especially—after she began to wrap her head in India-print scarves, even after her face looked like a drawing to which someone had taken an eraser, rubbing away her eyebrows and lashes, the color in her cheeks. Her features took on a stark, bold clarity, the luster of a portrait by Vermeer. After she and I and Rico shared dinner, sometimes I would put a movie in the player for him; at the video store in Ledgely, I'd purchased a batch of discarded Disney tapes. I'd moved the television from Poppy's dressing room down to my study. Sarah and I would go upstairs, undress, and lie together in bed. I would make her unwrap her head. She was almost but not completely bald. A scant few tenacious hairs, silver or dark, remained rooted in her pale pink scalp.

"I should shave them off," she said, "but I'm superstitious. As if doing that would contradict wanting it all to grow back."

"I like them," I said. "They are the stalwarts."

She laid a palm on my chest. "Percy, you are so strange. Nothing can derail you from your eccentricity, can it?"

"I hope not. Though Trudy is trying to reform me. I think she worries that someone at St. Matt's will report me to the authorities for making politically inappropriate jokes to the nurses."

"I hope she fails," said Sarah. "I like your inappropriate jokes. Chantal thinks you're wonderful."

"Balderdash."

This elicited the first giggle I'd heard from her in weeks. "She does, though. She says Trudy could use a little of your irreverence."

"I think that might be dangerous, given her line of work."

Mostly, as we lay in bed, we would talk. This had become the only time we really talked—talked in the timeless, delighted way we had during the early fall. Time was now strictly mapped out for Sarah: she kept a calendar telling her when she was to take which pills, when to have her blood drawn, when—at the so-called nadir point of each cycle—she was to coddle her immune system by avoiding crowds, contagious illnesses, and certain raw foods.

"As if you're touring in Sri Lanka," I said.

"Without the palm trees."

"Or the political crackdowns."

In bed, we could still laugh wholeheartedly. We embraced, but Sarah was reluctant to make love, and though she might be exhausted, she never came close to napping. She removed my hands if they strayed near her breasts; they were still whole, still so lovely, but the lump—that evil Reggie Kosinski with his puck-shattered tooth and cheap shiny switchblade—was still in residence. She was also mindful of Rico, keeping an ear out for his footsteps below. She could hear them through the most overblown of children's movie sound tracks.

I still did not ask how she was paying for her treatment, and she did not mention it. This worried me, but not enough to disrupt the harmony we'd found. As long as I was taking her to the hospital on the schedule ordained by Trudy, as long as she was taking her many pills, as long as I could see her eat a meal, I felt she was as safe as she could be. She was silent more often than before the cancer, but still I hadn't seen her cry.

The letter arrived the day of Sarah's third bombardment. She had agreed, this time, to come home with me first, to rest a bit before resuming her life as a mother. I had lured her with the prospect of a roaring fire, a cup of the herbal tea she now favored over coffee, and maybe the last of Helena's oatmeal scones, if Clover hadn't filched it.

As usual, Clover had brought my mail in and left it on the kitchen table. This was her habit, since she fetched E & F's mail from the roadside box that overshadowed mine. Sarah had collapsed on the couch, bundled in the homely quilt Clover had made for her mother in seventh-grade home ec. I'd lit the fire that I had so cleverly laid that morning, and now I had only to put on the kettle and hope to find that scone. I had my secret stash of Oreos as backup.

To spot a personal letter among one's mail nowadays is rather like glancing out the window to spot a hummingbird dining at a blossom. A rare sight, arresting and sweet. This particular piece of mail, the envelope unusually oblong in shape and the palest green in color, was addressed to me in dark violet ink, in a bold and declaratively European hand. I could not resist picking it up at once—to discover that, as typifies European correspondence, it bore no return address. It had been postmarked, however, in Matlock.

I forced myself to set it down again in order to get the kettle going. Once I'd found Sarah's tea and tossed a few spoonfuls into the pot, I sat down at the table and tore open the envelope (lined in a violet paper to match the ink).

Dear Percy,

I hope you will not find the intent of this letter uncourteous or rash. Although we have met but a few times, *en passant,* I have been hearing antidotes of your charms and wits from Evelyn for many a year—even preceding your act of superb generosity to Elves & Fairies last summer— and so feel as if I have spent hours in your company. (You—I venture— do not share this illusion!) It has been our intention to invite you for a quiet dinner these many past months—we must beg your forgiveness for our negligence and delay. Such an invitation will be following soon—and quite irregardless of how you may receive this overture I propose.

Alors—to the point then! During one of my early visits to the barn— when I was investigating its spaces and moods—divining its soul—I was with your daughter Clover. I remarked to her how I have been curious about your house since a very long time—how I have driven past and wished for an entrée to explore the premises. Perhaps she also caught me, *en pointe,* trying to see into your windows—now I confess too much!

She took me one day for a quick tour of the house—where she so happily spent the days of her earliest youth—and I must tell you that I fell in love. It was—as we French say of that magnetic moment between two lovers—*le coup de foudre.* I was therefore among the first in line at the house tour last month—and my feelings at that re-encounter did not diminish. The lines of the roof—the windows with their many ancient lights—the kiltering stairs—the grand hearth; in your house, I find myself *bouleversé*—there is no other word—in the most exuberant way. In this world, everything—all the things we love, over time—must change. And yet, your house takes a stand against time.

You will now have yourself deduced that I approach you—humbly— with the offer that if you might feel it tempting, I would like to discuss the purchase of your house.

As an architect, I know that this may sound like a request to purchase your wife, or your child—so if my request offends, I beg your pardon. I also know what you will be thinking: Is this the same Maurice Fougère of the glass house high on the hill—*that* Maurice Fougère? I can only assure you that I am a man of wide-ranging aesthetics and that it has always been my longing to one day live in a house that was built many generations in the past. Were I still in my native country, I would perhaps be courting a house medieval in its pedigree—but here I am—thanks to my wife and children a happy American now and for always—courting yours.

And I hardly need acknowledge that to take on the stewardship of the house would marry my dreams to those of my wife—house and barn—to put a fanciful spin upon it—conjoined as a single Eden.

The final paragraph was a litany of the various numbers and addresses through which he would be eagerly and patiently and humbly (emotions underscored by his Dickinsonian love of the dash) awaiting my reply.

The kettle had begun to mutter. I got up and turned off the burner, poured the scalding water into the teapot, stirred the leaves. I opened the breadbox and (eureka!) retrieved the scone, opened the cupboard and retrieved a mug. I arranged everything on a tray and carried it to the living room.

Sarah lay on the couch, quilt pulled to her chin, but she was awake. Though she tried to resist, I helped her into a seated position.

"So do you think that there could possibly be any antidotes to my charms and wits?" I asked her.

She did not demand to know what I meant. She said, "No chance. They're far too potent. In some cases fatal."

"Thank heaven. I was worried there for a minute."

I pulled the letter from my back pocket and tossed it on the table. "Maurice Fougère wants to buy my house. Apparently, he became 'exuberantly *bouleversé*' when Clover saw fit to enable his snooping through the place. Frankly, that's a sensation I like to restrict to the bedroom."

Sarah, who was blowing on her tea, paused to say, "Me, too. Even if I have no idea what it means."

I sat on the stool beside the fire screen, longing to be hot after the chill of the kitchen. "Maybe it's high time I let go of this place. Take the money and run. Prices are so high these days, it makes you wonder if someone discovered oil under this swampy town."

Sarah looked appalled. "Percy, this house *is* you."

"Now that's an absurd notion, isn't it?" I said. "And think of all the cash I'd have to fling about."

"What a wonderful image. You, of all people, flinging cash. You who dress in the same clothes you wore when the Beatles were learning to walk."

I looked down at my attire. "I beg your pardon. These pants were obtained at TGO no earlier than the year of poor John Lennon's death."

But that was when it occurred to me: if I sold the house, I could cover

Sarah's treatment no matter what it cost. I could cover trips to foreign countries for treatments involving rare botanicals or sutras bestowed by monks in holy places accessible only by pack burro or parachute drop. If that's what Sarah needed. Or wanted.

I could move to a rental cottage like the one on Dorian Van Otterloo's little estate on Quarry. I could overrule my absurd phobia and buy a loft overlooking the river in Packard, with buckets of lucre to spare—only, of course, if Sarah and Rico would join me.

Forget Maurice; I could put the house on the market and cause a commotion. Since the tour (and Mandy Pinkerton's fawning column), I'd begun to notice cars slowing at the foot of the driveway, windows rolled down, arms pointing. All of a sudden I was "on the map."

"I don't think I ever got to have a midlife crisis," I said. "Can I do that now? Is there an expiration date on such essential rites of passage?"

Sarah laughed. How I loved that sound. Her lips were caked with crumbs; she was halfway through eating the scone.

Her delivery of my mail notwithstanding, Clover had become elusive. In some ways, I was relieved not to know what she was up to other than working diligently (thank heaven) at E & F, planning the gala auction the little school held every spring to raise big bucks from sentimental parents, entry to their mutual funds lubricated with cocktails passed on trays of sustainable silver.

I did not wish to bring up Maurice's letter with anyone other than Sarah, but I was vexed at Clover. I ambushed her at last when, three days later, I saw her striding along the driveway.

"Daughter," I called out the back door, "come in, would you?"

"Daddy, I have a million calls to make—"

"Won't take five minutes."

As she stood in the bright kitchen, she had the nervous look of an animal cornered in unfamiliar surroundings.

"So then," I said, "when you gave that stealth tour of the house to Master Builder Fougère, which was his favorite room?"

"Stealth tour? You mean, the house tour? I wasn't here."

"I refer to the private tour you gave Evelyn's husband last summer."

"Daddy, I'm confused."

"As to whether you live here full-time and have my permission to traipse your friends and acquaintances up and down stairs as you please? Through rooms with unmade beds and underdrawers scattered about and—"

"Daddy! What's made you so mad?"

I sighed. Why was it hard to stay angry at Clover? Was it her fawnlike demeanor or her endlessly resurgent sense that life would go her way?

"I have tried, amid the upheaval here"—I swept an arm toward the back of the house, the barn—"to maintain my treasured privacy, just a morsel or two. Now I learn, through a very odd letter from Maurice, that you gave him a complete tour of this place, on which he's apparently had a covetous eye."

"I'm sorry if it's pissed you off," said Clover, "but I thought I had sort of a right—I've lived here, too, after all—to show the place off when somebody we knew admired it and was, like, eager to have a peek. He's an *architect*. Houses are his *business*. Honestly, nobody noticed any messy sheets or anything like that."

" 'Nobody'?" My ire rose again. "So how many other people joined in? I hope you charged admission."

Clover's mouth became a vise. "I don't have to listen to you get hysterical about something this silly, Dad. I know you're going through a rough time with Sarah, and I can understand if you feel a little on edge. Is she doing okay?"

"Sarah has nothing to do with this."

"Daddy, I have a billion phone calls to make before five. I promise never to show the house to anybody ever again." She laughed. "Well, a little moot now that it's already been a museum. Maybe you worried that Maurice was casing the joint, for a theft of some kind?"

"That remark is uncalled for."

"I'm sorry." But she didn't look sorry in the least. She looked ready and eager to bolt from my company.

"Don't let me keep you from your job," I said, feigning forgiveness. "Are the children up next weekend? Can I take you all out for dinner?"

"They were here this past weekend. You just missed them. But the weekend after. I'll take a look at our plans."

"Please do that."

I watched her walk down the hill toward the barn, pulling her coat close, inching her way along the icy path. She wore shoes that were utterly inadequate for winter footing in New England.

15

When you wish for something too hard and too long, against God's intentions for you, the wish may come true after all—but not in the way you would like. Celestino's mother would say this to his sisters whenever they complained about wanting a bigger house or a car or finer clothing.

So it was that Celestino finally saw Isabelle face-to-face.

It was an unusually warm Sunday for February, the sky a summery blue, the sun melting the last of the snow remaining from a recent storm. This meant that the earthen driveways and the lawns in Matlock would quickly turn to mud, that Monday's work would involve, for most of the guys, sanding and towing, the pruning of broken limbs; Celestino would spend the day checking on a dozen or more empty houses. Loud's "vacation care" service had caught on, and this week the children of Matlock were out of school—many of them away with their parents, skiing in the north or playing on beaches far to the south.

Celestino had decided that he would go to her apartment. If he telephoned, his voice would fail him. (Had he ever spoken to Isabelle on the phone when they lived together? Not that he could remember. He had wanted to call her from New York, but he would have had to get past her mother.)

Irving Street was lovely—not quite as lovely as the street on which she had lived with her parents, but the trees were tall and sturdy, the houses large. Several were painted in three or four colors, a fanciful tower here, a stained-glass window there.

He stood on the sidewalk a few doors down from the house where Isabelle lived. Once, it would have sheltered a large family in great luxury, but you could tell even from where he stood that it had been divided into apartments. Behind the windows hung curtains and shades of too many different kinds. On the porch were stacked several blue recycling bins; four bikes were locked to the long, battered railing.

He was gathering courage to approach the house when Isabelle walked out the front door. There she was, no mistaking her for anyone else or anyone else for her. She stopped in the sun to close her eyes and savor its warmth. Then she walked down the steps and onto the sidewalk, straight toward Celestino.

Her head was bare, her hair long and loose over a red wool coat. The coat ended just above her knees, knees in yellow tights, beneath them tall black cowboy boots. She fussed with a heavy-looking satchel, adjusting it on her left shoulder; she scowled, talking quietly to herself. As she came closer, she noticed him, looked him briefly in the eye. "Morning," she said, a greeting to a stranger, and she walked around him without hesitation.

Celestino, stunned by the ruthlessness of the moment, turned quickly to look after Isabelle. He saw her, an instant later, stop and do the same. They stared at each other. He struggled to speak, at least to smile.

Isabelle pressed her hands against her mouth, then shaded her eyes. "Celestino? Is that you?"

"Yes, Isabelle, it's me."

When she did not move, he approached her instead, though he sensed there would be no embrace, no touching.

"Here?" she said. "You're here?"

He could not tell if she was angry or simply confused.

She said, "Have you been, all this time, here?"

"No. I was in New York for years. Now I live . . ." What should he tell her? Because he had been here, approximately here, a long time now. She spared him a quick decision by interrupting.

"New York? New York City?" Her voice rose. She squinted at him, against the sun. "Good God."

He allowed himself to breathe. He had to breathe to speak. "I've missed you. I was sorry that I ran away. But I didn't know how to . . . run back."

"My God. Celestino."

"I'm sorry to startle you. I should have called." How foolish, just to show up at her doorstep. Foolish yet again.

"Come here," said Isabelle, her voice urgent. She walked past him, back toward her building. "Come here. I can't stand in the sun like that."

She sat on the bottom stair—in the center, setting her bag beside her, leaving no space for Celestino. He faced her, standing. He realized that when they had both been standing, she was taller. She'd grown by inches since they had been together. She had, after all, still been a child. Her mother had been right about that.

"Celestino? Oh my *God.*" What if this was all she could say? She leaned back, elbows on the stair behind her.

He had to say something. "I should never have gone away, I know that. That was a mistake."

"Jesus, we looked for you. You know? We drove everywhere. We called your school, everyone we knew who'd met you. After a week, Maman sent a *telegram* to your father. We never heard anything from anyone. Do you know what a nightmare it was? For me especially?"

Celestino's mother had never mentioned a telegram. When he'd finally called, all she wanted was for him to come home. Later, it occurred to him that maybe she had never shared his father's desire to move the family away from their simple home. Certainly, if she had heard stories from some of the cousins, the ones who did return, she'd have had reason to believe it was a foolish dream. Everybody knew someone who'd paid a fortune to get in, then came home anyway, poorer than ever, especially in spirit.

"I was scared," he said. "Young and scared."

Isabelle shook her head. "I was *terrified.* And younger than you. Maman was . . . For a while, I thought she'd lose her mind."

"She would have kicked me out on the street. She had reason to do that."

"Jesus, Celestino, she'd have made you move out—move somewhere else. Put an end to our seeing each other, I'm sure. But did you think she'd, what, deport you?"

He did not answer. Had he really been so stupid? But why should Señora Lartigue have wanted him anything other than gone, forever? "I did not think she could forgive me. Or should."

"This is . . . Okay, this is surreal." She looked at her watch.

"Isabelle, I was so . . ." Celestino squatted on his heels. He couldn't stand talking down to her this way.

"Sorry?" she said.

"In love. I was in love with you."

Isabelle looked at her feet, the sharp toes of her boots. "I thought you'd vanished. I thought you might be *dead*. And then . . . I went to college and you faded. Like so much else. You were part of the past I was planning to shed like a snakeskin." She smiled quickly. "That's how we all felt. Then."

She glanced up and down the street, as if worried that someone might witness their reunion. "I'm supposed to be somewhere." She stared at him, her expression neutral. And then something seemed to cross her mind. "Celestino, just now—were you coming to see me? Is that why you were here?"

"Yes. I found out your address only a month ago."

"Well." Her eyes filled with kindness and concern, but not the tenderness he wished for. Then she blushed and looked away. "Oh boy."

Isabelle reached into her bag and took out her phone. "Hang on, okay?" She went to the far end of the long porch and made a call. She spoke for a few minutes.

"Let's go down the street," she said when she returned. "I'm hungry. Do you remember Fido's? Didn't we go there together?"

They walked beside each other, Isabelle's bag between them. She asked him where he lived now; hadn't he mentioned New York? He told her that he lived in Lothian, that he had a job in Matlock. At the door to the café, she stopped to face him. "Matlock? That's fancy terrain, out there. Horses, woods, mansions."

The café was crowded, but the hostess knew Isabelle and took them to the one open booth in a back room. Isabelle threw her bright coat onto the bench and sat. She combed her hair back, impatiently, with her fingers. It was darker, more reddish, than he remembered.

Around her neck, inside the crevice of her blouse, she wore the same gold cross, the one she'd inherited from her grandmother and had never, when he knew her, taken off. He had touched it, held it, licked or kissed it, dozens, maybe hundreds of times.

Isabelle caught his gaze. "Yes, and I'm still a heathen. But then, Maman still goes to the watered-down Congregational church, so she's a heathen, too."

She examined the menu, as if food was her most important concern.

Celestino realized that he had isolated himself so much in recent years that his habit was to think far more than speak. But now he had to speak. "I've thought about you all this time," he said.

She laid her menu down. "And only now you let me know?"

"No excuse except fear. Many fears. Forgive me."

She stared at him. "Fear is forgivable, Celestino. But years of total silence . . . vanishing? I don't know. Is this supposed to be a romantic reunion? I'm not laughing at the notion, but don't you think—"

"Then don't forgive me."

"But if I don't, what's left?"

Celestino had removed his coat as well, and he could feel her assessing his plaid shirt, noticing his gray hairs, his nicked hands and battered nails.

"To let me be with you, like we are now. Know each other again."

Isabelle raised her eyebrows. What did this expression mean? Her face was so much the same, even if it was older—yet it seemed to convey emotions he'd never seen there before.

The waitress came. Isabelle ordered a bowl of soup, Celestino a chicken sandwich. "And a glass of the house red," said Isabelle. "I don't care if it's not even noon." Celestino shook his head when the waitress glanced at him.

Isabelle took hold of the salt and pepper shakers, one in each fist. She rolled them around each other, then apart, then together, as if they were dancing partners. "So what do you do in Matlock?"

He thought about his answer. "Care for trees and houses."

"Trees, that's good," she said. "Lots of trees in Matlock. A whole lot more trees than houses. It's nice out there."

"And you are here as a student?"

"Psychology. I'm studying PTSD," she said. "Traumatized children from abusive families in cultural isolation. In a nutshell." She pushed the shakers aside, unfolded her napkin. "I'm going to France in three months. I'm going to work in an Algerian community in Marseilles."

"France." The word, in Celestino's mouth, felt as if it were made of glass.

"Cut the umbilical cord, only to return to the womb. Absurd and ironic. But my French turns out to be my biggest asset. *Merci bien, Papa et Maman.*"

The waitress brought Isabelle's wine and a basket of bread. Immediately, Isabelle tore a piece off the loaf. She pushed the basket toward Celestino.

"I can't believe I'm looking at you across this table." She chewed as she spoke. "Celestino, I was so crazy about you. My friend Ceci—remember her?—she thought I'd die of a broken heart. Losing Papa, then you. Etienne clueless and snotty about it all, Maman in this personal cone of anger. That's what I called it, the cone of anger. I was so totally grounded after you vanished. For months. She must have thought I'd run away and find you, or maybe you'd climb a trellis and spirit me away. Ceci came home with me after school almost every day. Sometimes I wonder if Maman bribed her to keep an eye on me."

She said all these things cheerfully. "I guess it sounds like I *have* forgiven you, doesn't it? You know, there's this saying I remember from Grand-mère. *L'absence au coeur, c'est comme le vent au feu.* 'Absence to the heart is like wind to the fire.' A little fans the flames; too much puts them out. . . .

"I'm sorry," she said, interrupting herself. "I've eaten all the bread. I was at the library practically all night. I skipped dinner." Standing slightly, she waved at the waitress and pointed to the basket. Then she said, "I can't figure out if I should tell my mother I've seen you or not. I think she'd have a heart attack."

Celestino knew he should ask about Señora Lartigue. But he said, "I've never fallen in love with anyone else."

Isabelle stopped what she was doing (gathering the crumbs before her into a small, neat pile) but did not look at him. Was she hiding her face?

He would have to ask, because he had to know. "Are you with someone now?"

When she looked at him, he could tell she was anxious again, the way she'd been back on her doorstep. Her voice had tightened. "I've been with a few guys. After you left, I was at college, Celestino, not a convent. But right now—no. No one now. I work too hard. I figure the love part has to come later."

All this talk began to make him feel miserable, trapped, yet what could he do? Invite her to his drafty attic in Lothian? Take her to a movie?

"Can I ask you something, Celestino?"

"Anything, Isabelle."

"Did you finish school—in New York?"

"No."

She nodded. "I wondered about that. That's a shame."

She drank the last of her wine. The soup and the sandwich arrived.

"You know," Isabelle said softly, "Maman isn't heartless. Once—it was after they dedicated the gallery in the museum to my father, and there was this huge exhibit that included photos from the dig, and there was one of your father and his crew—anyway, we were at home together, and I was back from college, so she probably thought it was safe to mention you. She said she was haunted by the thought that you fell off the path my father put you on. She said she warned Papa not to get so involved with other people's fortunes, she said he was playing God. He argued that if you can change one person's life for the good— not counting your children's lives—then you've fulfilled one thing you need to do in your life. Maman told him he changed lots of people's lives by being a teacher. He said it wasn't the same thing, that his students would have learned whatever they learned, more or less, from somebody else if not from him."

Celestino thought of Dr. Lartigue going over his earliest compositions in English, the famous professor sitting in his study with a fifteen-year-old boy, a wild boy from the jungle. "A Portrait of My Village." "The History of My Family." That first year, all the topics Celestino's teacher assigned were strangely personal, something he hadn't expected. Dr. Lartigue had helped him think of details about his life that he had never noticed. The man's generosity and patience had never seemed unusual to Celestino, because they came to him as a legacy of sorts, shown to his own father first.

"Your father was so good to everyone," he said.

"To many people, yes," said Isabelle. "But he could be brutal when it came to ambition. Not all his colleagues loved him, I can tell you that."

She ate several spoonfuls of soup. Celestino forced himself to finish half of his sandwich.

"Can I steal some of your fries?" she said. Her fingernails were trimmed, modestly short, and lacquered a milky shade of pink. As Arturo had said, she wore no rings. Celestino and Isabelle had shared french fries a dozen times when they had roamed into the Square like friendly siblings—and later as secret lovers. Then, he would have grabbed the hand that took the fries from the plate, held it under the table. Now he just looked at her hand with mournful longing.

"What comes next, Celestino?" She held his gaze. "This is too sur-real."

What he wanted to come next was going back to her apartment with her—or anywhere, really: to the library if that's where she had to go, to the place she went when she wanted her hair cut, her nails painted. He wanted not to leave her again.

"I wish to see you more," he said.

"Are we friends, then? I don't get that feeling from you."

"No," he said.

"Not friends?" she said tentatively.

He answered quickly, "Friends, yes, of course. We are. I did not mean—"

She blushed again. "We could sit here, stammering like this, forever, couldn't we? But I'm afraid I do need to work. Celestino, I really am leaving for France, and I had planned on having almost no life before going. I was supposed to do an interview, for my thesis, this morning. I put it off till this afternoon." She signaled the waitress. "You know, this feels like a dream."

"Yes," he agreed. "But it is not."

She played with the shakers again. "If you had stayed, if we had known each other all this time . . ." The shakers clicked: together, apart, together. "All I know is, it would be different."

"Different how?" Though he could guess many ways how.

"Celestino, I'm no oracle. I can't really say. I just look at you and you don't . . . I don't know how you fit in my life. If that's what you're asking."

"Yes," said Celestino, seized by an urgency he hadn't felt in years, "yes, that is exactly what I am asking."

She had one hand on her coat, but she did not put it on. "Oh boy. I can't get my brain around this." She rummaged under her coat for her bag. She took out a notebook and pencil. She opened the notebook and pushed it across the table. "Give me your number."

"I can call you whenever you say," said Celestino, dismayed that he would have to reveal how unrooted he was. "Write your number."

"But what if I want to call you first?"

The waitress set down the folder with the check; Isabelle gave her a credit card without looking over the charges.

"No," said Celestino, reaching.

"Let me," said Isabelle. "Please. I mean, look at us. Who has the advantages here, who's the spoiled one?"

This, too, dismayed Celestino. When they had lived under the same roof, her advantages had been those of culture, language, education; they presented him with a heady struggle to make himself even with her, not the feeling that he would always lag behind. Now she must judge him to be poor, uneducated, inarticulate . . . desperate.

She put a hand on his, as if guessing the pathetic turn his thoughts had taken. "Let's be real with each other. We're old enough now."

He willed away her obvious meaning. He said, "When can I see you again? My work takes all my days except Sundays, but I am free any evening."

"I need to be able to call you—or e-mail? Do you have e-mail?"

"I am living carefully, saving for my business."

"No communications? That's rather Spartan! You run your business by word of mouth?" The look on her face was kind yet mocking. This older Isabelle alarmed him. At seventeen, her bravado had been charming, even sweet. Now her honesty felt harsh.

"It is not yet off the ground." A worn memory rose with his sense of shame. The night Señora Lartigue had ambushed them, she ordered Celestino to leave the room, preparing to deal with her daughter first. Isabelle had shouted, "Don't go! Don't obey her; we are in this together!" But he had obeyed. In this painful memory, Isabelle was the one who had guts. Perhaps she was also the one without shame.

"Well," she said now to the silence between them. "Let's head out."

He followed her onto the street. In the sun once again, he tried to see more deeply into her face. While they had been apart, had she ever burned with passion, pined away? The telltale lines of sorrow were absent from her beautiful skin. He was the idiot romantic, she the practical one, pushing forward in her life, waiting for no one. But would he have wanted the kind of woman his cousin called *la condesa en el castillo,* whose passions quickly turn leaden, into needs, demands, disappointments?

"I'm going to run," she said. "You know where to find me. I'm listed. We'll see each other again, I promise."

She hesitated, and then she hugged him; how impersonal it felt through the puffy insulation of his coat. He smelled not her neck but the wool of her brilliantly patterned scarf. She hurried toward the Square.

Loud had walked him through Mrs. Connaughton's fancy security system. She would be gone for a month. She had a cat to care for, in addition to her plants. "She'd love it," said Loud, "if you sat and, as she put it, 'snuggled a teensy bit with Horace.' " He laughed and shook his head. "Not sure I like paying you to snuggle, *hombre,* but ten minutes won't hurt, especially if it keeps the creature from crapping on these priceless rugs." They'd walked through the entire house. In the attic (its sloped walls white as clouds, like the lime-washed walls of a country church), Loud showed Celestino the places he should check for leaks, especially the trapdoor at the top of a ladder leading to the roof.

On his own now, Celestino entered the house carefully, punching the code into the box as quickly as he could. He was startled immediately by the cat, which leaped off the sofa in the living room. "*Hola,*" he said gently. The cat flashed him an offended look, then ran to the kitchen.

He followed it, treading lightly. In the kitchen he would find everything he needed: watering cans, cat food, lightbulbs, fuses, a flashlight. After every storm, he was to check not only the attic but the dark cavelike cellar. Steep stairs led down from the kitchen, and then he had to crouch on dirt.

In four rooms, there were seventeen plants to water; he had counted, so that he would not forget a single one. The cat had wet food, dry food, water, a litterbox. Tending to those needs took no time at all. But how was the creature to be "snuggled"? It fled from each room Celestino entered, yet seemed to wait for him in the next. It was a hairy cat, with a flat nose and black, fathomless eyes.

He spoke gently to it, announcing his intentions as friendly, asking silly questions about its favorite foods, the secret life of its mistress. Did she have many lovers? Did she like to walk naked around the house when she was alone? Did she eat cake in the middle of the night? He whispered, as if the walls might be listening.

In the bathroom off the kitchen, he changed the litterbox, the cat watching from a distance. He poured food into the animal's dish. He filled the watering cans.

The living room, which faced the open lawn, drank in the most sunlight. The plants that loved sun had been gathered on tables next to these windows: two gardenias, a hibiscus, a sprawling red geranium. As he misted the gardenias, Celestino could sense the cat sneaking closer from behind him. When he finished with the plants, he turned slowly. The cat retreated to the dining room.

When he went upstairs, the cat followed. Every time he turned from his task, he found the cat closer than before, yet always it bolted to another room.

After twenty minutes in the house, Celestino put on his coat. He was about to leave when he decided to try something. He went into the living room and sat on the sofa where the cat had been resting when he entered. He leaned back and closed his eyes. He thought about Isabelle, their meeting the previous day: her skin, her loose hair, her breasts beneath her blouse. Though this was what he'd been trying for, he was startled when the cat jumped up beside him.

He sat up slowly. He looked at the cat, staring at him, crouching low on the cushion beside him. "*Gato,*" he whispered. He could not remember the cat's name. He sat perfectly still for some time, and then the cat touched his hand with its cold snub nose. Still he did not move. It climbed into his lap, but when he moved to stroke its fur, it leaped to the floor and ran into the kitchen.

Celestino laughed. He got up, reset the security code, and left the house. Halfway to the road, he turned and looked back; the cat had climbed up among the plants inside the window to witness his leaving. It struck him then, forcefully, that the strange cat was too much like him: living its life aloof, in fear, watching from a distance, approaching and retreating over and over.

That night, he went to the sheltered pay phone in the park, with his phone card. He waited until nine, a time when he hoped she would have left the library but still be wide awake.

She recognized his voice, though she sounded surprised.

"Celestino, I've thought about you so much since yesterday. Where are you calling me from?" (Did she hope he was calling from nearby, so she might invite him to come to her?)

"Near my apartment," he said. "Lothian."

"Lothian's quaint now, I hear. I hear it's almost fashionable. Cambridge is the stodgy place to live. Practically Republican."

"I don't know," he said—though why shouldn't he? Why shouldn't he act as if his choices (where he lived, what he did for a living) were deliberate?

"Celestino . . ." Her hesitation sounded dark.

"Yes, Isabelle?" He spoke firmly.

"Are you hoping . . . ? We didn't really get to the heart of the matter. Yesterday, I mean."

Celestino looked beyond the phone to the desolate, weedy park, one of Lothian's many places you'd hardly call "quaint"—in better weather, a place for teenagers searching out trouble. "Hearts," he said, "*are* the matter."

"Oh, Celestino," she said, and this time he did hear her heart in his name.

"See me tomorrow, for dinner. We can meet in that café again."

"I think it's too soon. I wish you could know what I've been feeling."

"I wish that, too. That is why we should meet."

"Or why we shouldn't," she said. Another long silence. All he could do was wait; he couldn't insist.

"Celestino, are you . . . all right here? I mean, are you here, in this country, aboveboard?" She waited for a moment. "Legally?"

He tried not to betray his anger, that she should ask him this, now. "We can talk about it tomorrow."

"Tomorrow's not good for me," she said. "But one thing I need to say, and I know I'm being intrusive, is that I worry about you. I know a good lawyer here. I wanted to offer you—"

"Isabelle! I am fine where I am! I am working!"

"I know!" she shouted back. "Don't be angry! I do want to help you."

Help him? This was what she wanted? "It's not your help I look for," he said. Or was she so practical—this woman concerned with helping children who had little to hope for—that her first thought was to protect him, so she could be sure not to lose him again?

"All right. Thursday night," she said. "And yes, let's meet at Fido's. That makes it easy. I can be there at eight."

"Eight," he said. "Thursday."

They agreed on that much—that was enough, it would have to be enough—and they hung up.

Wednesday morning, Tom Loud assigned Gil, Pedro, Felipe, and Celestino to reconstruct a stretch of old stone wall toppled by a driver going too fast for Matlock's twisting roads.

Whenever a job required muscle, the man in charge was Gil. He decided they would take apart the damaged wall, down to the ground, sorting the stones into four piles according to their shape—the thin flat ones, the thick angled ones, the smaller and larger rounded ones. The stones that had been exposed were laced with lichen, which tore at the surface of Celestino's gloves, and his shoulders felt as if the joints were giving way. Yet that day he was relieved to do nothing but follow orders. He also found himself taking unusual interest in the stories the other men traded as they worked. Gil was Brazilian, Felipe and Pedro a pair of *chapines* from Huehuetenango. They spoke together in English, broken at times, mixed up with Spanish at others.

Gil's parents and siblings lived in Manaus, where one of his brothers had just found a job with a company that took travelers for "canoe adventures" on the Amazon River. The brother would maintain the boats and supply fish for the cook. Pedro had a sister who would be getting married that summer, to a schoolteacher who owned a small house already. Felipe, the youngest, had married the year before; his wife, Rosalba, was in Texas, in line for a green card, thanks to a rich employer whose elderly parents she cared for. The employer was paying for her to take nursing courses.

Another Dr. Lartigue. Everywhere Celestino turned in his mind this week, he returned not just to Isabelle but to her father: his generosity, his passion for the past, and what were surely the very high expectations he'd had for a future to be lived by his son and daughter. Now that he was dead, how much greater those expectations must weigh on Etienne and Isabelle. Dr. Lartigue's grandchildren would not have a father who "cared for trees and houses."

The three other men did not speak to Celestino unless he spoke to them. And the heavy lifting left them ultimately short of breath, shorter on words. Once they had sorted the stones, the challenge of fitting them together, making them balance and stand as a wall, took all their focus.

Celestino might have told them that it looked as if one of his sisters, too, would marry. He had spoken with his mother two weeks before, and though she had complained, as always, about her various ills, she had informed him that she was—despite the arthritis now plaguing her hands—beginning a panel of embroidery for a wedding dress.

A wedding dress? Whose wedding?

Oh, his mother had told him casually, at the hotel there was a young fellow, nice young fellow who drove the tourists to and from the airport. He made good money from tips. Marta liked him.

Marta? This young man, he intended to marry Marta?

Oh, they spent time together when they were off work. He had taken Marta for a drive, on his day off, to a zoo. . . .

Celestino's mother loved to throw bad news at Celestino without restraint; the good news he had to chisel from her, bit by bit. This was her way of punishing him for his distance, and he no longer allowed himself to lose his temper. If he did, she would answer with a litany of all that he missed by making the choices he had. And then he would remind her about the money he sent. And she would tell him that his sisters took care of her well enough. If he were to return, they would find him a good job, too.

They'd had this argument too many times.

When Loud came by, at four, they were not quite finished. He idled by the side of the road without leaving his truck. "Lookin' fine. Light should last till six." He nodded at Celestino. "Let me drop you by Mrs. C.'s place."

Walking down Mrs. Connaughton's driveway, he could see that the first timer had clicked on already, lighting the front hall. He could also see, on Mr. Darling's side lawn, Robert and Arturo. They stood at the foot of the beech tree.

Arturo had spotted him, too. "Hey, hey. *Mucho gusto!*" he called out. "Get over here, amigo."

The two friends were making plans to decorate the tree house for a big party to celebrate the school.

"The theme is Woodstock," Arturo told Celestino. "Now, I mean, give me a break. The parents at this school were in diapers when that took place."

"So?" said Robert. "They could've chosen the court of Marie Antoinette, or the Jazz Age, or the Italian Renaissance. It's just an excuse to get dressed up, act silly, spend too much money. Costumes lower inhibitions. Open checkbooks."

Arturo nodded. "Word."

Celestino nodded as well, pretending to care. He had helped them build this fantasy for the children, but it remained a part of the world he considered Tom Loud's more than his. He remembered the satisfaction of fitting and bracing the wood among the branches—not unlike fitting the stones in that wall—but for all the sense of building something solid, meant to last, this tree house might have been made of smoke.

"So what do we think, Celestino? Should we project a big image of Hendrix onto the tree, set up a sound system blaring out his greatest hits?"

"No audio," said Robert. "Clashes with the band."

Arturo leaned against the tree. "What band?"

"They're called, get ready, Never Smoked Never Surfed. NS Squared. They're like four dudes in their early fifties who made truckloads of money doing stuff with other people's money but always wanted to be onstage. Now they are. In Matlock, if that counts."

"Money talks. I guess it plays the drums, too."

Robert shrugged. "Yeah, but Clo says they're surprisingly good. And free, because one of them has a kid in Ira's class. They'll play all those covers our parents like to dance to. Beatles. Temptations. You know. Blood Sweat and Tears. Earth, Wind and Fire. Elvis One and Elvis Two."

Arturo groaned.

"Speak for yourself, Mr. Girl from Ipanema."

Celestino envied these boys their friendship, but it also seemed like a play to him, a script they followed to secure themselves in a place they knew.

Arturo startled him by reaching out and shoving his shoulder. "What're *you* thinking, Silent One?"

"That I am behind on my work."

"I see no lawns to mow or gardens to tend."

"I am caring for Mrs. Connaughton's house."

"Gone to someplace swanky like Boca Raton," said Robert. "Hey, Turo, doesn't that mean Rat's Mouth? Could be a new nickname for

Mistress Lorelei, who's back on Granddad's shit list. He is wicked sorry he agreed to that house tour." He turned to Celestino. "Cool place, though, huh? Her house is the rich big brother to ours."

Celestino nodded. He noticed that Robert claimed ownership of his grandfather's house. Inheritance: another thing to set him apart.

"Go have a look," Robert said to Arturo. "It's like stepping back in time."

"Yeah?" When he saw the look on Celestino's face, Arturo poked his arm again. "You are too paranoid, amigo!"

Celestino had no choice but to follow Arturo toward the house.

Inside, once Celestino turned off the alarm, they removed their boots and set them in the copper tray. In the living room, Arturo whistled. "Razzle-dazzle, Paul Revere." He examined the paintings on the wall, the antique fire tools, the china figurines. The many pieces of silver had been removed from the mantel and shelves; Celestino had spotted them, wrapped in plastic, packed in a crate, hidden away in the cavelike cellar.

"Don't touch the lamps," he told Arturo. "Some are on timers."

"Won't touch a thing. Won't leave a fingerprint! Promise."

The cat leaped out from the kitchen and hissed. Arturo jumped back and laughed. "Puss, you're a fierce one."

Celestino went about his jobs, ignoring the cat. It followed him from room to room. As he pinched spent blossoms off the geranium, he could hear Arturo's footsteps above him.

He returned to the kitchen to refill the watering cans and take them to the second floor. Arturo stood in Mrs. Connaughton's bedroom, looking out the front windows at Mr. Darling's house, the barn, and the pond. It was a wide and beautiful view, the kind you might see on a postcard.

"The things some people take for granted," said Arturo. Abruptly, he turned around. "But hey. Now that I have you alone. Have you tracked her down yet? Did you follow my advice?"

Of course he would ask. Perhaps this—his curiosity about Isabelle, both helpful and meddlesome—explained his following Celestino through Mrs. Connaughton's house.

"I saw her, yes. Sunday." Celestino watered the African violets and cyclamen on the dresser.

"Saw her?"

Celestino finished watering. He could have turned around, but he didn't. "We ate lunch together."

"I'm so glad. I'm optimistic for you, dude. I am."

It was clear that Arturo expected something. Gratitude? Friendship? What did this rich, intellectual boy need from him?

Celestino returned to the kitchen and took the flashlight into the cellar. It hadn't rained or snowed in the past two days, but he would let nothing sabotage the trust he'd won from Loud. When he came up into the kitchen, he found Arturo seated in a kitchen chair, the cat purring on his lap.

When she walked into the café, ten minutes late, he rose from the bench inside the door, determined to embrace her. She allowed him to hold her, but her face was turned to the side.

As soon as they sat down—or as soon as she had ordered a glass of wine, Celestino a beer—she began talking.

"I've thought about you all week." Her face was a mask of worry, not joy. "And here's what I need to tell you—"

"No," said Celestino. "I need to tell you first. I need you to know that I understand we are more different than we were before. I know you are going away this summer, but before then I want us to know each other again. It will be different. I know this." He wished he could say they would be *enfants* together, once more, but of course they wouldn't.

She sighed. "Celestino, you were my first. I wanted you to think I was worldly, that I was . . . a precocious seductress or something. I was in awe of how still you were, how nothing in this whole new world made you panic. How you listened, really listened, to everything and everyone around you. How much you were willing to sacrifice—your home, your family, your language—give that up so you could learn, have a richer life. Not money rich . . . you know what I mean. I fell for all of that."

He wanted to reach across the table and take one of her hands, but she kept them in her lap.

"I thought you were so . . . profound. Graceful, even. And also—"

The waitress came with their drinks. She asked if they knew what they wanted. Isabelle said, "Give us a minute," and picked up her menu.

Celestino knew what he wanted, and it wasn't on the damn menu. "I should have come to find you sooner," he said. "I did not realize how much I hurt you when I ran away. It was stupid on top of cowardly. You must have thought I didn't care."

"Well, you could have called." She buttered a roll. "But Celestino, in the long run it wouldn't have made any difference. What I came to see was that in a way—without realizing it—I used you. I wanted to subvert my father's pure intentions for you, I know that now. It sounds like therapy talking, and partly I guess it is, but I was headed straight toward hurting *you*. If you hadn't gone."

"We were in love with each other," said Celestino.

"It felt that way, it really did. Oh God, it really did." Isabelle blushed. Her hair was tied back this time, so that when she leaned down, staring at the table to avoid his eyes, he could still see her face. Her eyes were closed, her mouth set. "Oh Celestino, I don't see how we can go back. This notion that we could be friends . . . I can feel that's not what you really want. And I hate what I see of myself when I look back at who I was with you. Especially now, now that I know how much damage I did. Apologies seem so shallow. But I'm sorry. I am."

The waitress returned. A burger. A Caesar salad with grilled salmon. Dressing on the side. Water, please. Tap.

"I've made you cry. Oh God." She reached across the table then. She seized both of his hands. "I should have had you to my place, I was just . . ."

"Scared. Of me. Of what I might do." He should have pulled his hands away, but he didn't.

"No!"

"You thought I would become angry and hurt you."

"That's not true. I would always trust you."

"Why?" said Celestino. "I ran away from you."

"I see now that you did what you had to."

"No. We are here because you did not want me to see more of your life. Your furniture, your pictures, your kitchen, your—"

"Stop. This isn't fair."

"Why fair? What would be fair?" Now he did pull his hands away. He was careful not to raise his voice. "I am a day laborer, in the words of the newspapers. A lawn soldier, I have been called. I prune trees. I seed lawns." He hesitated, already sorry he'd said so much, but he had to go on. "You. You are a university scholar who will go out into the world to save the poor children. Isn't that how you see us?"

"I'm incapable of saving anyone, not even myself," she said quietly.

When the food arrived, they stared across the table, not at each other but at each other's dinner. Celestino noted the perfectly parallel grill lines on Isabelle's fish. He willed her to eat first. Despite the day's work—removal of a fallen tree—he had little appetite.

Finally, she lifted her fork. "I'm sorry. I made it sound as if I'm to be pitied. I'm not. Not at all." She cut into the salmon.

Celestino waited for a moment, watching her. Then he ate: slowly, carefully, with his best manners. Looking at her again, he wished he could burn away the younger Isabelle, see her now for the very first time. She would not seem so different from the equally smart, equally pretty women who served him sandwiches and tea on their lawns.

"Now you're scaring me," she said. "What are you thinking?"

"How does it matter? You are sending me away."

She put down her fork and knife. "I will feel guilty no matter what I do now. But I want you to have something." She pulled her purse into her lap. She pushed a blank envelope across the table. He tried to ignore it.

"In there," she said, "is the name of an amazing immigration lawyer. He helped our housekeeper. He works for almost nothing. I worry that you'll need someone like that."

He began to eat his fries.

"Take it. Do not throw it away. I need to know you'll have somewhere to turn if things get ugly for you. Because, in a minute, they can."

He smiled bitterly at the envelope. "Ugly," he said. He realized that he had probably grown ugly to her. He could imagine the taller, better-dressed men who had kissed her, shared her bed, in the past eight years.

"Excuse me," he said, "but I will go now."

"Please don't," said Isabelle.

"What is there to stay for?"

She had no answer to this, only a plea, a look of desperate sadness.

"You will have a book to keep you company while you finish your dinner," he said, gesturing at her bag. "If I leave now, I will catch the next train." He opened his wallet and put a twenty-dollar bill on the table. He put on his coat.

She stood when he began to walk away. She grabbed one of his arms and held out the envelope. "Take this. Do me one favor only and take it."

He took it. He folded it in half and pushed it into a back pocket of his jeans.

16

Sometimes I thought the mud would drive me mad. I share Mr. Eliot's low opinion of April: it is indeed the most maliciously fickle month, but I am sorry to say that lilacs have little to do with it. Lilacs do not bloom in these parts until the cruelest month is a calendar page in the recycling bin. We may as reasonably expect a four-alarm nor'east blizzard as we may a respite of winsome blue skies—though such skies will mock what lies below: the earth dark and sodden, a stew of peat, sand, rotten leaves, and petrified long-lost mittens.

Sarah soldiered on. She'd grown accustomed to the surprisingly wide-spread loss of hair—her limbs were slippery smooth as those of an infant—but she had begun to complain of a leaden sensation in her legs, of toes and fingers that prickled intermittently all day. "Like my nerves are cringing," she said. Sometimes, when she ate, she would cover her mouth and gasp; food that was either too cold or too hot sent needles of pain through her teeth. Now the meal she liked best was a plate of tepid mashed potatoes alongside a grilled sandwich of cheese and spinach on soft bread.

I remained her chauffeur on treatment days; how guilty my pleasure at knowing I would see so much of her and then, if she came back with me to Matlock for a rest, lavish her with tenderness. The weather was so awful that she no longer had the heart to banish me from the hospital. Once she entered Trudy's funhouse of toxins, I would often read a book on one of the waiting-room couches. I had abandoned Henry James; I'd begun to find him, as Robert would say, a major downer. Craving a more picaresque source of entertainment, I turned to Iris Murdoch's most farcical novels, their comedy dark, even diabolical. Poppy had loved Iris Murdoch.

If I lurked about, Chantal would include me whenever she ordered lunch for "the girls." Once in a while, Trudy would emerge and sit with me for a few minutes; I had not been invited back to the inner sanctum since Sarah's first day of chemo. Trudy treated me gently, as if in her eyes I had suddenly become a certifiably *old* man. She would greet me not with a casual "How's it going, Dad?" but with a sotto voce "Dad, how are you feeling these days?"

"Put upon," I told her that day in early April. "Mired in the muck, of my overly trafficked driveway and the ordeals of those around me. Although it occurs to me that I hardly ever see your sister."

"Clover's wrapped up in her quest to move the children north."

"Still?"

"She has a lawyer in New York now. I have no idea where she gets the money to pay him." Trudy sat next to me and leaned close, speaking softly.

"At least she talks to you," I said.

"No," said Trudy. "What I know comes from Todd. He called because he's worried about Lee. He says a teenage boy shouldn't be the object of a tug-of-war. No one talks about it in front of him, but he's old enough to sense that someone's up to something. Todd says his grades are down."

"He's a boy," I scoffed. "He wants to be an athlete. Perfectly normal."

"But Todd wants to get him into a good high school. It's very competitive there, even for public."

These were pressures I'd never endured. I had not worried about my daughters' education; I'd worried about their happiness. I suppose the two are related, in the long run, but I never thought about that. Perhaps this explained Clover's plight; should I have pushed her to get better grades, so that she, like her sister, could have gone to an Ivy League school?

"Well, I've never doubted Todd's judgment," I said. When Trudy agreed, I felt a twinge of betrayal. "Listen to us. Poor Clover."

"She does not deserve your pity," snapped Trudy, though she spoke in a whisper. She placed her hands on her thighs, one of many practiced gestures to signal that she must move on. I'd come to know them all. "Okay, Dad. I just wanted you to know that Sarah's doing beautifully. She's very strong. Body and spirit both. Many women at her stage of treatment would be in far worse shape all around. I wanted you to know that, from me."

"Horse's mouth." I put my hand on Trudy's white-coated knee. Our fingers touched, awkwardly, but I did not pull away. "Thank you, daughter."

"You're welcome, Father." She kissed me on the cheek.

I went back to *The Flight from the Enchanter,* in which a capricious young woman becomes enthralled with two brothers. Ah, duplicity, I thought oh-so-smugly: there's *one* concern I do not have.

On the way out of Boston, Sarah slept. I listened to a classical station, content to have her beside me, belted in safely, gently snoring. Her head drooped sideways, displacing her makeshift turban. At the intersection of Route 2 and the turnoff to Matlock, I stared at her until the light turned green. Veins glowed blue and lavender just inside her naked scalp. I felt as if I were in love with every inch of her bloodstream, every pore in her skin.

Because of the unforeseen ravaging of my long dirt driveway (which I could see would now have to be paved), I'd asked Tommy Loud to install a barrel of sand beside the mailboxes. I'd pull off the road, get out of the car, and strew several coffee cans' worth of traction onto the mouth of the driveway. This was where the parents' cars idled as they came and went, exacerbating the muck.

Sarah woke as I performed this new ritual. She was confused. "Where's Rico?" she asked through the open door of the car.

"At home," I said. "Don't fret."

She frowned. "Gus with him?"

"Yes, your mysterious and reliable cousin, whom I seem destined never to meet."

She lay back against the passenger seat. I drove us to the front door. Though she tried to protest, I carried her into the house. *Like a bride,* I almost said. She fell asleep for another hour on the couch, and then I made her eat a bowl of noodle soup. "From a can," I confessed. "But organic. The preservatives are grown in petri dishes blessed by the Dalai Lama."

She rolled her eyes. "Funny hurts right now."

"Then humor is off the menu." I swept an arm through the air.

I watched her eat. Even though I'd let the soup cool a bit, steam rose and brightened her face. Why *not* a bride? Why not a new bride, a new house? My glance shifted briefly to the mantel. The surface of the large silver bowl had reverted to an iridescent tarnish. Behind it I had tucked Maurice Fougère's impetuous letter. It had been sitting there, unanswered, for over a month.

When Sarah finished the soup, she asked to go. For once, I looked forward to releasing her, to being by myself, to pursuing my sudden scheme.

As soon as I returned from Packard—where Sarah never let me take her farther than the door of her building—I retrieved the letter. It was six o'clock, but I had a suspicion that Fougère's elves worked at his studio all hours of the day and night.

The elf who answered the phone informed me that the master had just flown to Dubai; could an assistant help me? No, I said. The matter was personal. I carried the letter into my study and opened my computer. As I clicked on NEW MESSAGE and watched the blank sheet of virtual paper flash onto my screen, I felt as if I had no time to lose.

Sometimes forbearance sneaks around behind you and gives you a rude, well-placed kick. *Take that, you self-satisfied prig. Ha!*

A few days later, Sarah came down with a cold. Almost immediately, she developed a fever. Trudy ordered her to visit a lab in Lothian where technicians could draw blood and look at her white-cell count. I learned this after she called to tell me that she'd flunked the count.

It was Saturday. We had planned on taking Rico to the science museum, and I saw no reason to cancel that expedition. Now, however, we would drop Sarah at the hospital so that she could receive an injection of some warlord drug that would muster the immune troops pronto. The nurses would watch her until her temperature dropped. Rico and I would head to the museum on our own and pick her up later.

"I now know why people talk about being held hostage to a disease," said Sarah. "So if the museum closes before they unchain me, maybe you could take Rico somewhere for dinner." I told her I'd be thrilled to do that.

At the museum, the first exhibit we entered was devoted to the human circulatory system. Hordes of children were cavorting through felt-lined tunnels representing veins and arteries; fleece platelets hovered in the tunnels, along with other microcellular organisms rendered in fabric and foil. Video screens embedded in the walls showed a miniature movie taken inside the human heart—fuzzy and dark, like a bad art film from the sixties—along with cartoons of lungs and other organs doing their proper jobs to maintain the body's irrigation network. All around us, like sci-fi Muzak, played the contrabasso of a beating heart.

I tried to steer Rico to the upper floors, where we were promised dinosaurs, the solar system, a special show about robots in movies. But no luck. The lub-dub sound track had him in its thrall.

After he'd made a round of the tunnels and caves, he found a display where he could push a button that set off a 3-D simulation of the heart performing its intricate valvular tango. Rico pushed the button over and over.

"Mom's blood is filled with drugs that slay the tumors," he said when he finally turned away. "The drugs can find them *anywhere*. They can't hide."

"That's good to know," I said. Perversely, I thought of the wily, malignant bin Laden, of Green Berets and Navy Seals searching those Afghan mountain ranges until the end of time.

"Some people do die of cancer," Rico said, leading me at last toward the elevator.

"Well, fewer and fewer, now that they have such excellent drugs, like the ones your mom is taking."

Rico looked at me coolly. "But some do. It's a fact."

I wondered if I was supposed to placate him by saying that his mother would not be among that "some" or affirm that he was right. Sarah had given me no guidance here, probably assuming I would never be alone with Rico when the subject came up. But why not? Why *hadn't* she prepared me for this? Yet again, I felt wounded, left out.

I was about to tell him that my best friend had had cancer many years ago and was now completely cured when Rico said, "If anything happens to Mom, I'll live with Gus. He'll be my dad. Gus is very healthy. And he's younger than Mom. He has almost the same birthday as me."

We had entered the elevator. Rico punched the number that would take us back to a much safer time, when monsters ruled the planet. People did not die of cancer then, because people did not exist.

I had no idea what to say to Rico's news. But I knew what to feel. Indignation. I said, "Gus is your mom's cousin, right?"

Rico frowned at me. "No he's not. I don't have any cousins, and

Mom says she's got no cousins, either. Lots of people have cousins, like lots of people have brothers and sisters. But we're just us. Us is plenty."

"No cousins," I echoed. "Gus is a good friend, then."

Rico pondered this. "Yes, but he got married to Mom. Mom doesn't live at his house, and I don't, either, but we used to. So maybe we'll live there again. If she gets really sick. It's okay. There's a playground with sprinklers."

"Married?" I said as the elevator doors opened. We faced a very hungry-looking allosauraus, jaws agape, pincers reaching out for prey. *You'll do fine,* said the red glass eyes.

Rico ignored my question. He ran ahead of me past the looming carnivore. "Come see the stegosaurus!" he called, and I followed. When I insisted we stop to rest on a bench, he explained to me the evolutionary relationship between dinosaurs and snakes. Snakes, I knew already, were his favorite animal.

"Snakes," I said as we made our way toward the advent of mammals, "are powerful symbols in many fairy tales and myths. I'll bet I can dig up some wonderful stories about snakes at my house." I made my best effort to sound chatty and bright.

"You mean like sea serpents," said Rico. "Like the Loch Ness Monster."

"All kinds of snakes," I said. "Very ordinary snakes, in fact. The kind you might meet in your own backyard."

"I don't have a backyard. But Gus does."

I heard a phone ringing inside my jacket. This phenomenon still startled me, but knowing it had to be Sarah agitated me further still. Rico watched me closely as I answered.

"Percy, hi." Barely a sigh. "They're going to set me free in about an hour, but we have to go straight home. No restaurants for me. Can you buy Rico a snack on your way over? Anything other than candy is fine."

"No candy," I said to her, winking at Rico.

"I hate this," she said. "I just hate this."

I wanted to tell her I hated this, too—this inability to tell her what Rico had told me, demand that she straighten me out. "I know you do," I said, doing my level best to sound sympathetic.

"French fries," said Rico the minute I pocketed the phone.

"This we can arrange." I took his hand and squeezed it. I wished I could tell him how much I loved his mother; it didn't matter how angry I felt. As we passed the exhibit on primates, I wondered if I was just another sad, predictable male Homo sapiens, wanting this female all the more because suddenly it looked as if I had competition. Then again, I might already have lost her.

Robert had said he was "heavy duty into chem" but that he could meet me for a sandwich. "No Fac Club, Granddad. No time to spiff myself up." We agreed to meet at a deli near the T.

"Everything okay?" said Robert as soon as he saw me. His backpack made a loud *clomp* when he tossed it into the booth where I'd been waiting. The sound seemed to accentuate the weight and importance of the obligations from which I had waylaid him.

"Why is it," I said, "that members of your generation evaluate everything by such a feeble standard? And why should 'everything' fall into a single basket for evaluation? One's health, one's daily occupations, one's property—"

"Yo. Hey," said Robert. "Granddad, what's going on?"

"As always, not a great deal." I tried to sound contrite. "In fact, I wonder why I thought it a good idea ever to retire."

Robert nodded. "That's a tough one, yeah. You're like practically twenty years younger than you really are. But you could travel; that's what I'd do. Hey, travel with Sarah! Take her to Paris or somewhere really romantic. I mean, after her treatment is over."

This left me speechless, but Robert wasn't waiting for an answer. "So I'm famished. I'll go order. What's your pleasure? The pastrami's great, though I'm trying to give up meat."

"Fine," I said. I scrutinized a poster of the Heimlich maneuver while Robert stood in line at the counter.

When he sat down again, he put two glasses of water on the table. He stared at me for a moment. "You do not look happy, G."

"I am neither happy nor miserable. I'm numb."

Robert looked nervous; much as he loved his grandfather (revered him, I like to think!), he did not want to plumb the murky depths of an elderly soul.

"Number One Grandson," I said, "give me an honest answer. What would you think if I were to sell the house?" For an instant, I thought I saw tears in his eyes. "If it would upset you too much, I'm not sure I could. Not that I'm sure I could under *any* circumstances. But you're the only one who—"

"Granddad!" he said, as if he were calling me away from danger. "It's your house, to do with whatever you want. Doesn't matter what I think. Or anybody else. That's the truth."

I smiled at him. "What would your mother think?"

The overworked waitress dumped two paper plates before us. Robert picked up his sandwich at once. "I think she'd be sad but sort of relieved."

"What is *that*?" I asked. The contents of his sandwich looked predominantly gray.

"Eggplant. But are you serious, G.? You're like putting it on the market?"

"No. I am done with people traipsing through my home like a pack of stray dogs. Maurice Fougère wants to buy it. The architect. Or thinks he does." I laughed. "One step into that cellar should change his mind. It could be colonized by skunks, for all I know."

"Wait. Mr. Skylights Galore? The dude who did the barn?"

"Yes, dear Robert, that very dude."

"Wow." *Did* he have tears in his eyes? "Well, here's what I say: take him for all he's worth. But where will you go?"

I shrugged. "Sky's the limit. World's my oyster. Right?"

Now Robert looked worried. "Not, like, far away. . . ."

I hadn't eaten pastrami in ages. For a moment, I savored its leathery texture, inexplicably pleasant; the sting of the mustard in my nose. "All I wanted was to ask what you thought. Please don't mention it to anyone, certainly not your mother. I haven't even spoken to Fougère. He's halfway around the world." We'd exchanged only a few e-mails, yet Maurice, ever efficient at global operations, had arranged for Matlock's toughest home inspector to conduct a walk-through later that week.

"Well," I said, "on to you. Have you plotted out your summer yet?"

Robert told me that he wanted to spend the summer in New York and would be interviewing for a couple of internships at save-the-poor-trees organizations based in Manhattan. He planned to drive down with his roommate for a long weekend.

"We're staying with Uncle Todd. Which I have to admit is weird."

"You'll see Filo and Lee. That's good. No need to feel any guilt."

"Mom says Aunt Clo's going off the deep end and has too much time on her hands." He shrugged. "Mom's hard on everybody who doesn't work an eighty-hour week."

"I venture to say that your aunt *is* working awfully long hours, contrary to your mother's assumptions."

Robert had finished his sandwich and was eyeing the second half of mine.

"Take it," I said.

"Nah." He took my pickle instead. "Simply giving up beef is like one of the biggest steps you can take toward reducing carbon emissions."

"Oh. So who recommended that I order this sandwich?"

"You get a pass."

"Because I'm teetering at the edge of my grave and will shortly amount to nothing *but* a carbon emission?"

Robert smiled. "No. Because that way, at least I got to smell the pastrami."

We laughed. I felt marginally better, more connected to the world.

"Gotta split, Granddad. Thanks for coming into town. If you want to see something cool, check out the Carpenter Center. A friend of Turo's has this amazing video up. About the Great Barrier Reef."

"How it's being destroyed by the evil humans, I suppose."

"No! It's like a celebration of all that *life*. It's a major up. You need that." He shrugged on his backpack. He clapped me on the shoulder. "You'll like it, I promise." And then he left.

Robert had not asked after Sarah. Perhaps, despite his youthful oblivion, he sensed that this was not a good time to do so; more likely, I remember thinking, he was transfixed by his own, far safer concerns. Later, I would realize that I'd had it backward: I was the one with pedestrian concerns, I the one who ought to have probed more deeply into *his* affiliations and plans for the future.

I'd called Sarah the day before, at eight o'clock the Sunday morning after our day in Boston. Once again, it was too muddy for running; had I been able to burn off some of my anger, my enervating confusion, our conversation might have ended differently.

I did not care if I woke her, but she was already up. "I need to see you today," I said. I did not ask how she was feeling.

"Percy, I'm spending today with Rico. He gets dragged all hither and yon these days. He needs a day of doing nothing, with his mom, at home. I feel bad enough I had to miss the museum." She paused. "Rico had a nice time with you."

"I have to talk to you, Sarah."

"I am so grateful for everything you're doing, Percy, and of all people, you deserve to have me on tap—but only after Rico. Today I belong to Rico. And to this hideous drug they gave me yesterday, which made me feel like my bones were imploding all night."

For the first time, I had no patience for her disease, how easily it became her shield. "Then we'll talk on the phone. Now. Is Rico with you? Right there?"

"He's watching a video. The idea was that I could lie down for an hour."

"That hour will have to be postponed."

"Percy, don't talk to me like this. What is this attitude all of a sudden?"

"Your attitude might be called on the carpet before mine," I said. "Your secrecy, your withdrawal—not because you got this terrible news but because, if not for me, you might never have heard it. Or so you think. You've been killing the messenger, haven't you? But slowly. Torture him first, by all means."

Sarah's laughter was desperation, not mirth. "I knew you'd reach the end of your rope, sooner or later. I can't blame you for venting. But Percy, you have it all wrong. I know it looks like I'm blaming the cancer on you, and in the beginning I did have this childish sense—"

"We're past that point," I said. "Gus. That's where we are now. Or where I am. Finally! This cousin, right? Or did I get it wrong? Is he simply a 'friend'? Or even more than that?"

I could hear Rico's movie, the hammed-up voices of actors lurking behind animation, a world where the laws of physics do not apply.

"I should have introduced you to Gus months ago. I'm sorry."

"Why didn't you?"

"Because we used to be . . . involved. But we'd broken up long before I met you. Months before. He's known Rico since he was a baby, so we stayed friends. But mostly Gus and Rico. Rico could stay overnight with him. That bond was too important for me to cut. Can you understand that?"

"A friend of Rico's," I said. "Would that explain why Rico tells me that you and Gus are married? It's a fantasy then. He only wishes that Gus were his father? Or am I the wishful thinker here? Please. Set me straight, Sarah." I laughed at my inadvertent pun. "Why, that's your name, isn't it? Sarah Straight. Sarah the Truthful." (Oh God, had I conflated Sarah with Trudy?)

"We need to talk this out in person."

"We talk it out now. Or I come over there now."

"Percy."

"Are you married to this man? Yes or no."

"All right, Percy, the technical answer to that is yes, but—"

"Thank you. Then let your technical husband be your cancer slave."

"Percy!" She lowered her voice. "Percy, I love you. I haven't said so enough, but it's true. It's been true almost since I ran into you, dripping wet, in that ridiculous pink bathing suit."

It was my turn to shout. "Oh what is *love*, Sarah? What is a proclamation of love but something for a sonnet or a maudlin TV show? What does that mean to me, your telling me you love me, when your entire being, in my presence, tells me otherwise? Love is deed, not word, Sarah. Even *you* are old enough to know that by now."

If we had been together, not on the phone, we might have been calmed by the ability to see and touch. Instead, anger had won us both over.

"Shut up, Percy. Shut up for two minutes," whispered Sarah. I could tell she had taken the phone somewhere far from Rico's movie. I pictured her locked in her tiny bathroom, staring at herself in the artful mirror, framed in a gaudy mosaic of glass. "I married Gus to have his insurance. He offered. And to lend me money for the first months, before . . ."

"Before what!"

"Until my treatment is actually covered. Listen!" she said desperately. "We went to the courthouse, downtown. No friends, no family, not even Rico. It's not about being married; it's about saving my life. Or stretching it out a bit longer."

"This man offered you all that because he loves you!" I said. "Don't be a fool. He wants to be married to you, honestly and truly married, doesn't he?"

"Percy, this is about what I need, not what I want."

I am ashamed to say that I did not even wish to believe her. "You're the one who broke it off with him, aren't you? He's always wanted you back. That's what you've been hiding, why we haven't met."

"He loves Rico. He's doing this for Rico."

"That's nonsense. Extravagant, trumped-up nonsense."

"You can think what you want, Percy. And you can do what you want. Never see me again—whatever feels right to you. I don't have the energy to persuade you of the truth. The only lie I ever told you was that Gus is my cousin. That was stupid, and I'm sorry. I couldn't bear the thought that you might get jealous. I didn't know you well enough then."

I was sitting in Poppy's dressing room, staring out the window at the series of puddled ruts my driveway had become. Mistress Lorelei's house looked prim and lonesome; she'd been away for weeks.

"I could have been the one to marry you," I said. How could I convince her now that, just a few days before, I'd been planning to propose?

She said nothing.

"Why didn't you tell me you were going to do this, Sarah? Why didn't you give me any choices?"

"Percy, you've made it clear that, however much you love me, you intend never to marry again. I understood that. I respect that."

"Things change, for God's sake!"

"Don't go talking to *me* about change." When I made no reply, her voice softened. "Percy, you want to believe, and so do I, that Trudy will cure me—but maybe she won't. Chances are good I'll be dead in five years. I have to make plans for Rico."

I wanted to tell her that under such unthinkable circumstances *I* would be a father to Rico; I could be just as good a father to him as this Gus fellow, this guttersnipe who had spirited Sarah to city hall like Hades abducting Persephone. (My mind grappled backward. When had this marriage taken place, what day?) And then I remembered Rico's remark that Gus was "younger." Despite all of Sarah's protests when we had been in the throes of passion, of course my age mattered. It mattered very much.

"I have one more question, and then you can go take your nap," I said.

"As if I could possibly rest after this."

"Does Trudy know about Gus?"

Sarah hesitated. "Trudy was incredibly generous to me when I thought I had no coverage. She helped me think things out, my options. I was desperate. I didn't want to go to any other hospital, to a doctor who . . . Percy"—her voice broke and, God help me, I wondered if the sob was feigned—"Trudy is one of the most amazing doctors I've ever met, and I know—"

"Did she meet him? Did Trudy meet Gus?"

"It doesn't matter. Trudy may be your daughter, but she's *my* doctor." Her voice had hardened again. "And you know what? For that alone, I will always be grateful to you."

"Sounds like I'm already part of your past. Receding in the rearview mirror."

Sarah burst into tears, the grief as genuine as her rage. "All I care about now is the future," she sobbed. "You want to give me something? Give me the eighteen years that separate us, Percy. Give me those years, just that many, in which to raise my son. Hang on to the decade or more that you've got left, fine, squander those years whatever way you like, but let *me* live to be seventy. And God help me if I'm half so patronizing when I get there."

Stunned as I was, I realized that finally I'd heard Sarah cry—because I had made her cry. Before I could think of anything else to say, she hung up.

Ironically, I turned seventy-one the following week. Clover slipped a card into the mail she left on the table. Trudy e-mailed to ask if I had plans. Norval phoned to ask the same. I told them both that I did have plans. I spent the night of my birthday eating sausage pizza in front of World War II. *Mrs. Miniver,* to be exact. I needed to witness nobility and courage (intensified by such fine British accents), since I possessed not a whit myself.

17

obert was packing for the weekend when Turo walked into his bedroom. "Have I got a surprise for you." He sat down at Robert's desk and opened the laptop. It glowed to life. Turo clicked and typed furiously, then spun the chair halfway around. "We are on YouTube, dude."

"We?" Robert took Turo's place in the chair.

"The DOGS, man. Look." Turo reached over Robert's shoulder, moved the cursor, clicked. The enlarged video became a mosaic of pixels. "You need a better machine," muttered Turo.

Nevertheless, Robert saw right away that someone's shaky hand-held camera had captured, by day, the "action" at the swimming pool in Ledgely (the banner pulled back, the roadkill bobbing in the water). At the far edge of the pool, near the top of the screen, two or three sets of shoes walked back and forth. Abruptly, the scene shifted to the lawn they'd covered with bottles in the shape of a giant footprint. It had taken a week for Robert's right hand to recover from the ache caused by anchoring the necks of those bottles in the half-frozen turf. (Their hands had been gloved—a cautionary order—but this did nothing to soften the stress on his wrist and forearm.) Again, the footage, a few scant minutes, had been shot by day as people milled around. The third scene was one that Turo hadn't described to Robert: a large powerboat, propped up off-season in someone's secluded driveway, had been wrapped entirely in . . . "Toilet paper? Is that toilet paper?" asked Robert.

"About a hundred rolls."

"Jesus, wouldn't you say that's wasteful?"

"Makes quite a statement. But I wasn't in on that one. That was down in Cohasset."

Robert absorbed this news for a moment. Did the DOGS have *chapters* or—what was that creepy CIA term—*cells*? Turo was evasive or jokey whenever Robert asked for such details. ("We are legion, my friend," he'd said in an ominous whisper when, after the pool MnM, Robert had asked outright how many people were involved.)

The video was accompanied by a sound track of Peruvian pipes. "What's with the music?"

"Oh we have no idea who made this video," said Turo, "but wait. Look!"

Two pairs of hands held between them a huge hand-painted banner: GO FOR THE JUGULAR, DOGS! Fade to black.

Turo said something emphatic, triumphant, in Spanish.

"Made by an insider, wouldn't you say?"

"Nobody's laying claim to it, but who cares?" said Turo. "We're going viral—culturally speaking. We are multimedia. We are *out there*."

"Well, I don't think the cops in Matlock or Ledgely—or Cohasset— would disagree with that." Robert remembered the flurry of letters to the *Globe*. The DOGS were out there, all right.

"Man, you are losing the fire," scolded Turo.

"Hey—let's get going. You ready?" Robert closed the laptop and slipped it into his pack, sandwiched between a chem text with the heft of a cinder block and *Love in the Time of Cholera*. He threw the car keys to Turo. "It's parked on Walker."

NPR was half presidential primary, half Eliot Spitzer mop-up. Nothing new under the miserly late-winter sun. They surfed stations, listening to a hodgepodge of music, talking about the summer ahead.

Turo had an interview in New York as well. He wanted to work for an environmental law firm: part of his long-term plan to outsmart the system with its own tactics. He'd decided not to stay in Brooklyn with Robert but to crash with a friend at Columbia, a classmate from Exeter. When Robert heard this, he felt a twinge of release. Lately, he'd OD'd a bit on Turo's monomaniacal passions. He'd started to reward himself for long hours at the library by playing squash with a guy he'd met in his psych class. He no longer worried if he came home at midnight to a dark apartment. Maybe Turo had learned to get by on two or three hours of sleep. That's the only way Robert figured he could survive academically. Or maybe he was one of those rare geniuses who got his work done in a fraction of the time it took everyone else. Even during sophomore year, when two of their courses had overlapped, by spring he saw Turo less and less in Loker, the reading room they'd staked out as their favorite place to cram.

Robert had begun to wonder if he wanted to continue living with Turo when they returned for senior year. Turo's assumption seemed to be that if they both found jobs in New York, they could share a summer sublet. Robert was hoping to work for the NRDC or, failing that, a group whose lofty mission was to "save the Adirondacks." His mother had offered him work at St. Matt's, but if he was going to consign himself to a life lived in hospitals, he knew he'd be smart to stay away from them until it was necessary. She couldn't disagree.

She'd taken him out to dinner a week before, and as soon as they'd ordered their food, she had asked him about his "professional intentions." She'd never been so blunt about it before, and Robert was startled. He'd almost wanted to ask if she didn't trust him with his future anymore. But he could tell she was nervous about bringing it up, and she hadn't mentioned Clara once, so he'd gratefully told her about his interest in psychiatry. She seemed surprised, maybe disappointed. She allowed that pharmaceutical advances made the field more exciting than it had been during her years of med school. Robert told her that pills had nothing to do with it; he wasn't interested in becoming a glorified drug dealer. That made her laugh.

When he mentioned that he'd be staying with Uncle Todd in New York, she'd said, "Please give him my best. I miss him. Or maybe I miss his sanity. Speaking of matters psychiatric. The more time goes by, the more I think he held Clover together."

"What, she's falling apart?"

"That would be an exaggeration. I guess she still loves that job—thanks to Dad, which I think she forgets—but I gather from Todd that she has some lawyer buzzing around his lawyer about trying to split custody of your cousins: one semester of the school year with her, one with him. She's deluding herself."

"You talk to Todd behind her back?"

"How else could I talk to him? Listen, sweetheart. I was related to him long enough that I do not plan to drop him. He can marry five more times and I'll still regard him as my brother-in-law. One day you'll learn about how complicated family gets when people make rash decisions."

Robert flashed on her former reluctance to let go of Clara. What if he'd stayed with Clara for five years and *then* they'd broken up? Yikes. He said, "So what does Uncle Todd say?"

His mother hesitated. "You know not to mention any of this to him when you're there. Or, God forbid, to Filo or Lee."

"Jeez, Mom."

"Well, he certainly has no intention of making the kids split the school year. What a ridiculous notion. But he's also convinced Moira to skip the big June wedding. I think they're planning on eloping the week after your visit."

Robert thought about this for a moment. Why was it such a big deal? Did Clover actually harbor hopes of getting back together with her ex? He didn't dare ask his mother this question. Everything she said about Clover made Robert feel hugely disloyal just to be listening.

"I think you're too hard on Aunt Clo. I get why you're mad at her, but like, she's the only sister you'll ever have." He saw the expression on his mother's face and said, "Duh of the century. Okay. But she's always been generous to me. And when I was little, I thought she was so cool."

"She is cool. She's too cool. That's her handicap, Robert. She's a butterfly. All that style and flashy romance, or whatever you'd label her outlook on life, it doesn't make for stability or, in the end, contentment."

Robert wondered what insect his mother would be. If the sisters were in Aesop, what would the fable be called? "The Ladybug and the Butterfly"? "The Earwig and the Butterfly"? Joseph, a fellow bio major, was crazy for insects. He told Robert that earwigs exhibited family-oriented behaviors. They were nurturers as well as workers. Ants and bees hogged the entomological spotlight, quite unfairly. You could actually blame Shakespeare for that, said Joseph.

How strange it felt to set foot in Aunt Clover's apartment when she no longer lived there. Turo went in with Robert, to use the bathroom and say hello to Lee, whom he remembered fondly from their midnight ski adventure. Lee and Filo had just returned from school, and their stepmother-to-be was out at the market. "She's going to make paella."

"Cool," said Robert.

"If you like it," Lee said grimly. Filo had turned on the TV.

Turo looked around. "Great house you've got." The apartment occupied two floors of a wide, bow-fronted townhouse. The street windows looked into the dappled branches of a sycamore tree.

"It's okay," said Lee, "but Dad says the maintenance is too high. He says we're going to look at houses in New Jersey. Moira wants a garden."

Turo gestured at the branches nudging the window; unlike branches in Cambridge, they were already leafing out. "Feels like Eden right here, man."

Robert carried his pack through the kitchen to the tiny back room where he'd stayed in the past. The twin bed was still there, made up with a new quilt in pastel colors; no more funky black chenille. A sewing machine monopolized the desk, and a bulletin board displayed new photos—obviously Moira's. She was pretty in a totally different way from Clover: dark pageboy hair, tea-colored skin. She looked part Asian—but she was plump, just a little, which made her look more suburban than Far East exotic.

Turo stepped into the room. "Gotta be off, man."

Robert walked him to the nearest subway stop. They made plans to meet up for the return trip; they wished each other luck with their interviews. Turo took the stairs that led down to the F train. He took them two at a time: as usual, certain of where he was headed.

Back in the apartment, Robert looked around the living room and began to notice the absence of specific objects (an eclectic gang of pillows on the couch, a pink glass chandelier) and the presence of their replacements (a small dark sculpture of a generic father and child, a delicately flowered wing chair). The TV was off; presumably, Lee and Filo had gone to their rooms.

Robert knocked on Lee's door. His cousin's room was painted navy blue, the walls a backdrop to posters of sports figures: Jeter, Favre, Nadal, Beckham, and a fierce-looking martial artist with a face twisted into a grimace and a leg raised toward the camera at an angle that looked totally impossible. "Dude!" said Robert. "Can you do that?"

"I'm not even a brown belt. I'll have to quit anyway, if we move."

"New Jersey has karate," said Robert.

"Tae kwon do."

"Sorry. But that, too."

Lee shrugged. He was lying back on his bed, an iPod tethered to his ears.

Robert sat beside him. "So. How is she? Your dad's girlfriend?"

"Moira?" He shrugged again; did everything matter so little? "She's cool. Tries hard to make us like her, so how can we not? Mom says that might change after they're married. She says to prepare ourselves for if they have a baby."

"She lives here now, though, right? You'd have seen the cracks if she were a phony, dude." Robert was appalled to think that Clover had started an evil-stepmother smear campaign.

"Whatever." Lee sat up. "Want an energy bar or something?" He freed himself from the iPod.

In the kitchen, Robert took a banana from a big cheerful fruit platter (also new), and Lee ate a bowl of dry multicolored breakfast cereal—which would have made Clover flip out.

He had to stop superimposing Aunt Clo on this scene.

"So your friend's like kind of an extremist, isn't he?" asked Lee.

"Turo's a believer in acting out your passions. He's dedicated to saving the earth. I mean, you know, working for people who do more than just talk about the environment, the habits we have to change. Like that."

Lee chewed busily for a moment. "At Thanksgiving? When we were skiing? Like he wanted to connect me with some group down here."

"What group?"

"They do recycling and composting and hand out stuff about saving energy. I've seen them in Prospect Park. I told Dad, and he says the soup kitchen's plenty. Except I have to do that with him and Moira. So I was thinking maybe this summer, after I get back from Mom's, I could maybe volunteer."

Was there no end to Turo's zest for recruiting?

"I think you've got enough going," said Robert. "I mean, with sports and school. I worked my butt off starting about your age."

"You're a genius, though. Mom says everybody doesn't have to go to

Harvard, that it's a lot of money spent on mostly social connections. She went to U. Mass. and did just fine."

The sound of the apartment door spared Robert from deciding whether or not to defend his school.

"Someone is shoveling again!" The scolding was loud but merry. Lee put down his spoon. Robert turned around. Here she was, the flesh-and-blood Moira, holding two shopping bags against her chest. Paper shopping bags. Doubled. (He had to stop superimposing Turo everywhere, too.)

"Robert! The famously brilliant Robert!" she cried. "A banana? You must be starved!" There followed an awkward physical clash of putting down bags, hugging, introductions, covert assessments, offers of more food. Moira struck Robert as a happy-to-the-core, energetic, overtly maternal woman. She had a midwestern accent and wore, under her coat, a close-fitting beige wool dress you saw only on women who work in business or finance.

In a blink, she'd put a plate of M&M cookies on the table. Homemade. "I'm putting the groceries away, no argument," she said. "But then I'll put you to work. Can you devein shrimp?" she asked Robert.

Weird but true: he liked her. Aunt Clo, in any context, would have loathed her on sight.

Robert hadn't laid eyes on Uncle Todd in two years. He looked exactly the same, except for more gray hair. TV handsome: smooth skin, ordinary features, like he'd stepped from an ad for a Camry or premium cable. Robert couldn't help remembering Clover's claim that her husband might be gay. Did the guy look remotely gay? Robert tried to put this out of his mind as they ate and talked.

Todd acted completely comfortable with Robert—wanted to know all about Robert's parents, about Granddad. Robert told him the big news: that Granddad had a girlfriend. He decided not to mention the cancer. When he'd last seen Granddad, they hadn't talked about it. Robert had been afraid to ask. He knew his mom was treating her, but of course she told him nothing.

"Kudos to Percy," said Uncle Todd. "Fantastic news. It's about time. Though I have to confess, your mom did spill the beans on that."

"He's maybe thinking of selling the house," said Robert. "Maybe moving in with her. He didn't say so, but that's my hunch."

"Wow. That's even bigger news. Leave that house?"

"It's kind of huge for him, and she's this stained-glass artist. She lives in her studio. I went once, with Granddad. It's pretty weird to imagine him hanging around this funky loft all day."

Moira was in the kitchen, making dessert.

"That house," said Uncle Todd. "Clover and I used to have a fantasy we'd end up there. She called it the house of her mother's heart. I don't know how we thought that would happen. Well, obviously, it wasn't meant to be. Either way."

"Guess not." Robert glanced nervously toward the kitchen. How much did Todd and Moira talk about Clover? Because of the kids, maybe a lot. His cousins would now have three parents.

Over strawberry shortcake, Uncle Todd asked Robert about the jobs he was applying for. Robert explained his strategy: do work on the nature side of biology, rather than the medical, up to graduate school.

"If you get one of these jobs, you could live with us for the summer."

"Really?" Robert looked quickly at Moira.

"Moira's idea," said Uncle Todd. "She thinks you'll be a good influence around here." He glanced at Lee's bedroom door. (The cousins had been sent to do homework, which would earn them their share of shortcake.)

Careful to use his napkin, Robert wiped cream off his lips. "But Filo and Lee go to their mom for the summer, right?"

"Well, Filo's off to that riding camp, but Lee's going to stay here through mid-August. He's nearly failing English and social studies, so we're enrolling him in a kind of summer academy. It's right around the corner, here in the Slope. There'd be nothing like it in Matlock."

"We wouldn't charge you a thing," said Moira. "You're family. And I'd get that clunky sewing machine off that desk. All I sew anymore are curtains, and we've got plenty. For the moment anyway." She smiled at Uncle Todd.

Was Robert being signed up as Big Brother? Did it matter? He had practically zero savings. There was no way the stipend from either internship would cover New York expenses. Unfortunately, what this deal might cost him were Aunt Clo's affection and favor. He'd think about that later.

"Wow," he said to Moira. "I don't know what to say."

The whole changing-partners thing had to be something you never got used to, Robert thought as he pulled García Márquez from his pack and turned down the sheets (daisies!) on the narrow bed. Yet people did it all the time, made the necessary adjustments. Did this handicap his parents, who could barely remember anything before Psych 101 back in college, their fateful assignment as lab partners? ("From lab to life. The first thing we shared was a white rat!" Robert's dad loved to say.)

The event Robert had dreaded for months finally came to pass: two weeks before, stopping in the Gato for a double dose of brain-revving caffeine and chocolate, he'd seen Clara, at a table with that guy who'd lived down the hall in her freshman dorm. Stuart Something. Tall as a totem pole. Varsity crew. Button-down shirts under wool sweaters straight from a catalog. Christ, *he* was straight from a catalog. The kind of guy Robert and Clara used to make fun of.

Their linked hands, on the table, framed a plate of carrot cake.

"Hey," said Stuart Something, spotting him first.

"Yeah. Hey," said Robert. He didn't want to look at Clara, but he had to.

"Hi," she said stiffly. "How's it going?"

Robert saw Stuart Something, blushing cotton-candy pink, try to withdraw his hands from Clara's, but she was holding on, making her statement.

"It's going along just fine," Robert said. "For you, too, I see."

His voice shook. Fuck.

She heard it, and her tone softened. "Good to see you."

"Good. Yeah." Only by sheer force of will did he manage to get into line at the counter, rather than flee back out to the Yard. He kept his back to her as he paid and moved toward the door. But when he paused to set down the coffee and put away his wallet, he felt her gaze. Turning briefly, hot-faced, he got the message loud and clear: Clara would never forgive him—and why should she? It was way too late even to apologize.

That night, Turo said, "She is now a callus."

"What?" said Robert.

Turo placed four fingertips on the heel of his opposite hand.

"Each relationship shed leaves a callus, man. Toughens you up."

"Thanks. I don't think I 'shed' her so much as ran her over a few times and left her for dead."

"I'm sorry, man. I don't mean to be cold. Clara was smart. Pretty. Sexy."

"I know what you're going to say. Lots more where she came from."

"You know it's true, my friend. Something we all learn."

"Yeah, and I know I have to learn a ton of stuff I am going to *hate* learning to get any decent job in this cruel world. I know lots of stuff I'd rather not but have to. Don't you?"

"Indeed I do. The next part is sorting out the stuff that really matters."

"Turo? Dude? Can we skip the life lectures just for tonight?"

Thankfully, Turo had dropped it.

Robert's interviews went well. He liked the Adirondack people best—and if he got that job, he'd get to do some fieldwork, collecting water and soil samples, camping out in the woods—so now he didn't know which he'd rather have. To his surprise, he received no texts from Turo before they left the city. In his free time, Robert went to the new MoMA and the Museum of Sex. He went to Williamsburg one night and stayed out late with a girl from his bioethics class who'd found out he was down there, too. No sizzle, but she was cool. He followed her back to a party at a loft where everybody was dancing and smoking weed. Robert was relieved when she left with another guy. He arrived back at the apartment just as Uncle Todd was getting up Monday morning to go to the gym. (A gym obsession; was that gay?)

"Bet you need coffee. Big-time," he said, and simply poured an extra cup.

No awkward questions. They ate toaster waffles and shared the *New York Times*. After Todd left, Robert made breakfast for his cousins while Moira showered and dressed. In a flurry of zipping backpacks, brushing hair, locating boots, they were suddenly gone, leaving Robert blissfully alone. He crashed.

The other two nights, he stayed in the apartment with his cousins, playing games, watching movies. Uncle Todd thanked him for "facilitating two date nights in a single week!"

Yikes. But not gay. *Negativo.*

"Man, you look bleached, like you've been up since I saw you on Friday!" Robert said when his friend got into the car. "No way you are driving."

Turo grimaced. "I took advantage."

"Of whom? Half the frosh co-eds at Barnard?"

"No names, amigo. No names."

"So. No more *senza ragazza?*"

"I didn't say that," said Turo. "I am still free as a condor."

"Poetic. I can see you've been waxing poetic."

Turo leaned back.

"How'd the interview go?"

Without opening his eyes, Turo said, "They loved me."

"Don't they always."

Turo slept from the Henry Hudson Bridge to the toll plaza at the exit from the Mass. Pike. "Thank you, my friend," he said quietly when he came to. When Turo was groggy from sleep, the Spanish inflections rose in his speech. Robert would remember, then, how one of the things that had drawn him to Turo in the first place was his unusual history: exotic, though not to be envied.

That night, after they entered the apartment and went their separate ways, Robert pulled his laptop out of his pack and plugged it in. He'd forced himself not to check his e-mail in New York, aware that he had recently become as much an addict to connectedness as the average modern citizen. When he recalled his months off the grid in Costa Rica, sometimes he felt mournful, even depressed. It seemed as if no one— well, not counting Granddad—shared his ambivalence about the dense, sinewed matrix of communication enfolding Robert and everyone he knew. By contast, he thought of his net-shrouded hammock, his tent, the jungle: the industrial symphony of insects at night, monkeys at dawn, birds all day. Was this, too, part of what had drawn him to Turo: nostalgia for life in the tropics?

Predictably, the e-mails were all missable: somebody from chem lab checking an assignment; his mother wondering how his interviews went;

his dad sending him (and, according to the address line, *27 more*) a joke about Bush and Katrina. Plus three spamlets that had squirreled their way through his filter.

He was about to close up when an IM from Turo flashed onto the screen. *Big MnM cmg up. U WILL b pt of it!*

Robert sighed. He wondered whether, in the utopia Turo pictured, the ways in which to broadcast your words—your voice, images, avatars, aliases, whatever—would increase or decrease. Maybe you had to go off the deep end to find your way toward something simpler, more humble.

18

The women around Ira were losing it. Their grip, their composure, their stamina, their footing—each falling out of balance in some essential way. Begin with Joanna, his high-finance sister, who'd lost her job two months ago and had fallen into major debt, maxing out credit cards on consolation shopping. For the moment, she'd moved back in with their parents, leading to calls of complaint and worry from his mother.

Evelyn was the easiest to deal with: she was simply freaking out about holding E & F's first auction in this new location. (*Freak*, as in *control freak*, was part of her job description, so in a perverse way she was behaving responsibly.) Her first concern was how to situate a party tent on the sloping lawn between the house and the barn. The one truly level bit of land was the fenced area, down near the pond, that held the swings and play equipment, but you could hardly ask young masters of the cosmos to dance in and around the miniature castle-with-moat or duck beneath the monkey bars en route to the hors d'oeuvres.

Her second concern was food. Years ago, this event had been a potluck supper; then, for several auctions in a row, a caterer mom had contributed a lavish spread. When the last of her kids outgrew the school, no one could bear going back to noodle casseroles and vats of gazpacho. Nowadays, someone with bottomless pockets shelled out for professional food. In keeping with the Woodstock theme, the auction committee had wanted "sixties food," but what did that mean? Sloppy joes and deviled eggs—or tofu stir-fry and eggplant stuffed with barley?

So they'd settled on Thai, from the restaurant in Ledgely, the only place around that served decent food with any kind of panache. (As Marguerite's mom put it, "Anything Eastern is sixties, right? *Siddhartha*, TM, sitars . . .") Evelyn's current worry, looking over the approved menu, was that so many dishes included nuts. E & F was a "nut-free zone," and didn't this mean they had to honor the ban 24/7?

"I'm sorry, but you cannot have decent pad thai without peanuts," declared Ezra's mom, head of the Refreshments Committee, as Ira passed Evelyn's office on his way out the door.

At least the classroom projects were complete. Heidi had photographed them so that pictures could be uploaded to the online auction catalog Clover would send to all the parents. Ira was pleased with the Birches' self-portrait milk bottles, tucked in their tall rustic case; as an object, it felt like Joseph Cornell with a dash of Warhol. He had secret hopes that it would outprice the ikat quilt, the decoupage toy chest, and the set of ceramic nesting bowls glazed with footprints and flowers. (Would you really want to eat from a bowl imprinted by actual feet? Hands, okay, but the crinkled feet of dirt-loving, shoe-loathing children?)

"Oh Ira, I'm so glad you're still here." Clover stood just inside the door to her tiny office. She looked wan and fretful.

"You okay?" said Ira. "Don't let this silly auction eat you alive."

"God, Ira, it's not the auction. The auction is keeping me from jumping off a cliff. I never thought I'd see cocktail napkins and barware and folding chairs as life preservers, but that's the pathetic truth."

He had no choice but to step into her office and ask what would tempt her to jump off a cliff—even though he could already guess.

The walls of the tiny room were crazy-quilted with charts and lists pertaining to the Big Event. The only window, a perfect circle, contained a view of the house and the lawn. It hadn't occurred to Ira till now that if, in the course of a day, Clover wanted visual relief from her work, her only resort was to look at her childhood home. Claustrophobic or what?

"My husband got married, just went ahead and did it."

Ira ignored the absurdity of her statement. "That must feel awful."

"And the worst fucking thing is that I had to hear it from my own sister. Or *her* husband." Clover laughed bitterly. "Actual, not ex."

She told him how she'd summoned the courage to ask her brother-in-law's advice on mediation for custody. She was running out of money to pay a lawyer, and now it turned out—again, her *sister* knew this first!—that she wouldn't even have her son for the usual two months of summer. Without consulting her, Todd had enrolled him in some tutorial program.

Her eyes filled with tears. "And get this. My nephew—Robert, you know him; Robert who I always thought was completely on *my side*—is going to be living with them in New York!"

Ira saw her plaintive look and knew what it meant. She wanted him to call Anthony to her rescue. "Clover, I'm so sorry. That sucks. But Robert will be hanging out with his cousins, remember that, and he's one of your biggest fans."

"And so?" Clover's voice rose, petulant.

Ira glanced at the board behind her, unable to look her in the eye. His gaze landed on a list of items for the silent auction: symphony tickets, a harbor cruise, eye surgery, architectural advice, a lava lamp, a Lalique decanter, a Derek Jeter dartboard. . . . He forced himself to focus.

"Clover, don't you get to a point where you just want to make the very best of what you have? And you have so much. You do."

Not surprisingly, her frown deepened. "What?"

"I know this place you're in feels terrible. I can't imagine being away from my kids so much—I mean, of course I don't have kids, so I can't really—"

"No. You don't. You don't, and you can't. You're right about that."

Ira felt as if he could see her indignation rising like a vapor from her face.

"I don't know you that well, Clover, but I do know you're an attractive, talented woman with great kids who are doing fine even in the face of—"

"Of my having deserted them. Right?"

"No. Of their parents having decided to make separate lives but still respecting each other's—"

"And how can you say they're 'doing fine' when my son is apparently in danger of flunking out of school? That's something you do know about—school performance. As related to *home life*."

Ira folded his arms. "What do you want me to do? Tell me. I'm clueless."

"Be a friend. Don't call me on the carpet. I have a therapist to do that. I have *life* to do that."

Ira stood and held his arms open to Clover. What else could he do? She stood and let him hold her. It felt insincere to him, the coward's way out, but it was all he had to offer. He gazed miserably at the wall, over her fragrant hair.

. . . a tour of the WGBH studios in Boston, a set of Bose speakers, six sessions of equine massage (what?), a child's bike, a silver tray . . .

When she stopped crying, she said quietly, "I wish you weren't gay."

"Sometimes I wish that, too," said Ira, "though it's mostly when I have to deal with the car mechanic."

She laughed. Thank heaven.

The hardest by far was Sarah: partly because Ira's attention had to stay on Rico, partly because her determination made it hard to tell how sick she really was, and partly because Ira couldn't figure out what was going on with the two men in her life—and he didn't dare ask.

Since Sarah had started her treatment, Ira had seen Gus a couple of times at dropoff and pickup, but then he came along with Sarah for the springtime parent-teacher conference. He was the kind of guy you'd describe as rugged or strapping, built for an outdoor life of chopping down trees and turning them into cabins. He had pink, oversunned skin, carroty hair, and a shrub of a beard. He dressed in new jeans (his "dressy" ones, Ira imagined) and wore dainty, old-fashioned spectacles that harked back to Henry Thoreau.

He spoke with scholarly precision, and though he seemed to have sprung from nowhere, like a genie from a bottle, he also seemed to know Rico as well as Sarah did. In fact, he spoke of Rico as if the boy were his son.

"We're concerned," he said, "that Rico might feel markedly different from the other boys and girls because of his mother's cancer—even ashamed of that difference." And when Ira asked Sarah how Rico was sleeping, Gus was the one who answered, "He's become acutely reattached to his snake, Balboa. When he stays over at my place, he drags that creature into my bed at two or three in the morning. But I haven't noticed nightmares, no terrors or accidents, no talk of death or dying."

"Balboa's stuffed," Sarah said.

"Well, phew!" said Ira. Snakes, stuffed or not, were the least of Ira's concerns about Rico. During the conference, Sarah spoke less than Gus did. Sometimes she just watched him talk about her son as if she were an impartial witness, a home-study consultant or a distant cousin.

That night, Sarah phoned him at home. Few parents took advantage of Ira's accessibility; this was a first for Sarah.

"I owe you an apology," she said. "You must have wondered what the hell was going on there. I didn't know Gus would be coming along until this morning. He insisted."

"Well, you might have noticed my double take." He was grating cheese for Anthony's asparagus risotto.

"I don't know how to explain this," she said.

Ira waited.

"Okay, Gus and I are married—but it's so I can have his incredible health insurance. My treatment is going to be long and expensive. Gus has known Rico since he was tiny, and he really cares about him. They really care about each other. I mean, they're genuine friends. We're all . . . friends."

He tapped the grater for the last flakes of cheese. "So Gus is like a godfather."

She did not agree with this statement but said, "You must wonder about Percy, too."

"I do, but it may be none of my business," said Ira. What he thought was, Young lumberjack trumps elderly librarian; what's there to wonder, honey?

"Anything that affects Rico is your business, right?"

"That's Evelyn's line, but it's not so simple." Ira handed the bowl of cheese to Anthony, who stood at the stove, stirring the rice.

"I'm hoping Percy will still be a big part of our lives," she said, "but for now he's very angry at me. Which I understand. And I have to fix. But I think Rico hasn't noticed yet."

"Noticed . . . ?"

"That Percy and I are in a . . . hiatus."

Hiatus! It was perfectly clear that Gus regarded himself as Rico's de facto dad. "Sarah, children see a whole lot more than we think—or than we want them to see. You know that." Did he sound harsh? He added quickly, "Whatever you have to do to get better, to get through this ordeal, you do it."

"I wish it were that easy."

"Please," said Ira. "No judgments here. Just keep me in the loop."

"I will."

He waited for her to say good-bye, but she said, "Rico adores you, Ira."

"Thank you."

"No. Thank *you*."

As soon as Ira hung up, Anthony said, "No judgments on what?"

Ira started to think about how he would tell the story of Sarah and Rico and Percy and Gus. Had he even mentioned Sarah? Anthony had met Clover and Evelyn and two of Ira's fellow teachers, but none of the parents. "Anthony, you know what? You've got to come to this auction."

Anthony sprinkled the cheese into the pot. "Did I ever object?"

Ira crossed the kitchen and leaned his head on Anthony's shoulder. "I'm sorry," he said. "I'm sorry for all the craziness."

"I'm glad you're sorry," said Anthony. "I won't lie. But please set the table—and refill the peppermill, would you?"

Considering his level of exhaustion, Ira felt oddly cheerful. He obeyed.

"Oh—my turn to apologize," Anthony said as they sat down. "I forgot to tell you your mom called before you walked in. I spoke with her. Not urgent."

"Joanna?"

"Joanna."

"Good news?"

Anthony shook his head. "She's going through retail withdrawal. Driving your mom insane. You should probably call her back after dinner."

Ira sighed. "This is delicious. You've outdone yourself."

"I might have to agree," said Anthony.

Ira realized that what he felt wasn't cheerful, or not entirely. What he felt was safe.

19

On the morning of May first—children were beribboning a maypole down by the barn—Maurice Fougère stepped from his shiny blue low-emissions chariot onto my driveway with all the confidence of a New Age pacifist warrior. Not to be outdone by the Toadstools, June-bugs, and Nightshades frolicking and trumpeting their pagan joy, he pressed both hands to his chest and exclaimed, face toward the sun, "How perfect a day is this!" He then aimed his blue eyes and his right hand in my direction. His advance was so sure that I nearly beat a remorseful retreat. I'd only happened to be outdoors, inspecting damage to a shrub that looked like the work of a very large woodchuck. In the disagreeable contemplation of how to deter one of these clever, undeniably winning creatures, I'd let the appointment slip my mind.

"I am so very glad we're meeting in a proper fashion at last!" said Maître Fougère as he gripped my hand. I could only hope that he was not alluding to the few occasions, the previous summer, on which we had *almost* properly met, on which I had seen his car glint past a window and had hidden somewhere deep in the recesses of my house. Evelyn, with whom I did speak often that summer, said that her husband was sorry he kept "missing" me.

Close up, he looked no less attractive than he had in the PBS documentary about modern architecture which Clover had forced me to watch after my first tour of the repurposed barn. His skin was so glossy and evenly tanned that it rivaled the sheen of an expensive handbag. His dark hair was thick and alert, his teeth even and bright (hadn't he grown up in fluoride-free Europe?).

I did note that I was definitely taller.

Looking up at the face of the house, he said, "Yes." And again, "Yes."

I cleared my throat. "I haven't said that word to you, not yet. Let's get that straight."

He turned to me again. "We have much to discuss, I know this."

I led him through the front door. I wanted to get him seated, pinned down, but he wanted to roam the place immediately. His designated inspector had been through the house two weeks before, banging, prying, peering, frowning. I had tried my best to ignore the fellow as he clomped upstairs and down; I'd even gone running in the middle of the afternoon.

The resulting report was a hefty document, though such is the norm for a house with deep history—rather like the medical file of any elderly patient. And indeed, when I read the first sentence of the opening summary, I couldn't help recalling Sarah's jest that the house *was* me. I like to think that my doctor would assess me in terms parallel to those of the house inspector, who wrote: *The foundation remains sound, and though many angles in the premises, particularly in wooden structures, would indicate extreme alteration from original building lines, nearly all such structures (see exceptions in Sections E and K below, related to cellar stairs and purlins supporting rear roof) appear to have settled solidly, without significant compromise to overall integrity.*

Fougère strode eagerly through the living and dining rooms, with a detour through the study. I followed on the heels of the master (shod in black hightop sneakers), unable to find any conversation to halt the exuberant stream of nonverbal praise flowing from his mouth. In the kitchen, he faced me once again, put his hands on his hips, and said, "Percy, my friend, I am ready to proceed with a contract, and I hope that you are similarly disposed. I am in love with this house, and I will treasure it like a child."

"Well," I said, resisting the urge to point out the grammatical ambiguity of his statement. Would he or the house be the child?

From inside his jacket, he extracted an envelope and placed it on the table. "Herewith is my offer. I find it more civilized to give people time to consider numbers in private, wouldn't you agree?"

"Well," I said again. "Well, yes. I'd say that's wise. Although . . ." I was puzzled that he had no desire to walk through the second floor again, to reassess the closet space (almost nil) or the state of the roof from within.

"You do not succeed in my business without being bold about what you like—*eh bien*, what you love—and what you want. I do not teeter on edges."

"No teetering." Except that our business wasn't funny, I'd have laughed.

This was when Clover walked in the back door. She wasn't carrying the mail, and the surprise she expressed when she saw Fougère was transparently phony. I'm sure she'd spotted his shiny, pert little automobile.

They exclaimed about how happy they were to see each other, exchanged French pecks on their cheeks.

"Maurice, will you be here for the auction?"

"It has been on my calendar, in red, for months," he said. "Which is to say, my good wife would assassinate me were I not present!"

He grinned. Clover grinned back. I saw her glance at the envelope on the table. Unlike the envelope that had carried his first letter to me, this one bore the printed return address of his firm; my name was typed in widely spaced italic capital letters across the open field below.

M. PERCIVAL DARLING.

Did the extra air between the letters lend me greater importance?

An awkward silence preceded Fougère's declaration that while he regretted his hasty departure, he had to catch a flight to Washington.

"Remaking the National Gallery?" I said.

"Ah no, but the Phillips would like a consultation. We shall see!"

Clover followed us as we retraced our steps out the front of the house. As we approached Fougère's car, Mistress Lorelei advanced on it as well. "Maurice! Hello, hello!" she called out as she crossed from her yard to mine.

"*Salut,* Laurel," he said, and they, too, enacted the kissing ritual.

"Maurice, I am dying to talk to you about joining in our historic architectural awareness program," she said. No beating about the bush.

"Oh yes? What an honor. We must make an appointment to discuss this, absolutely," he said. "And will I see you at the auction next week?"

She giggled. "Much as I love the little ones and their cause, I think it's a good occasion for me to scoot. Edgar and family will be in New York, so I'll join them. I hardly ever get to see my grandchildren—speaking of little ones. Though if I could corner our very own Frank Gehry, it might be worth staying!"

"Laurel, you flatter me to excess." Fougère was at the wheel, starting his car. How much fawning could the man endure—or did he thrive on it?

Through the window, he told Clover that he liked her dress, told Busybody Lorelei to call his secretary, then turned to me. "We will emerge from this as comrades, I assure you." One of his celestial eyes actually winked.

We three inferior beings watched Fougère drive away, his left arm, in its designer denim sleeve, bidding us a backward *au revoir*.

I found it easier to address Laurel than Clover. "So, barely back, and you're off again?"

"Percy, I've been back now for ages," she said. "Are we overdue for a shared supper, perhaps?"

"Perhaps we are," I lied, thinking about one more advantage of moving.

Clover watched Mistress Lorelei retreat. "So what was that about?"

"Well, it wasn't about a budding romance, let me set you straight on that." I assumed that news had traveled through E & F about my estrangement from Sarah.

"Daddy, I mean Maurice."

"No romance there, either. Alas for me. Is that man irresistible or what? Those eyes. Do we suppose he wears tinted lenses?"

"Daddy, you are so impossible sometimes. I just wondered what in the world you'd be doing with Maurice over here. I mean, you treated him like a leper when he was around making plans for the barn. . . ."

"Yes, and that was childish of me. Just making amends."

She stared at me as one might examine a specimen through a microscope.

"How are you, daughter? We're passing ships these days."

"Overwhelmed. That's how I am." She looked away.

"I hope to see more of Lee and Filo soon. When do they finish school?"

She frowned slightly. "Middle of June. But before that, I have a small mountain to move." She sighed, as if in a play. "And I'd better get back to it."

As she walked away, I thought about Clover and Sarah in unison, about how gratitude—for something enormous, something seismic— can sour into resentment. I've never seen myself as possessing a generous nature, yet if called upon to give something to someone I love—a favor or concession, even a sacrifice—of course I would always say yes. Yet what if such acts led to my feeling as if I'd betrayed the people I love? What then?

I did speak with Sarah, once, after our terrible conversation about Gus. She phoned me the following week, the day after my birthday. She had to, because I'd been scheduled to drive her into Boston for a checkup with Dr. Wang, who wanted to "start the dialogue" about Sarah's surgery, which would take place after the chemo, to be followed by radiation. (Never an end to the rides at this amusement park! I'd already remarked to Norval that his cancer ordeal had been, by comparison, a sunset picnic at Tanglewood.)

"I should have called you to say happy birthday," she said. "I'm sorry."

"I spent my birthday with the courageous Mrs. Miniver. Both of them."

"Percy, why are you always so arch when things get serious?"

"Because arch," I said, "is like a straightback chair. Dependable. No give. The easiest seat from which to rise."

"Okay. I guess that tells me something. Me, I always choose the soft chair, the couch." I waited for her to scold me. "Percy, I'm in a miserable place here."

"I know that, Sarah." I tried to say this gently.

"Don't condescend. I am talking about me and you. Not me and the cancer. Me and the insurance people. Or me and . . . Gus's parents, who think—"

"I don't want to hear about Gus's parents. Or Gus."

"Okay."

"Good."

"I'm asking somebody else to drive me to my appointments."

"I think that's a good idea."

"Well, that makes one of us. Or one and a half."

I waited. *No give,* I reminded myself.

Sarah said quietly, "Did you talk to Trudy? I mean, tell her?"

"I have not spoken to Trudy about anything of late. I have not spoken to much of anyone. Except Maurice Fougère. I think I'm going to sell him the house. He wants to write me a very large check."

"And have you told Trudy—or Clover—about that?"

I wanted this conversation to go on forever, yet I knew it mustn't. "Sarah, are you planning on continuing to give me advice? I can't think of any reason for my continuing to take it." I forced a laugh. "If I ever did."

"Percy, I don't want this to be over."

"I'd like to tell you, Sarah, that I'm wise and mature enough to handle this marriage-for-insurance deal of yours, but I am not. There, that wasn't so arch, was it?"

"No."

"My dear," I said, wanting for a change to sound as old as possible, "timing is everything."

"Oh Percy, what the hell does that mean?"

I wanted to say that it meant she couldn't have her cake and eat it, too, that she ought to have faith in true love, that God laughed when you made plans. . . . I wanted to level every proverb in the book at her wish for saintly forgiveness, to tell her that I was sick of lying down on my alarmingly rut-riven driveway to let myself be driven all over by every woman I'd known since losing my wife. But I said, "What it means, for now, is that I'd like you to call me after your appointment with Dr. Wang and tell me how you're feeling. Call me when you need to. I'm not going anywhere." Or maybe I was. "And I'm not going to be calling you." It felt good to sound definite. Resolve begins as a matter of persuasion.

I have always been an avid and fairly ecumenical reader of fiction: I relish the pretend, the invented, the convincingly contrived. Some will regard this affinity as Oedipal—my choosing the mother's turf over the father's—but as I have said before, I had a docile, ingrown childhood during which, as the years passed, I became increasingly conscious of how grateful I should be, if only for the harmonious cohabitation of my parents. Like everyone else who knew them, I tended to see them as a single unit: Alva & Betsy, Betsy & Alva. Only after I moved away did I contemplate the wonder of their sharing a workplace as well as a home.

Perhaps they were more like siblings than spouses. In certain novels I have read, that is what they would have turned out to be. (In one sort of novel, they would have lived chastely, I their secret foundling. In quite another, I would be a clandestine sailor's knot of genes that knew one another far too well.)

One of the more heated arguments I'd had with Sarah was about the way in which I viewed my youth. Sarah believed firmly that the happy childhood is a myth, that in order to grow not just up but out and away, children must reach a point of conscious discontent. Ideally, she said, that point comes late, or gradually, or with the turgid hindsight of adolescence.

"You," she said, "are turning a blind eye to how incredibly lonely you must have been at times—even shut out, left out, by parents who seemed so perfectly matched. Don't tell me you weren't lonely a lot of the time, didn't wish for a sibling."

"Didn't," I said. We were eating in my kitchen. My mouth was full.

"Probably, you buried that loneliness in books." Sarah pointed a fork at me. "In fact, it occurs to me that your parents might have been doing the same with their own loneliness. I doubt it was the perfect marriage you envision."

"And why do you suggest I dredge up all this alleged discontent—excavate these artifacts of sorrow?"

"To know yourself better. That's part of the momentum of life, isn't it?"

"My momentum is running, swimming, and getting up and down that staircase several times a day." I pointed at the steep stairs leading from the kitchen to the bedrooms.

Sarah sighed. "For my sake, I'm so glad you never remarried, but I'm willing to bet that if you'd fully faced the solitude your parents enforced on you—not that they did it meanly, I'm not saying that—then you would have found another wife within a few years of Poppy's death."

I chewed my food to calm myself. After a moment I said, "Speculate all you want about my childhood, but leave my marriage alone."

"All right, Percy. Then let's just say you belong to a club of one. The Club of the Perfectly Happy Child. Don't tell me *that's* not lonely."

"Let's change the subject."

"By all means." We finished our spaghetti in silence.

This was during the week before Thanksgiving, when she knew she was to meet my daughters—and they to meet her—and when I was trying to coax her to see a doctor. Sarah had told me about her own childhood: raised by grandparents from age five, after her parents were killed in a fire at the hotel where they worked in the rooftop ballroom. No siblings, no nearby cousins; three uncles with whom she lost touch in her thirties, once her grandparents died. "And Worcester. Do you know how much fun it was to grow up in Worcester in the nineteen-sixties?" she said.

Like Poppy, like me, Sarah was an only child. And Rico—I assumed he would follow suit. Did we possess a built-in homing device, we onlies (or "singulars," as we're dubbed at E & F)? I'd always heard that we are supposedly drawn to mates from large, chaotic, rambunctious families, where every gathering incubates a drama or two, where alliances shift as readily as clouds.

The night I made up my mind began like a scene from a novel I might love. Imagine this: Moon or no, the sky is dark as a bog. A storm rages, and wind flings rain against the clapboards of a very old house. Inside, the solitary occupant reads his book. Grateful for shelter, he hears windowpanes shudder in their mullions, water cascade from drainpipes, gusts of air whistle through the dryer vent. He tries not to personify the storm, not to see it as a spiteful spirit seeking entry through shingles, sills, and cracks in the stones that support the foundation beneath the stalwart floors.

He leaps at the sound of the front door latch, its urgent rattle.

He sets down the book and goes to the nearest window. A car is parked out front, but the rain is so fierce, the darkness so greedy, that he cannot begin to guess whose car it might be. Now the knocker strikes the door.

He is no coward, has nothing to fear; he unbolts the door and opens it. . . .

"Jesus, Dad, since when do you lock it?" shouted Trudy, pushing past me out of the squall. She stood on the rug in the foyer, her raincoat dripping.

"Since the wind blows it open," I answered. "One more thing that needs fixing around here."

"Jesus Christ, Dad." She continued to stand there, just staring at me. Was her face wet from the downpour, or had she been crying?

Belatedly, I felt the terror of her presence. It was only nine o'clock, but Trudy never arrived unannounced. To get her to Matlock at all required a major occasion.

Or an emergency.

"Not Robert," I said.

She looked at me impatiently. "Robert? What about Robert?"

"Robert's all right?" Or Sarah—was it Sarah that had brought her here?

Trudy tore off her raincoat as if it were covered with bees. She threw it on the bench. "So I happened to talk to Todd this evening, and he happened to mention that you're selling the house. Selling the house? Is that true?"

"Come in, would you?" I returned to the living room, magnanimous with relief. "I could light a fire. Make tea."

"Don't. Don't do anything. Just sit down and tell me what's going on."

I sat on the couch. Trudy sat across from me. She pushed wet hair away from her forehead.

"You seem perturbed, daughter."

"Dad, I am more than perturbed. I'm pissed. You're leading a life completely apart from the rest of us these days, making huge choices without consulting anyone."

"In case you forgot, I'm used to making huge choices. All on my own!"

"Come on, Dad. Selling the house?"

"That's one huge choice, yes, and one to which I don't believe Todd was privy. But never mind. What other choices of mine are enraging you?"

"I could go into a whole context here, but I won't. Some of this I am not ready to discuss. But Dad, the house?"

"Yes. The house. It's too large for me, as you know—"

"Any larger than it's been for the past twenty years?"

"And it's now surrounded by litters of human puppies and their extended families, a whole community I never—"

"Community is good for you, Dad. I didn't like that decision at first, the whole crazy nursery-school invasion, but Douglas convinced me it's a good thing for you to be surrounded by other people. Have your privacy at the center of it all—have the best of both worlds, that's how Douglas put it."

"How nice to know you and Douglas approve of my life," I said. "But didn't the two of you urge me, for years, to move somewhere more 'practical'?"

"Dad, I gave up on that long ago."

I heard the shade on the window in Poppy's dressing room, directly above us, snapping against the casement.

"Are you worried about where I'll go, is that it?"

Trudy didn't answer. That's when I had a hunch that this was as much about her mother as it was about me.

"I came to believe we'd always have this house," she said. "I realized I was wrong to ever wish that you would leave."

"And if I died here? Would you and Douglas move in? Is that it?"

She leaned back in the armchair and closed her eyes. "I don't see that, no. But the idea of you, anywhere else . . ."

"That's an odd idea, isn't it? But odd is the flavor of my life these days. As Robert would say, I've decided to roll with it. The oddness."

"Dad, please don't get all clever on me now. Please."

I removed the screen from the hearth. "Let me get this going," I said. It had been unusually cold all day, and for the first time in weeks, I'd laid wood for a fire. But then, looking for newsprint to twist beneath the logs, I'd been distracted by the *Grange*. The police log had contained nothing juicy in ages; what caught my eye was a page of houses for sale. I'd abandoned the thought of a fire and, instead, combed the real estate listings, trying to ascertain if Fougère's offer was profligate or stingy. I was completely out of touch with the financial realities of Matlock, the "value" of living in my privileged town, my enclave, yet I resisted the notion of hiring an appraiser. I was finished with strangers poking my heirlooms, stroking banisters, peering into cupboards.

Lighting the fire gave me time to think. Trudy let me go about my routine. Once the kindling caught (ignited by Matlock's latest brides and christened babies, sacrificial victims all), I returned to the couch.

"Do you remember the night your mom died?" My heart felt like one of the panes of antique glass in the windows, under assault from the storm.

Trudy's face registered fear, which gave me a certain degree of petty consolation: my ironclad daughter turned fragile.

"I assume you've never forgotten the way you heard what you thought was a voice, sent me out into the night like the good girl you were."

"Dad, we don't need to talk about this."

"I suppose we don't *want* to."

"I didn't blame it on you, if that's what you think. Or maybe I did at first, but I understood later . . ."

"How much later? Can I ask you that?"

"Aunt Helena wouldn't let us blame you one bit. And she was right."

I poked at the fire, though it didn't need my help to burn.

"She should have been a mother, Helena."

"Yes," said Trudy. "For a while there, she was kind of our mother. Clover once said that even though she liked Uncle Norval, she had a fantasy that he would die and you would marry Helena."

"Not a bad fantasy," I said. "But I would never put up with goats."

Trudy didn't laugh. "I thought Mom was pregnant when she died."

My lungs seemed to shrink. "What do you mean?"

"I heard a conversation. That week, I think. Or the week before. On the phone. I don't know who she was talking to. She said she loved the idea of having a son. But another daughter, she said—another daughter would be fine, too. She thought three children would fill this house perfectly. She said she sometimes felt as if someone else was waiting to be. Like the opposite of a ghost. That's what she said."

I waited for Trudy to tell me that Helena, or someone else, had set her straight. She said, "So I thought that, thought she was pregnant, for years. I thought about the conversation I'd heard—"

"Did you hear her *say* she was pregnant?"

"No, and I knew it; I mean, I knew that I didn't know for sure. I didn't even tell Clover. No one. After the funeral, when everybody was standing around talking about Mom, I listened to see if anyone said anything about it. But they didn't."

What if she *had* been pregnant? What if the argument we'd had before the party that night had trumped her telling me this? What if Poppy had been so angry, through the whole party—during which she drank, but didn't everyone drink through pregnancies then?—so angry at me for my boorishness about Clover and her looming sexuality . . . what if she'd been so angry that she'd drowned from rage? The sheer *weight* of rage, fueled not just by liquor but by all those volatile hormones?

"Dad, are you okay?"

I shook my head violently. "What is it with everything being judged as 'okay'? Of course I am not 'okay.' Are you 'okay'? Is okayness what made you drive through the tempest to scold me as if I were your child, not your father? Your father whom you fit into your busy doctor schedule now and then? Your father from whom you hide important details like the cockamamie insurance schemes of the woman he thought *he* might screw up the courage to marry? Doctor-patient privilege my ass."

"I'm sorry, Dad. Dad? Oh God."

"Go home," I said. "Please go home."

Trudy moved to the couch. "Dad! I didn't mean to upset you by this—"

"I'm the one who brought it all up, right?"

Trudy sighed heavily. "So listen, Dad. I know you're mad at me about Sarah, but I can't talk about that. I really, really can't. But I have one more thing to say about Mom. And then I'll go if you want." She waited for a moment. "Okay. When I started med school, I realized that if Mom had been pregnant, it would be in the autopsy report. You saw the report, didn't you?"

"Of course not." My face was in my hands. Why, I wanted to yell at Trudy, would I have wanted to see a list of the contents of Poppy's stomach, a catalog of her scars, an inventory of organs that had failed in quick succession? But I had done my yelling.

"Dad, she wasn't pregnant. It would have said so. I went and looked. I had to know for sure. I hope that doesn't make you mad."

"Please go home," I said. "This was my fault, this horrid conversation."

Trudy squeezed my right hand and stood.

"I'll talk to you about the house another time," I said. "But I believe I'm going ahead. I'm signing the purchase-and-sale on Thursday. I'm selling it to Maurice Fougère."

I heard her surprise, a reaction that would be echoed by everyone who knew Maurice and his flair for the ultramodern. Perhaps the anticipation of this surprise figured in his delight. I could imagine him telling me that another reason for his success was *always keeping zem on zair toes.*

"Please let's talk before you do that," she said. "Please. But I'm glad we had this conversation. Aren't you?"

"I don't think so, Trudy. I really don't."

"Don't be angry at me, Dad." She stood on the foyer rug again, pulling on her raincoat. "And please tell me you'll be all right."

"I'm not angry at anyone right now," I said, though this wasn't true. Yet it was true that I felt differently, more tenderly, toward Trudy: toward my little Trudy, the daughter who'd put on fishnets for her mother's funeral, meaning no harm or disrespect. I wished that only Dr. Trudy Barnes would leave, that I could remain in the company of just that little girl.

"Dad, I'm going to call you in the morning, and I'm going to have Robert do the same," she said. "I wish—"

I opened the door. "I'll be fine. Or should I say, I'll be *okay.*" I was glad of one thing: that the rain had diminished to a drizzle. "Please drive safely," I said.

20

"Wait until it gets dark. There's going to be quite a show." Ira stood beneath the tree house, Anthony at his side.

"My God, sweetheart, you really built this?"

"Not without help. As you know." Ira wore black jeans, a threadbare Grateful Dead T-shirt on reluctant loan from his nostalgic Uncle Sy, and a fuchsia corduroy blazer he'd found at Lothian's funkiest thrift shop.

"Ah yes. You and those three young studs. Will *they* be here?" Anthony wore a cheap, chunky pendant, peace sign as Olympic medal—another loan from Sy, who'd tripped out at the real Woodstock—over twenty-first-century khakis and button-down shirt. ("I am not going overboard for this," he'd warned Ira.)

"I don't know," said Ira. "Robert and Turo cooked up the surprise."

After checking that his class project was looking its best in the live-auction lineup, Ira had taken Anthony for a tour of the school. Anthony had been gratifyingly amazed. He'd loved the artwork in Ira's room, the view from the window, the birch-bark album containing photographs of Ira posed with the Birches up in the tree house. "That tree house, I've got to see it!" Anthony had exclaimed, so they'd made their way back outside and through the festive obstacle course: the party tables lined up along the face of the barn, the displays of silent-auction items, the dance floor cantilevered—thanks to Maurice—against the sloping lawn. The party tables were draped in cloths tie-dyed by two Cattail moms. On each one sat a large bowl of handmade fortune cookies, each of which could be purchased for five dollars. Most contained lame-duck sixties clichés—*Feelin' groovy*; *Drop acid, not bombs*; *Power to the people*—but a few contained prize outings with teachers. (*Mr. Ira will take you to the Franklin Park Zoo!*)

Staff members from My Thai were setting out their chafing dishes, members of the dad band were tuning up by the pond, and Clover was sprinting hither and yon, looking happy but hysterical. Guests would begin to arrive in fifteen minutes.

Ira wondered if tonight would be the night he finally said yes to Anthony. Later, of course, when they were alone together at home—though Ira knew well enough how plans could be derailed by the smallest of mishaps. He thought of your average straight guy with the jeweler's box burning a hole in his pocket, of bended knees, of dowries and stammering permission sought from fathers. At least they were spared the torture of such antiquated rites.

Ira heard Evelyn calling his name. "Think you can fend for yourself?" he asked Anthony.

"Can't promise I won't run off with the next Bob Dylan who walks by."

Ira laughed and jogged down the hill. The weather couldn't have been more accommodating: warm and breezy, the pond rippling in a light that promised the onset of summer. It was early enough in the season that mosquitoes were scarce, yet late enough that even after dark the parents would linger to drink and dance in the open air while spending money to give their four-year-olds precocious access to theater outings, ballet lessons, pony rides, possibly even stained-glass lessons from Rico's mom. The breeze rose to occasional gusts, but they were refreshing, not sharp.

Rosemary, that was her name. He'd met her at the squash courts. For the second time that night, she smiled openly at Robert from across the room as he tried to concentrate on reviewing theories behind the evolution of human estrus and gestation, the orchestrated rise and fall of hormones. (How ironic that his pituitary gland was sabotaging these efforts.) Eventually, he'd have to go to the men's room, which would take him directly past her table. If she hadn't left.

For now, he stayed faithful to his computer screen. The reading room was nearly full; they were halfway through reading period, exams a week away.

What kept him from absorbing the finer details of his class notes wasn't Rosemary, however; it was his exhaustion and the pressure of a poorly timed head cold. The night before, he'd helped prepare for the "big action" Turo kept talking about.

They'd had dinner at the apartment first. Turo had made tamales, a favorite meal of Robert's whenever they ate together (something they did less and less often). On the radio, while Turo cooked, they heard a story about an American couple in Guyana. The wife, a labor nurse, had set up a prenatal clinic to serve a community of Rupununi Indians. The husband, a botanist, had launched an ecotourism outfit. His true goal was to teach the Indians how to safeguard yet profit from the unspoiled wilderness around them.

"Wait till the government gets wise to the larger implications. Mr. and Mrs. Smith can kiss their visas adios," said Turo.

"What do you mean?"

"Let's see. Ecotourism . . . lumber and pharmaceuticals. Hmm. Which one yields a greater GDP?"

"Man, you are one hardened cynic," said Robert.

This vaulted Turo into a big jag about how, having started out life where he did, he'd seen firsthand what terrible, irreversible things people could do to the places where they lived. "I mean, not to belittle your conscience, man, but flying over a million acres of forest reduced to red earth, it's not like watching a bunch of ugly ranch houses go up in Newton or Matlock. I hear your granddad when he rails against people who 'destroy history,' I get where he is, but it's peanuts compared to what goes on in places like Brazil and Argentina. Nature is history writ macro, nature is way the fuck bigger than history. In the balance, history's puny."

Robert ate and listened. He didn't argue that Turo had mostly grown up in Gold Coast Chicago and Exeter, New Hampshire. Robert had his own illusions to nurture.

After dinner, in the car, Turo directed Robert to Everett, to pick up Tamara.

"You hear about New York yet?" Robert asked. He had yet to tell Turo that he'd just accepted the internship with the Adirondacks outfit and planned to live with his cousins in Brooklyn. It had just occurred to him that the lease on their Cambridge apartment wasn't up till the end of August, and whether or not they renewed it, they had to find tenants to sublet.

"Change of plans," said Turo. "This summer I'll be here, then . . . Depends on how things play out."

"What things?"

"I'm thinking of taking next year off."

"Dude. That's news to me," said Robert. "Don't tell me you're selling your soul to this . . . to the DOGS." He still found it hard to utter the name of the organization with any degree of seriousness. Though serious it clearly was, or he wouldn't be blowing off work on his Borges paper.

Turo snorted loudly. "Look after your own soul. Mine is not for sale."

"Can I say something, dude?" Robert asked as he waited for a light to change. "It's like you've gone and joined the army."

Instead of acting insulted, Turo said, "Well, yeah. It's that rigorous, if you make the commitment."

After they picked up Tamara, Turo drove them out to Lothian, to a warehouse near the train tracks. There, they joined two guys named—if Robert had heard correctly—Skunk and Boots. They were maybe in their thirties, Skunk a goth-looking guy, Boots a reggae type, dreadlocks down to his butt. They made no small talk, didn't even shake hands.

They were doing what Turo called prep work, as if this were a restaurant kitchen. At least they didn't have to go creeping through the pitch-black woods acting like commandos. If anybody was in charge, it seemed to be Boots, who gave Robert the weird task of tying newspapers into fat cylinders. Boots then stuffed them into four massive tires, the kind you'd see on a semi. At the other end of the huge empty space, Skunk and Tamara were painting the signature banner. Turo came and went from another room.

After two hours—no beer, no talk, and the place was a frigging freezer—Robert helped Boots load the stuffed tires into the back of a van, along with a crate of extension cords. He felt cross-eyed with fatigue, his fingers numb. Boots wasn't hostile, but he hardly spoke. The cooperative silence grew creepy.

Once the van was loaded, Robert crossed the space to have a look at the banner, but it had already been folded. "Dowels in the truck?" Tamara asked Skunk. Skunk nodded. He wasn't exactly loquacious, either.

Just as unceremoniously as they'd all come together, they parted. Turo drove. "So where does this 'big action' take place?" asked Robert.

"Won't know till we meet tomorrow, back at the warehouse."

"It's like we're special ops, at risk of blowing our cover," said Tamara.

"I think special-ops guys know everything before they go in," said Robert. "They are torture-proof. Which, come to think it, we are not. Or"—he glanced at Turo and laughed—"I am not. That's for sure."

"I have input, but I've learned to go with the flow," said Turo.

"Oh, that'll be the day," said Robert.

Turo hadn't responded. As they'd cruised into town, the three of them had slipped into a sleepy inertia. Robert dozed off, barely waking when they dropped Tamara at her place.

"Get your beauty sleep, friend," Turo told him when they got home.

He'd awakened that morning with a nasty sore throat and a cough. Turo had left a note on the kitchen table: *HERE AT 5!* Robert had groaned.

He'd taken a hit of DayQuil and packed for the library. He had to study for his medical anthro exam and finish a draft of his lit paper, or he'd be screwed. Midmorning, he tried to call Turo but got his voice-mail. "Man, I am wiped, and I've got this evil cold," he said. "I don't think I can make tonight."

When he took his next break, to buy a sandwich at the basement cafe-teria, he checked his phone and found a text from Turo: *B THR. NO OUTS.*

"Give me a break," Robert said aloud. He texted back, *b thr if i can. don't count on me.* Almost immediately, Turo replied, *NEED CAR.* Robert answered, *SORRY.* Enough of this textual Ping-Pong. He punched in Turo's number; weirdly, he hit voicemail. Maybe this meant Turo was in a library. "Finally, man," muttered Robert.

At five, he felt his phone vibrate. Not without a hint of guilt, he put the phone in his backpack. Turo would have to save the human race without his help that night.

Now he looked at the clock on his computer: only 8:15. His body felt like it was 3:00 a.m. Where was Turo now? On the lawn of some McMansion out in Ledgely? Down on the Cape? Why had they been meeting so early? Robert had to wonder if his appointed place in this MnM had been crucial; probably, all they really wanted was his car. All he did was follow orders. Anybody could do that. It *was* like the army. None of the men in Robert's family had "served in the military," as the press liked to put it. How weird was that? No war stories of any kind. Maybe he was a sissy at heart, didn't have the guts to give in to whatever unpleasant work it would take to effect any positive change. Maybe he simply didn't have the warrior gene.

"You need coffee. So do I." Her whisper, so close he could feel her breath on his ear, nearly knocked him out of his chair. Rosemary stood behind him.

Robert laughed quietly at his physical panic. This girl was so stealthy, *she* should work for the DOGS. She was right: he did need coffee. But more than that, he needed distraction.

He closed the computer, slipped it into his backpack, and followed her out of the reading room.

The band was playing—by request!—"In-A-Gadda-Da-Vida." Roughly two hundred adults dressed in silly, colorful getups were dancing to this undanceably interminable song, drinking together on the swings, and crowding around the silent-auction tables, trying to snare their fencing lessons or Red Sox tickets before the bidding closed. (Was that Jonathan Newcomb, venture capitalist, wearing the fake sideburns, bandanna headband, and ripped overalls?) Ira had bid three times on a gift certificate at Trader Joe's, but he quit when the bidding reached twice the face value. He was still in contention for a year's membership at the gym to which he and Anthony belonged. (They had secured this donation.) Last time he'd cruised by the table, he'd noticed that three separate people were vying for the equine massage. Go figure.

Evelyn took his arm. "Heidi's rounding up the other teachers, to introduce their projects. Are you ready to cue the tree?"

"Light my fire, baby."

She laughed. "These Earth Shoes are killing me. I cannot believe I ever wore them for more than five minutes." Over her ducklike shoes, Evelyn wore a paisley maxidress and a jean jacket with Joni Mitchell appliquéd on the back. She had long ago discarded a garland of fake daisies that made her scalp itch. Ira was feeling the same way about the thrift-shop jacket. Oh God, not fleas, he thought as he started toward the house.

After an incendiary sunset, the sky had finally darkened. Maxwell's dad had laid down all the extension cords that afternoon, anchoring and covering them to make sure no one tripped. Percy had been kind enough to let them use power from the house, since the tree was so far from the barn. He'd told Ira that he had other plans the night of the auction but would leave the back door unlocked.

Ira had noticed Rico's mom earlier; like a few other parents, she wasn't in costume. Well, who could blame her? If you were going through chemo, what energy would you have to dress up as Sergeant Pepper or Janis Joplin? (One couple, the Plotkins, were sporting what looked like canary-yellow Dr. Dentons, with hoods, makeshift periscopes strapped to their heads.)

Ira had watched Sarah as she wandered around the auction tables. She appeared to have come alone, yet he'd also noticed how often she looked up at the house. Percy had left lights on for Ira, so he wouldn't have to stumble through the dark to flip the switch. Sarah probably thought that Percy was home but refusing to attend the auction. It was still a mystery to Ira, what had happened between those two; clearly, the news wasn't good.

He stood on the porch, waiting. A crowd began to gather for the live auction, timed to occur when people had drunk just enough to loosen their purse strings but not so much that they'd doubt their own decisions. Maurice Fougère, wearing bright pink Indian garb that made him look like a sultan ripped from *The Arabian Nights,* stood by the mike where the lead singer had, a few minutes earlier, tried mightily to channel Iron Butterfly. Evelyn stood beside him. Maurice had agreed to be the auctioneer. This Ira couldn't wait to see. That thick French accent should make the spectacle extra amusing.

Anthony stood near the front of the group below. He waved at Ira. Ira blew him a kiss. They'd agreed to bid on the Nantucket weekend (honeymoon?).

Anthony was having a good time. He'd bought two fortune cookies, yielding strips of paper that read, *Kookookaju!* and *Go ask Alice.* ("Can I work here? Please," said Anthony. "Definitely not," said Ira. "One of us has to stay in touch with the real world." "And that's *me?*" said Anthony. Ira had kissed him, quickly but easily. " 'Fraid so.")

The crowd was impressive. Clover had done a good job of roping in not just current parents but a sizable number of alum parents as well as members of the Matlock community seeking idle entertainment and maybe a few good deals on acupuncture or Swan Boat rides.

Evelyn signaled Ira. Maurice spoke into the microphone. "*Attention, my psychedelic friends! This is the moment when we ask you to cast all financial caution to the wind, in the behalf of our wonderful children!*"

As the applause began, Ira entered the house and went to Percy's study. On the desk sat a power strip from which four extension cords snaked out through the window. Ira flicked the switch: four beams of light shot up into the branches.

Black lights had been Arturo's suggestion; he'd even told Ira where to rent the fixtures. The teachers had spent an entire afternoon cutting giant flowers, peace signs, and doves from heavy white paper. Climbing into the tree house that morning, they'd pinned and hung the shapes throughout the branches. Now these ghostly silhouettes glowed and shifted in the breeze. The effect was ethereal and joyful. Perfect.

Ira heard more and louder applause, the childlike exclamations of awe. There was something shameless about this degree of excitement over something so frivolous, yet here was a community of people who put the kind of value on their children's lives that so many other people, sadly, did not. Ira could not discount the effect of the wine, yet in that moment he realized how glad he was to belong in a place like this. Because he did belong.

He hurried back through the kitchen to the porch, eager to get to the main event, to see the tree from below, as it was meant to be seen. As he walked through the back door, he heard the applause and the cries of delight rise still further; had Maurice started the bidding?

No one was looking at the tree; even Maurice faced in the opposite direction. There appeared to be a pillar of fire in the middle of the pond—no, two. Flames rose from a pair of dark objects floating across the water from the opposite shore. Ira laughed. This was over the top; had Clover arranged this second surprise? Too much spectacle would distract from the auction itself.

He had yet to reach the crowd when he saw the next two pillars of fire ignite. At first, it looked like they were in the middle of the sky, over Laurel Connaughton's house.

Just as Ira realized that the fires had nothing to do with the auction, light struck Laurel Connaughton's house across its entire white façade.

The first thing he saw was that the twin flames appeared to emerge from the two chimneys—or from objects that sat like crowns on top of the chimneys. At the same time, an enormous piece of white fabric, whiter than the house, seemed to fling itself down over the front of the house, stretching from the roofline to the rhododendrons flanking the door. Some people gasped; others laughed.

Ira stood midway down the hillside, so transfixed that he couldn't move forward, couldn't look for Anthony in the crowd beneath him. He was aware that it had begun to disperse at the edges, that figures were running chaotically here and there.

Anthony reached him and held his arm. Neither spoke. They were looking at the curious message painted on the banner, lit by a pair of footlights similar to those illuminating the upstaged tree house.

FIDDLE-DEE-DEE, ROMANS:
WILL YOU DANCE WHILE
YOUR CHILDREN'S PLANET BURNS?

"Romans," murmured Anthony. *"Romans?"*

"Nero. It's a reference to Nero," said Ira. "Oh my God."

People around them were talking rapidly into cell phones. Clover passed them, glancing tearfully at Ira. She ran toward her father's house.

That's when a gust of lovely warm wind ferried a luminous tangle of sparks from one of the fires on the pond toward the light show at Mrs. Connaughton's. It drifted into the edge of the banner, which appeared to recoil before catching fire. The word BURNS was the first to be consumed.

The sound of sirens swelled rapidly; almost instantly, the flash of the fire engines pierced the trees lining the road. By the time the trucks drove in, the banner was a sheet of flame, yearning toward the shingled roof. The great columns of fire that had burned so fiercely at the outset—both those on the pond and those supported by the chimneys—had died down to quietly brazen embers. But the burning banner had a cause all its own, the fire a robust complaint, as if raging against the house itself.

"Oh my God," said Ira. "What if they can't put it out?" In an attempt to stop trembling, he took Anthony's hand. He let go when he saw Sarah running up the hill toward Percy's house.

Ira caught up with her at the back porch and said, more loudly than he'd intended, "He's not home."

She looked miserable. Ira tried to think of something else to say, but both of them turned toward the neighboring house when their attention was captured by an odd noise, a grating and crumbling.

One of the chimneys began to slump forward. Embers from the pyre resting on top poured like rough jewels down the steeply pitched roof; a large dark object fell to the ground. A new gust of wind ripped the entire flaming banner off the house and carried it, twisting, through the air. Like a gaudy specter, it passed over the fire engines, over the row of maples separating Percy's property from Laurel's. It loomed closer, rising steadily, still burning, until the crown of the beech tree, the highest point before open sky, snatched it from the air. Sparks rained down through the branches, and the tree house, its exterior composed so frugally of long-dead timber, caught fire after just a slight, suspenseful pause, along with the playful paper cutouts gleaming in the purple light.

Celestino made himself a pork chop, with beans and peppers on the side. He turned on the radio, tuned it to the college station, based in Lothian, that played a strange jumble of music: jazz, hip-hop, sometimes a song from a musical, a piece of opera. You never knew what to expect.

Before him lay a catalog of courses for a "business and vocational" school. You could study electrical engineering, bookkeeping, hairdressing, auto repair. Everything taught at the school seemed to be about fixing things, though not the things that Celestino wished he knew how to fix. But here was a section on landscaping and gardening. *Shaping Public Spaces. Running a Nursery. Science of the Modern Lawn. Understanding Trees.*

Celestino liked to think he understood trees. Loud had even said so: "*Hombre,* you understand trees, you've got a friggin' knack."

The day had been beautiful, and as he did on all the beautiful days this spring, Celestino had tried to absorb the pleasure of the sun, the first warm winds. There were no indoor jobs this week. Loud sent him back to Rose Retreat, the garden by the church. He'd already removed the salt hay, unwrapped the bushes, folded the burlap and returned it to Loud's storage shed. He'd left the bushes alone for a few weeks, to let their canes loosen, relax into their natural posture. Today had been the best part: clipping out the deadwood, pruning back. Thousands of tiny new leaves, shiny and red as blood, had begun to assert themselves. Buds would form surprisingly soon. Roses, when they flourished, were a source of deep satisfaction. Celestino dug compost and lime into the soil, still faintly moist from the rainstorm several days before.

The sound of the gate had startled him: two women. "Oh, hello," the younger one called out. "We're just looking. Is that okay?"

Celestino smiled and waved to indicate that she wasn't intruding.

The two women were mother and daughter, searching for the right place in which to hold the daughter's wedding that summer. They talked as they followed the circular paths. The mother wanted a big wedding, with more guests than the garden would hold. The daughter said she saw no reason to invite anyone who didn't know her and her fiancé well.

"Why do you want to pay for a lot of strangers to see me get married?"

"They're not strangers, they're part of our family circle. Your father and I have known some of these people for years. This wedding isn't just about you."

"No, it's about me and James. And we can always elope."

"I'd call that an empty threat. That dress of yours in my closet tells me so. That registry list at Williams-Sonoma."

Celestino's sister would be getting married in a month. He wondered if Marta and his mother were having arguments like this one, arguments about the details. It occurred to him that his own life lacked details—or the kind of details shaped by things like "family circles." This made him think of the Christmas party the Lartigues had held for the French families, the ones with whom they shared their culture. He remembered the way that Isabelle had enfolded him into those parties, though he would never have belonged. He wondered if she saw those families still. In France, would she find yet another circle? For Isabelle, friendship was easy.

After eating dinner, he went downstairs. Mrs. Karp had left him a note, asking him to hang the kitchen curtains she had washed. Celestino got the step stool out of the broom closet and slid the yellow fabric onto the rods, clicked the rods onto the brackets. Mrs. Karp went back to her TV show.

When he returned upstairs, the college-student deejay was reading the news. "And this just in," said the boy, deepening his voice as if acting in a play. "A major fire involving two historic homes in Matlock, continuing to burn as I read this news to you." When the boy named the street, Celestino sat down on the nearest chair.

The stunned revelers, those who had driven to the auction, had no choice but to walk the half mile back to the library parking lot; the shuttle bus that brought them over would never be allowed past the cordon of fire trucks and squad cars spilling from the two driveways onto the road in both directions. Ira wondered what it must look like to anyone driving by: a procession of shell-shocked people dressed as flower children, martyred rock stars, yellow submarines.

Stranger still was the scene they left behind. Folding chairs and tables had collapsed. Tie-dyed tablecloths had blown into bushes. Lime-green paper plates had scattered in every direction; some floated on the pond like Day-Glo lily pads. The party tent, so painstakingly mounted over the cantilevered dance floor, had been caught in the deluge of pumped water and buffeted down the slope toward the playground, slumping over the miniature castle. The one exception to the mayhem was a row of gift baskets, sprouting colored tissue and ringlets of ribbon, that stood undisturbed on a table at the opposite end of the barn.

Laurel Connaughton's house had burned down to a heap of smoldering antique rafters and planks. Of the two chimneys, one still stood, pointlessly resolute. The other had shed bricks and leaned askew, like a tall man in a posture of defeat.

Beside Percy's house, the great copper beech was a dark skeleton of its formerly glorious self, still—weirdly—illuminated by a single ultraviolet footlight. Percy's roof, at least what Ira could see from the rear, glistened black, its surface wet but thoroughly charred. Most of the panes in the old windows on the second floor had been shattered by the pressure of the water, and no doubt the furnishings in those rooms were soaked. But the fire itself had been halted at the roofline. According to the police chief, that heavy rainstorm the week before had helped spare Percy's house; Laurel's had gone down so fast because of the fuel used in the pyres set by the terrorists. That's what Chief McCord called the perpetrators, as if he had a second 9/11 on his hands. Ira detected the stench of melted rubber along with the smells of burning pitch and spilled oil.

Now and then, an indifferent breeze stirred up the innocent fragrance of moist green grass.

The barn had survived without so much as a singed shingle; the eaves still dripped with cascades of water from the engine that had pumped water directly from the pond (leaving thick muddy ruts across the lower lawn when it departed). Evelyn's and Clover's offices, where the windows had been left ajar, were strewn with a pasty stew of ruined papers and books.

They were gathered now in Ira's classroom: Evelyn, Clover, and the seven teachers who'd attended the auction. All of them, even Evelyn, would have given anything to turn their backs on this nightmare at least for another eight hours. Most of them had spent every waking hour of the past few days in this place, preparing for a party that should have ended in showers of money, not cinders, flame-retardant foam, and cold, stagnant pond water. More than dancing or dressing up or chowing down on coconut shrimp, they'd looked forward to a good long sleep. What kept them there, however, were the urgent questions of Chief McCord, his counterpart from the fire department, and a Matlock police detective. Anthony, too, had stayed, and though he sat apart from everyone else, he had found a pad of construction paper and, ever the lawyer, was taking notes.

Maurice seemed to have taken off, but Heidi told Ira that she'd seen him up the hill, walking around the house, inspecting it. Perhaps he'd been assigned to wait for Percy's return. Clover had been standing by the house when she called her father's cell phone—and heard it ring through an open window in the living room. The police reached Laurel, in New York, by getting her number from a member of the Historical Forum.

Chief McCord had split them into two groups. Someone had dragged in full-grown chairs for him and his detective, but those who worked at E & F were accustomed to children's chairs and throw pillows. Anthony had claimed the couch in the reading nook.

You could put it however you liked, but they were being interrogated. The use of the word *children* on that banner meant, of course, that the DOGS' latest escapade—the first in more than a month—had been aimed squarely at the Elves & Fairies community and must therefore involve an "inside" connection or a grudge. Or so said Chief McCord.

"We are not maintaining that any of you are suspects," he said (immediately putting the opposite thought in Ira's head—and everyone else's, too, according to the looks exchanged across his circle), "but we need to know if you'd've seen anything suspicious whatsoever. We have detectives working over Mrs. Connaughton's residence, but if experience serves us here, it tells us these terrorists left no clues. We'll crack this one, however. We doggone will. That's a promise." (Actually, thought Ira, it sounded more like a threat.)

"One thing we can tell you is that Mrs. Connaughton's residence was fully alarmed, and the system wasn't violated. We suspect the terrorists could not create the setup they did without penetrating the premises. We are investigating that angle with Mrs. Connaughton, but if anyone here saw someone lurking around that house today—or anytime since she left on Wednesday—that would be of valuable significance."

Or significant value, thought Ira. During the silence that followed, he gazed around the room, his room. He did not like the careless way McCord and his men had thrown their jackets and paraphernalia on top of the book racks and baskets of children's drawings.

The chief tried again. "What about visitors here this week? You've had caterers, deliveries for the party, comings and goings of all kinds. Maybe visits from people claiming to be prospective parents?"

This would have been a question best answered by Clover (Evelyn was in the other half of the interrogation), but Clover was staring into space. She looked practically comatose with grief. Only the tears running perpetually and silently down her cheeks betrayed that she was conscious.

"She needs a break," Ira said to McCord. He reached across Heidi and touched Clover's knee. "Honey?"

She turned and stared at him. "This is too much," she whispered.

"Ms. Darling, can we get you a glass of water?" asked McCord.

"No," she said. She wiped her face with a sleeve of her peasant blouse. It was already smeared with soot.

"Can we please all take a break?" pleaded Ira. "A stretch?"

Ira crossed the room to Anthony. Through the window, he could just make out the equipment abandoned by the musicians. A large speaker had been shoved into the cattails at the edge of the pond. Would E & F's insurance pay to replace that stuff? Suddenly Ira feared for his job.

"Well," said Anthony. "I wouldn't have missed *this* party for the world."

"This is not the least bit funny," said Ira.

Anthony squeezed his hand. "Sorry. But I warned you about that idiot group of insurgents. I told you there'd be an implosion of some kind. Frankly, the whole thing smacks to me of school pranks gone haywire. These suburban cops want to believe they've got a homegrown Al Qaeda lurking in the privet—but I think it's more like SDS. I mean, SDS itself is back. There's been a whole revival—the same sort of nostalgia behind your Woodstock party."

Had it been only three hours ago when Ira felt so hopeful, so romantic? Yet as he absorbed Anthony's I-told-you-so, as he gazed out the window at the drowning audio equipment and then at the starlit pond, his knee-jerk anger faded. Ira remembered something.

Nothing but *nothing* would take this job away from him.

Chief McCord stood at the far side of the room, talking to Evelyn; her group had followed suit and were milling about, shaking out cramped limbs, drinking water from tiny cups. Ruth had volunteered to start a pot of coffee. Joyce had gone to her classroom and retrieved a tin of graham crackers and Fig Newtons.

Evelyn was attempting to make small talk with the chief about his family. Ira interrupted.

"I have something. Someone. To report." He spoke in a normal voice, but the room was small, with excellent acoustics, and everyone else stopped talking.

"Turo. Arturo. I think his last name is Cabrero, Cabrera. He's been around here a lot this year—too much." Ira tried to remember the substance of the strange conversation he'd overheard from the window back in the fall, but it didn't matter. Because he did remember seeing Turo emerge from the storage space that other time; seeing him in the nearby woods over Christmas vacation; seeing him, more recently, talking with Celestino on Laurel Connaughton's lawn.

"Arturo who?" asked Evelyn.

"He helped build the tree house."

Heidi murmured in recognition, and then Clover spoke. "Robert! Robert and his roommate! They . . . Robert. My nephew." Her tone silenced everyone for a second time; in half a dozen words, it went from hysterical to chilly.

"Not Robert," Ira said to Clover. "I'm certain Robert's not—"

"Yes," Clover said firmly. "He hasn't been the same this year."

Ira looked at Chief McCord. "Arturo—the roommate—he's the one I've seen around here more. Robert would be here because of his grandfather. I think they're pretty close. That you'd expect. But it's the roommate who—"

"What would you know about Robert?" Clover demanded angrily. "I've known him his *whole life.*"

"Clover, there is no way—" In his peripheral vision, Ira saw Anthony standing, shaking his head. (A warning? Disapproval? Hadn't Anthony accused him of being a coward when it came to speaking out?)

"I need names," said McCord. "Spell the names." He started to write. And then the fire chief—when had he left?—entered the room and said, "Cap, the basement of the house. The Darling house. We have something there."

Behind the fire chief, Percy Darling entered. He looked like a parent who'd just been told of a child's death. His eyes went straight to Clover. They expressed relief for only a moment.

"Daddy, it's Robert," she said loudly. "He's been brainwashed. We should have figured it out before this! Robert's ruined *everything!*" She started toward her father, but just as urgently as he'd entered the room, Percy turned his back on her and left. Ira heard him run down the hall, heard the door fling wide against the wall of the barn, the impact loud as a gunshot.

The DayQuil had worn off. He felt as if someone had jammed a moldy rag into the space behind his eyes and nose. His brain felt physically smaller. It was 1:00 a.m., and he'd wasted close to two hours—well, not *wasted* exactly, but robbed from the time he desperately needed to finish that paper—having cake with Rosemary at the new café on Dunster. She was cool: heavy into bioethics on top of her concentration in history and urban planning. She'd be spending the summer in New York, too, doing an internship at the Brooklyn Navy Yard. Her hair was like a jungle: dark and thick. Robert hadn't wanted to touch a woman's hair so much in ages. Her breasts—the tops of them, pushed up under her red blouse—were lightly freckled. She smelled like tangerines.

Would she have gone home with him? Probably his obnoxious cough had done him a favor there. He had to sleep, and he had to work. (He also had to face Turo, though hopefully not till morning.) He could take NyQuil and do the former or another hit of DayQuil and (maybe) the latter. Ah, the marvel of OTC drugs. He pondered the pros and cons of each choice as he turned onto Linnaean. A block shy of his building, he noticed the two police cars parked in front. Christ, not another break-in.

Too whacked to ask for details, Robert nodded at the officer seated in the first cruiser. He entered his building and took the stairs. He heard the voices, the abrasive bark of the radios, before he reached the third floor and understood that the cop-show sound effects were coming from the open door to his apartment.

The two uniformed guys in the hall saw him at the same time. One held up his badge.

"Hey. Jeez," said Robert. "What's happening?"

"Arturo Cabrera?" said the taller guy.

"No," said Robert.

"Robert Barnes?"

"Yeah, that's me." And then it dawned on him. "Oh my God," he said. "Turo, you total moron."

Through the door, Robert saw what his preconceptions, in two amazing seconds, told him he would see: everything, everywhere, rearranged, unplugged, pulled from walls, turned radically inside out. Every light was blazing. The *refrigerator* was open. One of the cops had already relieved him of his backpack—almost gently—and the other was frisking him, just the way you'd expect from TV. What Robert also knew from TV told him to shut the fuck up.

He heard footsteps on the stairs behind him. When he turned to look, one of the cops grabbed his arm, not at all gently this time, but when Robert saw the man jogging toward him down the hall, the wave of emotion that cut through his thickened senses felt more like joy than shame.

"Officer, that is my grandson you are about to arrest," said Granddad. "Whatever he may have done, he's a very good boy. Please bear that in mind."

21

A re you sure you don't want me to go in with you?"

"I'm sure."

"So—tomorrow. I'll pick you up at one. Yes?"

"Thanks." Robert wanted to close the door, but Anthony continued to lean across the empty passenger seat.

"I'll be fine," said Robert, even if he could no longer imagine what it meant to be *fine*. "You should go. Get stuff done you're supposed to be doing."

As if Anthony weren't being paid for this. Probably by Granddad. Robert's parents had posted his bail, but so far, till now at least, his mother had refused to speak to him, let alone see him. "She's more upset than mad," his dad had explained over the phone. But that was Dad, diplomatic by profession.

Robert continued to stand on the sidewalk after Anthony had driven away. His father's car was parked inside the open garage; his mother's car was gone. An Outback and a gargantuan SUV, strangers' cars, occupied the wing of tarmac partially screened by a rose-covered trellis. Car code, Robert had called it in high school, the way he'd know at a glance what was what, who was where. This configuration was the weekday norm: Mom at work, Dad in his office with clients. It meant that the kitchen door would be unlocked and no one would be there to greet him. It also meant that his parents had decided to follow their routines, as if nothing about today, about this particular homecoming, were the least bit weird. And what did *this* mean? Forgiveness? Contempt? Confrontation? Not denial. Robert knew that much about his parents.

Nothing the least bit weird in the kitchen, either, once he entered the house. Though what did he expect, a plate of home-baked cookies? A note of greeting? Well, maybe the note. He felt the flash of déjà vu: home from school, drop his backpack on the bench, toss his coat on a hook, beeline for the fridge. A glass of milk, cold pizza or chicken. A note of warning or instruction from his dad, on the counter: *Don't touch those cherries!* or *Please thaw the pork chops.*

He sat on the bench. He had no backpack, no burden—no physical burden—to drop here. Under the jacket he'd been wearing the night he was arrested, he wore a shirt and jeans that Helena Sorenson had bought for him. For the past four days, she'd acted the part his mother had refused: taken him in, clothed him, fed him, driven him to Anthony's office when Granddad couldn't. She was like a figure in a fairy tale, the kindly old lady in the woods who, no questions asked, welcomes the lost, wounded traveler (the guy who, unlike Robert, would turn out to be a prince disguised by a witch's spell). The Sorensons, his grandfather's friends, were people Robert had heard about forever, but until now, he'd met them in the flesh only once every few years—like last Thanksgiving at Granddad's house. Robert flinched at the memory of Turo sitting next to Mrs. Sorenson on the couch, exuding his flattering, flirtatious charm. His *pathological* charm. Anthony's word.

Robert hoped for someone, anyone, to enter the kitchen. Get it over with, he thought. As if that was all he had yet to face: his parents' anger and disappointment. There would be no jury trial, according to Anthony, but Robert should expect hearings and meetings, dragged out over weeks, possibly months, to arrive at a "deal" and ultimately a sentence. Subject, verb. Like *You are fucked.*

He listened for the murmur of voices from the ground floor, the sparring of a couple as they broke apart under his father's guidance. Nothing. No fights today. He wondered if any couples had ever reconciled after meeting with Dad. Robert's mother claimed that his father was a born peacemaker. He was the one who'd answered the infamous "one phone call" in the middle of the night. Robert had been hysterical; he'd assumed Granddad would follow the cops from his apartment and get him released, but that hadn't happened; or not till the following evening, when Granddad showed up with Anthony along. Earlier, though, when Robert had been so entirely alone, alone as a man in a labyrinth in a story by Borges, his dad had steered him away from the panic.

All he really wanted to do right now was to lie down, try yet again to sleep, really sleep. His first night at the Sorensons, he'd slept for ten hours straight. Since then, he hadn't slept more than a couple of hours before he'd wake, each time remembering or imagining some new unbearable thing. The warehouse in Lothian, his hands blackened by all that ink from the newspapers he'd dutifully, robotically bound into bundles. (Honest to God, what had he *thought* they were for if not to fuel a fire?) His apartment, trashed and abandoned, a web of crime-scene tape. The exams he'd prepared for but wouldn't be free to take. Ever. The literature paper he'd never finish. He might have finished it if he hadn't been lured away by that smart, beautiful girl in the red blouse. Rosemary.

If not for her, he might be facing a trial. He'd found her number on the back of a receipt, deep in the pocket of his jeans. Anthony had made him search. How humiliating was that: the call she got was from a lawyer, to ask for an alibi, not dinner, not a movie, not a walk by the Charles.

He thought of the summer job that would go to someone else. Where would Robert be in two months' time? Not camping in the Adirondacks, that much you could bank on.

All too often, he thought of Clara. When he did, it felt as if iodine or vinegar flowed through his veins. He imagined how condescendingly sad she'd be acting. He pictured her talking about him as she lay entwined in the orangutan limbs of that J.Crew model, telling him how she'd seen it coming, how Robert had turned cold on her, how he'd been duped by politics, chosen his crazy, hubristic roommate over her—and for what?

Turo. Really, it was Turo and only Turo who woke him in the night again and again. Turo was the star of all his dreams, a Turo as versatile as Meryl Streep: menacing, mocking, beguiling, blaming, seducing. In one dream, Robert was in bed with Turo and they were naked. In that one, Turo apologized. But they were all nightmares; it didn't matter what went on, how convoluted the plotlines. Funny, in a way, how this was the only Turo that remained, Dream Turo. The actual Turo had vanished. Escaped, said Anthony. *Absconded.* JFK to Manila, the day after the fire.

In the jail—where, contrary to TV lore, he'd had a cell to himself (too hot, the smell disgusting, the light blinding, all the surfaces hard; but his for the suffering alone)—Robert had thought of Turo mostly with frantic concern. Robert was pissed as hell, no joke, but he knew that Turo would be trying to reach him, trying to figure a way out for both of them. Maybe he was holed up at Tamara's place. Robert worried that the police, who had Robert's phone as well as his computer, might be able to trace the calls. He half expected the cops to drag Turo down the concrete hall and throw him in the cell.

Anthony was bent on changing the way Robert saw Turo, the way that maybe he had to see Turo to get through this. (He could hear Turo warning him about lawyers, the way they could "poison your virtue.") What was it Turo had said, that sooner or later someone would be caught and that's when the DOGS would go big-time? Why *shouldn't* the someone be Robert? So that morning, Robert had finally asked Anthony, straight out, if he would go to prison.

"I'm doing everything I can to avoid that. Some of it depends on what proof there is that you were involved in other . . . incidents. If that kind of evidence emerges, I'll have to get you a bona fide criminal lawyer." Anthony did nothing to hide his scorn for the DOGS and what he called their infantile approach to changing the world. "And some of it, maybe a lot of it, will depend on Laurel Connaughton, the woman whose house you helped burn to the ground."

"I didn't know—"

Anthony gave him a sharp look. "What you chose not to know, Robert, that's what got you here. And I mean *chose*." Anthony had made it clear to Robert that one thing he was good at, in his pro bono work, was winning mercy, or a second chance, for people who'd totally screwed up. If they got the right judge, and if Robert were contrite enough—made not a single excuse—Anthony was hopeful.

If not for Celestino, Anthony might have had nothing but contempt for Robert. Within an hour of meeting Anthony, Robert told him that he was worried about Celestino—that he knew Celestino had nothing to do with the DOGS but might, by association, be in trouble. Ira had already thought of the connection, but Robert saw Anthony's face soften as he nodded, reassuring Robert that no one, so far, had fingered Celestino.

His parents' phone had not rung; he'd still heard no voices from beneath the kitchen floor. The clock over the stove ticked loudly, as it always had. Robert had been sitting on the bench for twenty minutes.

Upstairs, he urged himself, forcing his legs to comply.

He opened the door to his room. Here, where he'd least expected it, this was where the accusations lurked.

Stacks of clean, folded clothing covered the surface of his twin bed. Four pairs of his shoes stood side by side where the bedspread met the floor, facing out. Like a firing squad, thought Robert. Cardboard cartons—five—were stacked by the window, four labeled BOOKS, one PAPERS. His father's handwriting.

Robert's desk, normally bare except for an old-fashioned blotter and an electric pencil sharpener, was crowded with a seemingly random assembly of objects. Only Robert would recognize them, right away, as things that had come from his bedroom in Cambridge. A this-is-your-life exhibition in a museum: a stapler, a gooseneck lamp, a can of tennis balls, a squash racquet, a Swiss army knife, a box of ink cartridges for his printer, a box of unused checks, a packet of envelopes, a roll of stamps . . . a carved soapstone box that Clara had given him for no particular reason and that contained—he looked and it still did—a box of matches and a sheaf of rolling papers. (Had Turo left weed in the apartment? Anthony would have known that, wouldn't he? Anthony had shown him a list of the incriminating evidence, so far. Did the police deliberately withhold unpleasant surprises? He didn't like the sound of that "so far.")

Front and center, dominating all these trite possessions, stood the microscope that Robert's parents had given him as a high-school graduation present. Mom had chosen a card with a black-and-white photograph taken in a lush, fertile forest, every leaf, every ridge of bark and clump of moss in riveting focus. In the card's blank interior (Robert's mother declared herself allergic to Hallmark sentiment, perhaps because so much of it came her way from patients), she had written, *Dear Robert, We love the way you look at the world (which we know you'll go out and conquer, however you choose). Now you can look at it even more closely. With so much pride and all our love, Mom and Dad.*

The sight of the microscope, deported to the realm of his suburban childhood, struck Robert physically, in the core of his gut, as almost nothing else had in six horrific days. All the plans he'd had, whether vague or specific—the casual ambitions of a privileged boy, which his parents had kindled and nurtured and, along with him, taken for granted—were moot, obsolete, kaput. He thought of the recent dinner he'd shared with his mother, where they'd argued the merits and the attractions of curing ills of the body versus those of the mind. Such choices were both trivial and lofty. Just like that, they were a thing of the past, not the future.

He felt as if he were reliving the moment, two days before, when Anthony told him that Turo hadn't been enrolled at Harvard since their sophomore year. He'd failed most of his courses that second semester. He'd flunked out. Had Turo known this before he asked Robert to move off-campus and share an apartment? Had Turo's mother known, or did he have money all his own, to live as he pleased?

Did it make any difference? The deception was so enormous that to accept it in any version was to step off a cliff.

Sitting in Anthony's luxurious office with its sky-high view of the islands in Boston Harbor, the planes angling away from Logan, Robert had been unable to respond. He'd felt his memory, like a bird that flies through a window and finds itself trapped in a closed room, darting helplessly and senselessly back and forth over the past year—a whole *year's* worth of lying. But had Turo actually lied to Robert, literally lied, ever? Or had Robert refused to see the obvious? Had Turo ever talked about the courses he wasn't taking? Made a pretense of reading any textbooks or walking into classrooms?

Precisely what Robert had failed to do was to look at the world around him, really look, never mind look closely. So much for that microscope.

He sank into the desk chair and swiveled it outward, to face the rest of whatever the room had to say about his life. How fitting that the walls were dark and, for the most part, blank. After Robert had moved to Cambridge, his mother (with his permission) had removed all his posters and painted the walls a stormy slate blue. The only picture she'd hung, over the bed, was an oil painting of a rocky coastline, a relic of her mother's childhood by the ocean.

Would he live here now, again? Would his parents even let him live here—that is, if he didn't go to prison?

He noticed a small red box on his otherwise barren dresser. He hadn't a clue what it was until he crossed the room and opened it. Aunt Clover's friendship ring.

"What the fuck *else*?" he shouted, as if the house itself had laid these boobytraps, turned his own belongings into something malevolent, each one a messenger of shame.

"Robert?" His father stood in the doorway. "Can I come in?"

Robert laughed bitterly. "It's your house." Instantly, he was sorry. His father was not the parent who'd denied him refuge for days on end.

Dad sat on the edge of the bed, toppling a stack of T-shirts onto the floor. "Oh dear," he said. He leaned over to pick them up.

"Leave it, Dad." Robert was relieved, yet sad, that his father hadn't tried to embrace him.

"I'm so sorry, Robert. I'm sorry if it seems like we haven't been there for you, but we are, you know. Your mother meant to be home before you arrived, but she—"

"You don't need to explain for her. It's okay," said Robert.

His father sighed. He looked as if he had perched deliberately, absurdly, in a nest of shirts and trousers. Robert's undershorts and socks spilled into Dad's lap and onto the floor. "I keep on wondering what we missed. You're such a damn good student that we always assumed . . ."

Robert waited to hear what they assumed, even though he knew.

"That you were a damn good kid, through and through. That you wouldn't do anything dangerous. I mean, anything that could . . ."

"I fucked up."

His father didn't try to contradict him. "We're glad you're home now. I know you doubt that, but really, son, we are. For as long as you need it to be, this is your home."

Robert slipped the box containing the ring into his pocket. He retained the childish instinct to hide it—though now, knowing how everything had gone down, how Clover had denounced him, the instinct made sense. However angry his mother was at him, he could only imagine the fury she felt toward her sister. He hoped that, for now, they could avoid the subject of Clover.

His father said, as if reading his mind, "One thing at a time, I guess."

Robert nodded. He saw that Dad was every bit as weary, as sleep-deprived as he was.

"Are you happy with Anthony? The Python?" Weakly, Dad smiled. "Small world. I never cease . . . to be amazed."

In that moment's hesitation, both of them raised their heads at the sound of the kitchen door closing.

Robert's father looked at him and saw his despair. "She won't yell at you. I promise. You might not realize this, but it's just that she's so heartbroken. She blames herself, really."

"Great," said Robert. "I didn't break any of her limbs, what a relief! Just her heart, that's all."

"Robert. Sarcasm won't help. Please try to remember that." Robert knew this was something his father told his clients. They turned together at the sound of footsteps on the stairs.

"Are you up here?" she called tentatively. "Douglas? Robert?"

There she was in the doorway, and then there she was crossing the room, holding Robert far too tightly, her face pressed into his left shoulder. Of course he held her in return. He felt rather than heard that she was crying.

"I'm going to start dinner. I thought I'd make something simple. A pasta," said Robert's father. When no one said anything, he added, "Arugula, bacon, and pine nuts. Sound good?"

Over his mother's graying hair, Robert said, "Anything, Dad." How much thought, he wondered, had his father devoted to supper for the prodigal son?

When Dad had left the room, he told his mother how sorry he was. She told him she was sorry, too.

"But if I'd seen you these past few days, I'd have said things I might regret," she said. "Not just about you. About all of us."

Robert was tempted to tell her that maybe all those things ought to be said—that there was nothing he didn't deserve to hear—but then he thought of the secret he'd already bullied from his mother. He waited to hear what she wanted to say instead.

She sat on the desk chair. Robert shoved the once-folded clothing to the foot of the bed and sat in the space he'd cleared.

His mother rolled the chair toward him and reached out. He thought she wanted to take his hand, but she pulled a T-shirt off the bed and held it to her face, wiping her tears, blowing her nose. "Robert, I always hoped you'd be daring in some way—but not destructive."

The words *I didn't know* filled his brain again, but he thought of the reprimand he'd received from Anthony that morning.

"I was so gullible," he said, though wasn't this an excuse, too? "I was naïve and . . . rash." The word surprised him.

"You know about Mrs. Connaughton's house."

"Mom, I've spent hours with a lawyer. And with Granddad. There's nothing you can tell me I don't know."

She regarded him mournfully. "Except about my conversation with your dean."

Robert said nothing.

She shook her head. "I'm sorry."

They stared bleakly at each other for a moment. Robert nodded. "Mom, school's not important right now."

"But Robert, it will be!"

"Can we not talk about that now?"

"Everything you want for yourself—"

"Mom!" He tried to sound urgent and gentle at once. "I fucked up, Mom, and if I'm lucky—lucky—I get to do community work and, I don't know, stuff to make amends somehow. I *need* to do that. First. Before whatever comes next."

"Next." She wiped her face with the T-shirt again. She held it in her lap and stared at it for a moment. Then she stood. "Okay. I'm going downstairs to help your father and make a couple of calls to patients. I'll be quick. Why don't you take a shower?" She motioned at the clothes on the bed. "Maybe put some of this away. Or just throw it in the closet. I washed everything that was dirty. I put your kitchen things in the garage."

"Thanks."

She left the room carrying his T-shirt. Robert went to the window. It was still light outside, though the sun had fallen beneath the tree-line. Across the street, a woman was changing sheets in an upstairs room. On the sidewalk, one by one, three dogs passed by with their owners. By habit—still, after several days—he reached into his pocket for his phone.

He thought for a moment. He took off his shoes. He walked quietly down the hall, past the bathroom, past his parents' bedroom, to the small den at the back of the second floor. Neither of his parents worked here, but on a corner desk they kept an extra computer, for checking their e-mail late at night or first thing in the morning. Robert opened Safari and went to his server, typed in his address, his password.

The password was denied. Of course it was. He stared at the screen for a few minutes, until it went dark. So. Time for another low-tech detox, this one enforced. This one without the romance of the jungle.

He sat quietly and took in the features of the room, its homely sofa and shelves of forsaken books. This unloved room, it occurred to Robert, would have belonged to his little sister. Thirteen: that's how old she'd be now. What a consolation she might have been to his parents at a moment like this.

Downstairs, radio jazz kept Dad company as he cooked. Something sizzled loudly in a skillet. Robert went to the top of the stairs. He stood there until he smelled garlic, then bacon. He hoped his father would serve bread.

In the bathroom, he turned on the shower. He stripped off his clothes and stepped into the tub. He made the water as hot as he could stand. Inhaling the steam, he wished he could wash away so many months—or, more than time, whatever insolence or impunity had led him to do such fatally stupid things. He remembered the day he had first wondered, almost smugly, if Turo was little more than a groupie, a Moonie, a galley slave for the DOGS, but in the end Robert was the blind disciple: not even a disciple; more like a yes-guy, a patsy, a cog. A moth to the flame of groupthink.

Whatever he did after this, if he could just make it across to the *after,* like the opposite bank of a rushing river, it would be something independent. No labs, no lectures, no group anything. Not if he could help it. He would do more than ask questions; he would insist on pinning down the answers. He would look at them as closely as he could.

22

"Small house. Big tree. Both a good deal older than I." Those were the first words I spoke in person to the young real estate agent I met at her office in Vigil Harbor on a gray day in early June. We'd traded telephone messages and e-mails.

"How old is that, exactly? As a point of reference." Though she appeared hardly old enough to drive a car, let alone help me find a place to live, Daphne did not treat me with the cloying respect so often leveled at me and my peers.

"Seventy-one."

"Well, that won't be a challenge. Piece of cake in a town like this."

I was reminded, with predictable sorrow, of the day I'd walked into TGO in need of bathing trunks. Daphne was half Sarah's age, but she had that forthright nature I've always loved in women who know themselves well. She had a head of boyishly short dandelion hair, a rose tattoo above her right ankle, and, on her left hand, an emerald the size of a peach pit.

She showed me five houses that day—two without the tree, for which I scolded her. "Just testing your resolve," she said.

The fifth was desperately in need of paint, its wide-plank floors scuffed and gouged, its kitchen and single bathroom—again to quote young Daphne—"a blank canvas if you're into renovation." I liked its back porch, the ratio of four fireplaces to three bedrooms, and, most of all, the katsura, a braggart of a tree rising like a glossy green phoenix from the lawn, roots breaching the ground for yards in every direction. Not much dared grow in its thirsty shade.

"There's some local legend about this tree that has to do with a shipping merchant, his daughter's dowry, and a fateful voyage to Japan," said Daphne, "but frankly, the minute I hear 'shipping merchant' in any story around here, I have a hard time not rolling my eyes. Historically—

if that interests you—this was a town of hardscrabble fishermen, not colonial Onassis types."

The house, dwarfed by the tree, was built for a blacksmith in 1813. A parched wooden plaque by the front door made this claim. That door opened directly onto the street; as we stood in the small parlor, a FedEx truck passed within two feet of the window. "Good Lord!" I exclaimed.

"Not to worry," said Daphne. "Those guys drive by the inch."

What privacy this house possessed was all in back. At the nether end of the long yard stood a swaybacked shed (reminding me, on a smaller scale, of that dear old barn before Poppy and I gave it new life). Beyond a splintering fence, stacks of yellow mesh lobster traps stood higher than my head. They reeked a bit, but absent a view of the shore, they were a plainspoken reminder that the ocean was just around the corner.

Daphne led me into a rugged crawl space to show me the furnace and the knob-and-tube wiring. "Are you prepared to see an inspection report for a house this old? It's not for the faint of heart," she said when we emerged into the kitchen, standing upright again.

"My dear, I could write that inspection report. This house is a youngster compared with the one I've lived in for most of my life."

She gave me a sly smile. "I'd say that's more than long enough to become an expert on just about anything."

"Young lady, anyone else would call you impertinent."

"But you're not anyone else, are you?" She brushed the dirt from the cellar off her manicured hands and drew the brass bolt on the door.

With those manicured hands, Daphne passed me her pen when, a month later, I signed at the closing.

Not long after we became engaged, Poppy and I planned our retirement. We were walking along the Charles River and passed an elderly couple feeding scraps of bread to a family of ducks.

"You rarely see that as a coeducational activity," Poppy remarked.

"She's brainwashed him," I said, "over years of her excellent duck à l'orange."

Poppy groaned. "What will I brainwash *you* into doing by that age?"

"Joining the Peace Corps. Something liberal and in vogue."

"What I do not want to do," said Poppy, "is sit around on park benches feeding the birds. You're not far off about the Peace Corps. If we have children and manage to wean them properly, we could head off to the Congo, or El Salvador, and help build houses for the poor."

"My young joints quake at the thought of being up to that task forty years from now," I said.

"We could teach English. Teach reading. You'd be good at that, Percy. You could start libraries in equatorial Africa."

"Perfect. Me shelving books in the Kalahari Desert. I'm so glad that's settled."

Poppy put her arm around my waist. "So now that we know we can agree on the end of the story—and we can't complain about the beginning, can we?—what's left to learn about but the middle?"

"The middle is the tricky part," I said.

"You are too pessimistic," she said. "The middle is where the filling is, the jam, the custard, the cornmeal stuffing. The scallop inside the bacon."

We realized that we were hungry, and chilly, so we walked to the Square for lunch. We agreed soup would be just the thing. "We're already in the middle, you know," said Poppy. "And look how easy it is."

"Thus far," I said. "Let's not get ahead of ourselves."

Two years ago, once I made the decision to retire, I thought about those impetuous plans, the way we'd scoffed at fate by letting them pass our lips. Certainly I had no intention of heading off to equatorial Africa, not even for a vacation. But I had a misguided daughter to care for— that was to be my first challenge—and then I had books to read (a pleasantly never-ending task) and grandchildren to amuse, intimidate, and, for as long as I could manage, entertain. That's how I saw it, then.

Little did I know that my retirement would very soon involve a sudden, most unwelcome familiarity with courtrooms and judges' chambers, none the least bit grand or elegant, in niches of the city I'd never visited before and hope never to visit again. In my vital effort to gain the goodwill of countless "officers of the law" and the clerks who give access to such people, I did what my daughters had tried but never succeeded in getting me to do before: I shed my so-called attitude. I spoke the plainest of English. I did not offer humor where none was required. (None was ever required, let me tell you that.) I learned to defer to lawyers and their legalese, and on the rare occasions when they permitted me to speak, I learned to beg through bargaining.

I did none of this without help. Without, to put it properly, counsel. The counsel of, specifically, Anthony Giardini. When I reminded him that I'd learned his reptilian nickname from Douglas, he was quick to point out that in our case he would be taking the role of supplicant, not predator. The goal was to keep Robert out of prison, not to win him a yacht, a country home, or the custody of children. The goal was, in fact, to get him more or less *into* custody, said Anthony: custody of a nonpenal nature. Robert wasn't a child, and that was the tough part.

At first, Robert insisted repeatedly that he had never been a "member" of these DOGS, but he had to admit to the judge that he had participated without coercion in their acts of vandalism. His efforts to help the police locate a woman named something like Tabitha Earth Girl led to naught; he'd apparently been to her down-and-out neighborhood only once, after dark. Similarly fruitless were his attempts to find the deserted building in Lothian where they'd prepared for the "major action," as he referred to the debacle in my backyard.

Robert spent most of a weekend in jail before Trudy posted his exorbitant bond. Insisting she was too distraught and angry to see him yet, she sent me to retrieve him. I followed Anthony to a part of Cambridge that I could never, at gunpoint, find again.

Anthony handled the endless paperwork; I was relieved to stand aside. As soon as Robert and I were alone in my car, I focused on finding my way back to anywhere I recognized. I said nothing for some time, and neither did Robert. Once I was on familiar roads, however, I found that I was as angry as his mother. I shouted, "What in the world could have persuaded you to be a part of it? A part of any of these foolish acts? Please give me something to go on!"

"I was stupid," he said quietly.

I couldn't disagree with that. "This boy you trusted, this—where is he?"

"I have no idea, Granddad. They took away my phone, my computer, any way he'd try to get in touch with me."

"You think he's doing that. Really." I tried, but failed, to curb my sarcasm. Anthony would be the one to inform Robert that the police had found several of that boy's belongings in my cellar; that he had apparently slept there at some point, used my house as his burrow (and the underside of my barn as a storeroom). I had been too upset to inspect the place myself that night. From the lawn, I'd watched the Matlock police, suddenly so self-important, attack my cellar, comb through the rooms in my house. I had stood there, numb, horrified, until it dawned on me that anything implicating that cruel boy would come down on Robert's head as well.

"I was stupid, stupid, stupid to get involved, but he really believes in what he's doing, okay? Believes that the only way to change stuff is to take a radical approach. Turn the world upside down to change it."

"Do you even know who this boy is, other than a cunning sociopath?"

"He's someone with a very complicated past, but he's my friend. He is not a sociopath." Robert's head lay propped against the car window on his side, as if it were too heavy for his body to support. Periodically, he would have a harsh fit of coughing or wipe his nose on a sleeve. I could have offered him my handkerchief, but I decided to ignore his discomfort.

"A *friend* chooses your grandfather's home as a target for mischief?"

"Granddad, it probably wasn't his idea. Or maybe it was, but it wasn't about you. I mean, even Turo heard you go on about how Matlock's become this refuge for the filthy rich, this, like . . . all those parents at the nursery school— Remember when you went on and on about Jonathan Newcomb, what he did to those fields?"

I pulled the car over and braked. "Are you even sorry? Or should I turn right around and hand you back to those wardens?"

Silence. Would he actually refuse to answer me? Then he wailed. How well I had succeeded in breaking him down.

"God, Granddad, I am so sorry, *so sorry,* I can't even tell you how sorry I am. I'm sorry, sorry, *sorry.*"

We were parked by the side of Route 2, in a weedy lot adjoining a long-defunct farmstand, another casualty of suburban wealth and developers' greed. I could remember buying tomatoes and corn at that farmstand with Poppy. Robert cried against the window, openly, loudly.

"Grandson," I said quietly, though I was still angry. "I understand what drew you in. I admit that when it was just fodder for the local media, I found it all amusing. So I was stupid, too. Or arrogant. Here." I gave him my handkerchief after all.

I drove on. By tacit, weary agreement, we abandoned words. I felt Robert look at me when I passed the turnoff for Matlock, continuing toward Ledgely. When we pulled into Norval's driveway, he said, "Granddad, is your house gone, too?"

"Let's just say that what remains of it will soon belong to Maurice Fougère. He tells me he will restore any damage with the utmost loving care. Something I cannot imagine devoting to anything or anyone at this particular moment, so bully for him."

Robert began to apologize all over again, but I didn't wait to listen. I got out of the car and started toward the house. Helena passed me with a look of sorrow. I cut across the grass to avoid her reach. I went upstairs, to the guest room with the twin beds that Robert and I would share like a pair of children (and aptly so) until his mother felt she could bear to see him—or until he was carted off to prison. Out the window, I saw Helena coaxing Robert from the car.

I no longer aim to run every day, but when I do set out, I enjoy learning the byways of my new town, where the houses, many two or three hundred years old, stand hip to hip, shoulder to shoulder, angled every which way like guests pressed together at a cocktail party, liquor having stripped them of all inhibition. Many yards are no bigger than a bedspread. My new road (a very old road) is a short one-way lane that leads off a colonial thoroughfare flanked by larger, more symmetrical homes. At the far end, it forks: right takes me to the harbor; left, toward the burial ground that occupies the highest hill in town. The oldest graves dominate the summit, where revolutionary patriots—in their day, insurgents and rebels—are lauded on one worn, tilted slab after another. Granite steps set into the hill take me, if I watch my footing, to a plinth erected in 1848 as a mourning and memorial for sixty-five men and boys who set forth from Vigil Harbor on a dozen fishing vessels and died together in a single storm, leaving—as the inscription so chillingly reports—*43 widows, 155 fatherless children, and many a heart cleft in twain*. Nothing like a hit of hardcore history to put your own troubles in perspective.

Continue down the far side of the hill (too rocky and hazardous for running) and one reaches the newest graves, though only plots reserved decades ago remain to be filled. At the insistence of her parents, this is where we buried Poppy's ashes. Their remains joined hers eleven and fifteen years later. There's not much space remaining in the family's allocation, but I doubt Trudy or Clover plans to end up here. We've never been visitors of graves; I'd always felt that if Poppy's spirit lingered anywhere, it was over that beautiful nameless pond in Matlock. Of the place I will have lived for most of my life, that pond is what I miss most.

My visit here in late May was the first I'd made in at least a decade. I did not even think to bring flowers. The very first time I faced Poppy's finished gravestone, alone, months after her burial, I thought, This is where the story ends. The only story that mattered then, and for some time to come, was ours.

Many days, I swim in the harbor. I clamber buffoonishly down a façade of rocks, wearing my conspicuously tropical swimsuit, and risk a dive, hoping that a wave won't hurl me back against the jagged ledge. I work my way in loops among the moorings and the vessels: the dinghies, pleasure yachts, waterborne gas guzzlers, a few stalwart fishing boats that somehow still bring their owners a living. (Or maybe the fishermen of Vigil Harbor, like the rock musicians of Matlock, rely on so-called independent income; I have yet to diagnose the socioeconomic quirks of this place.) I suppose it's not exactly prudent to undertake such an activity at my age, but it feels like an act of healthy defiance. If some yahoo in a motorboat splits my skull with his fiberglass hull, well, there are worse ways to go. Trudy could fill me in on several.

I was too busy playing Perry Mason (or Perry Mason's client) to pack my belongings. At Evelyn's recommendation, I hired a cheery group of teenagers who called themselves Girls on the Go. I'd stop by to check their progress on my way from Norval's house to Anthony's office or to whatever courtroom demanded my presence. Trudy showed up at meetings and hearings as often as she could, though Douglas did so more often. I spent more time with my son-in-law in three months than I had in two decades. We discovered that we'd both defected to the Red Sox after Yankee-loyal boyhoods (and that we felt secretly guilty). He gave me a set of barbecue tools for my new life and promised to help me use them. By e-mail, we began to share the titles of our favorite books.

Yet the hardest task I had before me wasn't spending my summer loitering in various fetid hallways of justice (always too hot or too cold); it was obtaining the mercy of Laurel Connaughton. Hell hath no fury like that of a woman burned out of an irreplaceably old and beautiful home, gone up in smoke her priceless antiques, family mementos, and inexplicably beloved dust ball of a cat. (The cat had been seen lurking elusively in the woods, but no one could catch him.)

In truth, for the first time ever, my heart went out to Laurel. I certainly did not blame her for wanting to see my grandson drawn and quartered. She had a lawyer, too, who made her intentions clear to Anthony. Someone would do serious time for this, and the only someone at hand was Robert.

Through her lawyer, I begged her to meet me for lunch at the Ledgely Inn. I asked the lawyer to tell her that I had something important to give her and that I would only give it to her in person.

She arrived at the inn first; I found her at the table, drinking sherry and eating bread sticks. I couldn't help noting that she looked fine for someone who'd just lost everything she owned. Her hair was freshly dyed, her cheeks pink—though, judging from the temperature of her gaze when she saw me enter the dining room, they were flushed with fury. She continued to stare at me as I seated myself across from her. She did not so much as glance at the shoebox I placed on one of the empty chairs.

"I'm here so you won't ever bother me again," she said.

"I appreciate it, Laurel, I do."

"Tell me what you have to say. I have nothing to say to you. I can't believe I ever thought you a *friend*."

"As you can guess," I said, ignoring a statement I had no right or desire to contradict, "I've come to ask that you let the judge show some leniency to Robert. You know he wasn't the mastermind. You know he wasn't even there that night. I think we've established those facts."

"The cleverest of criminals are never at the scene of the crime."

The waitress gave us our menus and a basket of popovers. I pushed the basket toward Laurel. I set the menu aside.

"Laurel, were you ever twenty years old?"

"No, I was not," she said. "Not in the manner that young people today are twenty. Irresponsibly. Narcissistically. Never having been taught self-discipline or sacrifice. That grandson of yours will learn the meaning of those things now."

"He'll learn them no matter what you or I do about this." I had to admire the eloquence of her scorn. Perhaps I'd met my match. Perhaps, I thought sadly, I'd never given her enough credit.

She tore a popover into pieces. She spread butter on one piece. "Edgar has suggested I move to Alaska. Alaska! Can you believe it?" Her laughter was brutal.

"You're not planning to rebuild? You can't replace the house itself, but surely you have more than . . ." I realized I'd be foolish to mention insurance.

"You haven't heard the news?" she said. "Maurice Fougère is buying my land, too. Maybe he'll turn the nursery school into a junior college." She glared at me. "I saw the drawings for what he plans to do to *your* house. He's using the damaged roof as a fine excuse to rip the back right off and put in a huge conservatory roof. Promises to look like a giant terrarium. It's not visible from a common way, so he can do what he pleases. The Forum is impotent to stop him. Though now"—she snorted—"who the hell cares. Not I."

I hadn't heard any of this. So that was Fougère's brand of tender loving restoration. Laurel watched me absorb the news, no doubt pleased at my dismay. Then she said, "Pete told me you have something to give me. Was that a ruse?"

"I do have something for you. But I want you to think about Robert first. I'm not asking you to let him off the hook; that won't happen in any case. You know he can't return to Harvard. Probably not to college, or a regular program, for a while."

"I'll think about it. I promise nothing."

I decided this was as far as I'd get. I reached for the shoebox. I held it in my lap while the waitress took our order. When she removed the menus, I set aside the lid and laid the first packet of letters between my fork and knife. "Truthful," I said. I laid the second packet beside the first. "Azor."

In their gung-ho pillaging of my cellar, the Matlock police had used a crowbar to pry open the cupboard in the wall by the chimney. Poppy and I, unable to force it open years ago, had assumed it was a long-abandoned storage compartment. The two packets of letters—his and hers—that emerged from the cupboard had been tied with ribbon and wrapped inside a lambskin, but after manhandling by the police, the skin had been lost and the ribbons had disintegrated. There were more than thirty letters in her packet, a dozen in his. Gently, I'd bound them with cotton twine. "I thought you'd be the best caretaker for these," I said. "You're the one, after all, who thought my house had a secret space. In a way, you were right."

Laurel could hardly hide her historian's hunger. Still, her reach across the table was tentative. "Truthful and *Azor*? My Azor? You mean Truthful and Hosmer."

"No. Azor. Looks as if they were in love, behind the brother's back, for years. I haven't read them all. I don't know if the story here has a beginning or an end." A middle, certainly. The custard; the jam; the scallop tucked in the bacon. The good wife of the younger brother had been in love, embroiled in clandestine bliss, with the older brother, the one with the bigger house, the greater fortune, the one who stayed a bachelor so unusually long. Poor Hosmer, the one who'd foolishly chosen farming, had been cast too predictably as the cuckold. Had he ever found out? I had read enough to understand the gist of the correspondence, but deciphering the minute, frilly handwriting had given me a headache. Now I wished that I had taken the letters to a copy shop. I doubted that Laurel would ever share the full story with me, as she would have so eagerly, over gin and salmon, only a few months before.

Laurel held the packet of Azor Fisk's letters, letters probably written in the house she'd loved so much. Except that women are more often keepers of the flame, they might have turned up in Laurel's house as readily as mine. She simply held them.

"Don't you want to have a closer look?"

"Not here." She gestured at the plate of butter curls. She clutched the letters to her bright blouse.

"I named a daughter after this woman," I said. "In tribute to her apparent virtue." How I wished Poppy had been there to appreciate the irony.

"Are the letters . . ."

"Racy?" I said. "By the standards of the time, perhaps. But that's not something I'd be qualified to judge. They're not exactly John and Abigail, not a pair of poets. But all the same. Remarkable how well ordinary citizens once expressed themselves."

"My God, Percy." Laurel was breathing quickly. "Put them back in that box. Here come our salads." Our fingers touched as I took the packet of letters to put them away. I felt, briefly, the electricity between the two neighboring households carried forward in time to ours. I thought of how tactlessly I'd shoved aside Laurel's amorous advances that long-ago night in my bedroom. How little respect I'd had for her loneliness, the way she'd been willing to risk her dignity. I had to wonder if I would soon learn such desperation myself.

Laurel leaned forward over her salad and whispered, "Did you tell anyone else about these letters? Former colleagues at Widener?"

"No. Laurel, it's been my intention to give them to you since the police gave them to me nearly a month ago. You wouldn't talk to me."

"So they're a bribe."

I thought carefully about my answer. "In a nutshell, yes. Though nuts come in many flavors. Walnuts do not taste a thing like almonds."

I learned that Laurel would be moving into Dorian Van Otterloo's charming cottage on Quarry Road. I told her that I'd bought a house in Vigil Harbor. She was surprised that I would leave Matlock, but I could also tell that the news made her secretly glad. Once we'd consumed our Indian pudding and I had paid the check, I suspected we would never see each other again. And she would not be sorry.

The Matlock police believed that Laurel had given me her security code and that it had been easily accessible to anyone poking around my study. They knew that even aside from his hobo encampment in my cellar, Arturo had stayed in my house, as a welcome guest, several times. Two of these three things were true. The evening she'd plied me with cucumber sandwiches, Laurel had given me a slip of paper with her code and told me to keep it in a secure place, just in case she ever needed to send me into the house while she was away. Forgotten in a pocket of whatever trousers I'd worn that day, her code had gone through the wash, emerging as a nugget of pulp.

It was Teacher Ira who, in a frantic call the day after the fire, told me that he feared Celestino could be blamed, along with Robert. (We did not need to wait for the next week's *Grange* to see Ira's and Robert's pictures on the front of a newspaper; the *Globe* was happy to oblige—

along with the painful caption *One DOG leashed; catcher is beloved preschool teacher in Matlock*.)

Ira, who got my cell phone number from Sarah, reached me at Trudy's house, where I drove after my failure to stop the police from apprehending Robert. I realized how brave he was to call me when, nearly hysterical, he began by saying that he'd never meant to harm Robert. I told him that it wasn't his fault; I should have had doubts of my own about the other boy.

Then he told me that he was terrified for Celestino. "I know he had nothing to do with this. He was used, like the rest of us. I'm so afraid he could get deported." Desperately, Ira had been casting about for any connection to Tommy Loud. I told him there was little I thought I could do, but I would try.

Laurel was the one who might have connected those dots; fortunately, she didn't. But Loud was shrewd; even as a child, he'd put me in mind of a weasel. I placed a call to his office and spoke to his mother. I would be needing someone to take down the carcass of the incinerated beech tree. How about the nice young fellow who'd worked at Laurel Connaughton's place?

Happy gushed freely about the "terrible, terrible, *terrible* news." But as for that particular fellow? "He's not with us anymore. We can get you an A-one crew, though, can have 'em there tomorrow."

Oh dear, I told her; I couldn't locate my calendar. My life was in such chaos! Falsely, I promised I'd call back. Let Fougère deal the coup de grâce.

The blacksmith's house had been empty for months when I saw it; Daphne assured me that the rooms, once furnished, would look much larger. The only memento of former owners was a mason jar, on the tank of the baby-blue toilet, filled with sea crockery. On my third fretful night after moving in (pacing, rearranging, wondering what in the world I had done), I poured these ceramic tidbits onto my coffee table and examined them. Stripped of their patina, some bore the ghost of antique china patterns, hairline stripes or petals or scrolling, but most were plain, blunt, and yellowed. Like old teeth, I thought, shaking a few in the palm of my hand. I could not bring myself to throw this odd collection away, so I poured them into the bottom of a large glass bowl and decided that I would collect more.

About a third of the furniture I owned had been destroyed by water the night of the fire; what remained just fit my reduced accommodations. As I've said, I don't believe in destiny, but when the last of my chairs was assigned its new room, it felt like a puzzle piece clicking in place. My most valuable possessions, those kept in my former living room and bedroom, had survived. When I unwrapped the silver bowl that had lived on my mantel, I saw that it must have been polished by a Girl on the Go. This made me smile. Perhaps some of Matlock's teens were raised right after all. I placed it on the kitchen counter, perversely pleased by the look of sterling on faded pink formica. I hung Helena's sketch of Poppy above my couch. An alcove under the stairs would serve as my study; the desk I'd bought long ago at a Cambridge thrift shop wedged in precisely.

Robert arrived near the end of July. His parents drove him up with a suitcase, two boxes of books, and a toolbox: surely less than they'd ferried to his dorm room when he started college. No one gave voice to such a comparison. We were awkward and polite, even bumbling, as I showed everyone to the room that would be Robert's. Douglas bumped his head on the ceiling at the top of the stairs; Trudy kept up an obsequious patter of praise for the architectural details throughout the house, though they were paltry and wanted repair. Much of the charm we see in such houses is but a legacy of the builder's necessary thrift.

The conditions of Robert's suspended sentence were many, and I intended to make sure that we followed them to the letter. He was not to venture beyond a fifty-mile radius of Vigil Harbor outside the company of myself or one of his parents; for at least a year, he was not to leave the state of Massachusetts, nor to set foot in Matlock, Ledgely, or Lothian. He was to have no Internet access except under my supervision. He was to report three times a week to work on the reconstruction of a public school that had burned in a town fifteen minutes away. As he no longer owned a car, I would drive him. I would drive him as well to meetings with his parole officer.

In addition to the judge's conditions, I determined a set of my own, largely related to housekeeping chores and shopping. Most necessary goods were available within a mile: groceries, pharmaceuticals, hardware, cold cash, as well as just about anything nautical in nature, from oars and life jackets to bracelets made of seashells. Come September, Robert would take two courses at a nearby state college. He chose courses in social work.

I also informed him that, along with Celestino, he was to build me another magnificent tree house, this time with grown-ups in mind. "I will pay you both, but in return," I said, "if this magnificent tree house, in this very visible location, inspires requests for further such projects— and I just bet you it will—then you will accept those commissions and share the profits with me."

"Granddad, I can't imagine—"

"And you will never argue with me when I am suffering a rare bout of optimism," I said, "or when I am telling you what's good for you. *My* imagination, for the time being, will be the boss of yours."

Gratifyingly, Robert looked as near happiness as I'd seen him in months.

I thought of the way he'd always looked—satisfied, confident, if just a little wolfish—in the company of that girlfriend he had for a while. Assuming that she would never last, I'd paid her no special attention. Now, though my assumption had clearly proved true (could one blame such a young woman for fleeing trouble this deep?), I felt guilty in retrospect. Angry as I'd been toward Robert, I was sorry to see his life stripped of so many pleasures at once.

Celestino had been living with me, already, for several weeks. I had given him the second-best bedroom. (Mine, the best and largest, looked out on the katsura tree.) He might have slipped through our hands if Ira hadn't searched the Hispanic neighborhood of Lothian. It turned out that Celestino shopped at a greengrocer run by a Mexican family whose daughters were once Ira's pupils. Oh, the invisible webs of the cosmos.

At first, understandably, Celestino's agreement to live with me was a matter of desperation, though he tried to hide his fear behind a façade of courtesy and diligence. Quite happily, I made use of his easy strength to put my new house in order. We spent most of our first days together engaged in physical work, which left us little breath or energy for conversation. But in the evenings, I compelled him to sit down at the kitchen table and let me cook for us. I tried not to interrogate him, yet I would need to know this young man if he was to continue sharing my roof. Whenever the phone rang, he would stare at it as if it were rigged with explosives.

He'd been with me a week when I'd had enough of the servile cheer he wore, and not well, as camouflage. I handed him his cheese omelet, accepted his gratitude, sat down across from him, and said, "You know, I do feel virtuous for taking you in. I do. If there were a heaven, I'd be racking up the brownie points."

His expression tipped toward alarm. He sat still, hands in his lap.

"But," I said, "if there's one thing I've learned this past year, it's the truth of that old cliché, about no good deed going unpunished. You know it?" I did not care if he did, and he did not react. "So, Celestino, think me an angel, or a sucker, or an old man pining for company—none of which I am, by the way. Think what you want, but do me a favor."

We stared at each other until he said, "Yes. I will."

I shook my head. "Don't ever agree to a favor till you know what it is."

This time his smile was genuine.

"So this is what I'd like from you. Act like you belong here. Because then, eventually, you will."

"I understand," he said.

"Yes. But do you know what I *mean*?"

I watched him consider me in a different light. At last he said, "I think I do."

"I suspect it won't be easy for you, will it?"

"No, but I will try it. I believe I have to."

"You do. Or we will both go out of our minds, I promise you that."

That was when, in our limited male fashion, we began to have real conversations, to shoulder open the heavy door between our lives. He began to surprise me, and I began to make him laugh.

Anthony told me he knew nothing about immigration law; judging from what he'd read—and from the xenophobic climate of the times—he couldn't imagine finding a way to redeem Celestino's residency status. But when Ira had worried that Tommy Loud would think of Celestino in connection with the fire, Anthony laughed. "Now there's a no-brainer. Name the guy as a suspect and risk turning the searchlight on your army of underpaid soldiers? I don't *think* so. That raid this spring on the kosher meat plant in Iowa? All Guatemalans, by the way."

Not until Ira and I sat down with Celestino, in Ira and Anthony's living room, did he tell us that he already had the name of a lawyer who might be able to help him. This was the fellow who arrived in Vigil Harbor the week Celestino moved in. He was skinny and bald, what remained of his gray hair grown painfully long and gathered in a most unsavory pigtail. He wore bulky shoes that made his feet look like paws and carried a canvas briefcase stained with coffee. "We live in a seriously paranoid, seriously fucked-up country," he informed me almost as soon as he walked through the door. "That's why I do what I do. My rayzon dettrah."

He met for an hour with Celestino, and then he called me downstairs. He described to both of us the long, delicate negotiations he'd begin on Celestino's behalf. He guaranteed no happy outcomes. "Batten down the hatches. Keep your heads low and your powder dry," he told us. "At least no one's actively searching for you. You're lucky there." My idea of sponsorship for Celestino's renewed education might work, but that, too, would take time. In the worst case, Celestino would have to return to Guatemala and start a longer process from that point. "We're talking years," warned Rayzon Dettra.

"If I go back, it is not the *very* worst thing," said Celestino. "But I would like to stay."

I understood that we would be seeing a good deal of this lawyer for some time to come. And even though he assured me that I need not worry about going bankrupt paying his fees—"You won't find me knocking back Captain Morgan at that swanky yacht club across your harbor"—I wondered if there might be a tree house in his future.

"Would you by any chance have a fine old tree in your yard?" I asked him as I saw him out the door.

He looked concerned, not amused. "You're crazier than me, man. I live in a walk-up in Somerville."

Another of my despotically arbitrary conditions was that both Robert and Celestino learn conversational French. The first morning that all three of us were to share breakfast as cohabitants, I went out for scones. I was waiting in line at my new favorite bakery, gazing at a bulletin board covered with notices about boats for sale, apartments for rent, music lessons, financial advice . . . when an artfully handwritten page caught my eye: *Parlez-vous français? Mais pourquoi pas?* I laughed. For a modest price, one Mlle. Madeleine Parquet convened twice-weekly groups at the community center.

I found Celestino and Robert standing in the yard with their coffee, staring up at the tree. I called out from the porch, *"Parlez-vous français?"*

They turned around. Robert frowned. "Granddad?"

"Mais pourquoi pas, mes jeunes amis?"

Celestino said, *"Je parle un peu."* This would have stunned me had he not told me about the Lartigues.

"Très bien. En fait, superbe!" I exclaimed. According to Poppy, my accent isn't half bad.

Last month, I bartered my weary Toyota for a used pickup truck. Robert had given me a condition of his own: they would build the tree house entirely from salvage. So now the three of us crowd together in our vehicle to comb beaches for driftwood and old rope, to search back roads for cast-off furniture and deadwood culled by storms. Robert calls construction companies and cajoles them into letting us haul off their scraps. Sometimes, driving through Ipswich or Gloucester on our scavenger hunts, we stop for fried clams or fish and chips. None of us aimed to live this life, but it offers us certain rewards.

My new pal Daphne is a well-placed informant. We hit a bonanza when she gave me a tip that an old barn was being taken down behind a house she'd sold. Robert, Celestino, and I were there before the demolition crew.

We returned to the house, with our third and final load, late that afternoon. We'd had nothing to eat since breakfast. While Celestino backed the truck down the alley connecting the street to our yard, Robert pulled sandwich makings out of the refrigerator. I went upstairs to use the bathroom.

The phone rang. I sat down on the chair in my bedroom and answered. "This better be good," I said. "I am dead with exhaustion."

"Percy, it's Sarah."

I looked down at my arms, blackened above the glove line. "Sarah. How are you feeling?"

"Well, I'm in pain," she said with surprising warmth. "There's no denying that. But I'm glad this part is over."

A month before, she'd had her surgery: her left breast "cleanly" removed, as she put it. I had paid her a visit in the hospital, taking a box of caramels, a bottle of hand lotion, and two good novels with happy endings (all by request). She'd been drugged, but she was glad to see me. I did not ask if I could help in her recovery; I was tired of her refusals. I knew she had others to take care of her, even aside from He Whose Name I Would No Longer Mention.

"My latest scans came back," she told me now, "and the news is good. If I were to adopt another boy, I'd have to name him Ned. This week, those are the most beautiful letters in the alphabet. No Evidence of Disease."

Just as she had shared my grief and listened to my panic after the night of Robert's arrest, I shared her happiness at this good news. I told her I was overjoyed. I was.

After a pause, she said, "How's your new life?"

"Different. No doubt about that." I told her that I was thinking of volunteering at the local library. "You could fit the place in my back pocket, but there's one thing it has that Widener never did: children. Children who have to follow rules, that is."

She laughed—politely, as if she couldn't wait to get off the phone. I made no attempt to mend the silence. Let her be the one to end our conversation. I noticed that the age spots on the backs of my hands were growing more pronounced.

Finally she said, "What I'm calling about, really, is Ira's wedding."

"Yes?" I said. "I'm going. As odd as it feels to be attending the wedding of two *fellows,* I do plan to be there."

"You don't disapprove, do you?"

"I'm told by Robert that I don't, and I'll roll with that."

In fact, my reservations about attending the ceremony, a smallish affair to be held at Rose Retreat in early October, had nothing to do with the sexual habits of the betrothed and everything to do with my anxiety about facing certain other guests. Sarah was one, but seeing her, possibly even on the arm of that conniving fellow, was not my greatest worry.

"So," she said, "what I wanted to say is that I'll be there on my own. Well, with Rico. But . . . just in case . . ."

I waited a bit before saying, "In case what?"

"In case it matters to you. Percy, you don't make things easy, do you?"

Laughter seemed to be the most diplomatic reply. I might have answered that I was not the culprit here when it came to making things hard. But I am getting better and better at holding my tongue. I am a man of too many words—no secret to anyone—but I am slowly learning to withhold them when it is wise. To wait rather than speak.

"I have hair again," she said. "A little. I look like Rico's GI Joe. Like I joined the marines."

"Lucky for you we live in an age of sympathy for the soldier." Again, I waited.

"Oh Percy, the world is such a strange and illogical place."

"As I believe you told me the day we met. You underestimate my memory, Sarah. And please don't tell me again how *complicated* everything is." I let my rebuke sink in for a moment. Then I said, more kindly, "I am learning to live with complications that just may rival yours."

"I want to hear all about them. I do."

"You will. But right now, one of those complications has made me a sandwich and I have simply got to eat it or I will pass out. I also have to pee rather badly."

"I'll see you at the wedding."

"You will," I said.

After eating two sandwiches, I put on my pineapple swim trunks and walked to the harbor. We were midway through September, but the Atlantic Ocean was as begrudgingly warm as it ever gets. I launched myself from my favorite rock and swam toward the lighthouse, the closest point on the other side of the harbor. The first lighthouse on the point was tended by one Ezekiel Darling, who Poppy insisted must be tangled somewhere in my bloodlines. As much as I like history, genealogy bores me, so I have never bothered to find out whether she was right, and I probably never shall. I suppose that if I'm ever invited to parties here where people care about such things, I'll be asked about the connection. One day soon, I'll dream up a story or two; why not lend myself a bit of local color?

The harbor is long and narrow: on a good day, I can swim across it in ten minutes—though this is a tricky proposition at midsummer, when boats are tightly moored from one end to the other. Then, you could practically cross it on foot, stepping from deck to deck. By Labor Day, however, the number of boats has visibly diminished. First go the flashy motorized hulks and the visiting yachts from far-flung ports like Halifax and Chesapeake Bay; then, one by one, the indigenous sailboats disappear. The few that linger are the trawlers, the rusty stinkpots that haul in whatever fish remain to be caught. This gradual winnowing, I've mused, is not unlike the deterioration of memory: the last recollections to go, if you're lucky, are the homeliest, the plainest, the ones that travel farthest, if slowly, and cast their nets deep.

In my early days of learning the town—repeatedly losing my bearings, reversing my steps from lanes that dwindled to private yards or scraps of pebbled beach—I found myself on the street where Poppy lived as a girl. She'd driven me here, once, decades before. I recognized it because of an eccentric fork in the road, but I could no longer single out the house. Several stood close together, all old, no two alike, yet countless coats of paint and the intervening years had stolen from me the details necessary to saying, *There. That's the place!*

Strangely, I wasn't sad. I recalled Trudy's odd story about something she'd heard her mother say: that the third child she wished for was the opposite of a ghost, someone waiting to be. Perhaps that's what Poppy was, here and now: the opposite of a ghost. She had brought me to a place of becoming, away from a place of having been.

Oh, Poppy.

I made it all the way across the harbor and back. I would be very sore, but I didn't care. When I returned home, both young men were asleep on the couch. The television was on, broadcasting a tennis match between two alarmingly muscular women. I stood and watched until one of them raised her thick arms in victory. Then the news came on, and right away I turned it off.

I had yet to subscribe to any newspapers, national or local. Sometimes I heard rumors when I shopped—that the world of high finance was about to implode, that Obama might actually win, that my new town would have to swallow a huge tax hike to pay for a seawall—but I'd had quite enough of headlines, enough of police logs and photographs of loved ones in trouble with the law.

Robert's restraining order from the town of Matlock will prevent him from attending the wedding. Ira wishes that Celestino could be there, too, but we know it won't be wise for him to show his face, either. Celestino tells me that he's cared for that garden through several seasons, that he knows exactly which roses will be blooming the day of the ceremony. He's promised me that next spring he will make a beautiful shade garden in our yard, despite the tyranny of the tree. He tells me there is one sunny corner for roses. He is already preparing the beds.

I will have to contend with seeing Maurice and Evelyn, both of whom I feel have betrayed me, if subtly; yet far more difficult will be my encounter with Clover. I have no idea how she will react to my presence, nor how I will react to her reaction.

After the fire, she wrote me a letter in which she told me how sorry she was about the damage to the house but how she did not regret having told "the truth about Robert." She told me she'd come to realize that I loved Trudy more than I loved her and loved Robert more than I loved her children. She said she could forgive me but would rather not have any contact with me for at least the rest of the summer. She asked me not to phone her.

I wanted to sit down and write her at once, to tell her how wrong she was on each and every point. Yet I also imagined telling her everything I'd honestly felt about her behavior over the past three years. I would withhold nothing. By happenstance, Douglas called that day, to give me an update on Robert's case. He could tell how upset I was, and he pried a confession from me.

"Dad, don't do that," he said. "Don't write her. Not yet. I can tell you what's going on. She's reached the stage of therapy where she's really grieving for her mother. And you're not looking too good in that scenario. How could you?"

I wondered how much Douglas knew from Trudy about the night of Poppy's death; everything, of course. But when he continued, I realized I had it wrong. "You're the one who stuck around," he said. "The parent who stays is the only one who can make the mistakes. Not fair, but what can you do? An absent mom can do no wrong. She'll get past this, Dad. She will." Douglas, my good-tempered ordinary fellow of a son-in-law, who called me Dad without a hint of irony, whom I had always liked but not well enough until now, blamed me for nothing.

So I let Clover be. I stepped back and, yes, held my tongue. And since the fire had deprived me of the few farewell weeks I'd expected to spend in the house, I would not bump into her, not by accident or contrivance.

I had my spies, however. It was Ira who told me that Clover would be spending July and August in New York, subletting an apartment from Ira's sister.

She is back from that summer now, back at Elves & Fairies, planning what Ira calls the "auction do-over." She will be at his wedding. She will be there with both of her children. Now there are two people I can't wait to see.

My young men are sometimes secretive, and both of them flip through the daily mail feigning disinterest. Celestino received a letter from France last week, forwarded by Rayzon Dettrah, addressed to Celestino in a flourishy hand that reminded me, odiously, of the letter I'd received from Maurice Fougère. He took it away to his room at once; I could not decipher his expression.

Robert has an e-mail account linked to mine. We check it—together, as required—every evening after dinner. I sit beside him as the list of new messages cascades from top to bottom, reminding me of the old-fashioned boards on which one still sees train schedules posted in places like Grand Central Station.

And one day, there it was. Neither of us recognized the sender, and we were about to delete it as spam. The subject line read, *regrets from afar.* Robert said, "Wait." He opened it.

```
i only recently learned what went down last spring. the
whole story. i had no idea you'd take the fall, believe
me. i am sure i never lied to you, though i understood
what you chose to believe. a lot of that wasn't true. it
became necessary truth in the light of things that had to
happen. i know enough to know that if you are reading
this, you won't agree. people will say i was not your
friend. not true but so be it. i owe you money and you
will receive it. i hope you are okay, i know you will
rise and thrive. that's you. you exist in a zone of
tranquillity & strength and all will be well. as for me,
i remain senza ragazza, and in a way senza patria too. my
own cross(es) to bear. be in touch with me—or not. i move
around at present, but wherever i'm staying, i keep tabs
on the world. nor have i ceased working for what matters
most. no choice but perseverance! i hope our friendship
remains, a small portion at least.
```

Faint, mostly inscrutable noises escaped from Robert as he read. I was breathing heavily, trying not to shout with indignation at the vile, smug, disingenuous miasma emanating from the words on the screen.

I could tell that he was reading the message over and over again. When he closed it, I reminded him that he must forward it to his parole officer. "I know that, Granddad." He struggled to speak without emotion. I watched him click on the white arrow and type Mike's address.

We moved on, without comment, to messages from Robert's mother; from a friend still at Harvard; from one of the many overwrought environmental organizations whose newsletters he reads and quotes, his passion for "doing the right thing" undiminished.

When Poppy used to reminisce about her childhood, she'd say that Vigil Harbor was a town of people who respect your privacy as long as you let them feel that they know your deepest secrets. Take a walk in this town on a balmy summer's night and you will pass many an open window spilling conversations directly onto the street. It's quite the opposite of living in Matlock, and that is, for the moment and possibly the rest of my life, precisely what I need.

It's what all three of us need. So while our arrangement may perplex the casually nosy passerby, I like to think that the neighbors have debated our peculiar triad and come to a consensus that offers toothsome fodder for speculation and yet, because we're so friendly and unguarded, spares us suspicion of anything truly perverse. We may be heard grilling hamburgers, arguing over television channels, cheering for the Red Sox (sometimes with Norval or Douglas present), and singing along with Tom Lehrer, Nat King Cole, Mercedes Sosa, Tom Waits, or Kanye West. (The things I am learning to tolerate!)

The young men may be heard practicing their achingly awful French, sometimes up in the tree. (*Passez-moi le—qu'est-ce que c'est, ce truc? L'ammaire?* Did I just ask you to pass me the ocean? The hammer, dude! . . . *Veux-tu prendre un break pour manger un peu de chips et salsa? Moi, je peux fabriquer du guacamole, peut-être. . . . Avez-vous une idée à propos de cette bizarre angle?*) I hadn't thought of French lessons as a way to get them laughing again, but *eh voilà*. I still have my flashes of genius.

Then again, the eavesdropper on the sidewalk might hear Spanish or even an Indian dialect whose name I have yet to catch: this would be

Celestino upstairs on the phone, most likely with his mother or one of his sisters. Celestino never sounds so spirited as he does in these conversations, which range from angry and exasperated to joyful and teasing. I do not need to understand a word to know that these are family conversations.

Ears that know our house must perk up a bit whenever a woman's voice joins in. It could be Daphne's; she lives two blocks away and drops in sometimes when she's walking her Jack Russell. She's invited us to a neighborhood party the weekend after Ira and Anthony's wedding. ("You will meet the high, and you will meet the low.") Or it might be Trudy's voice—though she is as busy as ever, and her office is nearly an hour's drive from here. And though my hunch may be a delusion, I am thinking that soon the occasional woman's voice will be Sarah's. Sarah's voice and her unbridled laughter, Sarah alive and as well as can be, drifting out into the streets of Vigil Harbor, over the harbor itself. Voices carry surprisingly far over water.

They stand on the highest branches that will hold them, each with an arm braced around the trunk. One arm rests comfortably on the other. Separately and together, they are shocked to realize how far below the ground is, how far they can see over the house and the lower trees in nearby yards. They see the harbor, the lighthouse, a small uninhabited island—and, on the crisp horizon, a massive ship aimed for open sea, its progress almost impossible to gauge.

Beneath them, through leaves that are brightening and falling, they can make out the framework of the tree house they're building; unlike the one they built in Matlock, this one they've approached with only the sketchiest of plans.

"Do we know what we're doing?" one of them says to the other.

The other one shrugs. "*Qui sait bien ce qu'il fait? Personne!*"

They laugh.

One of them is thinking about French women in general and about Madeleine, their bossy French teacher, in particular. At the first meeting she said fiercely, to the five people who showed up, "The only way you become any good at a new language is when you are perfectly willing to make a complete fool of yourself. You've got to shed your pride!" He sees her point, but he is thinking that there are certain places in his life where he will never shed his pride again.

The other one is thinking about what they might eat for lunch. These days he thinks often about pleasures of the moment: the pleasure of TV, of sports (where were those tennis courts they passed the other day?), of swimming in the ocean; definitely the more difficult pleasures of building the tree house. So much is uncertain, but not this: he is becoming a good carpenter.

"How about a stained-glass window? Old wine bottles."

"I like that idea."

"And a roof made of funky old license plates."

"Where do we get them?"

"We'll figure it out. That's the way we roll. *Comme ça.* We figure stuff out."

"*C'est vrai.*"

The snap of the screen door draws their gaze to the house. Percy Darling steps onto the porch, dressed for the wedding. He wears that vaudeville orange bow tie he wore at Thanksgiving, a white shirt, a blue jacket. He looks like a large songbird, in full courting plumage. When they call to him, he looks around in several directions, startled. It takes him a moment to see where they are. He shades his eyes and shouts at them to be careful. They are too high in that tree!

Their reply comes in French.

"*Ne t'inquiète pas!*"

"*Nous connaissons cet arbre bien!*"

He shouts at them, also in French, to be good while he's away. Or they think that's what he said. He gets into the pickup truck and backs out slowly.

Wind blows through the boughs of the tree, and it's as if the sound of the ocean has been tossed aloft, directly to them, for them alone. They watch the truck climb the hill, pass the graveyard, and turn out of sight onto the road leading inland, away from the shore.

Acknowledgments

For touring me through their respective worlds and answering my too-many questions, I am especially grateful to Barbara Burg, Lucy Curran, and Jennifer McKenna. Thank you all for your time and generosity. The thorough and engaging *Widener: Biography of a Library,* by Matthew Battles, was also enormously helpful.

A Note About the Author

Julia Glass is the author of *Three Junes,* winner of the 2002 National Book Award for fiction; *The Whole World Over;* and *I See You Everywhere,* winner of the 2009 Binghamton University John Gardner Fiction Book Award. She has also won prizes for her short fiction and essays, as well as fellowships from the National Endowment for the Arts, the New York Foundation for the Arts, and the Radcliffe Institute for Advanced Study. She lives with her family in Massachusetts.

A Note on the Type

The text of this book was set in Sabon, a typeface designed by Jan Tschichold (1902–1974), the well-known German typographer. Designed in 1966 and based on the original designs by Claude Garamond (ca. 1480–1561), Sabon was named for the punch cutter Jacques Sabon, who brought Garamond's matrices to Frankfurt.

Composed by Creative Graphics,
Allentown, Pennsylvania

Printed and bound by Berryville Graphics,
Berryville, Virginia

Designed by M. Kristen Bearse